THE
SECRET
CHORD

D0555861

Praise for Virginia Hale

Echo Point

...is a lovely Australian romance that has a lot of things I love: an ice queen that thaws, an age gap between the leads, and it takes place in a small town. The writing is smooth, the characters are compelling, and the pacing works very well. It also feels very Australian, rather than being a story that feels like it could be set anywhere. If you're looking for a new comfort read, I totally recommend it.

- The Lesbian Review

This is Hale's debut novel and she's got a great career ahead of her judging from this one. It's a story of recovery, redemption, and how you deal with unexpected tragedy that changes the trajectory your life was taking. I read this book in pretty much one sitting, which speaks volumes of firstly, how well it's written, and secondly, how much the story pulled me in. In terms of quality of writing, Hale's style is for beautifully written scenes that flow superbly... It's a great book, definitely not a fluffy romance but the romance it contains is wonderful. Highly recommended.

- Rainbow Book Reviews

Echo Point is a debut novel by Virginia Hale, but without any of the typical first novel shortcomings. It is a warm story of love, loss and family, set in the town of Katoomba in the Blue Mountains, a region west of Sydney in Australia's New South Wales. The setting is really interesting, very well described, and plays a nice role in the narrative. Overall, this is a lovely book, full of feeling and very well worth reading. A very solid novel which definitely did not feel like a debut. I very much liked it and recommend it.

- goodreads, Pin's Reviews

Beautiful love story set in the Blue mountains near Sydney in Australia. This is not just a romance: it's a story of loss, family ties and redemption. The author's description of the landscape is vivid and picturesque. The bushfires and intense heat are a metaphor of the passions at stake. Ms. Hale knows how to build up the tension and the chemistry between Bron and Ally rages like a bushfire: uncontrollable, hot and consuming. Overall, a very solid debut novel and a highly recommended romance.

– goodreads, Gaby's Reviews

The best way to describe this is a pure romance. While you are reading about characters dealing with a great loss of their loved one, this really is a feel good book. The characters are normal people with real issues. This book is not filled with unnecessary drama and angst, it is a really well written pure romance. I can absolutely recommend this to romance fans. I know people are going to enjoy this. Hale writes really well. This is great for a debut book, and great for a seasoned author. I will not hesitate one bit to read anything else by Hale.

- goodreads, Lex Kent's Reviews

Where There's a Will

I was also a big fan of the characters. Both have their flaws and were actually a bit opposites attract but I really liked them as a potential pair. …I have to give Hale props for not waiting to the 90% mark to mess with her characters. Her characters have drama, this is not an angst free book, but the way Hale did it is the way I wish romance authors would tackle this issue. The book flowed so much better for me the way Hale wrote it. If you are looking for a romance and storyline this is different than the same old, get this book. Hale is a quality author and I can't wait to see what she puts out next.

– goodreads, Lex Kent's Reviews

Where There's a Will is a very good second novel by the Australian author Virginia Hale. The main conflict is over a murder house they jointly inherited. Dylan sees it as her everything in life, but Beth wants to sell it to get out of huge debts. This creates a conflict between these two good people. Through the resolution of this conflict, the author gives us a very satisfying ending while also creating an interesting and warm story of interpersonal relationships. With all main elements done really good this makes another solid read by the author, very well worth reading. I recommend it, and am looking forward to her next book.

Other Bella Books by Virginia Hale

Echo Point
Where There's a Will

About the Author

Virginia Hale lives in Sydney, Australia. After a brief dalliance with Theatre Studies, she went on to earn a Bachelor of Arts in English Literature and a Master of Children's Literature. Virginia's debut novel, *Echo Point*, was a recipient of the 2018 *Golden Crown Literary Society Award* for Best Contemporary Romance (Short).

THE
SECRET
CHORD

VIRGINIA HALE

BELLA
BOOKS
2019

Bella Books, Inc.
P.O. Box 10543
Tallahassee, FL 32302

Printed in the United States of America on acid-free paper.

First Bella Books Edition 2019

Editor: Cath Walker
Cover Designer: Judith Fellows

ISBN: 978-1-64247-043-7

Acknowledgments

Endless thanks to my editor, Cath Walker, whose patience knows no bounds. Cath, your guidance makes me feel like the luckiest writer in the world. To the dedicated team at Bella Books, thank you for your encouragement and support.

CHAPTER ONE

"Is something wrong, Kate?"

Kate pulled her gaze from the approaching ferry and looked to the passenger seat of the convent van parked at the pier. She forced a smile for Sister Ruth. "Nothing's wrong." *Lying to a nun—that's a surefire way to get a one-way ticket to Hell.* She removed her black frames and buffed the lenses on the crushed shirttails of her white button-up. "It's just that I still have so much lesson prep for this week. I've been so busy trying to get everything together for the VCE Literature Extension class I'm job-sharing with Tilly that I haven't even started my lesson plan for VCE Music Performance." She fogged the glass with her breath and rubbed at the persisting streaks. "You know what it's like when the girls come back from holidays—I'll barely have a second to myself to think."

Kate pushed her glasses up her nose, the emerald hills of Mornington Peninsula suddenly much clearer in the distance. Remarkably, the nine-thirty passenger ferry was making perfect time as it tugged across Port Phillip Bay from Mornington Pier, headed straight for Lords Island. The sight of the small, coffee-coloured vessel left Kate's palms clammy, her hands shakier than when she'd woken at seven to make up the guest room bed for St. Joan's imminent guest. She bit back a sigh. Contrary to what she was selling—contrary to what Sister Ruth had too easily bought—Kate's nervousness was completely unrelated to the return of three hundred students to the island within the next forty-eight hours.

As Sister Ruth wound down the passenger window, the veil of her baby-blue habit fluttered in the cool October breeze. With a soft sigh, she returned her focus to her crossword puzzle. "You work so hard for those girls."

Kate smiled. "So do you, Reverend Mother."

Nearing seventy-five, Sister Ruth was like an Eveready battery. She was a wonderful headmistress and maths teacher—Kate could attest to that having once been her student. Although Sister Ruth had odd ideas and an even stranger manner of *articulating* those ideas, the students—the twenty-five boarders, especially—adored their principal like a grandmother.

Nine months before, when Kate had arrived to assume the year-long position of music teacher at St. Joan of Arc Catholic Girls' School, Kate's first impression of her former headmistress was that she seemed absolutely exhausted. One of the primary missions of The Daughters of Our Lady of Mercy was education of youth. If Kate had a dollar for every time she'd had to remind Sister Ruth that it wasn't her job to bear that mission alone, she'd have accounted for her highly coveted salary. Now, nine months into her contract, Kate often found herself awake at night wondering why *she* had decided to share that mission at all.

The salary had been incredibly attractive—that was what she'd told her mother and sister. But the truth was that a position at St. Joan's offered Kate an escape. If she could isolate herself on Lords, she couldn't be tempted to spend nights in inner city Melbourne with Elodie, her kind and attentive and loyal ex who had simply envisioned a future different to the one Kate desperately wanted—a future including children. If she relocated to Lords and took on the position of housemother from Monday to Friday, the breakup would finally be *final*—and they could both move on. And that was exactly what had happened—they hadn't spoken in six months.

Initially, she'd reluctantly relocated to Lords with a negative mindset. Knowing what her peers had been like at St. Joan's in the early noughties, she had thought her decision might prove to be a nightmare. But in the decade since Kate's graduation, the school had fostered a much more sisterly atmosphere. Kate was pleasantly surprised to find that these girls were decidedly less entitled than they had been, that the select twenty-five students who now boarded—just as Kate once had—lived almost as simply as the sisters residing in the convent beside the boarding house.

As housemother, the only noteworthy meltdown Kate had witnessed had occurred the previous month. During a ferocious storm, the Telstra tower had been struck, severing telecommunications for the entire island, including the pioneer village that sat at the edge of the two-lane causeway on the other side of Lords. With the Internet down, all hell had broken loose. Without Wi-Fi—Netflix, Instagram, Facebook—it seemed that Kate had Lucifer's progenies on her hands. She didn't have enough fingers to count how often one of the girls had stepped into her office and made a case to return to the mainland. Lexi, of course, had been first.

"I'm feeling really sick, Kate," she'd said. "I'm feeling the way my Nan felt when she got pneumonia. Like real bad sort of thing. I think I need to get the ferry back to the mainland to stay at my aunt's for a few days. She only lives a few suburbs away from Mornington. My parents would be totally cool with it..."

Glaring over the rim of her glasses, Kate had fixed her only Year Ten boarder with a look. "Lexi, I'd like to see how you would have survived Kokoda. I really would."

"If I wanted to hear my dad say that," Lexi had spat, "I'd live with him and not you!"

"Go for it," Kate had murmured, returning to grading music essays.

"This island is a prison!" Grace had informed Kate the next night. "You're the worst housemother! You run this place like a death camp!" Emma had claimed an hour before the connection returned. Like heroin addicts feeling their rush, the girls had gone from demons to angels, and once more, all was well on Lords. Lately, Kate had even found herself missing the Year Twelves who had recently moved back to the mainland to undertake VCE exams hosted at larger schools, reducing the cohort from three hundred-and-fifty to just three hundred.

Three months until Christmas and her contract would be completed, Sister Mary Patrick coming from Ballarat to take the reins in the music department next year. Kate was looking forward to returning to Melbourne, to a life where she didn't live tight-lipped about her sexuality, endlessly longing for the weekend when she could take off to the mainland to absorb enough adult conversation to survive a five-day week of *she leaves all of her hair clogged in the shower* and *she stole my bra* and *she Snapchatted a fugly picture of me even though I didn't give her permission*. As Kate watched the ferry chug closer, aware of *exactly* who was on board, something told her that these next three months were going to be harder than the last nine combined.

"It's a lovely time of year for Tilly to be coming home," Sister Ruth said, her gaze still focused on her puzzle. "Not too hot, not too cold. And the vegetable garden is flourishing like never before. Tilly will just love it! She was always an excellent cook."

Because she had no option but to become one, Kate thought, bitterness prickling beneath her skin. It wasn't as though Tilly had it tough but losing her parents in a car accident when she was five and being sent from England to be raised by her mother's sister on Lords had reaped Tilly a life of responsibility unfamiliar to the other boarders. Sister Hattie had been a deeply loving aunt, but she'd also wanted Tilly to learn about duty. By the time Kate had arrived at the island at fifteen, barely able to boil pasta for herself, Tilly had been a good cook for years. The legally-blind Sister Mary Joseph had taught her, and when she'd passed away when the girls were sixteen, Tilly had taken on the cooking responsibilities—boarding house *and* convent—to share with old Sister Mary Claire until graduation.

"Thank you for driving down with me to pick Tilly up," Sister Ruth said.

Kate shifted stiffly in the driver's seat. "No problem at all." What choice did she have? With Sister Caroline away visiting her terminally ill sister in Tasmania for the rest of the year, Kate was the only one left on the island who could drive a manual car. She couldn't very well expect Tilly to wait an eternity on the unreliable island shuttle, or heave her suitcase up the hill. Like her own, Tilly's fair skin had never taken well to the sun.

"I remember you two together," Sister Ruth said absentmindedly. Kate watched the corners of the Reverend Mother's lips quirk. "*You* were so hard to wake up in the morning. Tilly was always up and at breakfast, and she'd have to go back to your room to drag you down just before the bells rang. And your hair each morning in homeroom, my goodness! Like a charcoal bird's nest, Katherine…"

Chuckling, Kate rubbed her sweaty palms across her shorts. "Reverend Mother, I think you'll find that you're exaggerating." She'd never been an early riser, true, but in the later years, when they'd been two of the oldest students, she'd been up early each morning to help prepare the breakfast for the convent, desperate to steal as much time alone with Tilly as possible. Not even sharing a dorm room had been enough to satisfy her.

"Exaggerating?" Sister Ruth hummed. "Am I?"

Kate wanted to smile, but the closer the boat came to the cove, the harder her heart began to hammer. "I haven't seen her in almost twelve years," she murmured.

Sister Ruth looked over. She hesitated before she spoke, and when she did, her words were soft, as though she could comprehend the ache in Kate's heart beginning to catch like dry tinder to a blue flame. "You just missed her by weeks earlier this year," she started. "She always visits in January, what with how busy she is at St. Matthew's the rest of the year—you know how demanding the parishes in Melbourne get, with the feast days, and Easter of course…"

She hummed her acknowledgment.

"She visited just before you arrived, before she had to return to teach in the city. It was the first time she'd been here since we lost Sister Hattie—God rest her soul—and I think our Tilly was quite shocked to find that there are only five of us here now, that over two-thirds of the teachers *aren't* sisters, that so many of the rooms in the convent are…vacant." She paused for a moment, staring out at Port Phillip Bay, at the ferry that carried Tilly home. "I always thought she'd join us here, make one of those rooms her own. I truly did think it was the Lord's plan for Tilly. Really, I did."

She swallowed. "To join the order, you mean?"

"Yes."

Overlooking the secret she'd rather keep locked away for all eternity, Kate had to agree. She'd been shocked to learn from the sisters that Tilly had never taken her vows. She couldn't recall a time when Tilly hadn't had her heart set on becoming a nun. "I've already been called to it," Tilly had said each time she'd fallen to her knees between their beds to pray. And each time, the hole in Kate's heart had grown larger because she had been called to something else—a fantasy world where they shared a love deeper than friendship. Tilly had longed for a simple life and devoting herself to God. Kate had longed for a simple life and devoting herself to Tilly.

"Can I ask you something, Reverend Mother?"

"Of course."

"Do you know why Tilly didn't take her vows?"

Sister Ruth tapped her pen against the puzzle book. "I do." She scribbled an answer into the boxes of a vertical column.

As Sister Ruth's loyal silence settled in the van, she didn't press.

"I'm sure she wouldn't mind if you asked her yourself, Kate. You were always so close."

She cringed. When there hadn't been so much as a "Hello" exchanged in all that time, *Hey, Til, why didn't you end up committing to a life of poverty and abstinence?* seemed inappropriate.

The wooden rosary beads around Sister Ruth's waist jingled as she turned the page, deciding against attempting a difficult-level game of sudoku. "It's a shame you couldn't have gone to the same university, especially considering that you both studied teaching. You would have just loved a Catholic university, Kate. Such a small campus, like a family. You would have felt right at home."

She bit her tongue. She wouldn't have. Spending her teen years cloistered on Lords was enough Catholicism for three lifetimes, thank you very much. The memories of her adolescence—post her parents' divorce—were wonderful. She'd spent winter mornings slowly walking the rolling green hills of Lords, wasted summer evenings jumping from the pier into the crashing waves of the cove. Still, she'd felt suffocated. St. Joan of Arc had been the most loving, nurturing, picturesque prison possible, but a pretty prison was still a prison. University had been the opportunity to reinvent herself she craved. At first, being apart from Tilly had felt like she was missing a limb, but after a few months of separation, she'd moved on.

"And the vicar seems like a lovely man," Sister Ruth said. "*Anglican*," she added, "but lovely."

Kate clicked her jaw. "So she didn't just hitch a ride with him down here from the city this morning? They *know* each other?"

Sister Ruth sighed. "I'm not sure, Kate. I don't know a thing about it."

Perhaps that had been the greatest surprise of all, even more than learning Tilly hadn't taken her vows. Seeing Tilly in a habit would have been easier to digest—vows were expected, predicted, the fault in their stars. But this *vicar* thing? It had come barrelling out of nowhere and knocked Kate for six. Something about the fact that Tilly had followed a vicar from Melbourne to Mornington didn't sit right with Kate. It irked her to think what a perfect coincidence it happened to be that the same week the vicar was to be invested at the Anglican parish on the peninsula, Tilly's contract at St. Matthew's just happened to finish, enabling her to return to St. Joan's as a temporary teacher.

If Tilly hadn't joined the sisterhood, did that mean she was *with* the vicar? The thought of Tilly with a man, any man, be it a vicar or the goddamn Marlon Brando of Melbourne, was a concept difficult to swallow. Kate had heard the sisters say the vicar had children. A boy and a girl—young. That he just so happened to be recently widowed joined the dots. Tilly had always latched to a problem like flies to molasses, made it her job to fix things—situations, sadness, *people*. Sad people in sadder situations. The whole thing just reeked of some sort of Von Trapp situation, and the fact was simple: no one could solve a problem like Matilda.

As the ferry docked, the horn sounded, vibrating through Kate, a hot flush breaking out between her breasts. Sister Ruth closed her puzzle book and slapped it onto the dashboard. "Feel like coming for the walk?"

Kate slammed the driver's door closed behind her. As she followed Sister Ruth across the gravel of the slipway toward the pier, her legs threatened to give way. She hadn't felt this nervous since her last blind date—a set-up orchestrated by her sister with a woman who, at twenty-five, was five years Kate's junior. It hadn't worked out. It should have, there was no reason for it not to, but it hadn't.

It was the smaller of the two ferries this morning—the passenger ferry, not the much larger twelve-car ferry that always made the final ten p.m. stop en route to the more populated East Island. The bay was mapped like a wishbone—Melbourne at the pinnacle, Mornington and Portarlington at each point. Lords and East Islands sat between the stems, but unlike East Island, Lords was connected to Portarlington by a two-kilometre, stone causeway that stretched into the bay. Kate rarely crossed the convict-constructed causeway—her family lived on the opposite side of the bay, and taking the car ferry directly from Lords to Mornington was much quicker than taking the causeway and driving two hours via Melbourne around the bay—but most of the students caught buses across the causeway each morning, only a handful taking ferries from Mornington. St. Joan's heavily relied on the causeway—when the causeway was occasionally closed due to an exceptionally high tide, the ferries had to work double time to ship the cohort back to Portarlington. Thankfully, the ferries were always at their beck and call—if the sisters planned on going into Mornington on a weekday to visit St. Gerard's, the local church, they'd phone ahead to request the car ferry stop via Lords Island to pick them up with the van.

This morning, as Kate had assumed, the passenger ferry was stopping at Lords Island just for Tilly. Colin, the deckhand, hauled himself onto the pier, securing the lines to the dock cleats as he tied off, crisscrossing the ropes to get the right angle. A second later, a slender figure appeared in the doorway, steadying herself on the doorjamb of the cabin as she tugged a large suitcase behind her.

She traced her tongue over her dry lips. It was Tilly, undoubtedly. A dress, buttoned to her collarbone—almost matronly. A dark, delicate plait flying across her back as she accepted a helping hand up onto the pier, thanking the deckhand as he lifted two suitcases and a cabin bag onto the planks.

Her stomach flipped as an invisible rope pulled tight between them and, for the first time in twelve years, Tilly looked her way.

CHAPTER TWO

Desperate to avoid looking into the rear-view mirror, Kate focused on the road ahead. From the seat behind the driver, Tilly rambled on and on as she answered Sister Ruth's question about resigning from her position as head of the history department at St. Matthew's. Like a snap of electricity, Kate felt Tilly's closeness as she leaned forward to repeat part of her answer for Sister Ruth.

Don't stare, don't stare…whatever you do, don't stare… As Tilly settled back into the seat, Kate raised her gaze. *Well, I tried.* Tilly's heart-shaped face was free of make-up, her green eyes framed by lashes long and dark enough to incite envy. The sisters had called her "Tilly Longstocking" as a teenager but her auburn hair had darkened with age, the amber streaks no longer so prominent. With the van windows wound down, a few shorter strands had escaped from her plait to flit about her face. Kate's gaze flickered from the incline of the road ahead and back to the rear-view mirror. Captivated, she watched as Tilly smoothed the plait from one side of her neck to the other. There was something about seeing Tilly so very grown up that left her short of breath.

Her anxiety about seeing Tilly was something that she had anticipated—she'd always been fascinated by her. But she hadn't expected to feel so attracted in a mouth-dry, mind-deserted sort of way. They'd hugged at the pier, Tilly's body pressed so closely to hers that she'd worried Tilly could feel her heartbeat. She'd pulled Tilly against her with a chuckle, the scent of Tilly's soft, flowery perfume sending her dizzy with excitement—and dread. She didn't need this, not now. Why couldn't Tilly have returned to Lords in three months' time after Kate had gone? She'd spent twelve years trying to get over Tilly. And she had. *She had*. But, God, seeing Tilly all grown up had her stomach in knots.

Everything about Tilly brought memory flooding back in waves. In the reflection, the sun caught the solid gold of Tilly's crucifix—an eighteenth birthday gift. Sister Hattie had snuck into their dorm room just after the first ring of the convent bells, knelt beside Tilly's bed and planted kisses on her cheeks until she'd woken. Kate had sat up in bed, groggy with sleep, watching as Sister Hattie clipped the crucifix around Tilly's neck. That birthday, Kate had given Tilly a bottle of Chanel No. 5, and Tilly had treated it like a prized possession, using it sparingly for feast day masses, birthday dinners, graduation…

Kate spied upward at Tilly and followed her line of sight across their side of the island to the statue of St. Joan of Arc on horseback, the stone figure so enormous that, on a clear day, St. Joan and her raised bronze flag were visible from Mornington Pier.

"Your hair is still short, Kate."

At the sound of her name, Kate returned her eyes to the unsealed dirt road. "Oh, yeah," she said. "Doubt I'll ever turn back."

"It was so much longer in school. I still remember that day we met in the city, after you'd cut it…"

Their gazes met in the mirror. Kate smiled. The only reason she'd ever let her hair grow past her shoulders was because she'd loved the sensation of Tilly's fingers raking through it when she'd plait it. The first week of university, Kate had cut it off. After that, she'd seen Tilly just once.

Tilly leaned forward as Kate rounded the bend, passing the dirt road that diverged to the other side of the island—the pioneer village, the causeway and the tiny town that included just seventy homes, a seafood restaurant and a general store. "Has much changed since January, Reverend Mother?"

As Sister Ruth began to explain Sister Tessie's suspected dementia, Kate approached the break in the trees. The giant clearing stretched out before them—the convent, cottage, and boarding house on one side of the dirt road, the two-storey school, the sports field and chapel on the other. Kate headed for the driveway between the boarding house and the cottage. Both sandstone buildings had been built in the late nineteenth century by English convicts, the cottage once a teacher's residence, the boarding house an orphanage. Now, girls came from all over the Mornington Peninsula Shire to lodge in the warm, refurbished rooms of the four-storey fortress with its high and wide windows and dormitory wings denoted by all four points of the compass.

As always after eight a.m. mass with Father Rodney, who drove across the causeway from Portarlington each morning, three of the four sisters of St. Joan's were hard at work in the convent garden, bent over tomato bushes and raised lettuce beds. It impressed Kate how self-sufficient they were. It was easier now that the maintenance man turned up more often to work odd jobs—checking the water levels of the eight enormous rainwater tanks, cleaning the gutters, delivering firewood—but for the most part, the sisters managed for themselves. They were competent women with lifetimes of experience and were deeply admired.

Sister Ruth had worked as a maths teacher for ten years before joining the order. In her early twenties, Sister Mary Monica had worked as a trained nurse in the Vietnam War. When St. Joan's had hosted a winter craft market on Lords the month before, Sister Mary Monica had refused to let her Saturday work routine be interrupted by their hundred guests. Cloaked in her long blue habit, she'd climbed onto the ride-on mower and taken off, her veil soaring behind her. A reporter from the Mornington Sun had come to the markets to write a small article for the events section, but by Tuesday, a picture of Sister Mary Monica zipping across the sports field had graced the front page of the local paper instead. The title? "The Flying Nun."

Kate drew to a stop. Lockie's head whipped around, hopeful for the return of the girls who showered him with affection. Much to Sister Mary Monica's chagrin he came bounding through the veggie patch to the van.

Tilly laughed as she stepped out, crouching in her long skirt to greet the golden retriever. "Who's this?"

"This is Lockie," Kate explained. "He belongs to one of the girls—Emma—but he lives here with us. Emma's parents divorced last year—that's why she boards here—and her mother moved into a rental in Mornington that wouldn't allow dogs. So Lockie moved here with Em, didn't you Lockie?" As Tilly scratched her nails over his head, his eyes slipped closed in pleasure, tail dusting the gravel. "I really don't know what the sisters will do when he leaves with Em next year," Kate added. "He's everybody's now."

"You're a very beautiful boy, aren't you?" Tilly asked.

"The only boy on this side of the island. And I think it's safe to say he likes your nails." Her own were blunter than Sister Mary Monica's manner.

With one last rake of her fingers over Lockie's head, Tilly turned back to the van.

"I can get your bags," Kate offered.

"No, I can get them."

As Tilly's fingers beat her to curl around the handle of the nearest suitcase, Kate's gaze caught on the ring on Tilly's left hand. She paused, an uncomfortable weight settling in her chest. Tilly's eyes were on her face—she could feel it. "Let go," Kate implored, playfully swatting at Tilly's wrist.

When Kate had both bags on the ground, Tilly lifted the handles and began rolling the cases in the direction of the convent garden.

"Tilly?"

She turned.

"You're actually staying in the cottage with me."

"Oh." Tilly's gaze flickered to the small, sandstone building Kate called home, then to Sister Ruth. "I assumed I'd be sleeping in the convent. I did when I taught here years ago."

Kate frowned. "You've taught here before?" Why hadn't the sisters mentioned that?

"Only as a temp." Her gaze darted across the driveway to the sisters in the garden, discarding their gloves and rakes as they made their way to greet her. "Just for a month," she said distractedly.

"We can set up a spare room in the convent if you'd prefer," Sister Ruth offered, but Kate was already taking a handle from Tilly and wheeling the case toward the cottage.

Tilly glanced at Kate, her smile not quite reaching her eyes.

Kate wet her lips. "It's no trouble if you'd rather stay with the sisters. Truly."

"No, no." Tilly hiked her cabin bag higher onto her shoulder. "The cottage is just fine."

In the convent kitchen, introductions were made between Tilly and young Sister Ellie, the only one of the four sisters that Tilly didn't know. Of all the sisters, Kate got along with Sister Ellie best. A novice, Sister Ellie was a few inches taller than Kate, a stocky twenty-seven-year-old French and Food Technology teacher with the laugh of Elmo and a smile that wouldn't quit. "And your trip down to Mornington with the vicar?" Sister Ellie asked as she nibbled at a butter snap biscuit, the golden crumbs raining down on her apron. "How was that?"

With her back to Tilly and the sisters, Kate rolled her eyes as she reached into the cupboard for six cups.

"Well, he has two little ones," Tilly started. "The youngest, she suffers from motion sickness. Thank goodness that it's just over an hour from Melbourne to Mornington. I sat in the back with her for the entire drive. Poor little thing."

"Oh, no," Sister Ellie said, and Kate fought against a grin. Although the sympathy in her voice sounded genuine, Kate guessed that the woes of a car sick kid wasn't what Sister Ellie had been fishing for.

The kettle clicked, having boiled. Tilly cleared her throat. "Declan lost his wife last December to ovarian cancer."

Kate stiffened as her fingers wrapped around the handle of the kettle. Last year? And Tilly already had a ring on her finger?

"She was only thirty-five," Tilly whispered.

Christ Almighty, Kate thought as she listened to the sisters mumble a blessing for the vicar's wife. *He likes them young.* She'd heard from Sister Ellie that he was in his late fifties—maybe even early sixties. As she dunked tea bags in their cups, Kate stared out the kitchen window to the east, to St. Joan of Arc on her horse.

Tilly was engaged to a man thirty years her senior. Kate's mind reeled. *Thirty years. Tilly. Engaged. A man.*

"That's just awful," Sister Ellie said.

Sure is, Kate thought.

"Those poor children," Sister Mary Monica added. "Losing a mother so young. The vicar must have appreciated having you around to help make the move."

Ahh. Complete understanding dawned. And there it is, Kate thought—Tilly's penchant for seeing herself in every child who had ever known the loss of a parent.

"And you're good friends?" Sister Mary Monica pressed. "You and Declan?"

A long silence settled upon the convent kitchen. Kate guessed she wasn't the only one who had spotted the sapphire on Tilly's finger.

"We're engaged," Tilly said breathily, and Kate's hand faltered as she splashed milk into two cups.

"Oh, Tilly! Congratulations!" Sister Ruth exclaimed. As Kate turned and carried two mugs to the table, she watched Tilly smile bashfully.

Sister Tessie grasped Kate's elbow as she placed her tea down on the table for her. "What did she say?" she asked loudly, her Papua New Guinean accent still as strong as it had been the day Kate had started as a boarder.

Kate bent to speak into her ear. "She's getting married."

Tilly looked across the table at the exchange.

Sister Tessie pulled back. She squinted at Kate. "Engaged? To whom?"

Kate dropped her gaze. "To the new vicar at St. Vincent's."

As Tilly stood to hug Sister Ruth, their eyes locked over the Reverend Mother's shoulder. "Congratulations," Kate said as she placed the other cups down on the kitchen table for the sisters.

Tilly's gaze was unfaltering. "Thanks," she said breathily. There was something there in her stare, Kate thought, something that wasn't quite right.

"He's a very pleasant man, Matilda," Sister Mary Monica spoke up. "He'll make a wonderful husband to you. Most of us met him last week when he popped over after mass at St. Gerard's, and when he told us the story of how you were introduced to each other at mass at St. Matthew's, he spoke very highly of you."

Kate remained quiet. At the time of the vicar's visit, she'd been on the mainland at her mother's, skipping out on Sunday mass at the school's local church, St. Gerard's in Mornington—as always—under the guise that she attended Sunday mass with her mum closer to the city in Dandenong. In reality, her mum hadn't seen the inside of a church in over a decade, and if her unwed, pregnant sister dared step foot inside one, Kate was certain the entire establishment would burn to the ground. Kate had a feeling the nuns were well aware that mass didn't occupy a slot in her weekend itinerary, but they never pressed the issue or enquired as to which parish it was that Kate claimed to attend further up the peninsula.

As a teacher at St. Joan of Arc, it was expected that she attend mass regularly and live her life according to the good Lord's will—but in Kate's case, Circumstance turned a blind eye. It was difficult, it seemed, for the diocese to find a teacher of Kate's calibre willing to devote a year of her life to living relatively isolated on an island, house-mothering twenty-five teenage girls under the watchful eye of an order of nuns. It was simple—if the sisters didn't ask, Kate wouldn't tell.

"The vicar's just lovely, Tilly," Sister Mary Monica continued. "And very handsome! I believe Sister Ellie called him a 'silver fox'!"

"Sister Mary Monica!" Tilly gasped a laugh, and the sisters joined her. Kate smirked, grasping the back of a chair as she watched Tilly twist the ring on her finger. "We have our differences, what with Declan being High-Church Anglican and me being Catholic," she said, "but they prove for interesting theological debate."

Debate? Kate quirked an eyebrow. *You'd think they were Catholics and Scientologists.* "If only it weren't for King Henry the eighth and his annulment," Kate joked as she sugared Sister Ruth's tea.

"Oh, Katherine!" Sister Ruth shook her head.

Kate grinned at the sisters before setting her gaze on Tilly. "Five hundred years later and still a touchy subject." She tossed Tilly a wink as she patted the Reverend Mother's shoulder. "Tough crowd."

Tilly smiled shyly, her cheeks tinging pink—at what, Kate wasn't sure. Tilly had always been so reserved. But once upon a time, they *had* opened up to each other. She could still remember coming back to the island after the summer of their sixteenth year, Tilly leaning across the bed in the darkness and whispering all about how she'd "finally started to develop." Up until that point, Tilly hadn't needed a bra, a "secret" only Kate knew, but one she was sure the other girls had guessed. Tilly had gone bra shopping in Mornington over the summer with one of the younger sisters, and as she'd turned on the soft glow of their bedside table to show Kate her new undergarments, her face had been the picture of pride. They'd been plain, simple beiges and whites, the cups barely there, and yet knowing they were Tilly's bras in her hands had Kate's face burning so hot she'd been glad for the semi-darkness.

That had been the same summer Kate had paid two hundred dollars for a fake ID and waltzed into a lesbian bar in Melbourne, let a woman snake her hand into her underwear in a bathroom stall and faked an orgasm. But weeks later, back on Lords, sitting in the darkness of their shared dorm with Tilly's beige A-cup bra in her hands, it had felt like her true sexual awakening.

When it was her turn to hug Tilly congratulations, she fought the blush heating her cheeks. All eyes were on them, including those of Sister Mary Monica, who had always insisted their bedroom door be left open at night, who had paid no mind when the other girls had shut theirs. Still, it hadn't stopped Tilly from crawling into her bed on the odd occasion. Quickly, she released Tilly.

Sister Tessie grasped Kate's hand. "You're not running off are you? Stay with us for morning tea," she insisted.

"I have so much work to do…"

"You have to catch up!" Sister Tessie said, exasperated, gesturing across the table to Tilly as though Kate hadn't known she was there until that very moment.

"Tilly and I can catch up later." They'd be working together day in and day out, sharing a twelve-by-twelve cottage for the next three months. And then there was the other, more important factor—she had absolutely zero interest in making small talk with Tilly in front of the nuns. She couldn't do trivial. Not with Tilly.

She excused herself and started down the corridor of the convent, out the side door and through the small piles of fruits and vegetables the sisters had abandoned by the garden beds to greet Tilly.

"Kate!"

She pivoted before the garden gate.

"Wait a second!"

Tilly had her arms crossed, her hands wrapped around her ribs as though she were trying to hold herself together. "I just…" She released a deep exhalation as she rushed closer. "I just want to say how sorry I am that we lost touch."

Kate's heartbeat slowed to strong, pounding thuds. "Oh, gosh, don't worry about it." She waved a hand through the air. "These things happen. Nobody's fault."

"I know. But I'm still sorry. We should have tried harder."

It was true. They'd seen each other just once after boarding school, in their first year of university, right before the semester began. After lunch and a movie, Tilly had followed her back to the university campus. They'd gone up to Kate's dorm room. Her roommate had yet to arrive, and Kate had vibrated with a stupid sense of hope that, away from Lords, with a bedroom door they were permitted to close, *something* could happen. She'd even put fresh sheets on the bed, obsessed with the thought that her deepest fantasies—maybe Tilly's, too—could be realised in the privacy of the city.

Ever since they'd started venturing up to the convent belltower at night to kiss, she'd been confused about what it was that Tilly had wanted. That day on campus, Tilly had been different, almost nervous sitting next to Kate in the cinema. Kate thought it had been her newly cropped hair that had thrown Tilly, or her collared shirt that gave off the exact vibe she intended. But up in the dorm, Tilly had broken the news that she was going to defer university to work as a missionary in Papua New Guinea for a while. She was leaving in two weeks, she'd said, and she was terrified of what Kate would think.

After they'd talked it through, Kate had walked her down to the tram stop. In the darkness of night, they'd hugged long and hard, crying silent tears into each other's shoulders. As the St. Kilda to Flinders Street Station carriage had disappeared with Tilly aboard, Kate had known deep in her heart that was the last time she'd let herself see her best friend.

Now, as Tilly smiled warmly as she came closer, guilt crept up Kate's spine. She'd been glad for Papua New Guinea. Glad for the excuse it had given her to sever their ties. She'd been in love with a girl who could never give her what she so desperately wanted. She'd been *glad* that Tilly had gone.

"I want to know all about who you are and what you've done," Tilly said with a slight tilt of her head. "I want to know who you've become."

As their gazes locked and held, Kate swallowed. Tilly had always had a charismatic way of speaking.

"Well good thing we have a lot of time," Kate said.

Seconds ticked by.

"You look—"

"—Congratulations, again—"

"Sorry," Tilly said, her eyes widening.

"No, I'm sorry," Kate said. "What were you going to say?"

Tilly shifted her grip around herself. "I was just going to say that you look so different. Still the same but…you look very healthy."

It was hard to ignore the swell of pride that Tilly's comment provoked, the sincerity glowing in her eyes as she raked her gaze over Kate's body. Kate knew just how different she looked. In the midst of her parents' messy divorce when she had been sent to St. Joan's for repeatedly acting out in school, she'd been small and frail, riddled with anger, anxiety, and depression over the separation. A few months into Kate's first year at St. Joan's, the school counsellor had encouraged exercise, but she'd ignored it—she had Tilly now, and the days were getting easier, her grades better, her "bad attitude" improving. It had only been after graduation that Kate had learned how to use exercise to fight depression and anxiety, and spending time in city gyms had certainly helped her focus during the break up with Elodie. Now, at thirty, Kate was proud of her body, of her toned legs and strong back.

"Are you well?" Tilly asked tentatively.

"Totally fine. I'm in a really good place right now. Have been for a long time."

Tilly pressed a hand to her sternum. "Kate…I can't tell you how glad I am to hear that. After all you went through with your parents' divorce…"

A strange surge of melancholy hummed through Kate's body. She raked a hand through her hair. "When I came here for the interview they told me about Sister Hattie…I'm so sorry, Til."

Tilly's fingers toyed with her necklace. "Thank you."

"She was always my favourite of the sisters. She always checked in on me after my therapy appointments in the city, called home on the holidays to make sure I was doing okay. Sister Hattie did a lot to make sure I felt safe here. You *both* did."

Tilly waved a hand, dismissing Kate's gratitude.

"No," Kate said firmly. "I was too young to fully appreciate you at the time and…it's true. I really wasn't mentally well enough to be boarding here and you bore the brunt of that. You were a kid, not a therapist. I wasn't your problem."

Sympathy pinched at Tilly's features. "You were my best friend, Kate. I was happy to be there for you. It's what friends do."

The realisation of how deeply she had missed Tilly struck her, sudden and sharp. She forced a smile. "Again, Til, congratulations on your engagement."

"Thank you."

Kate stepped aside for Lockie as he wandered down the garden path toward the convent. "I, uh, I have a lot of work to do inside…" She gestured behind to the school.

"Of course," Tilly said. "When would you like to sit down and discuss the Literature class we're sharing?"

Kate thought for a moment. "I'd say tonight, but…is tomorrow afternoon okay? I want to meet half the boarders at Mornington Pier tomorrow morning and get them back here to settle in. Then I have the rest of the girls coming in on an afternoon ferry, and I'd like to fetch them, too… Can we say midday? We can go through the syllabus and I can introduce you to some of the girls."

"Midday is perfect." Tilly smiled. "Do you usually eat dinner in the convent?"

Nope. No. No way in hell. "Nah," she said casually. "I cook for myself. I can cook for you too. We can eat together. Tonight. I mean, if you want." *Jesus H. Christ…*

"Oh," Tilly said. "That sounds really nice, but the sisters are so looking forward to dinner tonight…"

"Right." Kate nodded. "Of course."

Tilly's expression brightened. "Join us."

"That's okay. I already have chicken defrosting." Kate shoved her hands into the back pockets of her shorts. "Anyway, I've put your bags in the guest room. Make yourself at home…"

"Thank you, Kate."

She turned from Tilly, her heartbeat quickening as she reached for the latch of the garden gate. It was her sweaty, shaky fingers that did it—her own dumb fault. She pressed too desperately at the lever, and in the blink of an eye, captured the pad of her index finger between the fixtures. A soundless squeal catching at the back of her throat, she tugged at the catch and released her finger, the tip already purpling in its agony.

Like a soundtrack to her anguish, the convent bells announced the hour. Kate mouthed curse words at the clouds until the fourth and final bell rang, drowning out her low groan. She turned back to an oblivious Tilly and forced a smile, relieved when Tilly disappeared back into the convent.

Kate yanked open the gate and started toward the school. When the Lord closed a door, the sisters constantly avowed, he always opened a window. Nothing had ever been said, Kate thought, about a bloody garden gate.

CHAPTER THREE

The deafening chime of the seven thirty convent bells had Kate blinking awake, struggling to get her wits about her as the notes played on, an eternal punishment. She groaned into her pillow. Come January, and back in the real world, she was actually *looking forward* to setting an alarm.

As the tail end of the final chime faded, she reached across her nightstand for her glasses and rolled onto her back. She pulled the covers up to her neck—the recent warm weather had been such a tease—and listened closely as she stared at the peeling bedroom ceiling. It was an odd thing, she thought, to hear the shower running in her own cottage.

Tilly had returned late the night before. From the living room window, Kate had watched Sister Mary Monica's bedroom light go out around nine, and it had been a good hour after that before the front door of the cottage opened. It had taken everything in Kate not to comment on the fact that Tilly had stayed in the convent long after the sisters retired. Kate didn't have to ask to know that she had been in there cleaning up after dinner.

Kate lay still. Just twenty-four hours ago—minutes before leaving to pick up Tilly—she'd sat on the edge of her bed trying to calm her breathing. *Ridiculous.* Now, with Tilly across the house in her bathroom, she felt completely calm—maybe even a tremor of a thrill. Not knowing what to expect had caused yesterday's anxiety, and her mind sympathised today. *And see, it was fine. It all worked out. She's fine, you're fine. It's not as uncomfortable as you thought it would be. She's forgiven you for not keeping in touch; you've forgiven yourself for never seizing the day and clicking "Add Friend" on that pictureless "Matilda Wattle" Facebook profile.*

She stumbled out of her room, her bare legs goosepimpling in just her pyjama shorts. As she boiled the kettle and made her first cup of the day, she stared out the kitchen window, slipping into a trance. Across the road, the tiny sandstone chapel shielded the fierce light of the morning sun, at least until nine when the sun crawled higher. She sipped her coffee, mentally preparing herself for the day. As exhausted as she'd be by the end of the week, she was excited to see the girls again, to be reunited for one last term together.

The bathroom door opened. The soft rays of light that warmed the cottage caught the cloud of steam lingering behind Tilly. With a towel wrapped around her head, she was already dressed for the day. Perhaps it was the length of her white dress, Kate thought, the fact that its hem brushed the ankle strap of her sandals, that made her look taller, almost Kate's five-six.

Their gazes touched. Tilly adjusted her towel, her collar gaping at the movement and exposing the slightest glimpse of porcelain skin below her collarbone. "Good morning," she said cheerfully.

"Good morning." Kate smiled. "You get up early."

"I wasn't sure what time you woke and I needed to shower and I didn't want to upset your routine…"

Kate shook her head. "This is your home too. You're not going to bother me." She gestured to the steaming cup on the sink. "I made you coffee."

"Oh," Tilly said. "I'm sorry, I don't drink coffee."

She looked down at the cup. "More for me," she joked. "I can make you tea instead?"

"No, no," Tilly insisted. "I can do it." She paused. "Do you shower?"

"Do I shower?" Kate grinned. "On the odd occasion, I suppose." She took another sip. "When the mood strikes."

Tilly rolled her eyes. "I meant in the morning. Do you shower in the morning?"

With a smile, Kate lowered her cup to the counter. "I do."

When she was finished in the bathroom, Kate opened the door to find the cottage empty. Holding her towel tight to her body, she spied through her bedroom venetians. Kate's chest tightened. In the convent garden, Tilly was bent over the tomato bushes. She looked angelic. *So soft. So warm...*

Quickly, Kate dressed and combed her hair. When she returned to the kitchen, so had Tilly. Slicing a ripe tomato onto four pieces of buttered toast, Tilly looked over her shoulder. Briefly, her gaze flickered to the buttons of Kate's waistcoat, her jeans. Was she surprised? What did she expect Kate to pair with her shirt? A skirt? Victorian brooch? Cardigan clip? Fat chance.

Kate usually skipped breakfast, but when Tilly slid her plate across the bench, she didn't have the heart to refuse the toast.

"Of course, the sisters have been up for hours," Tilly said, salting her tomato. "I could smell their breakfast," she added.

Knowing how Tilly's mind worked, Kate just couldn't help herself. She took a bite. "Yeah, it's amazing how the sisters have learned to cook for themselves without you being around to wait on them..."

Standing in the corner of the counter, toast pinched between her fingers, Tilly's lips pursed in amusement. She fixed bright green eyes on Kate. "Are you having a go at me?"

Kate shrugged. "Not at *you*."

"I never minded cooking for them."

"I know you didn't. But that still doesn't make it right."

"You make it sound like they used me as child labour."

"Didn't they?"

"Hardly." Tilly's head tilted as she chewed slowly. "Who cooks for the girls now?"

"The boarders?"

"Uh-huh."

"Sister Ellie."

"The novice?"

"Yep."

"She does *all* of the cooking? Alone? For twenty-five girls?"

Kate nodded. "We usually schedule the Food Technology classes for last period so the girls can help her with the prep before they get their buses home across the causeway."

"Still, that's a lot of preparation for one person…"

She could see the cogs turning in Tilly's mind. "Tilly…you're here as a teacher. It's not your job to clean up after the sisters and cook for them and all that."

"I know," Tilly said, but it was as if Kate's comment fell on deaf ears.

"So don't set a precedent on your first day here, okay?"

"Mmm."

Kate looked down at her watch. "I want to get the ferry over to Mornington to meet the girls." It wasn't a requirement that she chaperoned the boarders, but as housemother, she had always thought it polite to greet the girls and their parents on the boarders' first day back. "I'll see you inside at noon for our meeting?" she asked Tilly. "To introduce you to a few of the boarders?"

"Sure." Tilly smiled. "I'm looking forward to meeting the ladies of St. Joan of Arc." She turned back to the fridge.

Kate halted in the doorway, holding the screen door open. She could let it go. She could. She almost did. "Til?"

Tilly turned. "Yes?"

"This is going to sound silly…"

Tilly's brow furrowed. "What is it?"

"I try to avoid calling the girls 'ladies.'"

Tilly's eyes widened slightly. "Oh."

"It's just…" She hesitated. "It suggests that as teachers—as role models—we place certain qualities on a pedestal, reinforce particular patriarchal values. I guess, long story short, I think it's damaging. It has connotations, implies expectation."

"Expectation…" Tilly repeated.

Kate nodded. "They are girls, women. Not ladies."

Tilly reached for the last bite of her toast and leaned back against the counter. She winked. "Duly noted, Ms. York."

"Every time I see that stone freakin' statue, all I want to do is jump off the back of the ferry and drown."

Rolling her eyes, Kate rested her forearms on the deck rail as the passenger ferry made the smooth morning crossing from Mornington to East Island via Lords. She watched as Lexi's expression twisted into the scowl of a soldier conscripted against their will. "So glad to hear you're happy to be back, Lex." She grinned at Emma.

Emma tore at the wrapper of a muesli bar with her teeth and leaned back against the railing. "It's better than being at home," she said. "Two whole weeks…" She shook her head. "I was bored out of my mind."

Lexi sighed. "How the hell could you be bored on the mainland? You live in Mornington and you already have your Ps. I live on a goddamn *farm*. When I get my own car and I don't need my parents to drop me off at the pier, I swear to God, I'm not coming back to Lords until Monday mornings." She groaned, grasping the railing and extending her arms from her body like she was about to be seasick across the deck. "I can't believe I have another two years here." She turned her head and glared at Emma. "You're so fucking lucky that you graduate next year."

"Hey," Kate warned, "Language. There are children on the ferry, heading for the pioneer village."

In the cool morning wind, Emma copped a mouthful of Lexi's long blond hair. She swatted at her face. "God, tie your hair up, Lex."

Kate smirked as she watched Lexi gather her hair into a messy bun. It always amused her how the girls would return to the mainland dressed to the nines, readying themselves to meet boyfriends waiting for them at the dock. Returning to St. Joan's, they were in sweatpants—pyjamas in Lexi's case—hair wild and cheeks pillow-creased.

Lexi turned to Emma. "Hey, wanna hear what Holden told me last night on Facebook? You're going to be *really* impressed."

Kate sighed. "Lexi, I don't want to hear it. You want to tell her something scandalous?" Kate said. "Go starboard."

As the girls wandered further up the ferry, Kate turned. Sixteen-year-old Molly was seated on the bench, chatting to the relatively new Year Seven student, Cassie. She'd been pulled from her previous boarding school after being the victim of horrific bullying when Kate had first met Cassie last term. Her family and psychologist had all decided that changing schools was her best option. And she had done well at St Joan's. But now, Cassie's eyes were red-rimmed and although it was only ten fifteen, she looked exhausted from the near-anxiety attack she'd had hugging her mother goodbye at Mornington.

Kate watched Molly take a sip of her takeaway coffee, recalling how her heart had warmed at the sight of her buying Cassie a hot chocolate at the Pier café just before boarding. Molly's gesture had been very sweet, but it hadn't stopped Cassie from casting glances back at the coastline so often that Kate worried she'd jump ship to swim back to her mother. Now, as they docked at Lords, Cassie looked up the hill at the statue of St. Joan with enough dread to rival Lexi's.

It was only a few minutes' wait for Colin to tie off and help them lift their bags onto the pier before the group of ten was heading to the convent van, the suitcase wheels clonking across the thick wooden slats.

"Oh my God!" Emma groaned. "Seriously, Lexi, you just rolled your suitcase right over my toe!"

"Well don't get right up behind me while I'm trying to walk!"

"It's not me, you're under my feet! Christ!"

Kate pushed her sunglasses to the top of her head. "Hey! What are you two, five years old? Cut it out!"

"She cut me off!"

"Hey!" Kate snapped. "Does it look like I give a toss? You're going to give me a migraine before the day's out."

"*She's* a migraine," Emma said.

Lexi scowled. "*You're* a migraine."

Up ahead, Molly turned. "You're *both* a migraine."

With the sisters occupied inside the convent, Lockie was the only resident waiting to meet the girls when Kate pulled the van into the driveway. Molly and Cassie stayed outside with him, following him down the path and into the convent garden to his collection of tennis balls. A handful of Year Nine boarders disappeared into the convent, promising to be back to unload their bags from the van after they said hello to the sisters.

"God, it's so quiet in here…" Lexi murmured as she followed Kate and Emma through the heavy double doors of the boarding house.

"It *was*," Kate said, "until you arrived."

Kate followed the girls up the grand staircase, the wheels of their cases loud against the marble. "Lift, don't drag, please!" she berated.

"Em, I have to make a confession," Lexi said, already falling behind from the effort of carrying her heavy case up the two flights.

Emma turned on the stairs and stopped. With a huff, Kate moved around her.

Lexi drew a deep breath. "I watched some more of *Stranger Things* without you."

Emma quirked an eyebrow. "How much?" The corner of her mouth twitched.

Lexi visibly swallowed. "All of it."

"All of season one?" Emma clarified hopefully.

"And two."

Emma's suitcase slipped to the next step of the grand staircase. "Are you fucking *kidding* me?"

"Language!" Kate sighed.

"We stopped it at exactly episode six and you *promised* you wouldn't watch any more until we got back."

"I'll rewatch it with you!"

"It's not the fucking same, Lexi! It's not the fucking same!"

"Excuse me!" Kate said.

"You're a fucking traitor, Lexi."

Kate tossed her hands in the air. "Are my words just falling on deaf ears? Can we *please* stop swearing?"

"I wish I never gave you my Netflix password in the first place!" Emma spat. "I'm changing it!"

At the top of the landing, she looked down to the foyer. Cassie and Molly were stopped by the front door, Cassie's eyes wide as she watched Emma and Lexi disappear up the stairs to the west wing spitting vicious threats at one another.

"Mol," Kate said as she jogged back down to the foyer, "can you help Cassie with her bag?"

Kate grabbed Molly's smaller suitcase from the van and headed upstairs to the seniors' west wing. *At least one of them doesn't need to pack the entire collection of her closet to return to the island.* For Christ's sake, she thought, they wore uniforms. How many pairs of pyjamas did they need?

When Kate stepped through the door, Molly jumped from the bottom bunk. "I could have gotten it."

Kate set the bag down between the two sets of bunks. "It's okay." She ran a hand through her hair and looked around the room. "Amazing how tidy your room always is on day one." She grinned. She looked between Molly, Emma, and Lexi. "Think you can keep it this way?"

Molly smirked. "Nope."

The girls always completed their chores on Friday night before leaving for the weekend—cleaning the bathrooms, vacuuming the halls and bedrooms—but the state of their rooms throughout the week was another story altogether. Tilly wouldn't be pleased and Kate worried how that reflected on her as housemother. What if Tilly ventured up to the third floor and thought Kate was too relaxed with the girls? That she wasn't doing her job properly?

"Can we try to make our beds each morning this term?" Kate asked as she sat down on the end of Emma's bunk. "Keep the bathrooms tidier? Start throwing empty shampoo bottles in the bin?" She paused. "I feel like we need hall monitors or something," she contemplated.

"Ew, no," Lexi said. "What is this, an Enid Blyton novel? We don't need hall monitors. You already run this place like a war ship, Kate."

Kate sighed. "I run this place like a free-for-all and you know it."

Molly lifted her suitcase up onto the window seat. As she leaned over to unzip it, she looked down into the garden below. "Who's that woman?"

Lexi and Emma joined her at the window.

"That's Matilda Wattle," Kate said from her place on the bed. "She's your new Religion and History teacher until Cynthia gets back from Europe. She'll teach VCE Literature Extension with me too."

"Matilda Wattle," Molly repeated. "That's the Aussiest name I've ever heard." She looked to Kate. "Is she going to live downstairs like Cynthia did? Babysit us?"

"No, the pipes in Cynthia's suite haven't been fixed yet. Tilly's living in the cottage with me."

"So she's not a novice like Sister Ellie?" Emma asked.

Kate shook her head.

Lexi crossed her arms as she stared down into the garden. "She sure looks like one."

"No, she doesn't," Emma scoffed. "Novices wear habits."

"Not *all* novices," Lexi said. "St. Joan's is, like, one of the last convents to let go of the habit."

"Yeah, exactly—if she was a novice here, she'd be wearing one, wouldn't she?"

"Not necessarily. She could still be a novice and just be doing her own thing."

"You're literally contradicting yourself."

Kate sighed. "For God's sake, she's not a bloody novice!" she muttered as she left the room.

She wandered down the hall to the north wing. She rapped lightly at the open door of the second bedroom. "Hi, Cassie."

The petite brunette looked up from her phone. "Oh, hi," she said despondently.

"You're not unpacking?" Kate leaned against the doorjamb.

Cassie's mouth twisted. She dropped her gaze and picked at a loose thread on her bedspread. Kate chewed at her bottom lip. If there was one thing that made her feel out of her depth as a housemother at St. Joan of Arc, it was homesick kids. Cynthia, the religion and history teacher Tilly was filling in for, had always taken care of that. Although Cynthia hadn't been employed as a housemother, with her suite inside the boarding house, she'd always been a great support—and considering the fact that Cynthia was the only person who lived at St. Joan's other than the sisters, she also happened to be the only member of staff Kate was out to.

"I see you've got some new posters. What are they?" Kate tried.

"P!NK…" Cassie hesitated. "And, uhh, Zac Efron. When does Mia get here?"

"She's coming in this afternoon on the ferry." Kate had been pleased that Cassie and her roommate, also in Year Seven, had become good friends.

Cassie cracked a smile. Laughter danced down the hall from the west wing. Even Molly's cackle was loud. Kate couldn't imagine the raucous noise that Grace's arrival would bring later that day when she moved back into the west wing. Kate had never come across a person so at odds with her name.

Kate smiled. "Maybe a couple of the older girls can come in later and help you hang your posters before Mia gets here."

"Oh, that's okay. I don't want to bother them."

"Trust me," Kate chuckled. "They have absolutely nothing better to do. And later tonight, I think they're watching *Stranger Things* down in the lounge. That's the latest fad. You should go down and watch it with them."

"Maybe." She hesitated. "Is it okay if I take a nap now? Before everyone gets here?"

The poor thing probably hadn't slept a wink the night before. "Of course, you can. If you need anything, just let me know, okay?"

Cassie nodded.

With a smile, Kate closed the door behind her.

On her way back to the west wing to ask the older girls to keep an eye on Cassie, Kate stopped by a few of the dorms to let the southerly breeze through. As she lifted the windows, the draught teased the edges of posters, lifted single sheets of classwork abandoned on desks. In Hannah Simpson's room, Kate tore a Post-it from the top of a pad, scribbled *Excuse me, Ms Hannah, I told you to fill this out for holiday homework! Caught red-handed!*, and placed the Post-it and uncompleted sheet atop the thirteen-year-old's pillow.

From the end of the west wing corridor, she could see Molly, Emma, and Lexi on their knees at the window seat, peering down into the garden. Silent, Kate stopped in the doorway.

"Look at her dress," Lexi said, completely unaware of Kate leaning against the doorjamb. "She's so daggy she's almost hipster."

"Maybe she *is* a hipster," Emma reasoned.

"Nah, she looks too sweet," Molly said. "She's definitely just a dag."

"She's flatter than a washboard," Lexi murmured. "Even Emma has bigger tits than her."

"Fuck you," Emma said.

Kate cleared her throat.

She'd never seen three heads whip around so fast.

"Tilly is a lovely person. If I hear another negative word about her, I'll change the Wi-Fi password for a month."

Emma smiled as she climbed down from the window. She reached into her open suitcase and threw her toiletries bag onto her bed. "You wouldn't," she said, grinning.

Kate quirked an eyebrow. "Try me."

Just before midday, the heavy click of the double front doors echoed down the corridor of the boarding house to Kate's office. She spied out.

To the noise of the girls unpacking upstairs, Tilly stood in the middle of the sun-drenched foyer looking up at the chandelier. Her slender figure was bathed in sunlight, highlighting the auburn in her hair, her skin flushed from being outside all morning. As she tugged off her gardening gloves and set them on the side table, it wasn't so hard for Kate to remember Tilly standing in the same spot at sixteen, her white uniform blouse buttoned higher than the other girls, her blue tartan skirt an inch or two longer. She'd been so pretty as a girl. Now, she was stunning.

Something hot seized in Kate. She wanted to know everything about Tilly—her missions overseas, her time at university, her early years teaching. She wanted to know all that had built her up and brought her down, every small, insignificant choice Tilly had made in the past twelve years that had set her on the path that led back to St. Joan's, placing her here at the same time as Kate.

Fate's hand at her back, Kate started down the hall.

The moment Tilly saw her coming, her eyes snapped to Kate's. "You okay?" Kate asked.

Quickly, Tilly nodded. "Fine."

Noise swept into the foyer from every direction. The voices of her seniors in the east wing of the ground floor were distinct. "This way," Kate said, "I'll introduce you to a few of the girls…"

They ventured down the corridor, past the enormous dining room, until they reached the kitchen.

Seated at the counter island and sharing a bowl of green grapes, Molly and Emma laughed at Lexi, who, for whatever reason, had her arms locked around Sister Ellie's shoulders, playfully irritating her Food Technology teacher as she prepared lunch. When they laid eyes on Kate and Tilly in the doorway, the kitchen fell silent.

"Girls," Kate said, sliding her hands into her back pockets, "this is Ms Wattle."

"Hi," Lexi said cheerily. Molly and Emma smiled.

"*Tilly* is fine when we're in the boarding house," Tilly said.

The girls chorused their hellos.

"This is Emma," Kate introduced. She's our star athlete. You'll rarely see her here," Kate joked. "Em's always off at one state championship or another. And this is Molly. She's our prodigy. She's going to Edinburgh for a writing workshop at the end of December. One of just two Australians picked."

Molly dropped her gaze to the bowl of grapes, her cheeks colouring.

"That's incredible," Tilly said.

As housemother, Kate wasn't supposed to have her favourites— but they weren't *her* children, so she could be excused. She tried not to let it show, but she favoured Molly and Emma above the rest. They were mature, down-to-earth and free from the usual teenage angst. It disappointed her that Molly and Emma didn't seem all that close. Perhaps without Grace and Lexi around, things would have been different.

"And I'm Lexi." Lexi reached into the bowl of grapes and popped one into her mouth. "Not the prodigy, not the athlete— the other one."

Kate rolled her eyes. "Lexi isn't one of our VCE Literature girls, she's in Year Ten," Kate explained. "But you'll have her for History and Religion. And if you're lucky, Til, you may catch her at the piano. Lexi's very gifted."

Tilly smiled. "And is that what you want to do when you finish school, Lexi? Music?"

"Oh, no. I'm going to work in public relations."

"She wants to be a wedding planner," Kate explained.

"Are you very organised?" Tilly asked.

Molly and Emma snickered. "No," Lexi said, "I just read a lot of *Vogue*."

"Maybe Tilly will hire you," Sister Ellie said from the counter where she was slicing chicken fillets into strips for that night's stir-fry. "She recently got engaged."

Inappropriate, Kate thought.

Lexi popped another grape into her mouth. "Really? Can I see your ring?"

Tilly smiled as she extended her arm to Lexi.

"Woah, that's so fancy," Lexi said as she grasped Tilly's hand, turning it in her own as she appraised the sapphire. For the first time since Tilly's arrival, Kate looked at it properly. She couldn't see very well over Tilly's arm, but it certainly wasn't modern. The claws were too large and the band was marked with a vintage pattern. A family heirloom, perhaps.

"She's engaged to Vicar Armstrong," Sister Ellie said from the sink.

Lexi sank into a chair between the others. "The new vicar at St. Vincent's? But he's like sixty?"

Molly and Emma stiffened. Kate's eyes widened as she glared at Lexi.

"He's really hot in like a George Clooney way, though," Lexi added. "And I bet if you dyed his hair he'd look like only five years older than you at most—"

"Tilly, shall we get on?" Kate interjected.

In the small office reserved for the housemother, Kate reached for the broom beside her filing cabinet and banged the handle on the ceiling. Seconds later, the volume of the music lowered to a faint hum. "They're good girls," Kate assured Tilly as she gestured for her to take a seat at the desk that was far too large for such a small office. "And, by coincidence, Molly, Emma, and our other senior boarder, Grace, are the only girls who chose to take VCE Literature Extension."

Tilly's eyes widened. "We only have three Year Eleven Literature Extension students?"

"Well, I think most of the girls get their English lit fix with VCE Literature being compulsory."

Kate had gone to a great effort to prepare lesson plans for the Year Eleven Victorian Certificate of Education unit they were job-sharing. As it was, Tilly had a heavy workload working in other departments of the school—she'd be taking all grades for History and Religion, following the program Cynthia had laid out before leaving for Europe. She was job-sharing a few of the Religion studies classes with Sister Mary Monica, but still, Kate wanted to make the transition as smooth as possible for Tilly.

"Are you happy for us to start with *The Color Purple* for Lit Extension?" Kate asked.

"Oh," Tilly said. "Sister Ruth led me to believe we'd be teaching *The Glass Menagerie* to begin. I've never read *The Color Purple*."

"Really? That's okay—I have a copy in the cottage. I'd prefer if we started with *The Color Purple*. I mean, it'll take the girls a while to get through the novel—I doubt they've actually read it like they were told to do over the holidays. You can bluff them, though, teach as you read…"

Tilly laughed. "Well, that wouldn't be the first time I've had to do that."

Kate laughed. "Join the club." Sometimes even teachers had to turn to online cheat guides and chapter summaries.

Kate had reorganised the timetable as best she could, swapping a few of Cynthia's classes so that Tilly could have complete and half-days off rather than a handful of scattered free periods. "This way, you have the option to go off to the mainland on Tuesdays and Friday afternoons," Kate finished.

"That's okay," Tilly said. "I think I'd like to stay here to write anyway."

Kate edged her glasses up her nose. "Write?"

Tilly crossed her legs. "Sister Ruth didn't tell you?"

"No…" *Write?* "No."

"I have a series of chapter books, written under a pseudonym. A Catholic publisher, seven books so far. Informative novellas for children eight to ten. I'm working on a Caroline Chisholm manuscript right now. Anyway, it doesn't take up much of my time, don't worry."

Tilly dropped her gaze, and Kate's heart soared at her bashfulness. "I'm…I'm not worried. Tilly, that's amazing. I'm so impressed."

Tilly looked up. Her shoulders sagged as she laughed. "Thanks."

A knock at the door severed the spell. Tilly twisted in her seat. "Come in," Kate called out.

Lexi poked her head inside and looked between the two of them. "Cassie's upstairs and Molly says she's having a panic attack. She wants her Mum."

Kate stood, her chair legs scraping loudly against the floorboards.

"I can go," Tilly offered.

"No, no," Kate said. "I've got it."

"Honestly, it's fine," Tilly said, and before Kate could protest further, she was brushing past Lexi out the door.

Lexi looked down the hall after her, mesmerised. "She's like an angel," she murmured.

The soft, enchanting scent of Tilly's Chanel perfume lingered in the office. Kate cleared her throat. "Lex, go and ask Sister Ellie if she needs any help with lunch."

"Huh?" Lexi asked distractedly.

"Lunch," Kate repeated.

Lexi's gaze snapped from the corridor to Kate's office. "Oh. Sure. Oui, oui, *Madame Kat-er-in.*"

CHAPTER FOUR

"Are we having a barbecue?"

Squinting in the afternoon sun spilling through the windows of the second-floor music room, Kate looked at Lexi over the baby grand. "Uh-huh. For Hannah's birthday."

Lexi sniffed the air, as though the scent of frying onions wafting through the opened window from the school quadrangle for the last fifteen minutes had only just assaulted her senses. "I can't eat a barbecue."

Kate returned her gaze to the sheet music. "Excuse me?" she murmured. "You've eaten a barbecue every first night of term since I've been here."

"I'm vegan now."

Kate looked up. "Since when?"

"Since the holidays. My cousin hit a 'roo," she explained, and Kate's mind spun as she attempted to make sense of that logic. "So what's the meat substitute?" Lexi pressed.

Kate sighed. "I don't know, Lexi. If you didn't give Sister Ellie a heads-up before she took the island shuttle across the causeway to shop this morning, the *substitute* is whatever you can find in the fridge. Otherwise, I'm sure there are bread rolls."

Lexi cringed. "Bread is so fattening."

Exhausted by the first day back, Kate couldn't even summon the effort to roll her eyes. Thank God the cohort of three hundred had already escaped on afterschool buses across the causeway to Portarlington, or the Mornington ferry. Thank God only the twenty-five boarders remained.

"You think I can play once more for you before dinner?" Lexi asked hopefully. "Then we can finish."

Kate clicked her pen and set it down on her notes. "Sure."

For her end-of-year practical exam, Lexi had selected Carole King's *Beautiful*. Kate had been surprised by the choice, and then deeply impressed. She hadn't shared her hope with Lexi yet, but Kate could see her perfecting the performance to take into final year for the external markers. While Lexi's vocals were exceptional, she wasn't quite there yet as a pianist, always fumbling over the final few notes. But Lexi had time and Kate had faith.

The final bell rang just as Lexi reached the riff, but she played through it, her expression adopting a fierce determination that had Kate chewing at her lip in an effort not to grin. Lexi finished, groaning. "You don't have to clap literally every time, Kate. That was crap."

"I do have to clap each time. It may not have been as good as earlier today," Kate agreed, "but it was still very good."

As they gathered their work, the noise from the barbecue grew louder. "One day down, fifty-seven to go," Lexi sighed. "Oh, by the way, I had Tilly for History this morning."

"Yeah?"

"She said that you both boarded in our room."

"We did."

"She's really nice. I like her a lot. Glad I have Sister Ellie for French, though. You should have heard Tilly trying to pronounce the school motto earlier—well, attempting to."

Kate chuckled. "She always struggled with the accent." She turned in the doorway. "Are you coming down for dinner?"

"Yeah," Lexi said. "I just want to get one more practice in."

"Okay. Don't work too hard. Come outside soon for your bread roll, yeah?"

Lexi scowled playfully.

Kate stopped by her office inside the boarding house to drop off her notebooks. Even from across the road and indoors, the music was loud—the girls must have taken their portable speakers across to the quad. Was Tilly out there yet? Throughout the day, Kate had passed her in the hall a few times, wandered by her Year Eight History class after lunch, but they'd barely exchanged three words.

At the movement of one of her Year Nine boarders in the doorway, Kate chanced a quick glance up from checking her email on her computer. "What's up?"

The student slid her diary across the desk. "I have to get this signed by you."

Kate's gaze flickered briefly to the opened diary, to Tilly's perfect script in the bottom left corner of the day's date. "Tilly says my uniform is two centimetres too short."

Kate looked over the desk. The navy tartan skirt was a bit short above her knees, but hardly an issue. "It looks all right to me."

"Well, apparently it's not." The girl leaned across Kate's desk and lowered her voice to a whisper, as though they were sharing a secret: "She made us kneel on the floor and she checked with a *ruler*."

Kate raised an eyebrow. "She did?"

"It was *so* weird."

So weird was how the memory of being alone with Tilly in the belltower suddenly struck her. Kate, slipping her hands over the smoothness of Tilly's thighs, Tilly letting Kate's touch venture beneath the hem of her school skirt. Kate pressed it to the back of her mind. Reluctant to undermine Tilly, she signed the diary. "Get the hem taken down over the weekend, yes?"

"Fine…"

Outside, back across the dirt road and inside the school quad, Kate found Grace and Molly helping Sister Mary Monica and Sister Ruth at the barbecue, the two girls insisting they didn't need the aprons Sister Ruth attempted to slip over their heads to protect their uniforms.

At one of the picnic benches inside the quad, Sister Ellie was busy buttering bread rolls. "Don't butter Lexi's," Kate told her as she slipped up beside her and reached for a disposable cup. "She's vegan now."

Sister Ellie shook her head as she watched Kate pour apple juice from the picnic vat. "I give it a week."

Kate scoffed as she cast her gaze fondly over the girls' volleyball game across the quad. "I give it three days." Leaning back against the table, she looked across the quad in search of the woman who had been on her mind all day.

There she was, at the furthest table, fixing the blanket over Sister Tessie's knees. The downing sun cast Tilly's immaculately coiffed bun copper as she sat back on the garden bench, her shoulder pressed against Sister Tessie's, fingers clasped between the elderly sister's hands as Sister Tessie talked her ear off. The afternoon wind fluttered the hem of Tilly's skirt, the thin material licking at the base of her calves. Tilly bent for a moment to tuck it between her legs. As she sat back again, she said something. Grinning, Sister Tessie smoothed a hand up Tilly's forearm, rubbed back and forth like a proud, affectionate grandmother.

An ache grew in Kate's heart. It was nice that Tilly had come home just in time, she thought, that Sister Tessie could still remember who Tilly had been, appreciate who she had become.

If a cardinal sin had ever dared anchor in Lords Cove, it was pride. Kate could see it shining bright in the sisters' eyes each time Tilly spoke of her education, her career, her missions… Was it silly for Kate to feel proud of Tilly too? She had no business feeling such satisfaction. They hadn't been close for years. And yet, since Tilly's return, pride dangled before her like forbidden fruit. As reluctant as she was to admit it to herself, she wanted more than just a taste.

After they'd sung "Happy Birthday" and Hannah had blown out the candles on her cake, the girls cleared dinner's mess without being prompted.

"No, I can do it myself," Tilly insisted when Lexi reached for Tilly's empty plate.

"There's no dishwasher," Lexi said. "We wash our own, clean up after ourselves—it's not going to give me carpal tunnel to wash and wipe your plate too. Besides," she added, "if I don't, Kate'll lecture us about it for the next three months until she nicks off."

It was undeniably true. When Kate had arrived there had been a rotating roster in place that the Reverend Mother had implemented years before. The problem, however, was that Sister Ruth was oblivious to the fact that poor Sister Ellie always cleaned up *after* half-job cleanups. Deciding that hearing one more excuse of "those plates needed to soak overnight" would send her grey before her time, Kate changed the system—each girl would clean up after herself.

With the sisters retiring for the night and the juniors disappearing into the boarding house to squeeze an hour of television in before checks, only the three seniors and Lexi stayed out in the school quad at the fire pit with Kate and Tilly.

From her seat at the fire, Kate spotted Cassie coming under the arched entrance of the quad before the others did. Gaze dropped, arms wrapped about herself in the cool of night, Cassie looked exhausted. Poor kid, Kate thought as she watched Cassie cross the quad, her hands lost in the sleeves of her jumper.

"Hey Cassie," Kate offered. "How are you feeling?"

"Good," Cassie said unconvincingly. She paused. "I, uhh, I just wanted to say that I know it's not checks yet, but I'm going to sleep now. Thank you for dinner." She turned.

"Cassie?" Tilly called softly, and the girl backtracked. "Would you like to call your mum tonight?"

Cassie shook her head. "It'll only make it worse…I think."

Tilly reached for her hand and Kate watched as she gave it a squeeze. "I think that's probably a good idea."

"Hey," Grace said as she tugged on Cassie's other hand. "In fourth term, we never go to bed without hugs."

"We don't?" Lexi asked. "Since when?" Kate smirked as Molly shot Lexi a glare.

Reluctant, Cassie accepted Grace's warm embrace with a one-armed, half-hearted hug. "Nope," Grace said. "That's not a hug. Twenty seconds is a hug."

The longer Grace held Cassie, the quicker a smile spread across the younger girl's expression, and by the time Molly had announced the thirteen-second mark, they were all laughing. Across the low fire, Kate's gaze locked with Tilly's. Held. Tilly smiled. Kate's mouth grew dry. She looked away.

Kate lowered Tilly's tea to the coffee table and examined the flames jumping inside the wood heater. She looked to the closed bathroom door. Should she throw another log on before Tilly finished her shower? Would Tilly like that? Or was it already too hot? The cottage was only small... Another log, she decided, crouching to open the glass door. Tilly always was a cold frog.

When the bathroom door opened, Kate looked up from the fireplace. Her smile slipped at the sight of Tilly's concerned expression.

"I can smell marijuana," Tilly said.

Kate stood. "What?"

"In the bathroom," Tilly said, gesturing behind herself. "I opened the window to let the steam out and... Somebody in the boarding house is smoking marijuana."

Pot? At St. Joan's? No way. The girls wouldn't dare. It was probably just the smoke from the cottage chimney wafting back through. "Maybe Sister Mary Monica's smoking a joint for her arthritis," she joked.

Tilly pinned Kate with her gaze. "Do you not believe me?"

It wasn't that she didn't believe her, but Tilly identifying the scent of pot? It seemed like a long shot.

"You think I don't know what pot smells like?" Tilly's eyes hardened. "Because you think I'm naïve?"

Well that escalated quickly... Kate pulled herself from the lounge and followed Tilly into the bathroom, distracted more by the impulse to reach out and touch her fingers to Tilly's flannel winter pyjamas than the sudden aroma that assaulted her senses. Kate inhaled, her eyes widening as her gaze locked with Tilly's. "I'm going to kill them," she said. "I'm going to bloody kill them."

She stood on the toilet and peeled back the lacy white curtain. Nothing but darkness.

With Tilly at her heels, Kate stormed out the front door in her slippers. At the side of the cottage, she looked up to the second floor. The window was closed, as were the higher east wing dorm windows.

A gust of wind picked up the leaves raked at the base of the gum tree. Together they stood, silent. Listening. As Tilly wrapped her arms about herself in the cold night air, voices carried on the wind. Kate's gaze flickered a second time to the window on the ground floor. She inhaled sharply as the blind crashed against the windowsill. The kitchen window was open. The moonlight was weak, but it was just enough for Kate to identify a hand reaching through the window, settling the rattling blind.

"It was definitely marijuana?" Tilly whispered. "Right?"

"It was definitely marijuana," Kate mumbled. "Stay here, I'll deal with it."

The front door locked, Kate ventured around the side. She unlocked the back door as quietly as possible. As she neared the end of the east corridor, she realised that the kitchen door wasn't quite closed. A soft glow poured through the narrow gap, oozing into the corridor. Was it her Year Nines? They were a problematic bunch. She'd caught them with that bottle of vodka early in the year and having been forced to reprimand them, Kate hadn't bonded with any of them. Kate listened to the soft murmur of voices. It had to be the Year Nines. Lexi was the only boarder in Year Ten, and surely Kate's bookish Year Eight boarders hadn't gotten their hands on any pot. It had to be her Year Nines. It had to be.

She pushed open the kitchen door. "For God's sake!" She coughed harshly against the stench. They'd hotboxed the goddamn kitchen.

She flicked on the light and gasped at the sight of her three seniors—Grace, Molly, and Emma. And Lexi.

Her gaze flickered from Lexi, sitting between Emma and Grace on the island counter and spreading Vegemite onto bread, to the opened jars of jam and peanut butter beside them. Two loaves of bread, slices fallen out of their bags like dominoes. A tray of cooked sausages left over from the barbecue. *Bloody hell.* Just when she thought it couldn't get any worse than the time she'd caught Lexi and Emma snacking on unconsecrated communion wafers because they "were out of chocolate chip biscuits."

The blue flame burning on the stovetop glowed almost as strongly as the panic in Molly's eyes.

"Where is it?" Kate demanded.

"Where's what?" Lexi asked. Slowly, she lowered a half-eaten sausage into the barbecue tray.

"The pot," Kate growled.

Silence settled heavily. As Kate crossed the kitchen to turn off the burning jet, Emma avoided her sharp glare, staring down into the Nutri-Grain packet in her grasp.

"Is somebody going to tell me where it is?" Kate pressed.

Emma looked to Molly, then to Lexi. Grace buried her face in her hands and groaned.

"There's none left," Lexi said. "We smoked it all."

At least they're all too baked to lie. Kate exhaled. "How much did you smoke?"

Grace rubbed at her right eyelid. "It's okay, we only shared two joints."

"Oh, *it's okay*, is it?" Kate asked. She coughed, hard. And to think she'd been so proud watching them clean up after themselves hours before. "You are all in *so* much trouble. Get to bed."

They rounded the table, passing Kate at the stove. Lexi had the decency to avert her glassy-eyed gaze, but Emma was less sensible, exhaling audibly as she made for the door.

"You didn't just sigh at me," Kate challenged. "*Did* you?"

Emma's eyes danced in a haze, more bloodshot than Lexi's. "No."

"Good. That's what I thought. Go."

Kate pulled up the blind. Sister Ellie was coming in to prepare breakfast at six. Unless Kate wanted her to have an intensely spiritual experience at mass the next morning, she had no option but to air out the room. Just when Kate thought the girls had gone, Molly's voice ruptured the silence. "Are you going to tell my parents?"

Kate's head whipped around, surprised to find both Molly and Tilly standing in the doorway. Tilly's arms were crossed, and for somebody who had known the girls not forty-eight hours, she'd mustered an expression of disappointment worthy of an Academy Award. Or maybe, unlike Kate, she was upset rather than angry. Her hair was down, her concern so authentic that she hadn't plaited it before leaving the privacy of their cottage.

Kate turned back to the blinds. Her back to Molly and Tilly, Kate thought for a moment. "We'll see. Go to bed."

Molly's footsteps were soft as she padded away.

Kate could feel Tilly's gaze boring into her back, the judgement radiating off her like electricity. "You're not going to call her parents?" she asked.

Kate turned. "Oh, I definitely am. But it's midnight. If telling her I'm not stops her having a pot-fuelled panic attack and gets me some sleep, then that's what I'll do. And tomorrow…tomorrow I'll put the fear of God into them."

CHAPTER FIVE

At the double beep of the message bank, Kate sat forward in her office chair. "Hi, Ms Kirkpatrick. This is Katherine York from St. Joan's. Again. I'm not sure if you got my message this morning, but I'd like to have a chat with you when you get a chance. Emma's fine, no need to worry, but if you could give me a call back, I'd really appreciate it—"

The beep sounded. Kate drummed her pen against the edge of her desk in frustration. Well, she reasoned, three out of four were good odds.

Molly's parents hadn't been particularly concerned—apologetic more than anything. Molly was a good kid—a few puffs of a joint wasn't going to send her off the rails, and Kate had to agree. Grace's and Lexi's parents, on the other hand, had been irate, and when Kate passed the girls in the dining hall at breakfast, they'd looked very sheepish. It seemed their parents had followed through on their promises to contact their daughters privately.

Fourteen hours after the incident, Kate still hadn't punished the group as per Sister Ruth's instruction. Not because she was deliberating over a suitable penalty, but because she believed guilt was the most impactful sentence of all.

"Kate?"

Kate pulled her gaze from her marking. One of her Year Tens was standing in the doorway of her office. "What's up?"

Her student grimaced. "Um, Sister Mary Monica was wondering if you could come over to the chapel and fix a kneeler."

"A kneeler?"

"It…it broke again."

"Because you *stood* on it, correct?"

"It was Lexi!"

Jaw tightening, Kate pressed her pen closed. *You have got to be kidding me.* "How many times does Sister Ruth have to tell her to walk around it, not over it?" Of course Lexi had to break a kneeler on the maintenance man's day off. The last thing Kate felt like at two thirty on a Wednesday afternoon was playing jack-of-all-trades, but she couldn't very well expect Sister Ruth to get down on her hands and knees with a screwdriver just because one of the kids had decided to play walk the plank. "Go back to the chapel," Kate sighed, "I'll be there in a minute."

Taking the toolbox from the cleaning cupboard, Kate stepped outside for the first time in hours. She squinted in the afternoon sun.

From the strawberry patch on the far side of the garden, Tilly looked up. Swiping the back of her gloved hand between her brow and Sister Ruth's straw hat, she smiled. Kate bit her lip. She waved back.

On the field, Emma and Grace were kicking a ball around with Lockie, shouting calls to each other that were loud enough to be heard from Mornington. "Hey, you two!" Kate whisper-called. "Sister Mary Monica's class is still in confession, how about you lower your voices!"

"Sorry!"

Kate squinted at the far end of the field—Jeremy Nguyen, the PDHPE teacher—was with the rest of the class at the high jump mats. "Why aren't you doing high jump with Mr Nguyen?"

"Can't do high jump today," Grace called out. "I think I injured my coccyx."

Kate rolled her eyes.

As the arched chapel door shut behind Kate, the girls seated in the pews waiting to go into the confessional looked over their shoulders. Even the two at the altar kneelers swivelled. Kate dipped her fingertips into holy water and blessed herself, shot them all a look. Immediately, they returned their attention to the altar.

Kate started down the centre aisle, her sinuses tingling. Christ, the sisters were using enough incense to scent the Vatican. St. Joan of Arc was the size of a shoebox—and that was its charm.

In the left sector of the pews, Lexi was seated with another Year Ten student. Kate approached, bristling as she watched Lexi's lips move in deep conversation. Kate tapped her on the shoulder. Lexi swivelled. "Where's the broken kneeler?" Kate asked coolly.

Lexi looked up at Kate through her lashes. "It's the same one as last time."

Rolling her eyes, Kate continued down the aisle. Why did Lexi have to push the limit with everything?

She sat the toolbox down at the end of the pew and got down on all fours, straddling the broken kneeler. She pushed her glasses to the top of her head and looked into the dark void beneath the seat. The screw connecting the kneeler to the pew was halfway out. Sister Caroline had repaired it last time, but her poor eyesight and arthritis had obviously been an impediment.

Even down in the depths of the pews, she could still hear Lexi a few pews behind, chattering away at a mile a minute.

"Alexandra!" Sister Ruth berated. "Quiet. *Please*."

"Sorry, Reverend Mother."

"Father Rodney didn't have to come all the way back to Lords for a second time today after giving mass to us this morning, but he did—for you girls. Father Rodney isn't even our local priest, and yet, twice in one day, he's driven the causeway back and forth to save Father Peter the trouble of leaving St. Gerard's to catch the ferry from Mornington. The least you can do is keep quiet for half an hour!"

"Sorry, Reverend Mother."

Bent low, Kate turned her head down the aisle and watched as Sister Ruth's feet disappeared out the side door of the church. Within seconds, Lexi started up again.

"Far out," Lexi sighed, "it's not my problem old mate Rodney has to hike it here every morning at the crack of dawn to give the sisters their daily mass."

Kate shot up onto her knees.

The girls started. "Shit," Lexi whispered.

Kate locked eyes on her. "Did you not hear the Reverend Mother? Has the cannabis affected your hearing too?"

They dropped their gazes to their laps.

"Zip it!" Shaking her head, Kate returned to working on the kneeler, the stone floor icy beneath her palm.

Lexi leant forward over the back of the seat. "Are you still dirty with me?" she dared.

"I'm not *dirty* with you," Kate murmured, buried beneath the pew and practically on her belly. "I'm *deeply disappointed*. Now sit back in silence and think about all of the *sins* you can confess to when you step into the confessional and…"

Kate trailed off, her gaze darting to the side as a familiar pair of sandals came into view. Tilly stopped before her. A strong impulse gripped Kate—the need to reach out and skim her fingers over the delicate bones of that ankle, to trail her hand under the hem of that dress… Swallowing, she glanced up.

Dancing lithe fingers across the back of seat in front, Tilly smiled down at Kate. "Good afternoon."

Audibly, Sister Mary Monica motioned to Lexi and her partner in crime across the church, leaving Kate alone in Tilly's company.

Tilly held her gaze.

"Hello, Tilly Longstocking." Kate could hear the husk in her own voice. Immediately, she returned her eyes to the kneeler, trying to ignore the way her heart hammered against her breastbone. *Get a hold of yourself.* If she didn't cut it out now, she wouldn't survive the next three months feeling like she was going to combust every time she locked eyes with Tilly.

Tilly sank to her knees at the end of the pew. "Can I help?" she whispered, setting the straw hat on the seat.

Kate let her gaze flicker upward for a moment. Tilly's neck was flushed pink from being out in the sun. Kate wanted to kiss it, maybe even taste it, slide her tongue along the slope of the tendons there, against her pulse. *Congratulations, Kate. Thinking dirty thoughts in a chapel—you've officially stooped to an all-new low.* It wasn't Tilly, she told herself. It was just that she hadn't had sex in such a long time and here was Tilly, looking at Kate with those kind green eyes, and she was so gorgeous and sweet and they had a history fuelled not by passion but by pure love and unfailing care. She just needed to be touched. That was all.

Kate shifted back, placing some space between them. "Could you, uh, hold the end of the kneeler up for a sec? While I get the screw back in?"

"Of course."

Kate leaned down and tucked her head beneath the chair. "A fraction higher?" Kate asked, watching the drilled hole until Tilly lifted the kneeler high enough between Kate's legs so that the holes were lined up to fit the screw. "There," Kate murmured. "That's perfect."

"How did you go with the phone calls this morning?" Tilly asked softly.

Kate worked the screwdriver. "Spoke to all bar Emma's mum. I left a message, but I'm still trying to get a hold of her."

"I wanted to ask you about it at lunch, but I couldn't find you— you weren't in the staffroom with everybody else."

"I'm rarely in the staffroom at lunch—I prefer my office in the boarding house."

"But everybody eats in the staffroom."

"Not everybody. Clarissa eats in her science rooms, and legend has it that Marielle hasn't left the art room for lunch in seven years."

Kate focused for a moment on fitting the screw into place. "You're quite the handyman," Tilly remarked.

"Handy*woman*."

"Well, I was going to say *handylady*," Tilly played, "but I've been told such language isn't permitted at this school. I don't know if you've heard, but apparently there's a staff member here who is quite the staunch feminist."

Kate grinned as she tightened the screw. "Now, that couldn't be the same teacher roaming the grounds handing out uniform infringements, could it?"

"Oh no. I hear the two women are quite different."

Kate shrugged as she got to her knees. She sat beside Tilly on the seat. "I don't know about that..."

Kate lowered her glasses from the crown of her head and appraised Tilly. The corners of Tilly's mouth twitched, the creases beside her eyes all the more noticeable for it. Tilly seemed to be searching her gaze for something. Kate tilted her head in question.

"Your glasses are dirty," Tilly explained.

"Oh, they're always..." Kate faded out as Tilly grinned, reaching up to pull the plastic arms from behind Kate's ears. Kate's vision adjusted again as she watched Tilly buff the lenses on the polka-dotted skirt of her pale-blue dress.

Kate admired the way the sunlight streaming through the stained-glass window played across Tilly's face. The reds and blues of St. Joan before battle danced in Tilly's hair, on her nose, the shell of her ear. Tilly handed her glasses back. "There you go."

"Thank you." Her eyes dropped to Tilly's lips. It was easy to remember how they'd felt against her own, that soft, timid give and take that had come so naturally. Three times they'd snuck up to the belltower at night. Three times knowing that what they were doing was risky, that their decisions were heavy with meaning. Just *three* times. Did Tilly think about it?

Tilly reached out and pinched the cuff of Kate's shirt, rolled up to her elbows. Her fingertips brushed against the hairs on Kate's forearms.

Skin tingling, Kate adjusted her glasses. "What?"

Tilly's breath was warm on the line of her jaw. "Why do you dress like this?"

"Like what?"

"So...masculine."

Her gaze bore into Tilly's. Tilly stared back, unblinking. There was something there in her gaze, something unveiled, unguarded. Whatever it was, it seemed to be able to understand Kate better than seventeen-year-old Tilly ever had. Kate swallowed. She had questions, *so many questions*, and the desire to voice them showed no sign of waning any time soon. "Why do you dress so feminine?" she whispered.

"Matilda?"

At the raised whisper, they both swivelled. Sister Mary Monica had moved into the aisle, standing a couple of pews behind. She fixed her stare on Tilly. "Father is ready for you after Claudia," she murmured.

"Oh," Tilly said. "Thank you, Sister."

Sister Mary Monica's gaze darted between them. "Would you like me to let Father know that you'll also be seeking penance, Kate?"

Kate hadn't been to confession in months. When she had, it had only been to keep up appearances and she hadn't shared anything true. If she needed forgiveness, she'd ask the heavens for it while she was out on a run, not Father Rodney. Tilly shifted against the seat. Their knees brushed. "No thanks, Sister," Kate whispered.

Sister Mary Monica nodded shortly and moved along. Kate ran her tongue along her teeth as she watched her go. Why did she suddenly feel sixteen again, burning under the calculating eye of Sister Mary Monica? She turned her head. Tilly was looking past her, up to the stained-glass window above their pew. "I love the way the light comes in of an afternoon," Tilly said, her voice barely a whisper. "The way it plays across the altar…the tabernacle…"

Kate could feel Tilly's gaze on the side of her face as she stared up at the window of Joan of Arc in complete armour. "That one was always our favourite," Tilly whispered, "remember?"

She nodded. "I remember."

They sat in silence. For the first time since Tilly had been back, the moment felt heavy, like all of their truths were spilling into the silence between them. Kate gripped the edge of the wooden pew and fixed her gaze on pools of emerald. "I missed you, Tilly."

Tilly's lips parted. Kate watched the pulse jump in her neck. "I missed you too, Kate. I can't tell you how often I thought of you…"

Across the church, Claudia, a Year Eight student, exited the confessional. Sister Mary Monica looked across the church, and in an instant, Tilly stood. "See you later," she whispered.

Kate's heart pounded a hard, steady beat against her chest. "See you."

As she watched Tilly walk down the aisle, Kate prickled with anticipation of their first dinner together that night. For the first time, they'd be alone in the cottage and really get to talk. Just the two of them. Alone.

Tilly genuflected before the small altar, her long dress gathering across the back of her calf. As she stepped inside the confessional and closed the wooden door behind her, Kate watched her expression crease with…distress?

Kate gathered the contents of her small toolbox and headed out the doors of St. Joan of Arc. What on earth would Tilly Wattle have to seek absolution for?

Is it too much to set the table, Kate wondered to herself. She usually just ate on the lounge while she watched TV, but Tilly didn't know that. Kate looked across the living space to Tilly. Reclined on the lounge in her pyjamas, she was focused intently on marking

History tests she'd given that morning, her fingers mindlessly toying with her plait. Kate hunted in the cabinet beside the stove for the pasta strainer. Would Tilly mind sitting at the table to share a meal? They'd be able to talk more without the distraction of the TV. And if they set a precedent now—to sit together each night and talk over dinner—then Kate would have it to look forward to at the end of the day. The corner of her lips twitched with a smile. Yes, she'd definitely set the table.

The scent of Tilly's body wash was comforting as she slid up beside Kate at the sink. "Can I help with anything?" she asked.

Steam rose from the strainer. Kate swirled the pasta, the movement disguising the way her body jerked suddenly at the brush of Tilly's hand across the low of her back. "Nope. All done."

While she plated up their dinner, Tilly filled their water glasses. At the table, Kate picked up her fork and whirled it through her pasta. "So how was—"

"You don't say Grace?"

Kate looked up. Tilly's lips were pursed.

"Um…no." *But something gives me a feeling I'm about to start…*

Tilly looked to Kate's fork. Slowly, Kate let the pasta slide off and back into her bowl. *Message received.*

Tilly's eyes closed. She clasped her hands together. Running her tongue along her teeth in amusement, Kate did the same.

Tilly pressed her steepled hands to her breastbone. "Bless us, O Lord, and these, Thy gifts, which we are about to receive from Thy bounty."

Kate's eyes dropped from Tilly's lips to her collarbone.

"Through Christ, our Lord—"

"Where's your crucifix?"

Tilly's eyes snapped open. Instantly, she made to clutch at her pendant. She stiffened. "Oh no. It fell off in the garden but I thought I had secured it properly." Her eyes grew wide. "Oh, Kate," she said anxiously. "Aunt Hattie gave it…I…I can't sleep without it."

Something caught in Kate's chest at the grief in Tilly's gaze. She pushed back her chair. "The garden? It's okay, we'll find it." Taking the torch from beneath the kitchen sink, Kate smiled reassuringly. "Come on, let's go."

The torch battery was low. Kate bashed it against her palm, hoping the jolt would spark life. No luck. "Give me the torch and you use my phone torch," Tilly said, tossing her slippers off beside the garden gate. "My eyesight has always been much better than yours."

"Gee thanks."

As Tilly opened the gate, she swiped roughly at her jawline with her free hand. Kate's heart clenched. In the moonlight, Tilly's skin was wet with tears.

Tilly headed straight for the spinach patch. "I was in the lettuce bed for a long time, and then..." She inhaled sharply, her step faltering as she spun back to glare at the fruit boxes. "Oh no, I was in the strawberry bed, and tomatoes too..."

So basically the entire garden.

Kate gasped as Tilly stepped over the edge of the raised garden bed, a warning ready on the tip of her tongue as Tilly's toe *just* scraped the rim. She stumbled. Quickly, Kate reached out to steady her, but Tilly paid no mind, heading for the strawberries, her frustration growing.

Kate followed. "Hey, Til, hey..." Gently, she grabbed for Tilly's hand and stilled her. Goosebumps erupted on Tilly's skin as Kate rubbed at her arms. "Hey, calm down, okay? We're going to find it," she said with all the conviction she could muster. "We will."

Tilly's eyes wouldn't meet hers. Unfocused, her gaze travelled the garden. "We don't even know that it's here..." Her voice trembled. "Oh God, I wish I'd lost the ring instead."

Kate chewed her lip, a surge of bliss seizing her.

Tilly looked up. "I didn't...I didn't mean that," she whispered.

Kate nodded. She broke the eye contact and bent low to roll her pyjama pants to her thighs, just as Tilly had. "It's somewhere on this island and we're going to find it. I'll start in the strawberry bed and then the tomatoes. You go and start in the veggie patch, okay?"

Tilly nodded. "If God wants me to find it, I'll find it..."

Kate nodded tersely. Lately, she'd found herself thinking the same about Tilly.

They seemed to hunt for hours, and Kate was glad that Lockie was inside the convent and not hovering, kicking up the dirt as he moseyed about. The wind picked up, whipping Kate's T-shirt about her sides, licking at her pyjama pants, the red-chequered fabric already putrid with soil. As Kate came to the end of the orchard— much smaller than the veggie patch—she chanced a glance at Tilly. She was barely halfway through the second row of spinach. A shiver chasing down her spine, Kate adjusted her glasses. No way in hell was she going to leave Tilly alone out here in the cold, but Kate didn't know if moving over to join Tilly was the best idea. Knowing Kate had had zero luck across the garden would only upset her. Perhaps starting over in the fruit trees was the way to go. She'd be more thorough this time around.

Moving back to the first raised garden bed, Kate paused by the gate. She watched as Tilly rubbed at her bare arms.

Dropping her torch between the tomato stakes, Kate hurried inside. She took Tilly's cardigan from the back of the lounge and went back out. Gently, she drummed her fingers across Tilly's shoulders. "Put this on."

Tilly looked up, her expression clouded with frustration. "Thanks," she murmured, slipping her arms into the sleeves before returning to her quest with renewed vigour.

Barefoot and toes stiffening in the cold, Kate stepped into the raised tomato bed. Crouching between the bushes, she sighed. She flicked on the torch, danced the pathetic glow from stake to stake, and like lightning, the glint of gold caught her eye. Kate's eyes snapped up. There, hooked around a splintered tomato stake, was Tilly's necklace.

Quickly, Kate plucked the chain from the stake and crossed the garden, a heady mix of excitement and relief charged in her chest. She fell to her knees beside Tilly in the veggie patch.

Focused, Tilly scanned the ground. "I know we've been out here forever. I know that. I know it's silly to be looking in the dark when it'll be so much easier in the light of day but I just won't sleep wondering." Her gaze remained rooted to the soil. "You can go back inside and eat. I don't mind."

As Tilly moved to crawl forward, Kate reached out, let the chain dangle before her eyes.

Tilly's breath caught. Pushing herself to her knees, she launched her body into Kate's arms. "Thank you, Kate," she gasped. "Thank you so much. I'll have to get the chain fixed."

Tilly clutched at her back, her face buried in Kate's neck. Her skin was hot against Kate's, her freshly washed hair still damp. She breathed a sob of relief against Kate's bare skin and Kate shivered at the sensation as Tilly's hand cupped the back of her neck. Tilly's heartbeat fired against her chest, and Kate was grateful for the chain clutched safely in her fist, that her hands locked at the small of Tilly's back couldn't smooth over hips pressed firmly against her own.

Her short nails digging into her palms, Kate pulled back. She opened her hand and Tilly took the chain, her fingernails scratching against Kate's dirt-caked skin in a ticklish pinch that shot heat straight between Kate's legs.

Tilly clipped the chain around her neck, her eyes slipping closed in relief. She breathed a little sigh as she held the pendant to her skin. Kate's mind whirled as desire tightened in the pit of her stomach. It was impossible to focus on anything but the need to press her lips to Tilly's, to run her hands over every inch of her body and never stop. *But you have to stop.* You have to stop this right now, she told herself. *She is your friend. Your straight, engaged friend. Your straight friend engaged to a vicar…*

Kate scooted backward on her knees and flicked off the torch.

"Oh my goodness," Tilly laughed, letting Kate pull her to her feet. Her eyes dropped to Kate's dirt-caked knees, then her own. "Look at us!" she said, swatting the soil from her shins, her elbows. "We're filthy! We're going to have to shower all over again!"

Kate chuckled. "I call first shower after dinner."

"I may have to join you—we'll have wasted that much hot water!"

Kate swallowed harshly. That image wasn't doing much to alleviate the problem.

Seemingly oblivious to what she'd said, Tilly looked up from turning off her iPhone torch. "I'm so sorry that it took so long. You must be starving."

"Yeah," Kate said, laughing breathily as she bent to retrieve their slippers from behind the garden gate. "Starving."

CHAPTER SIX

It was during fifth period on the following Wednesday when Tilly stopped in the doorway of the music room, her face flushed and a book tucked beneath her arm.

"Hey," Kate said as the last of her Year Seven Music students passed Tilly on their way to their next class.

Tilly popped open the top button at the collar of her dress, the lapels parting. "There's something I have to discuss with you," she said, exhaling deeply as she stopped before Kate's desk.

"Sure," Kate said. "The VCE girls will be here in a few minutes but you can have me until—"

"Who prescribed *The Color Purple*?"

Slowly, Kate slipped the marked pages of the Year Seven girls' music assessments into her fifth period folder. "I already told you. Cynthia and I selected the texts together..."

Tilly set *The Color Purple* down on the edge of Kate's desk. "And have you read it?"

Kate quirked an eyebrow. "Of course I've read it."

Tilly tapped the cover with her fingertip. "And you approved it as a prescribed text?"

"Obviously."

"Well," Tilly huffed, "it was banned."

Seriously? "So what if it was banned? We studied *The Catcher in the Rye* and that was banned. In fact, I vividly recall Sister Mary Margaret teaching us Salinger. Remember?"

"Of course I remember."

Kate looked at Tilly over the top of her glasses. "I take it you also had a problem teaching *Dracula*."

"I haven't taught *Dracula*—I'm not usually an English teacher."

Kate looked up and focused on Tilly's hardened expression. *Wow.* She was genuinely irritated. What on earth had just happened across the quad in VCE Literature Extension?

"This is a Catholic school," Tilly said confidently, as though she'd rehearsed her argument on her way to the music room. "We need to adhere to Catholic teachings."

Kate scoffed. "This isn't the eighties—"

"There are explicit sexual references."

"Tilly, a small passage from *The Color Purple* isn't going to make much of an impression on these girls, trust me. We have much greater cause for concern—a copy of *Fifty Shades of Grey* has been making the rounds for months. I'm sure it's under one of their mattresses. I just have to find it…"

Ignoring Kate, Tilly swiped the novel from the desk and flicked through it, her cheeks hollowing as she bit the insides of her mouth. Suddenly, she stopped turning the pages, her eyes focused on a particular passage. "It says…"

"It says?" Kate prompted.

As her gaze locked with Kate's, Tilly swallowed overtly. She stood taller and squared her shoulders. "Pussy."

Hearing the word fall from Tilly's lips sent a charge through her. Quickly, it faded as amusement tugged at the corners of her mouth.

"Don't laugh at me, Kate! I'm serious about this!"

"I'm not laughing at you."

"The girls certainly were!"

"They laughed at you?"

"It's not just…the 'pussy' thing." Her voice lowered. "We were discussing the theme of sexuality…"

Kate raised an eyebrow.

"And that's fine," Tilly assured her, "that's *expected*—it's a senior English literature class. But then Grace *insisted* we discuss the passage in which Celie looks at herself…" She hesitated. "Between her legs, with a mirror…"

"And?" Kate prompted.

Tilly held her gaze for a long moment before she extended the novel to Kate, opened to the passage.

Tilly tapped a paragraph with her fingernail and Kate made a disgruntled sound of acknowledgment as she began speed-reading. A young woman learning herself while her trusted friend advised her from behind a closed door—so what? The passage was beautifully written and integral to character development. Kate could feel Tilly's sharp eyes scanning her face. She could only imagine the immature giggles the passage had received from the girls. But what had gotten Tilly so riled up?

She returned the book to Tilly's hands. "Whatever the girls said, they're just stirring you up."

"Yeah?" Tilly pressed. "Just stirring me up? Then why, when I explained the metaphor of Shug's *button*," she air quoted the word, her cheeks tinging pink, "did Grace say, 'The button she's touching isn't a metaphor, Tilly.' In fact, I believe Grace's words were, 'The button is pretty *f-ing* literal.' So if they're just *stirring me up* as you claim they are, then why did they find *that* so hilarious?"

Kate chuckled. *Wow, Tilly, pulling out the big guns…*

"Don't be arrogant, Kate. Why?"

Kate's gaze shot up. "What?" she asked, confused.

"Why did the girls laugh at that?" Tilly repeated, completely serious.

Kate blinked twice. Hold up. Was Tilly not being sarcastic? Was she *genuinely* asking Kate what Grace had meant? Did she *really* not understand? "Seriously?"

Tilly arched a brow, waiting.

"Til…in the book…she's talking about her clitoris."

"Excuse me?"

She wet her lips. "Her button…it's her clitoris."

Tilly's brow furrowed as she stared at Kate. Lowering her gaze, she reopened the novel and began flicking for the passage.

Kate watched, gobsmacked, as confusion crossed Tilly's face. Hail Mary Full of Grace…had Tilly really not known? She was thirty…how was that possible? The passage was so clear, it seemed almost impossible that the meaning could escape her.

Tilly stopped on the page, her long lashes fluttering against her cheek as she placed what Kate had told her into context. As understanding dawned, something turned behind Tilly's eyes. "Oh. I supposed I overlooked that," she muttered.

Overlooked that? How the hell could she overlook something like that? Had she tried to read a copy in braille?

Tilly looked up. "This is filth."

"It's a *classic*. It's…" Kate paused. She shook her head and averted her gaze.

"What was that look for?" Tilly demanded.

The sixth period bell was shrill as it rang out through Kate's office. Down the hall in the language classroom, there was the loud scrape of chair legs against the hardwood floors as girls shot from their seats.

Kate shifted the file of essays beneath her arm. "No reason. I'm just surprised that something like this warrants such a reaction."

"Why wouldn't it?"

Kate cleared her throat. "It's just that, well, you didn't seem to be so scandalised by *The Joy of Lesbian Sex*."

She could summon the memory in a heartbeat—returning to their room one night after a shower and finding seventeen-year-old Tilly at their shared bureau, *The Joy of Lesbian Sex* spread open in her palms like a hymnal. Kate had made the purchase in Melbourne that winter, hidden it at the bottom of her underwear drawer upon her return to St. Joan's. It was a vivid recollection, the way Tilly's eyes had widened when she'd realised she was caught, Kate mumbling something about forgetting something in the west wing bathroom and retreating. When she'd returned, the drawer had been closed and, like the subject of Kate's sexuality, the book had gone undiscussed for all of eternity.

A pink blush crept up Tilly's neck. "Are you trying to unnerve me? So I'll back down? Because—"

"—I'm not trying to do anything—"

"—because I'm not going to back down."

They fell silent. Regardless of the fact that Kate's time on Lords was quickly running out, she wasn't about to let Tilly keep her from bringing St. Joan of Arc well and truly into the twenty-first century before she was gone. It was her English class too, not just Tilly's. "It's being taught," Kate asserted. "*The Color Purple* may be the most important novel ever written. If you refuse to teach it, that's fine, I'll teach it during my lessons and you can pick up poetry during yours. But it's being taught."

At the suggestion that she didn't have to teach the text *herself*, Tilly visibly relaxed. She dropped the novel onto Kate's desk. "Fine. Which poet do you suggest I teach in the meantime? Otherwise, I could always begin with *The Glass Menagerie*—it's on your prescribed list for this term too."

"No. I just said that I'd like you to start with Gwen Harwood, please. We'll move on to *The Glass Menagerie* in early December. The Melbourne Theatre Company is doing a production in the city and I'd like the Extension girls to see it before they start studying it. Lexi will come too—she's studying Laura Wingfield for her Year Ten Drama monologue."

"Fine."

Kate dropped her gaze to her sixth period folder. "Great."

"I'm not happy about this. Look at me, Kate."

At the fierceness in Tilly's darkened gaze, her stomach flipped. This was new...the confidence. Tilly hadn't been like this as a teenager.

"I'd really like you to reconsider," Tilly said.

Kate pushed her shoulders back as she glanced through the door and down the corridor. "Tilly, I appreciate your opinion, but I'm not changing the text list. We're done talking about this. I have a music class. And honestly?" Their gazes locked. "I thought you were more progressive than this."

The hair on the back of Kate's neck bristled as she watched Tilly's face fall.

Kate's entire body hummed as she watched Tilly spin on her heel and disappear down the corridor. She'd never been in conflict with Tilly before, and the feeling was disturbingly foreign. Tilly had changed. There was a fire in her eyes, a charge in her determination. Kate had only ever seen Tilly react so angrily once before.

They'd been young—fifteen, sixteen at most. A girl in the church band at St. Gerard's in Mornington had applied to board at St. Joan of Arc. Father Jeffrey, the priest at the time, had more or less threatened the girl's parents—he would sponsor the girl's enrollment under the condition that the parents contributed a sizeable amount of money to the parish donation envelopes each week. The girl had never ended up attending St. Joan of Arc, and weeks later, she'd changed parishes. Tilly had been so riled up that she'd been hell-bent on confronting Father Jeffrey about it when he'd come to host confession for the girls later that month. *I'm going to do it today,* she'd told Kate. But when the great and powerful Father Jeffrey had stepped into their tiny church, Tilly had chickened out. She'd sat beside Kate in the pew, so furious with herself that she was close to tears. Kate could barely stand it. So, she'd taken it upon herself to fix the problem.

"Bless me, Father, for I have sinned," she'd started, sweating beneath the armpits after slipping into the anonymous confessional. "It's been two weeks since my last confession and these are my sins…" She paused to draw breath, to gain control of the quiver of her voice. "Father, I blackmailed a less fortunate family from St. Gerard's."

The grate between the boxes shadowed as the man on the other side inched closer. "You did?" he inquired.

"Yes, Father."

"And how did you blackmail this family, child?" he whispered solemnly.

"I told them that if they didn't start contributing to the weekly donation envelopes, I wouldn't sign their daughter's sponsorship to attend St. Joan of Arc."

Silence. The thud-thud-thud of her heartbeat in her ears and the vision of Tilly's smile behind her closed eyelids. It had taken all of Kate's courage to turn her head and spy through the wire to make out Father Jeffrey's reaction.

The moment stretched like elastic pulled to its limit. "Did you?" he said.

"I did."

A pause. The shadow on the grate receded as he sat back. "Well, child, I think six Hail Mary's and an Our Father will absolve you of your sins."

Screw you, Jeff. "Thank you, Father. I'll make sure I light a candle for you once I've said them."

She'd pushed open the door to the confessional with such a shove that, in the front pew, Sister Mary Monica's eyes shot up from her Bible. "Katherine!" she'd berated. "Gentle!"

Gentle.

"Kate?"

Kate looked up from her desk and met Grace's eye. She'd been so lost in thought that she hadn't realised the girls were ready to begin the lesson.

She blinked. "Do you have a question, Grace?"

Grace's expression twisted. "No. But I, umm…well, we think we may have offended Tilly last period."

With a sigh, Kate dropped their essays down on the top of the piano. "You *think?*"

Kate popped two extra-strength Panadol and chased them down with a gulp of water.

At the other end of the kitchen counter where she stood waiting for the kettle to boil, Tilly nervously pinched at the lapels of her pyjama shirt. "Headache?" she asked.

Nodding, Kate leaned into the corner of the counter and studied Tilly's face. Hours after their argument, she still seemed tense. "So I don't know if you know this," Kate started, "but I'm a huge proponent of never going to bed upset."

Tilly looked across the small kitchen. She seemed to think that over for a moment. "Have you lived with somebody in the past?" she asked. "A…partner?"

"Yes." For three years, she'd lived with Elodie. And two with Britta.

"Oh," Tilly said. She stared out the kitchen window at the illuminated field across the road where a few of the boarders were playing touch footy. "I've always lived alone. I mean, I've had roommates, but never a…" Trailing off, she dropped her gaze to her slippers. "I'm not trying to fight you on the novel for the sake of it, Kate. And I am progressive—I would hate for you to think I wasn't. I just…I felt so silly," she said, her voice whisper-soft beneath the loud hum of the boiling kettle. "I've only ever taught in Catholic schools with very strict and conservative curricula, and I've only taught English once—we studied Keats and Austen." She looked up. "I usually understand the sexual references. I'm not stupid. But today…" She rubbed at her temples, as though she had a migraine fit to compete with Kate's. "The thought of going back into that classroom tomorrow, with those girls just waiting for me to trip up again…" She sighed. "Sixteen-year-old girls understand their bodies better than I understand my own," she rasped, her eyes wide and bright. "And they know it."

As she watched Tilly bite her lip and draw a hand over her plait, Kate understood the bigger picture.

Their eyes locked, held.

"I'm not ashamed, Kate."

"Ashamed?"

"That I've saved myself for marriage."

The kettle came to a boil, clicked. A lump formed in Kate's throat. She had assumed it to be the case, but to hear Tilly admit that she had never been touched drove the breath from her lungs.

Tilly exhaled a nervous laugh and Kate set her glass down, reached out to offer a hug.

Sighing softly, Tilly relaxed in her arms. "Tomorrow is going to be fine," Kate said, relishing in the sensation of Tilly's heartbeat against her own. "Trust me. The girls have already forgotten it." And if they haven't, Kate thought, I'll make sure of it.

CHAPTER SEVEN

"You're getting old, Kate!"

Pressing on at Molly's call from the top, Kate scoffed. The great hill was always a feat on foggy mornings. It was psychological, of course—Kate knew that. She had climbed it on much colder mornings without a problem. But there was something about seeing the fog paired with the way the crisp sea air broke in her lungs that always set a struggle. A daybreak run was supposed to wake her up enough to get through the last day of the school week. So why did she feel as though she was sleepwalking through a sea of moss?

A Friday morning jog was the icing on the cake of an already long week. Kate was exhausted—mind, body, and spirit. All she wanted was a Friday morning with Tilly at the kitchen table, drinking coffee and eating breakfast. Why the hell had she promised Molly she'd pull herself from bed at six? Molly—being Molly—had been stretching at the garden gate at five fifty-seven, complaining that it had been impossible to wake Emma, who had been up all night writing an essay.

Sunrise was breaking over the hill behind them, bouncing its blood-orange glow off St. Joan's bronzed sword. Kate squinted as she jogged the incline with wavering determination, wishing she'd swapped her glasses for her prescription sunglasses.

"Come on!" Molly called out.

Kate neared the top of the hill to the base of the statue, heart pounding as she drew a sharp breath. She could walk from here. Yes. Walking. Walking was good. A good idea.

"Seriously?" Molly teased. "*Walking?*"

"All that pot has done wonders for your stamina!"

"What? Suddenly you're allowed to joke about it but we're not?"

"It's been a month," Kate panted, her thighs tingling as she slowed to a stop. "I'm entitled to joke about it now. You have my permission to start making cracks at the three-month mark and not a moment before."

"I'll be in Edinburgh then," Molly pointed out, her hands on her hips as she stood on the spot and squinted up at Joan of Arc on horseback.

"So? That's why God invented Skype. You're not planning on Skyping me from Scotland? That's just plain rude. I'm your English teacher—I edited your entry half a dozen times!"

Molly laughed, collapsing to the ground, her dark, curly ponytail swinging as she sprawled her legs out in the rustling grass. "If you're lucky, Kate. If you're lucky."

From the top, Kate looked down into the bay. Waves rushed against the rock wall that guarded the tiny cove, spurting water high as the surf lapped in and out of the calm, protected bay. Last week, when Kate, Emma, and Molly had reached the statue, they'd looked down to find Tilly swimming with Sister Ruth and Sister Ellie. Treading water in the bay, they'd waved, and Kate had felt overwhelmed by the sight. This week, the weather was too cold for a morning dip in the ocean. Kate had left Tilly sound asleep in the cottage. She'd be awake by now though, Kate thought. She'd probably even found the cup of tea Kate had made for her just before leaving. By now, it would be the perfect temperature.

Kate grasped her knees with both hands, her breath quickly returning. She looked at Molly, watched as her talented student stared up at Joan of Arc intensely. Suddenly, Molly dropped her gaze. Her brow furrowed as she picked mindlessly at the grass between her knees. "You want to know what I pray for every morning?" Molly asked.

Kate had a feeling she knew where this conversation was headed. "Only if you want to tell me…"

For a long moment, Molly didn't speak. Then: "I pray that I'm going to be good enough," she said softly. "I pray that they chose me for the right reasons, not just because I'm a girl, or because I'm Aboriginal. Not because I fill some sort of quota."

Kate straightened. *Oh, Molly…*

Molly looked up from the grass. She searched Kate's gaze, not for a response, not for validation. Kate had already given her that in bucket loads. As Kate looked down at her, she hoped her stare conveyed what Molly needed. *I hear you. You're heard.*

It was already November. With the passing of each day, they were drawing closer to the end of the school year, and then to New Year's Eve when Molly would be leaving for Edinburgh. Kate knew Molly was nervous, that she was doubting herself. Whenever Kate mentioned the trip, Molly fell quiet, withdrawing for a few hours. Kate had read Molly's file—she knew what was going on. The first year of boarding had been hell for her. The poor kid had been so riddled with anxiety that a child psychologist started visiting once a week. It had come as a bit of a shock to Kate when she'd read it. She'd only ever known Molly as a confident, settled person. But now, with Molly heading into an unfamiliar environment, Kate harboured concerns that it could all prove too much. Over the next few weeks, she'd have to keep an eye on her.

As Molly pulled herself to her feet, Kate reached out and grasped her shoulder. "You don't need to pray for that, Mol. Come on. Let's go home."

Just before the end of second period, Kate was making her way to the music room, morning tea in hand—socialising in the staffroom was one of her least favourite activities—when she stopped in the corridor. The door of Tilly's Literature Extension classroom was open just enough for Tilly's voice to swim out and reach Kate's ears. She was reading poetry. Gwen Harwood's *At Mornington*.

Slowly, Kate retraced her steps down the empty corridor. She pressed her shoulders against the plaster wall and listened.

Tilly's voice had a quiet strength as she recited the poet's memory of being taken to the sea for the first time as a child, leaping from her father's arms, fully clothed, into the waves of Mornington Beach. Kate rested her head back against the wall. The breeze from the window at the end of the corridor washed over her like the notes of Tilly's voice. Kate closed her eyes.

She grasped her Tupperware container tighter, imagined Tilly's lips at her ear, whispering poetry, her voice firm, mouth hot against the shell of Kate's ear, against the pulse in her neck…

"Are you okay, Kate?"

Kate's eyes snapped open. Grace stood before her, a curious glint in her eye.

"What?" Kate asked.

"Are you okay?" Grace repeated slowly.

Tilly's soft cadence continued to slip through the opening in the door. Grace looked toward the classroom.

She pushed off the wall. "I have a migraine," she lied. "Where are you supposed to be?"

Grace nodded toward the crack in the door. "In there with Ms Wattle—Tilly. I just went to the bathroom…"

"Well hurry up," Kate whispered. She started back down the corridor to the music room, heart humming as Tilly's voice trickled after her.

She left the door to the music room wide open.

With Tilly's Friday afternoons always free of classes, Kate assumed Tilly would be busy writing in the cottage until day's end. So, when Kate stepped back into the music room just after three thirty—she'd only popped out for a second to take a phone call with a parent—she was surprised to find Tilly at the piano with Lexi.

Over the past month, Lexi had taken to Tilly like a moth to a flame. It had only been last night in the common room that Kate had overheard Tilly telling Lexi that she'd love to hear her recital. Not twenty-four hours later, here they were.

Tilly moved from the piano seat and crossed the room to lean against a student desk. "Mind if I join you both for the tail end of the lesson?"

Kate shook her head. "Not at all."

As the crescendo swelled, Kate looked across the room to Tilly, focused intently on Lexi's performance. Kate's gaze dropped low, to where the small curve of Tilly's behind rested on the desk. Taking a sip from her water bottle, Kate raised her gaze higher, to the dip of Tilly's back where the end of her plait tickled low, almost to the high waistband of her floral skirt. Kate held back a sigh. God, she looked so lovely today.

When Lexi finished, she gasped a deep breath and sighed dramatically. She reclined across the length of the seat, arms dangling at her sides, fingertips skimming the floorboards. It wasn't hard to miss the way the corners of Lexi's lips curled at Tilly's enthusiastic clapping. Tilly and Kate shared a knowing smile.

"And you're being graded next week?" Tilly asked.

Lexi turned her head and looked over at Kate. "Unfortunately."

Kate rolled her eyes. "It's only me grading you."

"Yeah," Lexi remarked. "That's the problem." She turned to face Tilly. "Do you know how well she plays? She can't sing to save herself, but she's like Chopin on the keys."

Tilly smiled. "Yes, I know." She locked eyes with Kate. "When we were your age, she used to play every Sunday morning at St. Gerard's."

Lexi snorted. "Seriously? *Kate* played *at mass*?"

Tilly looked to Lexi. "She even wrote her own harmonies and played them at the end of communion."

Kate's face heated. "Tilly…"

"Do you know Leonard Cohen's song *Hallelujah*?" Tilly asked Lexi.

Suddenly, Kate's throat grew tight.

Lexi nodded.

"Well," Tilly started, her eyes drifting back to Kate, "We studied music performance together, and we performed *Hallelujah* for our final."

"You and Kate?" Lexi asked.

"Yes," Tilly said softly. "Sister Hattie, my aunt, used to say that Kate was just like King David—she knew the secret chord."

"King David?" Lexi asked. "The guy who killed Goliath?"

"Yes," Tilly said, her eyes trained on Kate. "And he also happened to be the only one who could soothe Saul with a song—"

The second the bell rang, Lexi shot up, the legs of the piano seat screeching against the floorboards. "Thanks for coming Tilly, soz, gotta run, gotta pack…"

Kate looked down at her watch. "You still haven't packed?" The four-thirty car ferry to Mornington would be pulling in in no time and Lexi was a prefect—Kate relied on her to escort the younger boarders across to meet their parents, or buses, at the end of each week. "You have twenty minutes before the van's leaving," Kate called after her. She crossed the room to the window. In the driveway, a few boarders were ready with their bags. Kate looked across the room. "The end of that class passed quickly! Sorry if she pulled you away from your writing."

"I don't mind at all." Tilly joined her at the window. Smiling, she bumped her shoulder playfully against Kate's, then leaned so close Kate could feel the heat radiating off her bare arm. "Do you still play piano?" Tilly asked.

"Not as often as I used to."

"That's a shame." She turned. "I suppose I should get back to writing…"

Kate's fingers reached out and curled gently around the fine bones of Tilly's wrist, stopping her. "By the way, I finished your books."

Tilly's eyes glossed over with surprise. "You did?"

Kate nodded.

Tilly settled against the windowsill. "But I only gave you the set last week?"

"I've been reading one a night."

"I haven't seen you reading them." She paused. "Now that I think about it, you *have* been going to bed earlier…"

Kate took a seat beside her on the windowsill. "I don't know how you do it, Til. To have written so many books and have the teaching résumé you do."

Tilly's cheeks lit pink. She dropped her gaze, a bashful smile playing at her lips.

Grinning, Kate ducked her head in an attempt to catch Tilly's eye. "What?" she asked.

"Nothing, really. It's just that nobody has ever read my books."

"Of course people have read them—they're best sellers."

"Well, nobody that I know…"

"Seriously? Not even the sisters?"

Tilly shook her head.

Kate hooked her forefinger beneath Tilly's chin. Their eyes locked. "I think you're amazing."

Tilly's tongue snuck out to wet her lips. "That's very nice of you—"

"Don't do that."

Tilly swallowed, her chin bobbing beneath Kate's finger. "Don't do what?" she whispered.

"Don't be modest. Not with me."

Tilly blinked. "With you…"

A craving to be touched by Tilly seized her, just as it had during assembly that morning when their eyes had caught across the school hall. Just as it had the day before when she'd passed Tilly in the library and caught her bent over a student desk. Just as it had the day before *that* when she'd—

At a loud call down the hall, Kate broke the gaze and retracted her touch. "I better go and pressure the girls to hurry down to the van."

She pushed off the windowsill.

"You're coming back after you drop them off?" Tilly asked, a hint of hope in her voice. "You aren't leaving now with the girls? Taking the car ferry and driving the van out to your mother's?"

Kate shook her head. "Nah, I think I'll just leave first thing in the morning. Stay tonight…"

Stretching both palms out at her sides on the windowsill, Tilly smiled. "Well I'll just be here," she said, crossing her legs at the ankle, "waiting upon your return."

There had been a time, not so long ago, when Kate had waited all week for Friday afternoon to arrive, to leave on the four-thirty car ferry to Mornington and return when the boarders did on Sunday night. She'd enjoyed lunches with her family, dinners with her friends in St. Kilda. But with Tilly around…well, Kate's priorities had changed.

Friday nights at St. Joan's were quiet, peaceful, *theirs*. The sisters retired early—they rose each night at one a.m. for prayer before returning to bed for another four hours of sleep—so after eight thirty, there wasn't a chance of one of them rapping loudly at the cottage door, or in Sister Ruth's case, waltzing in unannounced. Friday nights were a reliable constant.

Tilly was always home; she had dinner with the vicar on Tuesday nights, and spent the weekend with him. A strict routine that, in four weeks, had yet to be disturbed by spontaneity. It was strange, Kate thought. *Regimented.* Even more bizarre to Kate was that, when Tilly went to Mornington, regardless of the fact that she was spending both Saturday and Sunday with Declan, Sister Ellie claimed Tilly always returned on Saturday night. She caught the ferry back to Lords, walked up the hill to the cottage in the dark of night and repeated it all the next day.

"Why don't you just spend the night at Declan's?" Kate had asked one Sunday night on the ferry. "Seems like a lot of effort, going back and forth."

Tilly had looked at her, aghast. "I couldn't stay."

"Why not? You're engaged."

"Engaged," Tilly had said. "Not *married.*"

Kate parked the van and started up the path to the cottage. The desire to ask Tilly to venture across Lords to the seafood restaurant burned on the tip of her tongue. Unless Kate was taking the causeway across to Portarlington, she very rarely went into the tiny town of Lords, but the idea of escaping St. Joan's with Tilly for a few hours was enticing. Perhaps, if Tilly was feeling adventurous, they could even take the causeway into Portarlington...

Halfway to the house, she spotted Tilly at the clothesline at the side of the cottage, Kate's pale blue bed sheets curling around her form in the wind as she reached up to peg.

Moving quietly around the outdoor bench, Kate grasped Tilly's waist through the sheet. She shrieked in surprise, her hand clasping Kate's as Kate lifted her off the ground, twirling her inside damp cotton. Tilly's ribcage expanded with laughter as Kate's hands smoothed over the dampness of the sheet. "Kate, let me go!" Tilly laughed.

Between the sheets, Kate locked eyes with Sister Mary Monica in the convent garden. Quickly, she lowered Tilly to her feet.

Tilly peeled back the sheet and grinned up at Kate, fixing her hair. "That was a quick trip," she said, breathless.

Smiling widely, Kate reached for the dangling point of the sheet and reached for a peg. "I don't muck around."

She could feel Sister Mary Monica's eyes on them across the way, her thick eyebrows furrowed in disapproval. Kate looked up, but Sister Mary Monica was too quick, returning her attention to winding up the garden hose.

Together, they picked up a fitted sheet and waved it between them. "What are you thinking about for dinner?" Tilly asked as they pegged the corners.

Kate licked her lips. Suddenly, with the image of Sister Mary Monica's expression burned into her mind, the idea of asking Tilly to dinner—let alone asking her to cross the causeway—felt like crossing a line. She reached into the basket for Tilly's pillowcase. "I was thinking those steaks you asked the sisters to grab us."

"Oh." On tiptoes, Tilly reached up to the line to peg Kate's pillowcase. "I was actually planning on using those for lunch tomorrow."

Tilly wanted her to hang back long enough into Saturday to have lunch with her? Satisfaction swirled in the pit of her stomach, dizzying like liquor. "Sure. We can do that. But there are enough for tonight and for lunch tomorrow, don't you think?"

Suddenly, Tilly's arms dropped from the line. "I mean…Declan is visiting tomorrow. For lunch. He's bringing the children to the island…"

The old peg snapped in Kate's hand as she clipped it over the sheet. *God damn it.* She reached into the basket for another. The vicar had robbed Kate of the love of her life and now he was taking her prime rib, too? "Right…"

"Will you be here?" Tilly asked, confused. "I thought you'd be well and truly gone by lunchtime…but if you *are* still here, I mean, that would be great. I'd love for you to meet Declan and the kids…"

Oh, hell. Kate's mind raced to find an excuse to get out of *that*. Thank God she had an appointment with the real estate agent in St. Kilda. It wasn't until three, but she could make herself busy on the mainland until then. "Sorry, Til, mind blank there. I can't stay for lunch. I'll be gone by ten. *Have* to be gone, I mean. I have an appointment."

Tilly frowned, utterly trusting. "That's a shame. I know he's curious about you. I talk about you so much. *Too* much, maybe." She laughed. "In fact, he had to stop me the other night."

Kate stalled as she reached into the basket for one of Tilly's skirts. He'd had to *stop* her? Smugness settled between her ribs. Was he jealous?

"I know you'll be at your mum's on Sunday, but you should drive over for the welcome mass," Tilly said. "All of the sisters are coming to St. Vincent's—Declan's welcoming all congregations. Catholic, Anglican—he says it shouldn't matter when we're all God's children."

CHAPTER EIGHT

From three pews behind the sisters, Kate watched as Tilly made a subtle, unsuccessful attempt to pull away from Sister Tessie for the second time. The elderly sister had been hanging off Tilly's arm since Kate had watched them disembark the public bus outside St. Vincent's. When they'd first stepped foot into the Anglican church, Tilly had asked Kate to save her a seat beside her—she'd just help Sister Tessie to her seat and be back in a moment. A moment, however, had passed five minutes ago.

Kate glanced to the back of the church. With most of the parishioners having already taken their seats for the mass, a few of the clergymen meandered in the narthex, awaiting the vicar's arrival. Kate returned her gaze to the front. Was she going to have to sit through the entire service alone? Was all of this worth it, just to satisfy her burning curiosity?

Finally, Sister Ellie wandered down the aisle, smiling across the church as her eyes met Kate's. Kate inclined her head in the direction of Tilly and Sister Tessie, and, ever so perceptive, the novice nodded. She slid in beside Sister Tessie and Tilly seized her chance.

As Tilly started quickly down the aisle toward her, concern etched on her face, Kate's newfound relief disappeared in a blink.

Tilly slid into the pew, her long plait flitting about the shoulders of her white linen blazer. "What's wrong?" Kate whispered.

Tilly adjusted her skirt around her knees. "Sister Tessie just asked me what all of these people were doing at St. Joan's," she murmured, her breath warm on Kate's jaw.

Swallowing, Kate watched as Tilly redirected her attention to the altar. "Did the Reverend Mother hear?" Kate asked.

Tilly's lips set into a straight line. "She heard." She paused. "Anyway. How was your Saturday with your parents?"

"Good, thanks. Went to the movies last night with my sister and niece. I'm happy to report that I *still* fall asleep in animated films."

Tilly smiled. "Heading straight back to your mum's after this?"

Kate nodded.

Across the aisle, a little girl was turned in her seat. Wide-eyed and hopeful, she stared in their direction. "Um…Til?" Kate whispered.

Tilly only had eyes for Sister Tessie. "Mmm?"

"That little girl is looking at you."

Tilly followed the direction of her line of sight, and Kate watched as the surprise on the little girl's face grew. Tilly cupped her hand in a tiny wave that only served to foster the child's delight. "That's Declan's daughter, Lily," she explained. "She's five."

With the first notes of the organ, the congregation stood. Kate cast her gaze around the church. It was nowhere near as beautiful as St. Joan's. Instead of stained glass windows, carved wooden statues stood between high, narrow windows. Banners of St. Vincent adorned the walls, the canvas fluttering from the exposed brick under the gentle force of the high, wire-cased fans.

The altar boys and acolytes passed first, and then, there he was, at the end of the procession—the illustrious Vicar Armstrong.

Kate stiffened at the sight of him. He was handsome, cleanly shaven with salt-and-pepper hair and a sharp jawline above his clerical collar. And he was tall, at least six-one. Even dressed in the starched black cassock, it was just as simple to imagine him commanding a different setting altogether. He could just as easily be a lawyer or a businessman, or some kind of executive, feet elevated on the edge of his desk and a cigar burning between his fingers, calling out to his secretary to fetch him a coffee. Okay, she thought, maybe you're being a tad dramatic.

It was obvious why Tilly had fallen for his charm. In welcoming the sisters of St. Joan, he was charismatic and confident, and it wasn't long before his gaze found Tilly—and Kate.

When the time came to give his sermon, he took full advantage of the cordless microphone, moving from behind the decorative lectern to explain the scripture. Matthew Chapter twenty-three went down a treat, Kate thought sardonically. He used Jesus's denunciation of the Scribes and Pharisees, the ancient communities that had allowed power and authority to go to their heads, to segue into seeking donations for the Christmas mission to Vanuatu. He wasn't asking for textbooks or clothes, he clarified—shipping containers cost a fortune—it was monetary donations of which the church was in need. From the back of the church, a baby wailed. Usually, the requests for donations came with the final five minutes of a service, when church newsletters were passed around and the final blessing was granted. Not in the middle of the goddamn homily. People like this guy, Kate thought, are the reason people join cults.

When children between six and twelve were called out to Sunday school, the church grew noisy with the loud whispers of children bidding farewell to their parents, kneelers creaking beneath the weight of the youngsters as they shuffled out into the aisles, eager to escape the hour of sacred silence.

"There's Mason," Tilly said, "in the blue shirt." Kate searched for Tilly's future step-son as the group headed out the side door in single file, but there were at least four boys in shades of blue. Impossible.

"Did you see him?" Tilly asked.

Kate shook her head.

Regardless of how welcoming the vicar was in inviting everybody to take communion, like the sisters down the front, Tilly remained in her seat beside Kate. It was blasphemy, they'd always been taught, to receive the sacrament from a non-Catholic priest, and Kate had been curious to see what Tilly would do when the time came. As the queues of parishioners dwindled, Kate watched as Declan's eyes flickered searchingly to his fiancée. Had he really thought that Tilly would take communion from him?

For the duration of mass, Kate and Tilly had an audience in Lily Armstrong. She went from sitting ramrod-straight, to turning to make sure Tilly was still watching her, then back again. When mass was over and Kate and Tilly's row exited after the sisters of St. Joan's, it wasn't long before Lily came bounding from the side door, a hand raised to her forehead to block out the sudden onslaught of sunlight as she weaved her way through the small crowd in her search for Tilly.

Tilly swept the tiny girl up into her arms. "Lily, don't you look lovely in your new dress!" she said, fixing the double lining of the floral dress around Lily's knees. It was odd—Kate had no reaction to seeing the child across the church, but now, up close, she felt a strange sense of relief that Declan's daughter looked nothing like Tilly. With golden curls and a fair complexion, Lily's face was much wider than Tilly's had ever been. Mostly, it was in the eyes, Lily's grey-blue so very different to those of the emerald-eyed child framed on the convent mantelpiece. Other than both being petite, it was hard to mistake the two for mother and child.

"Kate," Tilly said as she adjusted the little girl on her hip, "this is Lily."

She smiled. "Hi, Lily."

"Hi." Lily's gaze settled upon Kate. "You're not a nun."

Kate chuckled. "No."

"You just drive their bus?" Lily asked.

"No," Tilly said. "Kate is a teacher, like me."

"Oh. On Tilly's island?" she clarified.

"Yes…"

It was difficult to give the child her undivided attention when, across the grass, the vicar's eyes were on them. Over Tilly's shoulder, Kate could see him in conversation with a pair of elderly women, but his attention was divided. She pretended not to notice when he crossed the grass toward them, the sun reflecting off his clerical collar—and looking Kate up and down.

Kate feigned interest as Lily told Tilly all about her week at school, what she'd taken for show-and-tell. As he approached, his hand sliding around Tilly's back, Kate grew uneasy. "Hello, darling," he said, pressing his lips chastely to Tilly's cheek.

As the term of endearment reached Kate's ears, her heart splintered—Tilly's relationship with Declan was deeper than she let on. Little comments had been littered here and there about the time she spent with Declan—something funny Lily had said when they'd picked her up from preschool together, a restaurant where they'd eaten lunch—but Kate hadn't fully realised until now. Tilly fit so seamlessly into life at St. Joan's that it was hard to comprehend that she already had a family.

"Declan," Tilly said, "this is Kate York."

His smile widened, showcasing a set of teeth so straight and white Kate struggled not to stare. They had to be crowns. *Or false teeth.* "Kate, lovely to meet you. I was sorry we missed you yesterday on the island."

Kate forced a smile. "Yes, I was in the city—"

"I was only saying to Tilly that you should come by for dinner one Tuesday night. I promise to have you both back to the ferry by final departure." He winked at Tilly.

"Kate has the convent van," Tilly said, his flirtation evading her. "You wouldn't need to pick us up or drop us off."

"Of course," he said, his gaze lowered as he watched his daughter toy gently with Tilly's crucifix. After a moment, he lifted his gaze and met Kate's eyes. "I'd invite you by this week, Kate, but I'm still busy trying to unpack and the house is a disaster…"

"Maybe in a few weeks," Tilly said, but her enthusiasm was weak, forced.

"Sounds great," Kate said. *It didn't.* Desperate to pull an excuse from thin air, she started a sentence and hoped she'd find the rest of it along the way. "Tuesdays, though, they aren't really great for me, having to be back for the girls—"

It was as though Kate's words fell on deaf ears. "Darling," Declan said, tilting his head in disappointment as he locked eyes with his daughter. "Let go of Tilly, please. You're a big girl, you don't need to be picked up."

His comment sounded like it was more for Tilly's benefit than his daughter's, and it seemed Kate wasn't the only one who noticed. As though she'd been scolded, Tilly immediately lowered Lily to her feet. Amongst a sea of chattering parishioners, they all fell silent.

"Lovely service," Kate offered.

"Thank you, Kate. A special one today, I think." He paused. "Did you get back to Lords last night?"

"No, I, uhh—"

"Kate drove from her mother's house in Dandenong to be here," Tilly added, gesturing across the car park to the convent van. "Isn't that lovely?"

Kate shifted from foot to foot, her cheeks warming. *Jesus Christ, Tilly, don't tell him that.* "No big deal," she said, wetting her lips. "It's only a forty-minute drive and I knew the sisters would appreciate it if I made an appearance."

Tilly fixed the strap of her small bag on her shoulder. "Where's Mason?" she asked.

"He's still at Sunday school with the other children," Declan said. He looked across the landscaped garden to the raucous noise that vibrated from the fibro cottage, then, brows furrowing, at his watch. "They tell me that Miriam tends to go overtime every Sunday, much to the children's distress. I don't envy her, having to contend with twenty children anxious to get out and run amok." There was that grin again, so perfect, so charming... Kate's stomach turned.

"Who knows," she joked, "that extra ten minutes in Sunday school might up their chances of getting through the pearly gates one day."

Tilly scoffed a laugh. Declan fixed his gaze on her. Suddenly, he turned to Tilly. "Oh, darling," he said, "I'm sorry to do this at such late notice but something has come up and I'm going to have to postpone our lunch." Gaze flickering between both women, he leaned closer, as though he were about to share the secrets of the universe. "One of the parishioners has been struggling after giving birth and her husband has asked me to visit with them."

Pulling back, Kate blinked twice. *Seriously?* When her little sister had developed postnatal depression at just eighteen, requesting a visit from the local vicar hadn't exactly been the top priority in getting Beccy the help she so desperately needed. "Maybe you could suggest she see a doctor," Kate said.

It made her blood boil, the way he chuckled condescendingly. "That's already been taken care of," he assured her, then held up his palms. "I'm *good*," he claimed, "but I'm not a miracle worker."

"*That we know of,*" Tilly inserted, and Kate's eyes snapped from Declan to Tilly. What was that, Kate wondered. Was that Tilly flirting? With her own fiancé? *The audacity.*

"I'm sorry, Tilly," he said. "I do hate to cancel our plans at the last minute…"

"It's perfectly fine," Tilly assured him. "Really, Declan, you needn't worry."

Needn't worry? Please. Tilly's demeanour was so falsely polite that Kate fought the impulse to roll her eyes. What was this? An interaction with her fiancé, or an audition for *Meet Me in St. Louis?* Kate slid her hands into her front pockets. *Should I expect Judy Garland to show up? For Tilly to ride off to Mornington Pier singing The Trolley Song?*

"I'll call you later on?" he said.

Tilly nodded. She bent and kissed Lily, drew her into a tight hug that had the little girl giggling as Tilly planted kisses across her cheeks.

When Declan had gone, heading across the grass with his daughter to greet a group of parishioners, Tilly glanced at Kate. Forcing a smile, she exhaled deeply and looked around until her gaze landed on the sisters of St. Joan of Arc. The tight-knit group had congregated in the shade by the side door and were deep in conversation with a few parishioners. Quietly, Tilly watched the group, as though she were torn between joining them and remaining at Kate's side.

There it was, laid out before Kate and hers for the taking—the opportunity to have Tilly all to herself for the afternoon if she was brave enough to ask for it. She stole a furtive glance. The sight of Tilly's profile as she licked her lips set a fluttering low in Kate's belly. A sense of urgency gripped her. "Are you just planning on going back home now?" she asked. "To St. Joan's?"

Tilly's body angled toward Kate and their eyes met. "Yes." Her gaze remained locked on Kate's, as though she was waiting for Kate to grasp the opportunity to say more.

"Come with me," Kate heard herself say. "I'm going back to Mum's for lunch and Beccy will be there with my niece and they'd love to see you."

Pensively, Tilly glanced across the car park to the sisters, then back to Kate.

"The sisters know how to read the bus timetable without you, Til—they get the public bus all over Mornington. They'll just get it back to the pier."

Tilly captured her bottom lip between her teeth.

Smiling, Kate tilted her head. "Don't go back to Lords," she implored. "Come with me."

"Before we head back home, do you mind if we go a bit further into the city?"

In the passenger seat of the convent van, Tilly turned to face her. "Sure..." Her eyes narrowed. "Why?"

It was only three—they had hours before they had to be back at Mornington. As Kate made a left at the end of her mother's street instead of a right, she scratched at the back of her neck. "There's something I just realised I want to show you," she said. Truthfully, she'd been thinking about it all through lunch.

Tilly smiled curiously as Kate headed in the opposite direction to Mornington, onto the road that would take them to the inner-city suburbs. The St. Kilda terrace was only a thirty-minute drive from her mother's house in Dandenong.

As Kate parked alongside the curb half an hour later, Tilly looked at her, an eyebrow arched. "Why are we in St. Kilda?"

Kate pointed across the street to the ornate Victorian terrace house with the double-chimney.

"Are you pointing at the one with the *For Sale* sign?" Tilly clarified.

Kate nodded. The day before had been the second time she'd seen it, and she'd fallen in love with it all over again. Now, she was certain of what she wanted. "This is where I was yesterday," she said, and Tilly exhaled softly as realisation set in. "Do you like it?"

For a long moment, Tilly was quiet.

Kate unclicked her seat belt. "Do you think it's too quaint for me?"

"No," Tilly whispered, "I don't think it's too quaint." She paused. "I'm sorry but...this is going to sound so bizarre..."

As she watched Tilly's lips part in confusion, Kate's curiosity piqued. "What is it?"

"I just...

"You what?"

"I had a dream about this house. Years ago. *This* house. Those bars on the windows. The second-floor balcony. The veranda tile. Slate roof. All of it." She exhaled slowly. "Gosh, I must have been about twenty-five."

Kate expected Tilly to say something to the effect of the dream being a sign from God. Instead, she was quiet. "Weird," Kate said.

"Uh-huh…"

The urge to show Tilly inside grew. "Want to see the backyard?" she offered. "It's a rental at the moment and it's empty."

Tilly's eyes widened. "Oh, Kate, we couldn't."

"Couldn't we?"

Grinning, Kate unclipped Tilly's seat belt. "Come on, goody-two-shoes."

Just as it was the day before at the showing, the back gate was unlocked. With Tilly hot on her heels, Kate led the way around the side of the house and into the small backyard. Stepping up onto the low veranda, Kate cupped her hands against the kitchen window. Tilly followed suit.

"Oh," Tilly said, taking in the empty kitchen, the breakfast nook, the antique double-lights fixed to the walls. "It's lovely, Kate…"

The layout was narrow, the rooms small, but it was enough for Kate. A sun-drenched terrace was hard to find—but she had. "Can you see that second door to the left of the hall?" Kate asked. "That's an office, or study. The room in front of that is the living room."

"Where are the stairs to the second level?" Tilly asked.

"In the study."

"And what's upstairs?"

"The bedroom and the bathroom."

Tilly pulled away from the window and leaned back against the wall. "Have you put in an offer?"

Kate stuffed her hands into her pockets. "It's going to auction. It was supposed to go up next weekend, but there's a hold up with the owner going to Europe on business so they've had to reschedule. It could be a month or more. In the meantime, I'll get an inspection."

Her hands clasped behind her back, Tilly shifted against the wall. The breeze toyed with the hem of her skirt. "Do you mind if I ask how much it's worth?"

Kate bit her lip. "One point three million."

Tilly whistled. "You can afford that?"

"I can afford a mortgage."

Tilly laughed.

Together, they sat in the shade on the top step of the back veranda. The wind picked flowers from the jacaranda tree in the corner of the backyard next door and carpeted the small lawn mauve. Leaning against the veranda post, Kate balanced the low heel of her boot on the bottom step. The witchy melody of a neighbour's windchime was soothing.

"The breeze is nice," Tilly said, wrapping her skirt around her knees, cradling them as she gazed up at the clouds.

Kate watched as Tilly leaned back against the opposite post and let her eyes slip shut. The gentle waves of her chestnut-coloured hair danced on the wind as the sunlight caught on her dainty crucifix. Kate licked her lips, recalling the memory of her niece playing with it at lunch. Kate's heart had surged at the sight of Tilly, enamoured with Karlie.

Taking Tilly to lunch had filled her with a kind of peace she hadn't felt in a long time. Her family had always loved Tilly. As usual, Tilly had been incredibly polite, and despite her Catholic values, so understanding of the fact that Beccy was unmarried, a twenty-three-year-old single mother heavily pregnant with her second child. Twice, Kate had heard Tilly telling Beccy how intelligent she thought Karlie was, joking that she herself—an English teacher—was jealous of the five-year-old's vocabulary. You must be so proud, Beccy, Tilly had said as she'd helped pack the dishwasher. *So proud.*

Tilly at family lunch had been *easy*. Life with Tilly was easy—it always had been. Living with her was easy, working with her was easy, sitting in silence with her was easy. Loving her as *just a friend* was the hard part.

"I always wondered where you were," Tilly said, interrupting the silence as her eyes opened. "I wondered if you were close by to wherever I was at the time." Their gazes locked. "Tell me where you lived before taking the position at St. Joan's."

"Melbourne for most of the time. Inner city. Geelong for a while in the early years—my first permanent job was there."

Tilly's smile slipped slightly. "When you said you lived with a partner," she started, "… It was somebody you loved?"

Elodie's image swirling before her, Kate shifted against the veranda pole. "Yes."

"A woman?"

Tilly knew. She'd always known. She was simply searching for confirmation. "Yeah," Kate said. "My girlfriend."

As Tilly averted her eyes, indignation crawled beneath Kate's skin. Silent, Tilly stared up at the clouds. "Does that bother you?" Kate pressed.

Tilly turned back to her. "That you loved another woman? Why would that bother me?"

Kate hesitated. "I don't know. You just seem taken aback by an answer you obviously knew was coming."

Tilly's gaze locked on hers. "I'm not taken aback. I've always known, Kate…that you prefer women."

"The sisters don't know. Well, I assume they've always had an inkling, but I've never told them."

"Right."

"It's always been one of those 'don't ask, don't tell' situations." She chuckled lightly.

Tilly didn't laugh. "I'm sorry it has to be that way."

"It doesn't *have* to," Kate said, "but it is." She looked out at the backyard.

"Nobody has ever outright asked?" Tilly pressed. "Not even when you had your interview?"

It was surprising that Tilly was so inquisitive, so willing to talk about the one thing that had lived with them in the cottage for a month without ever introducing itself. Kate shook her head.

"And you're okay with that?" Tilly asked.

It was a loaded question. How simple things would be if it were all just a matter of being a closeted atheist, maintaining a façade to keep the job. It was more complicated than that. Keeping her job was about more than just collecting a hefty paycheck—she loved St. Joan's and, if she searched herself, she found faith. She believed. Perhaps not with the intensity and devotion Tilly did, but *she believed.* So the underlying homophobia…it wounded, just enough to leave a mark.

Like every religion, Catholicism certainly had its faults, but Kate adored the sisters of St. Joan's, their way of life, the wonderful values they imparted on young, impressionable girls. In Kate's perspective, everything about St. Joan's was all the good that Catholicism had to offer. Was her sexuality her own business? Yes. If asked, would she lie about who she was? Never. Kate shrugged. "I'm not *okay* with it, but it is what it is. And at the end of the day, it was my decision to apply. I didn't *have* to teach at St. Joan's—there are public schools, private schools that wouldn't blink an eye if they knew I was a lesbian. *I'm* the one who chose to apply to teach at a Catholic school."

Tilly tilted her head. "So why *did* you?"

Why had she put herself in that position? "I guess, when it all comes down to it—paycheck and position aside—I knew I'd feel right at home." She shifted. "Something in my gut told me that it was right for me, that it would make me happy." She smiled. "And it has."

"It has?"

"Yeah," she said softly. "I didn't apply to St. Joan's to change the world, or crusade for gay rights in the Catholic church. I just did it for me. I needed some quiet time, away from the city. But if, by the time I leave, a bunch of nuns can put a face to people like me, see that we live our lives as good, kind people and that we aren't so different, well, that's just an added bonus."

Tilly nodded. "Well, I won't say a word about what you've told me," she said, her tone turning serious. "I know it could mean your job."

Kate shrugged. "I don't really think it would make a difference to them now that I only have a few months left." She could hang a pride flag out on the sports field and she doubted she'd lose her position. By now, after almost a year, the sisters relied on her, maybe even loved her.

Tilly studied her. "I went to a lesbian wedding last year," she said all of a sudden. "In the Botanical gardens. They invited me." Kate watched, eyebrows raised as the tip of Tilly's tongue snuck out to wet her lips. "I know lesbians."

It took everything in her to hold back a grin. "Congratulations, Til."

Tilly shook her head and looked at her toes, her cheeks colouring. "I'm sorry, I don't know what I'm supposed to say…"

"You don't have to say anything."

They didn't, until Tilly spoke up. "Did it upset you greatly?" she asked. "In school… Father Jeffrey—God rest his soul—I remember that there were certain homilies…He wasn't very welcoming to homosexuals."

"I didn't…I don't think I really knew who I was then. I mean I knew before I *knew*, but still…" She paused. "And yet somehow, I do remember every hurtful thing he said."

"So do I…" Tilly murmured.

Kate drew the tip of her boot across the rim of the stone step, her heart beginning to race. "Did it hurt you?" she dared.

"Why would it hurt me?"

Kate looked up at her. She held Tilly's gaze, determined. "Because you used to kiss me, Tilly. Because we kissed in the belltower. All the time."

Like a curse, the words hung heavy in the garden. Tilly stared at her blankly, but Kate's stare was unwavering. "No," Tilly said. "It didn't hurt me."

You're lying. Tilly had been so responsive to her kisses, her touches. To hear Father Jeffrey's condemnation would have hurt her. How could they not? Tilly's faith meant everything to her. Kate's mouth grew dry. "I just thought maybe it had a little bit of an effect on you, you know, because the last night we kissed was the same day Father Jeffrey gave one of those homilies. I always equated the two, thought maybe that was why—because Father Jeffrey made you feel guilty about us, that it was wrong."

"I wanted to join the convent," Tilly said, her voice catching. "It *was* wrong."

"Wrong because you wanted to take your vows?"

"God was watching. What we were doing was *so* improper."

Hardly. They'd been two girls who had loved each other fiercely in ways they couldn't even understand. Two almost-adults, surrendering to their bodies' impulses. It had been nothing short of lovely.

Kate's voice was a whisper. "We were only kissing, Til. It was innocent."

Tilly shook her head, her gaze jerking down to her boots. "Kate, please. I don't want to talk about it."

It was like salt in a wound to think that Tilly regretted a memory that Kate held dear—those chaste, sweet kisses, Tilly's soft, gentle hands in her own, drawing her closer. Would anything ever feel as special?

Kate rubbed her hands across her knees. It was all so vivid—the two of them in their pyjamas climbing over the low wall of the belltower and onto the sloping roof of the convent. The lightning and the thunder, playing like an underworld extravaganza over the horizon of Port Phillip Bay. The night quickly growing dark, rain refusing to fall as flashes lit the night sky. Lying beside Tilly, their feet pressed against the tile as they stared into the moonlight, the stars, waiting, waiting, waiting. The Earth pulling around them. Shoulders pressed together, filthy tile against her palm, against her spine. The storm, stretched tight across the night sky like an elastic band, tension, tension, tension. Tilly's fingers on her cheek, her breath warm on Kate's jaw…

Kate drew a deep breath and pulled herself to her feet. "Are you ready to get going?"

Sunday nights were always the chattiest. Well past the excitement of returning to see their friends at the end of the weekend, the boarders were either asleep or already in bed playing on their phones. After bidding goodnight to too many LED-lit faces to count, Kate moved on to the exhausting task of demanding lights out in the junior wings. Ten-thirty checks quickly progressed to eleven-fifteen checks. Finally, Kate was headed out to the cottage when she noticed that the kitchen light was still on.

"Oh, Sister Ellie," Kate said, her hand falling from the light switch. "I didn't think anybody was in here."

Sister Ellie smiled shortly. "That's all right, Kate." She reached across the counter island for another carrot and began slicing, her eyes refusing to meet Kate's. "I couldn't sleep so I decided to prepare some things for the lesson tomorrow."

Kate stood in the doorway, an uneasy feeling suddenly seizing her. "Are you okay, Sister?"

Sister Ellie took pause. She placed the knife down beside the diced carrots. "I feel very conflicted about something, Kate."

Kate stepped further into the kitchen. "Should you talk to the Reverend Mother?"

Sister Ellie planted her hands firmly against the countertop. "I did speak to her, and heaven forbid, I have to say that her advice has brought no peace."

Kate took a seat on one of the counter stools. "Well would you like to talk to me about it?" she said softly. Sister Ellie was so much younger than the other sisters, just as Tilly would have been had she joined the order, and Kate often worried that Sister Ellie seemed lonely. If Kate could be someone to confide in, somebody like-minded, then she wanted Sister Ellie to know she was there for her.

Sister Ellie pressed a hand to her forehead. She looked to the doorway. "I worry that you're the last person I should talk to about this."

The last person? Worry prickled beneath Kate's skin. It had something to do with her? "No, no," Kate assured her. "You can always talk to me, you know that." She paused. "What is it, Sister?"

Their eyes locked. "The vicar," Sister Ellie started. "He's asked me to go with him to Vanuatu next year. For eighteen months. Maybe longer."

Disappointment gripped Kate. "Tilly's going to Vanuatu?"

Sister Ellie shook her head. She leaned over the counter. "No," she whispered. "He asked me not to tell Tilly. He'd like her to stay here—with his children."

Kate's eyes slipped closed. A flush of anger, red-hot and vile washed over her. Quickly, it was eclipsed, her heart aching for Tilly who was completely oblivious to his intentions. "But she already has a position lined up at St. Matthew's in the city for next year. It's a ninety-minute drive home to Mornington every night. And even if she moves the children to Melbourne, he can't expect her to teach full-time and raise two kids alone."

Sister Ellie swallowed. "From what I gather, he's expecting her to give up that position at St. Matthew's."

Kate traced her finger along the chopping board. "He's using her. He's using her and she's so good that she can't see it." She raised her gaze. "You can see it, can't you? I'm not being paranoid?"

Sister Ellie sighed.

"And why does he want *you* there?" Kate pressed.

"Because I can speak French," she said simply. "And I can cook. And I can do both very well. I suppose I have experience taking missions too."

Kate swallowed. "But have you thought, I mean, you're very young and very beautiful and he's not asking Sister Mary Monica, is he? He could be a sleaze—"

"Yes. I've considered it. But I honestly don't think so, Kate. If that were the case, wouldn't he just stay a while longer with Tilly? What interest would he have in me when he has a new lovely wife?"

Kate's stomach swooped unpleasantly.

Sister Ellie reached across the bench and took Kate's hands in her own. She was quiet. Gently, she squeezed Kate's fingers.

Like a dam opened, the confession spilled from Kate's lips in a rush. "I don't think I realised how much I missed her until she arrived. She was my best friend. I always knew I was going to lose her, that she'd never love me the way I wanted her to, but I was okay with that because I knew I was losing her to the sisterhood. She was hell-bent on choosing this life where she'd do wonderful things for people, important things, just like you do. And in truth, if I'm being really honest, I was bitter about it; that she was so damn compelled to save the world. It frustrated me that we wanted different things but I still understood it—why she needed to choose that life." She paused. "But *him*? There's something off about him, right? To know that she's being taken advantage of just kills me, Sister. It does. I'm not…I'm not jealous. I'm *livid*."

Sister Ellie's expression was compassionate as Kate's confession settled. But there, beneath the glow of the hanging light, was a flicker of something else in Sister Ellie's gaze, something that bore an embarrassingly close resemblance to pity. Behind them, the fridge hummed. "I hope you have somebody, Kate," she said, her voice catching. "Maybe somebody on the mainland who feels the way you do. Somebody who loves you."

The words set a lump in Kate's throat. Sister Ellie wasn't trying to embarrass her, of course not. Still, hyperawareness spiked, washed dread down Kate's back. Was that how she seemed to everybody else? Unfulfilled? Lonely?

Sister Ellie leaned forward. "Kate? Promise me that you won't tell Tilly? The Reverend Mother said I mustn't betray the vicar's confidence."

Anger sparked in Kate. How dare Sister Ruth aid his manipulation. Couldn't she see that what he was doing was wrong? Not only was he manipulating Tilly, but he had placed Sister Ellie in a terrible position. "I almost wish you hadn't told me," Kate rasped.

"The Reverend Mother said the very same thing."

Kate looked up. Their eyes locked. "If Tilly has expressed any reservations about getting married," Sister Ellie murmured, "any at all…then maybe somebody needs to make it clear to her, before she makes a mistake, that her concerns are valid." She hesitated. "I think, Kate, that somebody best be you."

CHAPTER NINE

The next weekend, Tilly took it upon herself to ensure that charity—quite literally—began at home.

Holed up in her office marking all day, Kate's Saturday had been long and lonely. Driving all the way out to Dandenong to see her family had seemed a pointless prospect—she'd only be up to her eyeballs in essays there, and five-year-old Karlie would certainly be a distraction. A loud, boisterous distraction. St. Joan's served silence on a silver platter—too large a helping, in retrospect. Tilly had left early that morning to spend the day on the mainland with Declan at a carnival fundraiser, and as far as company, Kate had only briefly spoken to Sister Ruth around lunchtime. So when Tilly knocked on the door of Kate's office at seven that night with a bowl of steaming stir-fry, Kate was more than glad to see her.

"Ms. York, I come bearing gifts."

Kate's gaze snapped up and she squinted against the onslaught of light as Tilly pulled the chain switch. Night had fallen so quickly that she hadn't realised the brightness of the computer screen had been placing such a strain on her eyes. "Til, I didn't know you were back."

"About an hour and a half ago…"

Kate glanced at the window. The lights of Mornington were like fireflies in the distance. "I didn't even hear the ferry come in."

Tilly gestured to place the bowl down beside textbooks and Kate quickly shifted her mess of papers to make room. "You didn't have to do this," she said as Tilly lifted the tea towel from the top of the bowl.

Tilly shrugged. "I was hungry too."

"How was your day?" Kate asked. "Take a spin on the Cha-Cha?"

Grinning, Tilly shook her head. "No. I worked the cake stall."

Kate leaned back in her chair. "Of course you did." She folded her arms over her chest. "The vicar at least try to win you a stuffed panda?"

Tilly looked to the floor. "I can't say anybody has ever tried to do that for me. And I can't say I feel that I'm missing out."

Kate grinned.

"It's cold in here," Tilly said.

"It's a cold night. Do you want me to pop back to the cottage and start the fire for you?"

Tilly pressed a hip against the edge of Kate's desk. "You very well know I can start the fire myself."

"Can you?" Kate teased.

Tilly didn't bite. "How long will you be here?" she asked.

"I just have to mark three more and I'll be over."

"So…an hour?"

Kate raised an eyebrow. What was with the third degree? "Are we entertaining guests?" she asked playfully.

Tilly planted both palms on the edge of her desk and leaned forward. She bit her lip. Her gaze was downcast, like she was too busy holding a secret close to her chest to look at Kate. "I want to watch last night's episode of *The Bachelor* with you."

Kate grinned. God, did she have to be so cute? "Okay, I won't be long. I'll chew *very, very* quickly."

Tilly nodded. "Don't give yourself indigestion," she said, and then she was gone, leaving Kate as endeared as she was confused.

Smoke billowed from the cottage chimney. In just a T-shirt, Kate shivered in the cold night air as she struggled to balance her glass and empty bowl atop her work folders, the spoon sliding about inside with each step she took down the cottage path. By the front steps, she did a double take as her eyes locked on a pair of dirtied work boots placed neatly to the side of the mat. *Male* work boots. *What in God's name…*

The moment she opened the door, Tilly shot from the lounge.

Kate wasn't sure what she'd expected to find inside the cottage, but it certainly wasn't the elderly stranger seated on the lounge, Kate's coffee mug in hand. Dressed in a bright tropical-printed shirt, his anxious gaze flickered between Kate and Tilly.

"Hello," Kate said. She looked to Tilly.

Quickly, Tilly's focus jerked back to their visitor. "Kate, this is Jim," she said, not sparing a glace to where Kate stood in the open doorway. "We met on the ferry tonight and I asked Jim if he'd like to have dinner with me."

"Hi Jim." Kate set her folders and bowl on the edge of the counter. She stared at the side of Tilly's face. "I thought you already had a fiancé?"

Tilly's eyes widened as Jim laughed. Kate looked between them as she closed the front door behind her.

"Kate teaches music and English, Jim," Tilly explained over the blaring volume of the television. "She lives here too."

Turning, Kate gripped the back of a kitchen chair. Stumped, she looked to Tilly.

Tilly swallowed. "So Jim is going to stay with us tonight so we can take him to Mornington train station tomorrow morning before mass."

Kate blinked twice. "Oh?" She paused. "I'm sorry." She shook her head, needing to clarify. "You've met before tonight?"

A pink flush crept up Tilly's neck. "No."

Kate's jaw set hard as she fixed Tilly with a piercing glare. She'd met a stranger crossing the bay and invited him to dinner and a sleepover? Had she lost her goddamn mind? Who was this person? Was she looking to be butchered in her sleep?

"So." Tilly shifted to lean a hip against the arm of the lounge. "It's just for tonight."

Over my dead body it is. No way in hell was he staying. He'd be on the next ferry out, no doubt about that. What kind of psychopath accepted a young woman's invitation to stay in her home overnight?

A serial killer, that was who. As Jim leaned forward to place the mug on the coffee table, Kate shook her head at Tilly so fiercely she almost jarred it.

Tilly ignored it. She sank into the corner of the lounge and plastered on a smile for Jim.

"I've organised for Jim to stay with St. Matthew's House in the city for a few weeks."

Kate stiffened. St. Matthew's House? *Oh God...Tilly, what have you done?*

Jim turned to face Kate. "I was lucky enough to meet Matilda. Like a guardian angel she is. I tried that St. Vincent's last night. They had the old shed behind the church and the minister there used to let me roll out my swag overnight, but the new minister wasn't too keen on that, sent me away..." He sighed. "What can you do? Can't just expect things of people."

Kate swallowed.

Tilly turned to her. "I rang ahead to St. Matthew's and they had a resident move out just this morning."

"Like fate," Jim inserted. He pointed a finger at Tilly, jabbed it playfully into the air between them. "I'll tell you what, they need more Catholics up in Canberra."

Tilly blushed.

As they both looked to her for a reaction, Kate forced a smile. Her gaze flickered to the pile of blankets by the lounge. *Matilda Wattle: solving Australia's housing crisis one step at a time.*

If the Archangel Gabriel had shown up in her office that evening and told Kate that she'd spend her Saturday night watching a DVR'd episode of *The Bachelor* with Tilly and a homeless stranger, she would have called his bluff.

From her place on the recliner, Kate glanced across the lounge, watching as Tilly explained to Jim the intricate politics of rose ceremonies and eliminations. Subtly, she let her gaze track Tilly's body. Tilly usually looked stylish and put together—even if the girls thought it dowdy—but tonight she looked flustered, frazzled. The collar of her highly-buttoned shirt poked over the neckline of the grey university jumper that swallowed her up. Paired with her long, matronly skirt and ankle-grazing slippers it was certainly *a look.*

"Tilly?"

Leisurely, Tilly pulled her gaze from the television. "Mmm?" she asked nonchalantly.

Kate fixed her with a deadpan glare. She stood. "Can you help me grab some more wood?"

"I don't think we need any more wood." Avoiding Kate's gaze, she reached for her teacup on the edge of the coffee table.

"It's about to go out and you know you like to wake up to a warm house."

"If you tell me where it is, I can get it," Jim offered.

"No need, thanks Jim." Smiling tersely, she took the cup from Tilly's hands and returned it to the coffee table. "Til?"

Torch in hand, she followed Tilly out the front door of the cottage and pulled it shut behind her. "Are you crazy?" she hissed. "Have you lost your damn mind?"

"Okay, I had a feeling that you'd react like this—"

"Of course I would!" She stormed down the garden path to the wood shelter at the edge of the bush, Tilly close at her slippers. "I can't believe you've brought a stranger here to sleep in our *home*."

Behind her, Tilly spluttered a noise somewhere between a gasp and a scoff. "You think I was just going to get off the ferry at Lords and wave him goodbye? Let him go on and sleep under the dock on East Island? He's almost completely deaf, Kate, what was I supposed to do?"

"Give him a twenty, I don't know. This," she jabbed her pointer finger back toward the cottage, "is not normal."

Tilly rolled her eyes. "I did it all the time in the city."

Kate halted before the tiny, poorly constructed wood shelter. When she'd lived alone? "Are you fucking serious?" Her stomach dropped. "You invited strangers into your house when you *lived alone*?"

"I had roommates for a while, don't get your knickers in a twist! You're here. It's safe."

"It's *not* safe!" The frame of the shelter creaked loudly as Kate planted a hand on the rusty, corrugated-iron roof. "Do you know how long it would take the cops to get across the causeway if something happened?"

Tilly sighed. "Kate, he's seventy-nine and he says he has severe plantar fasciitis. His feet are so painful that it took us almost forty minutes to walk from the pier to the cottage—he can barely move. He isn't going to do anything unsavoury."

Shaking her head, Kate placed the torch on the barrel of wood and dragged her hands over her face. "Thank God the girls aren't here on weekends."

"I wouldn't have invited him if the girls were here. Honestly, you're being overly dramatic." Tilly's breath was visible in the torchlight. "It's very offensive to assume that just because he's homeless he's inclined to rob us, or to be violent—"

"Are you kidding me?" Kate snapped. She squinted into the darkness of the barrel, hoping that her voice would have scared off any snakes taking residence inside. "It's not that he's bloody homeless. I couldn't give a toss if he lived in Windsor fucking Castle. *We don't know him.*" Suddenly, realisation struck her. She pulled her hands away. "Your bedroom door doesn't have a lock." How could she possibly sleep knowing that only a door separated Tilly and the complete stranger sleeping on their lounge? "You can't stay in the cottage tonight," she said firmly. "You're sleeping in the convent."

Tilly's expression hardened as she watched Kate pull down the sleeves of her jumper and begin gathering wood pilings in the crook of her arm. "Can you please just lower your voice? And you should be wearing gloves to do that."

"I don't need gloves and he's deaf and we're a mile away!"

"The bathroom window is open and his hearing isn't all that bad. And I can't go to the convent. The sisters would ask why and..." She hesitated. "They wouldn't approve," she said, the words falling from her lips in a rush. "I've done this before, with a different person and they...they overreacted."

Kate threw her hands into the air. "See!"

"He's harmless!"

"You don't know that!"

Tilly's cheeks flushed. "If he sees me leave, he'll think we don't trust him, that he's putting us out!"

"He *is* putting us out." Kate reached deeper for the wood. "I don't care what it looks like, it's not safe for you to be here."

"And it's safe for you just because you're so strong and masculine?" She rolled her eyes.

"*I* have a lock on my door."

Tilly folded her arms across her chest. "*You* may not care what it looks like for me to leave, but I do."

"I swear Tilly, I am not kidding about this—fuck!"

She pulled her hand back and examined her finger. She couldn't see a thing in the dark, but if the stinging throb was anything to go by, the splinter had pierced deeply. And it was *thick*.

Tilly clicked her tongue. "I told you to wear gloves!" She moved closer.

"Tilly, just bloody back off for a sec. Honestly, you're doing my head in."

"I'm sorry," she said sarcastically. Kate watched her shift from foot to foot, listened as the cogs turned in Tilly's mind. *Here we bloody go…* "I'll say you have a pull-out sofa in your room, that I'm staying in there."

Kate blinked twice. "What?"

"I'll say that I can't expect him to sleep on the lounge and I'll offer him my bed." She paused, eyes narrowing. "And you can lock both of us in your bedroom and *sleep soundly*," she said.

Kate swallowed. "You know, sarcasm doesn't look so pretty on you."

"You know, *bigotry* doesn't look so pretty on *you*." Tilly's stare bore into hers, an indelible glint in her eye that drew Kate's attention like a magnet.

"Fine. Go and get your mother's jewellery and anything else valuable from your room."

Tilly fixed her with a glare.

Laden with an armful of wood, Kate swiped the torch from the barrel and pressed it into Tilly's hands. "*Don't* be stupid about this."

When they returned, Jim was standing by the sink. He met Kate's eye. "I'm afraid the fire died while you were gone," he said, sheepish. "I tried to keep it burning but…" He hesitated. "I can leave if you'd prefer it," he offered. Carefully, he reached for Kate's cup on the drying rack and smothered the sudsy cup in the "Birds of Australia" tea towel Sister Tessie had gifted Kate all those months ago as a housewarming gift. "I mean, I understand why you wouldn't want me here. No harm done."

"No, no," Tilly insisted. "Of course not. We were just talking and Kate suggested that you take my bed tonight."

Jim shook his head adamantly. "Oh, no. I couldn't."

"Yes, you can," Tilly said as she took the tea towel and cup from his hand. She smiled warmly and rubbed at his shoulder. "Kate has a pull-out in her room that I can sleep on, and honestly, we'd both feel much better knowing that you were sleeping in a real bed rather than on the lounge." Her gaze brushed Kate's as Jim hobbled across the kitchen to return three cups to the rack.

Jim chuckled. He spared a glance at Kate as she lowered the fresh wood beside the fire. "Only if you're sure," he said sincerely, and embarrassment burned hot as it climbed Kate's neck. Perhaps she hadn't been as welcoming as she could have been. Perhaps she'd been a royal jerk.

Kate smiled widely as she arranged the kindling inside the heater. "One hundred percent sure. Til, can you grab me a fire starter?" she asked, desperate to change the subject.

Tilly pulled the box from the top of the fridge and squinted inside as she crossed the room. Reaching inside, she pinched one out. "Oh, by the way," she said as she lowered the cube into Kate's hand, "I know you offered, but are you sure you're okay to strip and remake my bed for Jim while I shower?"

Striking a match, Kate bit her tongue. *Nicely played, Tilly. Nicely played.*

Christ Almighty. Kate groaned internally as the end of the splinter broke off into her short nail, the rest still deep in her flesh. *Good fucking job, Kate.* She needed tweezers, and a magnifying glass, and more than the pathetic glow of her bedside light. She winced against the pain as she squeezed at it. If Tilly hadn't insisted on turning out the main light to get down on her knees and pray, maybe she wouldn't have broken the splinter in the first place. She looked to the ceiling in frustration as Tilly droned on with her prayer for Sister Ruth's arthritis. If Kate didn't pop a blood vessel trying to squeeze the damn splinter out, Tilly's never-ending repentance would get the job done.

"And finally, Lord, please bless Sister Tessie..."

Yes, finally. Kate glanced at her bedside clock. Prayer time was going on five minutes. At this rate, Tilly was giving Maria Von Trapp a run for her money. Kate ran her gaze over Tilly's face, watched as her closed eyelids fluttered with every word that left her lips. Like a veil, her hair fell over her high cheekbones in dark waves. She'd always prayed aloud, even when they'd shared a room as teenagers, but she'd never prayed for so *long*. Kate pulled her gaze away and looked back down to her throbbing thumb.

"Lord, may Sister Tessie find peace in her confusion, and with your love and guidance, may she remain with the sisters of St. Joan for as long as possible."

Halle-freakin'-lujah.

"And Lord, please bless Kate."

Kate's gaze snapped up to stare over the rim of her glasses.

"May she find the compassion in her kind and loving heart to open her arms to those less fortunate. May she find the goodness within not to judge—"

"—I told you it's not because he's homeless—"

"—those she does not know." She paused, the silence extended. "In God's name I pray. Amen."

It was hard to focus on Tilly's jab when she was pulling back the covers on her side of the bed, the long, creamy expanse of her legs so exposed in those cotton shorts as she slipped in beside Kate. Tilly sighed exhaustedly, her eyes closing as her head found the pillow. The sound twisted Kate's stomach into knots. Drawing her gaze away from the hollow of Tilly's throat, she threw the covers back.

"Where are you going?" Tilly asked.

Kate stopped at the door. On her tiptoes, she felt across the head jamb for the ancient key.

"Do it quietly," Tilly whispered as Kate slipped it into the keyhole.

Out of her control, the lock clinked heavily. As Tilly clicked her tongue in annoyance, Kate rolled her eyes. "He's already snoring."

"No, he's not."

"Listen."

Tilly propped herself up on her elbows, her brow furrowing. Even through the plaster walls, the irregular rumble was unmissable.

Kate shook her head as she padded back to the bed. "If he gets any louder, *I'll* sleep in the goddamn convent."

"Can you please not put those two words together?" Tilly huffed.

Kate folded her glasses on the bedside table and switched off the lamp. "You've already prayed for my soul for the night, I'll be fine."

"That's what you think."

I'm not so sure I *can* think right now, she thought as she settled in beside Tilly. Her bed was only a double. Tilly was so, so close. The warmth of her body, the scent of her...

"This bed smells like you," Tilly whispered.

"Like fairy-floss and popcorn?" Kate joked.

Tilly pushed herself up onto an elbow. Even in the darkness, Kate could feel the intensity of her stare as Tilly slid her other hand into the empty space between them.

Kate turned her head on the pillow. "What?"

"Do you remember when your mum took us to the fairgrounds?" Tilly whispered. "That Queen's Birthday long weekend?"

Kate smiled. "Yeah." Of course she did. The only reason Tilly had been allowed to sleepover at Kate's for the first and only time was because Kate's mum was running the Rotary barbecue. Disgruntled by the idea that Tilly would have to head back for the ferry and miss the nighttime events, Kate had gone alone to Sister Hattie's office and insisted they needed extra help at the food stall. What are they raising money for? Sister Hattie had asked. The homeless, Kate had told her. In truth, the proceeds had funded a local boy's trip to Canada to compete in an international chess championship.

"I was thinking about it today," Tilly said softly. "I think about it often. That was the one of the best days of my childhood."

Kate wet her lips. That day had fallen somewhere in the middle of their final year, between when they'd started kissing and when they'd stopped. Those blissful few months when hope had burned bright, when every touch, every look had mattered. When Tilly had stopped slipping into Kate's bed at night after checks because suddenly, it had seemed to mean more than it ever had before.

"I can't remember too much," Kate said. "But I remember the Ferris wheel."

Silence.

Christ... She hadn't meant for the comment to suck all of the oxygen from the room. Her heart pounded treacherously. So possibly not the wisest thing to say after the way Tilly had reacted in the backyard of the St. Kilda terrace...

She went rigid with surprise when Tilly's soft whisper filled the room. "Yeah," she said, her voice wavering ever so slightly. "I remember the Ferris wheel, too."

They'd stayed at the fairgrounds late into the night. She'd been high on the adrenaline of having Tilly clutching at her arm on the pirate ship, their hips brushing inside the barbecue stall as they'd collected donations. That day, they'd been soft with each other in ways they hadn't dared to be since Kate had first planted a kiss to Tilly's neck in the belltower. So, high up in the treetops aboard pink gondola number three, when Kate had summoned the courage to reach out and take Tilly's hand in the cloak of dark, it had felt like something had locked into place for good, forever. Tilly's fingers had relaxed in hers and Kate had vibrated with a nervous excitement that far exceeded the rush of satisfaction she got from kissing Tilly.

Tilly shifted down the bed and rested her head on the pillow. "There was a boy, working the stall with us…"

"There was?"

"Mhm. He was the son of your mum's friend."

Kate thought hard for a moment. "I don't know who that could have been." The memory of working the barbecue stall was vague.

"That was how we got the tickets for the Ferris wheel," Tilly said. "We'd used up all our own tickets on the swinging chairs and the Ghost Train." She paused. "Anyway, he gave you a pair of tickets he'd been given for free and he expected you to take him. And you took me."

"I can't remember any of that."

"Really? He kept flipping your ponytail all day, tugging on it. He was flirting with you." She shifted lower, the covers rustling. "Boys liked you," she murmured, and there was something there that hinted at irritation.

Kate smirked. "You make it sound like you were jealous."

"I wasn't jealous. You took *me* on the Ferris wheel, not him."

Her throat constricted. "I meant jealous that he was flirting with me and not with you."

The room fell silent. "It's bright in here," Tilly said after a long moment. "You should get curtains."

"The venetians work just fine."

"They *don't*," Tilly argued. "I feel like I need you to blindfold me."

Kate's eyes slipped closed at the comment. *As if this isn't already sweet hell.* Her thumb throbbed. There was no way she was going to be able to sleep knowing the splinter was in there. With a gruff sigh, she sat up against the bedhead and switched on the light. "Sorry, Til, I'll turn it off in a sec, but this splinter is driving me nuts." She reached for her glasses.

Tilly sat up against the headboard. "Come here." She took Kate's hand in hers. "Gosh you get obsessive when things don't go your way."

Kate brow furrowed. "That's not true."

"It is." Tilly's breath was warm on her wrist as she inspected her thumb. "It's your arrogant streak. If I didn't know any better, I'd swear you were an only child."

"I think you'll need tweezers."

"I have nails."

Kate cringed as Tilly pinched the skin of her thumb tightly. "*Fantastic*. Yeah, don't worry about being gentle or anything."

"Don't be a wuss. I see it," Tilly said without squinting. "You've gone and broken the tip off playing with it," she chastised, raking her long hair around to one side of her neck to keep it from obstructing her view.

Tilly's hands were so soft, her body warm as she pressed closer. Kate stared, transfixed as Tilly's teeth slipped over her bottom lip in concentration. She cleared her throat. "So what's your plan for Jim tomorrow morning when the sisters wake?"

Tilly sighed. "I'm trying not to think about that right now," she mumbled.

Kate winced as Tilly squeezed harder, determined. "I promised the sisters we'd take the car ferry and I'd drive them into Mornington for eight o'clock mass. We can't exactly leave him here. You think they're not going to notice when Grandfather Jim climbs aboard the nun mobile?"

"So I'll get up early, go into the convent and explain. Whether they like it or not, they'll just have to get over it."

"You could have just explained tonight. And gone and slept in the convent—" Her hand flinched in Tilly's grip. "Ow! Tilly! You did that on purpose!"

"I did not. There, it's out."

Kate ran the pad of her thumb across her skin. She was right. "Thanks," she grumbled.

"You're welcome." Tilly slipped low beneath the covers. "Now could you please turn off your light?"

Slowly, Kate's eyes adjusted to the dark. Her eyes slipped closed, but her mind ran wild.

She rolled over. "Til?"

"Mmm?"

"When you talk to the sisters in the morning, maybe don't tell them that you slept in here."

"Why?"

"…You know why."

Tilly was silent. "Well if they ask, I'm not going to *lie.*"

"Just tell them that we swapped rooms for the night and he slept on the couch."

Quiet.

"Til?"

"*What?*"

"Did you hear me?"

"*Yes*, I heard you."

"You won't say anything?"

With a tired sigh, Tilly rolled over. "Just go to sleep, Kate."

The first to climb into the van the next morning, Sister Mary Monica fixed Kate with a disapproving look as she hiked up her habit and reached for the support handle.

"Just for the record," Kate said, offering her hand to help Sister Mary Monica up the small step, "I did not encourage this."

Sister Mary Monica took her usual seat in the second row. "Tilly made that perfectly clear when she came to speak to us this morning at breakfast."

So what was with the dirty look?

Silence settled inside the van. Across the convent garden, Tilly, Jim, and the other sisters were slowly making their way toward them. "It's not safe," Sister Mary Monica said. "To do a thing like that."

Kate looked up into the rear vision mirror. Sister Mary Monica's gaze was focused on Lockie as Tilly locked him safely in the garden. Kate swallowed nervously. "I know. I tried to talk her into staying in the convent but she wasn't having it."

"Yes, she mentioned that you insisted she leave the cottage." She paused. "Especially considering that only your bedroom has a lock."

Christ... Tilly hadn't mentioned the fact that they had shared a bed, had she? Kate had explicitly asked her not to. "She wouldn't listen," Kate said, desperate to steer the conversation in any other direction than the one they were headed. "You know how she gets."

"Yes," Sister Mary Monica murmured. "I do know how she gets," she said bluntly. "That girl makes silly mistakes."

Kate's eyes widened slightly. *Wow. Harsh.*

"Thank goodness for the lock on your bedroom door," Sister Mary Monica said. "That she could sleep in there."

Kate slowly relaxed. Tilly hadn't told the sisters. *Thank God...* "Yeah. We just swapped rooms so she'd have the lock. No big deal." *Hurry up, Tilly. Put me out of my misery...*

"Swapped rooms?" Sister Mary Monica said. "That wasn't what Tilly told us."

CHAPTER TEN

Swiping seawater from her chin, Kate grinned as she crossed the sand. The closer she came to Tilly, sitting primly on one of the pale pink towels from their linen press, all the more evident was the thick layer of sunscreen Tilly slathered on her forearms.

"You're an English rose, Matilda Wattle."

As Kate reclined on her own towel, Tilly laughed. She raised a hand to block out the downing sun, her eyes crinkling into almond shapes. "Shh," Tilly said, nodding toward the students swimming nearby in the bay. "Let's keep my nationality a secret, please."

"Don't worry," Kate chuckled as she lifted the sides of the towel to swat at the water that tracked from her sports bra to her middle. "I won't tell anyone you're a pom."

Kate looked back at the girls in the water. Only a quarter of the boarders had decided to come down for an afternoon swim after school and that made for easy supervision. Unlike the west end of the island, the east was a safe bay, and although most of the girls were decent swimmers, they knew not to venture too far toward the mouth of the cove where the current began to pull.

She turned her head to meet Tilly's eyes, and instead, to her intrigue, found Tilly's eyes locked on her bare abdomen. Caught, Tilly pulled her gaze away.

Licking sea salt from her lips, Kate looked out at the sunlight glinting on the water. *What the hell was that about?* She resisted the urge to glance down at her belly, at the slightly apparent muscles above the band of her bikini bottoms.

"Remember when I got that portable CD player for Christmas and we'd come down here and dance?" Kate said, shivering as icy droplets chased down the back of her neck.

"*I* would dance," Tilly corrected, her long plait swinging between her shoulder blades as she reclined on her elbows. "You just lay back on the sand and watched."

Tilly shook her head, a small smile playing at her lips. "We went through so many batteries."

And sixteen-year-old me would have bought shares in Eveready if it meant spending the rest of my days watching you dance in the cove...

Reclined in the shallow water at the shore, Emma and Grace called out to Lockie, but he ignored their incessant calls, happy to lounge halfway out on the sandbar in peace.

Sighing, Kate shifted on the towel, her elbows digging into the sand. "I'm going to miss all this," she confessed. "I think this has been the most rewarding teaching position I've ever had."

Tilly held her stare before she looked out to the bay, the short sleeves of her denim dress fluttering in the breeze. "Mine was working at a small school in Papua New Guinea," she said. "But then an earthquake destroyed it."

Kate tensed, the revelation settling heavily between them. Tilly had never mentioned that. "I had no idea you were ever in danger..." she said. "Not like that. I don't remember ever hearing about an earthquake while you were there—when I thought you were there."

Briefly, Tilly's gaze flickered to hers, then away. "It only hit a very small part of the remote east coast, at night. Seven point two on the Richter scale," she said softly. "We lost so many children. Families..." Tilly's eyes brightened with tears. "I stayed for a while, to help, but I left not long after."

Kate watched Tilly's fingers twitch against the towel. "How old were you?" she asked.

"I came home to Australia a week before my twentieth birthday and started uni the very next semester," Tilly rasped. She drew the back of her wrist across her cheek and Kate's chest pulled tight. "That trip changed things for me," Tilly admitted. "It changed me."

As she looked out at the girls, Kate covered Tilly's fingers with her own. It was a helpless feeling—wanting to offer all the sympathy she was capable of giving yet knowing she would never fully comprehend the tragedy Tilly had witnessed, *endured*, at such a young age. "Of course it did," she said quietly. Their eyes locked. "It would change anybody. And, hey, if you ever want to talk about it all…I'm here."

Tilly's fingers linked with her own. "I know you are."

Kate broke their gaze and looked out at the drooping afternoon sun. She would always be there for Tilly, but it wouldn't always be easy like this, slow and simple and breathable. Soon enough, the sapphire on Tilly's finger and its glistening promise would come between them. Once more, they'd blame distance, the miles between them. And maybe, considering how greatly Kate struggled to think of Tilly as just a friend, it was for the best.

But who would be there for Tilly when Kate was gone? When Tilly was married? When Declan abandoned his new wife for Vanuatu? Tilly rarely mentioned friends other than the few from university, and those friends had taken up teaching positions in towns all over the state. Tilly didn't really know anybody in Mornington other than the sisters.

As a gust of wind picked up, Tilly released Kate's hand to tuck her dress beneath her thighs.

"Why doesn't Declan come here very often?" Kate asked. "To Lords?"

"I suppose it's a trip."

"An eighteen-minute ferry ride…"

"Lily gets seasick."

"Right…" To Kate, it seemed more like Declan wasn't willing to go out of his way.

"So do you have something lined up for next year?" Tilly asked.

Kate nodded. "I have an interview just after Christmas. Head of the Music Department. Grammar school in the city."

Tilly arched a brow. "You aren't going to tell me which school?"

"I don't want to jinx it."

Tilly laughed. "Well, I hope you get it," she offered.

"Oh, I'll get it."

Tilly laughed. She shook her head. "There you go again with the arrogance."

Grinning, Kate pushed herself up onto her elbows. She shrugged. "Your modesty balances me out, Ms. Wattle."

Squinting, Tilly looked out to Lockie out on the sandbar, his gaze focused on Mornington peninsula. "Is he okay?" she asked.

Kate raised a hand to her brow. "I think he's whale watching," she joked. She looked between the girls and the retriever. It wasn't all that long ago that she'd take the girls down to the water and Lockie would splash about, a firecracker ecstatic to spend the afternoon wrestling with the girls. "He's getting old," Kate said, standing. "I'll be back in a sec."

The further Kate walked across the sandbar, it became increasingly apparent that something was wrong. Ambivalent to Kate's approach, Lockie extended his front legs and lay down on the sand, the shallow water barely touching his paws as it rushed and receded.

Kate crouched beside him. "Hey, matey."

With a glance at Kate, he dropped his head to rest across his front legs.

"What's the matter?" Kate asked, smoothing her hand over his head and rubbing her thumb between his brows just the way he liked.

His eyes closed, his tail still. A pained whimper escaped him.

A lump grew in Kate's throat as she ran her hand down to his belly and felt his breathing. "Up, matey," she said. "Lockie," she encouraged gently. "Up."

Back at the shore, Kate could hear a few eighth graders shouting Lockie's name. "Come on, Lock," Kate said, scratching behind his ears. "Your girls want to play with you..."

His eyes slipped open and locked on her, and Kate's heart dropped at the fatigue swimming in sorrowful brown. Kate looked back at Tilly. Watching in concern, her hand was raised to her forehead to block out the sun. Lockie moaned again, and a flashback of losing her childhood dog hit Kate.

Christ. If only she had given in to the girls' request to drive to the beach, if only she hadn't insisted they all walk. She now needed the van—she could manage to carry Lockie back to the beach, but not all the way back to the school. What were her options? She glanced back to the shore. Tilly couldn't drive a manual, but Emma…Emma could. Months ago, when Emma first got her learner's permit, Kate had taken her for driving lessons around the island in the van. She wasn't licensed, but with Tilly's supervision… Kate waved Emma over.

Emma waded through the water, breathing heavily when she finally reached the point of the sandbar. "Yeah?"

Kate pushed her sunglasses to the top of her head. "Em," she said gently, "he can't get up."

Emma's expression crumpled. "He collapsed?"

"I think so," Kate said.

"Well maybe he's just tired…"

Kate swiped a hand over her mouth. "He's whimpering, hon. Something's wrong."

Emma's eyes welled. She slipped to her knees and buried her face in the fur at Lockie's neck.

"It's okay, it's okay," Kate assured her, crouching low again. "Don't panic," she whispered. "He's okay for now. *He is*. Em?" Kate gripped her shoulder. "Em, look at me for a sec."

Emma pulled back. Their eyes met.

"Don't tell the other girls, but I need you to go and tell Tilly to walk them back. You need to go with them. When you get there, I need you to get the van and drive it down here with Tilly—I don't want you driving alone. I'm going to stay with him—"

"—No, I can stay with him—"

"No. I will." If something happened to Lockie, the last thing she wanted was for Emma to be alone when it happened. "When you get back down here, we'll take him across to the vet in Portarlington."

"I can come with you across the causeway?" Emma asked. Hastily, she swiped at the wetness on her cheeks.

Kate nodded. "Of course you can."

Emma nodded. With one last kiss to Lockie's ear, she stood. "I'll be real quick."

Despair clutched Kate as she watched Emma and Tilly take the steep shortcut through the spindly grass of the dune to where she and Lockie sat back on the dry sand of the beach. *Oh God...* They had taken such a long time. Too long. Swallowing, Kate shook her head.

Tilly slowed in step, hand pressed to her breastbone as she hesitated. Emma quickened her pace.

Damp hair matted to the sides of her face, Emma fell to her knees in the sand. Slumping forward, she buried her trembling chin in Lockie's fur and whimpered a sound that twisted Kate's stomach into knots. "I shouldn't have gone anywhere," she cried. "I should have stayed with him." She looked up at Kate. "Are you sure?" she asked, eyes glossy with blind trust.

The cooling wind pulled at Kate's T-shirt. "I'm sure," she said softly. She wet her lips and tasted salt left behind from her tears minutes before. "I carried him up here about ten minutes ago and it happened not long after. I'm so, so sorry, Em."

Stopping just a few feet away, Tilly wrapped her arms around herself to rub at her bare arms. As the sea rushed up to tease her toes, Kate shifted on the sand. Streamers of kelp rolled up to the shore. The tide was coming in. Kate's eyes locked with Tilly's— they had to move. Kate looked up to the van parked high on the hill. *How the hell am I going to carry a thirty-five-kilo golden retriever up there?*

Kate watched as Tilly crouched and smoothed a hand over the back of Emma's head. "He was with Kate," she said, her voice candied with kindness. "He was okay, Emma, Kate was with him."

A shadow passed over the corner of the tool shed. Spinning around, Kate found Emma standing in the doorway looking exhausted. "Em, hey." She turned back to pulling garden rakes and brooms aside to get to the larger of the two shovels.

"I've come to help," Emma said.

Kate turned. "You don't have to do that, Em."

"No," Emma said decidedly. "He was my dog. I'll help."

Kate reached into the locker and blindly freed the first shovel. There was so much of herself in Emma, she thought. Refusing Emma's help would only upset her more. Kate handed her the shovel. "Hold this while I scrounge out another."

"'Kay."

Twilight quickly set in. Together, they decided on a spot between two gum trees at the edge of the bush. As Kate pierced the blade of the shovel into the soil and forced her foot down onto the step, she glanced up at the boarding house. The lights were on. Silhouettes passed by the study hall windows on the first floor and by the ground-floor common room. It was obvious that Tilly had advised the girls against venturing out to ask if Kate and Emma were ready for the service.

In silence, they dug until they were both knee deep in soil. "Have you done this before?" Emma asked, her voice hoarse. "Buried a dog?"

"Yeah, unfortunately," Kate said. "We had a border collie named Missy when I was growing up. When my parents divorced and I came here to board, Missy went to live with my dad. I didn't spend much time with my dad after the divorce so I rarely saw Missy, but I was home for the holidays in my final year and I was spending a few nights at Dad's. He had to go to a wedding one afternoon and left me to look after my little sister—she was in her last year of primary school."

She shovelled a heap of soil onto the growing pile on the grass and resisted the urge to tell Emma to try to keep it in one pile. "That night, we were in the lounge room and Missy was asleep in the kitchen. My sister went to mic the popcorn and Missy was just…she'd just passed away in her sleep. She wasn't as old as Lock, but she was still old." She cringed as a small clump of soil slunk into her shoe. "I didn't really know what to do, and it wasn't like it is now, you know, you couldn't just send a text or call your parents whenever you need to ask how long you need to boil an egg."

Emma rolled her eyes. "So *you* buried Missy?"

Kate nodded. "I was determined to take care of it myself."

"Why didn't you just wait until your dad came home?"

"I guess I was trying to prove to myself that I didn't need my parents." The words bubbled from within: "Their separation really did a number on me and I was super depressed. Actually, that's why they sent me here—so I could get away from that…environment."

Emma ceased shovelling. She speared her shovel into the dirt and stood tall. "I didn't know that."

"Yeah," Kate husked. "When I came here to St. Joan's, I was a mess. And I was acting out too. But the sisters sorted that part out quick smart."

Emma was quiet. She picked up her shovel and began again. "Do you see your dad much? I mean, I've heard you say that you spend weekends at your mum's, but..."

"I see him from time to time. But he lives in Queensland now. His brother and sister are up there."

"That sucks..."

"It does, but he likes his life up there, and I fly up to see him whenever I get a chance. What about you? Do you see your dad much?"

"I see my dad a lot. More than I actually thought I would, you know, when they first told me they were separating."

Kate smiled softly. "Good. That's great, Em." She tossed her shovel up onto the grass and pulled herself up. Emma followed.

Together they stood, examining their work. "I think it's deep enough," Kate murmured.

Emma looked over at Lockie, shrouded in a paint-spattered drop sheet the sisters had. She puffed her cheeks out on an exhalation. "Okay then," she said hesitantly.

Kate turned to her. "Want to go and get the girls and the sisters?"

Emma's expression hardened. "Not really." She sank to her knees and smoothed a hand over the speckled pink sheet, over Lockie's head. "He was my first dog." She raised her gaze. "Can you go get the others and I'll just stay here with him until you get back? Please?"

She nodded. "Sure."

The turnout for Lockie's farewell was more impressive than that of Kate's great aunt's. When the teary cohort of boarders was gathered at the edge of the bush, Sister Ruth insisted on conducting the "service." Twice, Kate raised an eyebrow across the circle at Tilly as the Reverend Mother droned on about an entirely unrelated parable, stopping to blow her nose into a handkerchief before she navigated a roundabout link to Lockie. As the sisters sang a tone-deaf rendition of *Ave Maria*, the girls drizzled handfuls of dirt into the grave.

When it was over, Emma lingered. She reached for a shovel but Kate took it from her. "This is the easy part. How about you go and shower and have something to eat?"

Emma's red-rimmed eyes narrowed. "Are you sure?"

Kate nodded. "Definitely."

When the grave was half-filled, with a heavy heart, Kate stopped her shovelling and raised her gaze to watch a colony of flying foxes soar overhead. A wicked, ominous feeling gripped her and she tried to squash it down. Returning to the high pile of soil, a flash of blue caught her eye. "Great," she mumbled beneath her breath, as she watched Sister Ruth cross the dirt road, "Just what I bloody need…"

"Don't you pull your back out again," Sister Ruth warned as she approached.

"I've never pulled my back out."

Beneath the plastic frames of Kate's glasses, sweat had pooled on the bridge of her nose. She pulled the frames off and tossed them down to the clean grass.

"April," Sister Ruth said, and Kate spared her a brief glance. Her sight impaired, Sister Ruth was nothing but a blur of blue in the moonlight. "I saw your Google search on the office computer," Sister Ruth continued. "Exercises for back pain. You can't get anything past me, so don't be deceitful, Kate," she said playfully.

"Deceitful?" Kate scoffed. She pressed her foot against the step of the shovel and collected a heavy mass of soil on the blade. "Maybe you should pass that line of advice over to St. Vincent's."

Kate heaved the mass of soil into the grave. Sister Ruth remained silent.

"It's going to break Tilly's heart when she realises she's being used—when they get married and he just takes off."

"Kate, the vicar told Sister Ellie in confidence. I can't betray that."

She swatted a mosquito from her forearm. *Son of a bitch.* "You encouraged Sister Ellie to betray Tilly—for him. We don't even *know* him."

She shovelled faster.

Sister Ruth cleared her throat. "The vicar is doing the right thing and we must have confidence in him. He's a man of faith, Kate, a good man—"

"He's an *asshole.*" With a grunt, she speared her shovel into the ground.

Silence.

Kate swiped the sweat from her forehead with the back of her hand. "I'm sorry, Reverend Mother."

Sister Ruth crouched by the clean grass at the head of the grave. Calmly, she straightened the rose the girls had picked for Lockie. "We all know that you care very deeply for Tilly, Kate."

Something in the Reverend Mother's tone brought a flush of heat to Kate's skin. "Yeah, well, she's my friend." Kate grunted with exertion as she filled the grave. "She deserves better. And you know what? I'm not so sure that I'm going to be able to keep quiet about this for much longer. *I* don't owe the guy anything."

"Kate..."

"I mean, Tilly almost took the wrong vows once, didn't she? Now she's doing it all over again." She looked up, trying to focus on the pale blur that was Sister Ruth's face. Even blind to her features, Kate could read the warning. She'd gone too far, said too much. Fuck it, she thought. It was time to be bold. To be brave. It was time to bury the reticence—including her own. "You know I'm gay, right?"

For a long moment, Sister Ruth stood in stunned silence. "Yes, Kate," she said. "We assumed."

Kate waited for the Reverend Mother to offer more, but nothing came. She stabbed the blade into the mound of loose soil in frustration. "Good," she said shortly. "Glad we've cleared that up."

"I don't think it really needed discussing in the first place, Kate." Her tone was clear—she had no interest in talking about it.

"Yeah? Well I think it needed to be brought up, and I'm sorry if you don't like that, but that's the way I feel." Her arms trembled with a dissociative mix of exhaustion, anger, and apprehension. "I'm sick of feeling like I need to keep a part of myself hush-hush, as though I'm constantly having to make sure I don't slip up when the girls ask why I'm not married, or about old boyfriends. Thing is, Sister, I'm so *completely* respectful of everything you have going on here at St. Joan's and I think that, considering everything I've done for the school this year, it's only fair that I should be extended the same, simple courtesy."

With a great, heaving sigh, she patted the shovel against the soil. She picked up her glasses and slid the frames up her nose.

Sister Ruth's expression was pinched with uncertainty, her lips parted as she struggled to respond. Exhaling harshly, Kate waited. "We respect you very deeply, Kate. It troubles me to think that you believe otherwise. That we treat you differently."

"You do, though. You *do* treat me differently." She paused. "Look, I'm not having a go, but I need to just put it out there, okay?" If she were honest with herself, it had been playing on her mind since her deep and meaningful conversation with Tilly in the backyard of the St. Kilda terrace. "You're happy to ask Tilly all about her past, but with me, you'd rather just turn a blind eye. You're always encouraging her to invite the vicar on over but in the nine months I've been here you've never once said, "Hey, Kate, is there anybody you'd like to have visit for the weekend?""

"We respect *you*, we respect *Tilly*, we—"

"I know you do, but..."

"But what?" Sister Ruth implored.

There were so many *buts* that Kate didn't even know where to begin. *But you just don't get it, Sister. But by asking me to hide who I am, you've given me no option but to set a horrible example for the girls. But you can't understand how it feels to live like this. But it doesn't have to be this way.* "But I wish you respected Tilly enough to tell her that he's planning on—"

"Oh, Katherine! What is this about? Your lifestyle? Or Tilly's engagement?"

Kate swallowed. "What?"

Sister Ruth shook her head. "One moment we're arguing over the vicar's plans, and the next you're asking for my blessing to live a homosexual lifestyle—"

She scoffed. "I'm thirty years old, I'm not asking for your blessing—"

"I can't keep up with you tonight, not when you're clearly so aggravated. I'm going inside," she said decidedly.

Kate blinked. *Why am I so surprised?* Sister Ruth avoided confrontation like the plague. Really, she should have been surprised they'd got this far.

"Now," Sister Ruth said, "will you be all right out here alone?"

Kate nodded tersely. "Don't trip in the dark on your way back," she grumbled.

As though they hadn't been deep in heated discussion a moment before, the Reverend Mother brought two fingers to her temple in a salute and, smiling, turned to leave.

Returning the tools to the shed, Kate headed in for a shower. Sand chafed in places sand had no prerogative being and her hands were still putrid with soil regardless of how hard she had scrubbed them at the garden tap.

When she opened the cottage door, Tilly's smile slipped. She pulled the phone away from her ear and covered the receiver, but Kate shook her head, mimed *Ignore me, keep talking, I'm not here, about to shower anyway.* She crossed the kitchen and reached around Tilly for a glass of water.

Making no effort to shift away from Kate's closeness, Tilly hummed in agreement with whatever Declan was saying on the other end of the line. At the surprising sensation of a warm hand against her lower back, Kate stiffened. Tilly's touch, innocent and sweet, smoothed over the thin skin of Kate's T-shirt. Desperately attempting to relax into the friendly touch, Kate fought against a shiver. Her body was alive with adrenaline—anger, need, desire— and Tilly's long fingers against her spine weren't helping quell the stirring in her stomach. She took a long gulp of water. For as wholesome as Tilly was, in her heart of hearts Kate knew that Tilly could match her passion with equal intensity, with equal fervour. And that knowledge…well, it was potent enough to be her undoing.

She set the empty glass back down on the table, relief chasing through her as Tilly's hand drifted low and pulled away. A short-lived touch, Kate thought for a second, but *no.* As Tilly shifted the phone against her ear, she reached out, teeth worried at her lip as she smiled shyly. In a maddening tease, her fingernail brushed against the neckline of Kate's T-shirt, traced the small patch of sweat high on her sternum before jabbing the cotton there gently, as if to tell her she'd sweat through. Tilly fixed her with a look she couldn't decipher and Kate's chest expanded in anticipation. This thing between them…it wasn't just friendship. It couldn't be. It was richer than ever.

His voice nothing more than a faint murmur through the receiver, Tilly's finger zigzagged over the dampened patch of cotton, and Kate pulled her gaze up. Tilly's nervous smile was gone. Their eyes locked, held.

"Declan, I'm sorry to cut you off but I have to go…" Her gaze held Kate's. "Kate's just come in."

Kate shook her head, gesturing for Tilly's conversation to continue as she backed away and closed the bathroom door behind her. As she stripped, the spray of the shower drowned out Tilly's voice.

They had less than two months left, Kate thought as she slipped beneath the warm spray. On autopilot, she picked up Tilly's body wash by mistake. She flipped the cap and brought it to her nose, inhaling the sweet scent of apricot as her eyes slipped closed. Carefully, she placed it back down and reached for her own. Eight weeks to figure out how to contend with a twelve-year love affair. Sixty days to figure out how to get the hell over it.

CHAPTER ELEVEN

It was Saturday morning—just days after Lockie's funeral—when the strangeness set in.

"Mind if I come in?" Kate asked. "I just have to brush my teeth…"

At the basin where she was rubbing lotion into her palms, Tilly stepped aside. "I'm ready to go whenever you are."

Reaching for the toothpaste, Kate paused. Tilly hadn't been waiting on her, had she? "I've decided not to head over to Mornington today, remember? I told you last night before bed…"

Tilly blinked. "Right. It slipped my mind."

"It's just that I have a heap of work to finish before the girls get back. Might go tomorrow."

"Right," she said absently.

As Kate flipped the cap back on the tube, she looked up into the mirror. Tilly's gaze seemed unfocused. *How did she forget in the space of eight hours?* Something was off.

"You okay, Til?"

"Fine."

Tilly's smile was forced. *Anxious.* "You're not having breakfast before you leave?" Kate tried.

Reaching for the bottle of perfume on the second shelf, Tilly shook her head.

Breakfast plans with the vicar? How very domestic. She shut off the tap. "I'll drive you down to the pier," she murmured around the head of the toothbrush.

Tilly didn't look up. "Okay."

"You sure you're all right?" She tapped her hand against Tilly's hip, making way to rinse at the sink. Instantly, Tilly shifted aside at the touch.

"I'm fine. Can we leave soon? I already called ahead for the nine o'clock."

They climbed into the van together. Kate tilted her head as she clipped her seat belt. "Aren't you going to be hot in that cardigan?"

"No. It's cool today."

"It's supposed to get to thirty-three by lunchtime."

"I know how to dress myself, Kate."

Kate raised an eyebrow.

Tilly was silent for the drive down to the pier. When they pulled up, the ferry was already docking.

"I'll walk down for you tonight," Kate offered. They'd started taking nightly walks around the island and she knew Tilly enjoyed it. Kate glanced down at Tilly's shoes. "I'll make sure I bring your sneakers. Might break an ankle in those…"

Tilly was quiet as she fiddled in her handbag.

"Or I could just bring the van…"

Tilly unclipped her seat belt. "You don't have to do either."

Stunned, she blinked. What the hell? "Well, I'd like to…"

"I…" Looking out at the ferry, Tilly drew a deep breath. "I have to go."

"All right," Kate said softly. "I'll see you tonight? Call me and let me know if you're on an earlier ferry and I'll come down earlier."

"Yep."

Kate watched as she walked the pier. The long skirt of Tilly's dress danced in the warm wind as she wrapped her cardigan around herself and let the deckhand help her onto the boat. She went straight into the cabin without turning to wave goodbye. Kate sat back in her seat. What the hell was her problem? Kate had never seen her in a mood like that. Had Sister Ruth confided in Tilly that Kate had come out to her? Did Tilly have a problem with the fact that Kate had demanded to be seen? Or had Kate said something, *done* something that had made Tilly uncomfortable? Oh, God, what if Tilly could see that she was secretly infatuated? *Am I that transparent?*

By dinnertime, Tilly hadn't called. It was the longest day Tilly had spent with Declan since she'd been at St. Joan's. Usually, when she left so early, she was back well before dinner. Kate ate alone, confident that she would be on the last ferry. Of course she would—half the parish from St. Gerard's was coming to the island for a special mass in the morning, and Kate knew how important it was to Tilly that she be there.

Kate left the cottage at nine forty-five. With Tilly's sneakers tied together at the laces and slung over her shoulder, she began the downhill walk. Without Lockie at her heels, or Tilly at her side, the walk was strange. As she reached the pier, she inhaled deeply. One day soon, she was going to miss the scent of the sea.

In the night sky, the moon sat high above the end of the pier. Kate wandered down to the end and sat against the corner pylon, let her feet swing off the edge. The ferry was close, its lights bright in the darkness.

Kate waited. And waited.

Confusion gripped her.

As the car ferry continued on, the answer became starkly apparent—the boat wasn't turning into Lords. Jealousy burned like ice as she watched the ferry cross Port Phillip Bay, headed straight for East Island. Well, she thought bitterly, that's that.

She turned, eyes flaming in the wind as she marched back up the hill. Tilly had chosen to spend the night with *him*. Was her impulse to avoid Kate so strong that she had decided to break her moral code? To miss tomorrow's special mass? Kate was beginning to think that it had less to do with Tilly knowing she had come out to Sister Ruth and more to do with the fact that Tilly was perfectly aware how Kate felt about her. Of course Tilly knew. After their moment in the kitchen on Monday night, how could she not? Maybe Tilly had known for even longer. Something had shifted between them in the backyard of the St. Kilda terrace the moment Tilly had demanded that she didn't want to talk about their romantic past.

Then there was the consideration that turned her stomach. What if Tilly's failure to return had nothing to do with Kate? What if Tilly really *was* attracted to him? What if she'd been so consumed by lust that she'd simply forgotten that Kate would be waiting alone at the pier in the dark? It wasn't a reach. Perhaps she'd been so tempted that she'd just…stayed.

As for those tiny, fleeting glimmers of hope that hinted at the chance Kate's feelings could possibly be reciprocated…well, maybe it was all in her head.

 The persistent rapping on the front door of the cottage pulled Kate from a deep sleep. She groaned in frustration as she checked the time on her phone. 7:47.

Kate threw back the covers angrily and kicked her heels against the mattress. For fuck's sake, it was Sunday. All she wanted was just a few hours of peace. Just a few fucking hours alone. Was that so much to ask?

"Kate?" Sister Ruth called loudly. "Kate, are you awake?"

The pounding increased. She slipped her glasses on. *God, I'm coming, I'm coming. Christ Almighty…*

As she opened the door, she squinted against the sunlight. She dropped her gaze, tried to focus on the baby-blue blur of the Reverend Mother's habit fluttering in the early morning breeze. "Sorry, Reverend Mother, I had a really bad night and—"

"Sweetheart, the vicar called. Tilly's in hospital."

Kate grasped the doorframe. "What?"

"Appendicitis last night. She was taken into surgery early this morning."

Kate's stomach dropped.

"She's out now and she's fine. Kate?"

Her eyes snapped to the clock across the living room. Ten minutes to eight. Adrenaline coursing through her veins, she pushed off the doorframe and stepped backward, grasping at the back of a kitchen chair. "Can you call through to Mornington Pier and let them know I want on the eight o'clock from East Island?"

Sister Ruth followed her into the cottage. "I can come with you."

"No," Kate said, rushing into her bedroom and stripping off her sleeping shorts. She yanked a pair of jeans from the end of her bed.

There was no way she was taking Sister Ruth along with her. "You have Father Rodney coming at nine to say mass," she called out to the kitchen. "Honestly, there's no sense in both of us going. I'll go alone. Please, Sister, can you just call through to the pier?"

Ward C, Unit 2, Bed 16. That was the information Declan had relayed to the Reverend Mother. Kate repeated it like a chant as she jogged the stairs to Tilly's ward—she didn't have the time for hospital elevators.

Like a sleuth, she slipped past the empty nurses' station. Visiting hours weren't for another hour and Kate wasn't sure how strict the hospital was when it came to making exceptions.

It was unexpected—the surge of emotion that took hold of her the moment she laid eyes on Tilly.

Sitting up in bed, eyes closed, Tilly looked as pale as her hospital gown. Her messy plait lay limp across her shadowed shoulder, dark against her gown. *God, she looks like death warmed up...*

Kate cast her gaze around the room. Two beds were empty, but directly across from Tilly, a younger woman was asleep, her curtain half drawn to bar the brightness of the morning sun.

Treading lightly, Kate moved to Tilly. An IV was in her left arm, the skin around the cannula bruised. She winced. Tentatively, she touched Tilly's knee through the cotton blanket, and in an instant, as though she had only been resting, Tilly's eyes opened. As she focused on Kate, her eyes began to swim.

"Hi," Kate whispered, her throat tightening as she sank into the padded vinyl chair at Tilly's bedside.

Her gaze raw, Tilly exhaled deeply. "Hi." Her brow furrowed. "You're wearing my T-shirt."

Kate swallowed. "Yeah. Sorry. I just grabbed whatever out of the washing basket."

Tilly chewed at her bottom lip. "You're going to stretch it."

Kate reached for her hand and linked their fingers together. "How are you feeling?"

"Stiff. And filthy."

"Well, you look gorgeous."

Above the blanket, Tilly smoothed a hand over her abdomen. "Don't make me laugh."

Kate's chest ached as their eyes locked. Regardless of the other patient asleep across the room, sitting at Tilly's hospital bedside felt like the most intimate thing in the world. Kate rubbed her sweaty palm on her knees. "Where's Declan?"

"He has a service this morning."

Mass? He'd left his fiancée to wake up alone after emergency surgery because he had *to say mass*? She burned to comment, but the last thing she wanted was for Tilly to feel even more alone. "Tell me what happened, Til."

Tilly released her hand. "I felt ill all day yesterday, since waking." *And here I was, obsessing over the fact that she was avoiding me...*

"I thought it was just cramping," Tilly continued. "I've never had menstrual cramps like that but I honestly just thought that was what it was. And it just became progressively worse, and quickly. I was in agony, couldn't concentrate on a word the children were saying, or Declan. And I just passed out at the dining table. Declan called an ambulance."

Outside Tilly's room, the hospital was coming alive. A laugh rang out from the nurses' station at the end of the corridor and the clatter of breakfast trays was close. But in Tilly's room there was only soft silence. "Did Declan come after the ambulance?" Kate asked. "To be with you?"

"No." Tilly paused. "It's difficult. With the children..."

"Right..."

"The nurse said he came by just after I came out of surgery at six," Tilly excused. "But I was in recovery for so long and he had to leave because he had the children with him and it wasn't visiting hours."

"He should have called us last night."

"I told him not to."

"He shouldn't have listened to you. I would have come, Til. I could have been here."

Tilly turned her cheek into her pillow. Her eyes slipped shut. "I was so scared, Kate. I was in so much pain I honestly thought God was going to take me to be with Him. To be with my parents..."

At the fear in Tilly's eyes, Kate's heart broke. Tilly didn't have a mother, or a father. She was an only child, and she'd lost her aunt, her only relative here in Australia. She didn't have anybody, and now, the person she was preparing to devote the rest of her life to had just watched on as an ambulance drove her away.

Kate moved from the chair, her breath catching. "Come here…" Gently, she slid her palms beneath Tilly's underarms and gathered her into her arms. Tilly's ribs butterflied against her fingers as she sighed shakily, her breath warm against Kate's jaw. Her chest tugged at the sound. Burying her face in Tilly's neck, she inhaled the lingering scent of apricot shampoo. The tips of Tilly's fingers pressed tightly to Kate's shoulders, and relief grasped her, sudden and sharp. "I love you," she breathed against Tilly's neck.

A beat. "I love you too."

Kate's eyes slipped closed. If only Tilly meant it the way she did.

When she felt Tilly relax, Kate pulled back. She forced a smile. "How long are you going to be here?"

"I can go home today."

"Really?"

"It was laparoscopic surgery. I just have to wait for my surgeon to come around and see me. The nurse said they'll probably discharge me after that. They want to keep an eye on my blood pressure, though, for a while longer." Her eyes searched Kate's. "Can you take me home?"

"Yes. Of course. I have the nun mobile parked just down the street."

Tilly rolled her eyes. She hesitated. "I need to ask something else of you too."

"Anything."

"My friend is visiting."

"Oh." A friend? Was it somebody from the city? That principal from St. Matthew's who had been like an older sister to her for years? "Well, we have time until they get here," she suggested. "Visiting hours haven't started yet. I sort of snuck in."

Tilly's brow furrowed. "No. I have…" She paused, a light blush creeping above the neckline of her gown. "I need you to go down to the chemist for me. The nurses have only given me…" She gestured weakly to a packet of large sanitary napkins on the bedside table.

Kate's gaze settled on the bedside table. For God's sake, were those maternity pads? "You have your period?" she clarified.

Tears welled in Tilly's eyes and she squeezed them shut, wet beads rolling down her cheeks. "I can't ask Declan. I need you to get me something smaller than *those*."

Kate tensed at Tilly's overreaction. Obviously, the anaesthetic hadn't completely worn off, and combined with the shock of emergency surgery, Tilly's mind and body were still struggling to make sense of the past twelve hours.

"Hey, don't cry, don't cry..." She leaned closer to rub at Tilly's calf through the cotton blanket. "It's done. It's all over."

Tilly swiped angrily at the wetness on her jawline, and Kate reached for a tissue on the bedside table. "Thank you," Tilly sobbed.

When the tears stopped and Tilly relaxed, her eyes slipping closed every few seconds, Kate stepped out. Downstairs in the chemist by reception, Kate filled a basket with anything else Tilly could possibly need. A toothbrush, toothpaste, mouthwash, lip balm, deodorant, a cheap, plastic comb. After leaving Tilly's antibiotics script with the pharmacist, she stepped outside to the coffee cart and ordered a cappuccino and muffin for herself.

Coffee in hand, she returned to Ward C to find that, not only had Tilly's IV been removed, but in the short time she'd been downstairs, her surgeon had been and gone. Tilly was sitting upright in bed, chatting away as the nurse wheeled her table across her lap and set her breakfast tray in front of her.

Kate placed the plastic bag on the chair beside Tilly's bed and smiled as the nurse disappeared back into the corridor.

Tilly raised an eyebrow at the fullness of the pharmacy bag. "Did you buy the entire chemist out?"

While Kate pinched muffin crumbs from a paper bag and Tilly sipped orange juice from a popper, Tilly relayed what the surgeon had said. All a success. Because Tilly's appendix hadn't ruptured, the surgeon expected a smooth recovery over the next few weeks. They were quiet as they spoke, mindful of the other patient who slept through breakfast, and miraculously, as the duty nurse checked her vitals.

As the morning passed and the effects of the general anaesthesia wore off, Tilly started to perk up, picking more enthusiastically at her breakfast. By eleven a.m., Kate was helping Tilly slip out of bed, to find her feet while they waited for the nurse to check her wounds before a shower. When Tilly laid eyes on the tiny, bright bloodstains on the front of her gown, her lips twisted in confusion. She looked up at Kate. "But I'm not in pain," she said, her green eyes searching Kate's for an explanation.

Kate chuckled. "I think the Endone may have something to do with that…"

When the nurse returned and decided Tilly's incisions needed redressing before a shower, Kate slipped outside the curtain to give Tilly privacy. It was fine to stay, Tilly insisted, but Kate shook her head. By the door, she listened to their murmurs, to the nurse's instructions for aftercare—the stitches in the smaller incisions would dissolve, but when the site healed, Tilly would need to see her GP to remove the stitches below her belly button.

After a few minutes, the nurse pulled the curtain back and disposed of the waterproof dressing packaging in the medical bins by the door. Kate smiled softly at Tilly. *You okay?* Tilly nodded. Scrubbing her hands at the sink across the room, the nurse looked over her shoulder at Kate. "I have to see a man about a horse. You can help her into the shower?"

Kate nodded. "Sure."

"Just be mindful of the back of her gown," she warned. "She's so slender that it swims on her, so you'll need to hold it together." She said it as though Tilly wasn't in the room. They both watched as the nurse yanked a paper towel from the dispenser and wiped her wet hands.

Tilly was steadier on her feet than Kate expected. At the sink, Tilly peered into the pharmacy bag. "Have everything you need?" Kate double-checked.

She nodded.

"You okay from here?"

Tilly looked up into the mirror. Staring back at Tilly's hesitant expression, Kate tilted her head in question.

"Can you untie my gown?" Tilly asked.

Kate worked on the double knot at the back of her neck. As she slipped Tilly's plait aside to see what she was doing, a blush crept up Tilly's neck. "It's only me, Til," she whispered. "You don't have to be embarrassed."

"I know." The bathroom fell silent. "It's just that I'm used to doing everything for myself…"

Kate licked her lips. "Well, you don't have to, okay?"

Tilly sighed as she dropped her gaze to the floor. "Okay."

Kate reached down to the sink and peeled Tilly's fingers from the edge. Gently, she lifted Tilly's hand to the tie at the base of her neck. In the reflection above the sink, their gazes locked. "I've loosened it. All you have to do is pull that one, okay?"

"Thank you."

The urge to drop a kiss to Tilly's shoulder was strong. "Do you want me to undo your plait?"

Tilly shook her head. "No. I'm okay."

"Okay. I'll be just outside if you need me."

Wired with hostility, she fixed the covers on Tilly's bed. Was the vicar so jealous of Kate that he'd rather leave Tilly terrified and alone? Or did he just not understand what Tilly needed? No. He was too intelligent to be unaware. He'd chosen what worked for *him*. There were a million ways he could have reached St. Joan's, but no, Tilly had to go into surgery panicked and alone because he couldn't stand the thought of Kate being the one upon whom Tilly relied. Pathetic. Kate detested him with every fibre of her being.

As she packed up Tilly's breakfast tray and returned it to the trolley in the corridor, she tried to calm herself. She could stew over it later, when they were home, when Tilly was asleep and Kate was alone. Now wasn't the time. It would just put her in a bad mood and Tilly would pick up on it. She always picked up on it.

Behind the heavy bathroom door, the low wheeze of the hairdryer ceased. Kate watched as the patient across the room shifted in her sleep.

Dressed in what she was wearing when she left the morning before on the ferry, Tilly stopped in the doorway, her dark hair wild. She sighed. "Can you plait my hair?" she asked, her face devoid of any embarrassment. "My arms feel a bit weak from drying my hair and I'm all too aware that I look like I've grabbed an electric fence with both hands."

Smirking, Kate patted the bed. "You should have let me dry your hair."

"It's okay," Tilly said, slowly shifting up onto the mattress. "I sat on the toilet to do it but I just feel…"

Kate took the plastic comb from Tilly's hands and moved around the bed, climbed up behind Tilly. She folded Tilly's collar down, found Tilly's neck bright pink from the heat of the hairdryer.

Taking a quiet breath, she gathered Tilly's lightly damp hair, let her fingers slide against her scalp as she sectioned the strands. Her thumb brushed the shell of Tilly's ear, and immediately, Tilly tensed.

"Sorry," Kate murmured, her pulse skipping a beat.

"That's okay," Tilly whispered.

The effect the tender contact had on Kate, how it set her blood alight, was inappropriate. Tilly needed her. She trusted Kate, implicitly. Still, as Tilly leaned back into her, barely a space between them for Kate to focus on Tilly's hair, she couldn't help the rush of protectiveness that overcame her. Squashing a pang of pride, she focused on the plait, the symmetry…

At the movement in the doorway, Kate looked up.

Arms laden with a mixed arrangement of pink carnations, Declan stood, watching. "Oh," he said. "Kate. You're here."

Kate's tongue grew leaden. For all the things she had thought to say to him while Tilly was in the shower, every cutting word she had ready and waiting, the intimidating sight of him struck her mute. Immediately, she slipped off the bed. She tied off the plait quickly. "Hi," she managed politely, hating herself for it.

He crossed the room and laid the bouquet at the end of Tilly's bed. Kate released the plait, her stomach bottoming out as, from the other side of the bed, she watched his large hand smooth between Tilly's shoulder blades. He pressed a kiss to Tilly's cheek, his touch so gentle that Kate had to look away. "Are you going home already?" he said softly.

"The nurse is working on my discharge papers."

He nodded. "And how are you feeling?"

"I just showered," Tilly deflected.

Chuckling he fell into the chair at Tilly's bedside. Turning to return the cheap plastic comb to the pharmacy bag, Kate rolled her eyes. *Hope I kept the seat warm for you, Vicar.*

Unease crawled beneath Kate's skin as he took Tilly's hand in his. "Are you in pain?" As she folded Tilly's still-warm gown, Kate could feel his eyes on her. Kate watched as Tilly shook her head.

"How is Lily?" Tilly asked. "I hope I didn't frighten her."

"She was very upset."

Kate's jaw set hard. *Don't bloody tell her that.*

"Tell her that I'm completely fine," Tilly said.

Yeah, Kate thought sarcastically, completely fine. Carefully, she folded the gown so the bloodstains weren't visible.

"Lily would like to see you," he said. "I promised I would bring her with me this afternoon to visit you. But now, I see that's unlikely…"

Tilly smiled apologetically.

"*Or*," he suggested, "if you think the discharge papers could still take a while, I could go back for the children. We could help you across on the ferry, back home…" Briefly, his gaze flickered to Kate. "I'd like to help, Tilly. I shouldn't have left you earlier and I'd like to make up for it, make sure you're comfortable. Please let me."

At the clear lilt of manipulation in his tone, Kate's eyes snapped up. She could feel the guilt radiating off Tilly, her incessant need to please. "Sounds like a bit too much excitement, Vicar," Kate said bluntly. "She's exhausted. I'm taking her home."

"I think what Tilly wants is up to Tilly, Kate."

Jaw tensing, Kate gathered the bag of toiletries. "Yeah, and she decided that's what she wants about three hours ago." Looking up, she fixed her gaze on him. "Back when you were across town giving mass."

Tilly released a weak, nervous laugh. "Declan, I appreciate the offer. Really. But Kate's already here. It would be silly for you to go to all that trouble."

He nodded. "If you insist." He turned his gaze to Kate. "She can't teach. Don't expect her to be up and about in a few days."

Kate stiffened. This guy, who couldn't put Tilly's needs before his own was telling *Kate* what Tilly could and couldn't do? As she looked down at Tilly's small hand covered by his, irritation consumed her. "Of course she can't teach," she said. "She isn't coming home to work—she's coming home to heal."

"I'm starting to feel it now," Tilly said, wrapping both arms around her middle. "It feels tight. Crampy."

From the bench at the stern of the ferry, Kate looked out at the cliffs of Mornington. Beside her, Tilly shivered slightly. Wrapping an arm around her, Kate encouraged Tilly's head onto her shoulder. Tilly sighed.

"The rocking probably isn't helping," Kate said, revelling in the warmth of Tilly's body pressed tight against her side. "It's rough out today." She could sympathise. Running on such little sleep, the choppy sea was twisting her own stomach into knots.

"I just want to be home with you already," Tilly said softly. "That's all."

A rush of possessiveness set a heat low in her belly, made her feel like she was on fire.

"Did you worry?" Tilly asked. "When I didn't come home last night on the ferry?"

Kate swallowed. Worry? She'd worried—that Tilly was avoiding her, that suddenly Tilly found herself so consumed by her attraction to *him* that she'd forgotten all about Kate. She'd been so wired with jealousy that she'd barely slept a wink. Her greatest concern though, had been that she was quickly losing herself to something more powerful than her self-control, something that was ready and strong enough to destroy her, destroy the relationship she had with Tilly. That worry had yet to settle.

"Yeah," she sighed, tightening her arm around Tilly's waist. "I worried."

CHAPTER TWELVE

"You'll tell me if I hurt you?"

Tilly looked down her lashes at Kate. Pulling the band of her pyjama shorts lower and baring more skin to welcome Kate's touch, she nodded. The plastic lid of the toilet seat crackled beneath Kate's weight as she shifted, gaze focused on the black thread Tilly had asked her to remove from the flat plane of her abdomen.

Two weeks had passed since the surgery. At Tilly's checkup, her GP had suggested leaving the sutures in a little longer—in a few days, she could remove them herself after a shower. It wouldn't be difficult, he'd said. Palms sweating, Kate pulled her gaze from the plum-coloured scar and met Tilly's stare. "You promise to say something?" she asked.

Tilly rolled her eyes, inching closer between Kate's splayed knees. "*Yes.*"

In her tight sleeping singlet, a sweat broke out between her breasts. "You know, on second thought, maybe we should do this in the morning light…"

"Kate, just do it."

Kate swiped her glasses off and placed them on the counter.

"You were there," Tilly said. "The doctor said it would be simple. I won't even feel it."

I wouldn't count on that. Kate bit the tip of her tongue and reached out to the inch-long line that descended from Tilly's belly button. At the brush of Kate's fingers against her skin, Tilly's belly contracted.

Kate's eyes snapped upward. "Sorry," Tilly said shakily. "I was expecting your hands to be cold."

"Sorry."

"You're sorry that your hands are warm?"

Kate swiped the tiny scissors from the top of the vanity. "Can we not tease each other while I have a sharp object so close to your skin?"

"Later then," Tilly played.

Against the back of her hand, Tilly's skin was hot from her bath. Kate slipped the blade of the scissors under the lower stitch and sliced through the thread on one side of the incision.

"Didn't feel it," Tilly assured her.

"This isn't the part I'm worried about," she mumbled, slicing another stitch open. "Are you sure you don't want to tweeze them out yourself?"

Tilly settled a warm hand on her shoulder. "I just need you to do it. Please."

Drawing a deep breath, Kate took the tweezers from Tilly's hand and, careful as ever, pinched the thread and pulled.

Tilly's nails dug crescents into the bare skin of Kate's skin. "Keep going," she encouraged when Kate stilled. "It's just the pull that hurts."

"Almost done," Kate whispered, her hand unconsciously reaching out to grip the curve of Tilly's hip in her concentration.

When she was finished, she encouraged Tilly to stay where she was—practically straddling Kate's knees—while she dusted antiseptic powder over the scar.

As Kate washed her hands in the sink, their gazes met in the reflection. Tilly smiled warmly and Kate thought back over the past two weeks. Since that first night, time had passed slowly. The students had been understanding, following Kate's strict instruction not to bombard an exhausted Tilly with visits to the cottage. In turn, Kate had taken on a heavier workload, accepting any and all essays Tilly had set prior to falling ill. Quickly realising double the work meant one a.m. bedtimes for Kate, for the first time in her life, she didn't feel so very fortunate to have such conscientious students. Now, with Tilly returning to work tomorrow, Kate was glad it was drawing to an end, and that for the most part, Tilly had returned to her energetic self.

Kate reached for the hand towel. "All over now," she said. "All healed."

It was on Tilly's first day back at work, a Friday, that it happened.

After lunch, Tilly returned to the cottage to rest. That morning, there had been a brief mention of the possibility of Declan visiting in the afternoon, this time without the children. His last visit, just days after Tilly's surgery, had been exhausting for Tilly. When Kate had returned from driving Declan and his children down to Lords Pier, she'd found Tilly in a deep sleep on the lounge.

So when Kate opened the cottage door at the end of the day, she expected to find Declan with Tilly. What she found instead, was entirely unexpected.

On her way from the bathroom to her bedroom, Tilly halted before the lounge, the long, ivory skirts of the wedding dress gripped in her hands as their eyes locked.

The room grew hot. Everything narrowed.

"It was Mum's," Tilly explained, her eyes growing bright with tears as she unclipped the veil. "Aunt Hattie kept it for me. The Reverend Mother gave it to me last night…"

Skin heating, Kate scratched at the back of her neck. "That's, uh…that's nice."

With her gaze fixed on Kate, Tilly chewed on her bottom lip. "Do you like it?"

Kate's heart ached. Did she like it? Of course she liked it. She liked it too much.

Until that very moment, the idea of Tilly as a bride hadn't made sense to her. It was too difficult to fathom. An alien idea. But with Tilly standing in the middle of their quaint, quiet living room, the cottage still and safe and *theirs*, nothing had ever seemed so sensible.

Tilly was waiting for an answer. "Yeah," Kate said. "I think… you look lovely, Til."

Seconds passed, and Tilly's gaze remained trained on Kate. Quickly, her expression blanked. "I'm going to change," she said suddenly, and in a flash of white, she was gone, her bedroom door closing behind her.

"So Declan was a no-show today?" Kate asked later that night as she slid onto the lounge beside Tilly and handed her a bowl of pasta.

"I'm going over next Tuesday for dinner," Tilly excused. "But I think I'll take this last weekend to be sure I'm one hundred per cent. Lily likes to be picked up and I don't think I have the strength yet. I don't want her to think I'm still unwell."

Kate fought the impulse to roll her eyes. "Well, you are unwell— you're not wonder woman. You *are* going to mass with the sisters on Sunday morning though, right?"

As she twirled her fork through spaghetti, Tilly shook her head.

"What? I thought you were looking forward to going to mass at St. Gerard's?"

Eyes trained on the TV, Tilly shrugged. "I think I'll stay here and join the sisters when Father Rodney comes to say mass tomorrow morning at St. Joan's."

"But what about Sunday mass?"

"Father Rodney says that it's fine to attend a Saturday service if you can't make it to the Sunday service."

"Right…" Kate blinked. Tilly missing Sunday mass? *Well that's new…* "I don't think I'll go over to the mainland either," she said casually.

"No?"

"My sister has a prenatal class on Sunday and Mum's going with her so they can't do lunch."

Tilly's gaze settled on her. "You're telling me that *you* don't want a break from Lords?"

Blushing, Kate brought her legs up beneath her on the lounge. "I mean, we have *The Glass Menagerie* in the city next Wednesday night—that'll be here before we know it." *And you'll be gone before we know it.* Their together time was limited and Kate wasn't prepared to give up having Tilly all to herself for an entire weekend just for a change of scenery.

And so that was what she chose—a weekend of sleep-ins and lunches in the convent, two blissful days spent marking essays and swimming with Tilly, Sister Ellie, and Sister Ruth in the cove. Saturday evening, when the sun swept low and the moon crept through the clouds, they went walking around the island, just the two of them.

Before Kate knew it, it was Sunday night and she found herself back inside the boarding house, checking her students in.

She arrived home to find Tilly leaning against the kitchen counter, the ancient telephone cord wrapped around her finger as she spoke to Declan. As Kate moved around Tilly to boil the kettle, his muffled voice on the other end of the line was like a pin to their bubble. Suddenly, with startling certainty, she realised that she would do anything to ensure she had a place in Tilly's world until it was time to move on.

But that *time* was still some time away.

So when Tilly pressed her hand to the receiver, and with hope in her eyes invited Kate to dinner with them on Tuesday night, she no longer had the good sense to say no.

Attempting to find her balance as she climbed up to stand on her swivelling, creaking office chair, Kate pulled at the cover of the air conditioner. Of all afternoons, when she had a parent-teacher interview in fifteen minutes, the system had to conk out. What a week, she thought. *And it's only Monday…*

She pulled roughly at the vent. *Come on, come on. Why aren't you working, you son of a…* Suddenly a cloud of dust wheezed powerfully from the vent, spraying the collar of her stark white shirt grey before the system shut itself off again with a dying groan. Spluttering, she swatted the dirt from her chin, her neck.

Plan B was suddenly looking good.

She charged two flights up to the common room and pushed open the double bay windows behind the lounge, sighing deeply as the cooling afternoon breeze swept in. She'd have to take the meeting up there. There was no way she could invite Mia's parents into her sauna of an office.

She looked down at her shirt. *Ah, hell.* She ventured out into the corridor and glanced at the grandfather clock. If she was quick, she had time to make it to the cottage and back again before the island shuttle pulled up with Mia's parents—

A flash of white at the end of the hall caught Kate's eye. Her gaze snapped to the end of the south wing. She paused… Had she imagined that? Were her eyes tricking her? *Please God, do not let it be another rat infestation—*

Her eyes widened as a tiny white rabbit scurried from the end room, nails raking across the floorboards as its fur brushed against the base of the trophy cabinet, against the skirting board. "You have got to be fucking kidding me…" Kate inhaled sharply as the rabbit disappeared into the room opposite.

Just as Kate began her march to the end room, Brianna Lasko stepped out of the room, and at the sight of her music teacher, stiffened. "Oh, shit…"

Kate's jaw set hard. "Why is there a rabbit in the boarding house?"

Eyes growing wide in fear, her Year Eight student turned quickly, her dark hair flying about her shoulders as she quickly headed in the other direction.

"Brianna! Stop right there!"

Brianna pivoted. "I swear to God, I didn't do it!"

"Well, you can go and tell *whoever did do it* that I want it gone within the next twenty minutes or there will be serious consequences."

"We *can't.* The Year Nine girls kept him because they think he's Lockie reincarnated."

Her mind reeled. "Reincarnated?"

"They found him sitting on Lockie's grave, sleeping there…"

Hail Mary Full of Grace, now I've heard everything. At her wit's end, Kate bit back a groan of frustration. She raked a hand through her hair and glared down at Brianna. "Why on earth are you in the boarding house before the last bell? Where are you supposed to be?"

"With Tilly in Religion."

"So why aren't you across the road?"

"We were helping put the Christmas tree up in the convent with Sister Mary Monica and I asked to go to the bathroom…"

Kate thought back to the day before, to the unusually high number of requests that had been made to visit the bathroom in each and every class—and all by boarders. It wasn't difficult to deduce what was going on. These girls were clever. Like shift workers, they'd arranged a very effective babysitting schedule.

"Get that rabbit in a cage," she growled. "I have a meeting now but I will deal with this as soon as it's over. You're to be in my office with whoever started this at five p.m. Understood?"

"But it wasn't me!"

"Bad luck, Donald Duck!"

She jogged down the path to the cottage, past the garden, a sweat breaking out across her lower back. *Reincarnated?* Kate shook her head as she pushed the front door open. For God's sake. *So much for Christian bloody ideals. Are we Buddhists now?* No wonder the lettuce beds had been budding so perfectly for the past week. What point did a goddamn rabbit find in hunting for his own dinner when he had a luxury five-star catering service and a penthouse suite inside St. Joan's? She threw a glance at the convent. If she had time to go inside and speak to Tilly about the situation before her meeting, she would. But it would have to wait until later.

The cottage was even stuffier than the school. Kate stripped off her shirt and swiped at the sweat between her breasts with the discarded shirt. Rounding the kitchen table, she headed for her bedroom. The moment Tilly got wind of the reincarnation thing, she'd probably side with the girls, encouraging their spirituality, empathising with the fact that they'd lost Lockie. *I just can't win, just can't catch a fucking break...*

Kate stumbled in the doorway of her bedroom, the sight that greeted her stealing the breath from her lungs.

Tilly stood before Kate's oak bureau, black leather straps loose in her grasp.

Kate's arms fell limp at her sides as their eyes met. Fisted in her hand, the dirty shirt fluttered to the carpet. Her gaze snapped from Tilly to her open underwear drawer, and back again to what Tilly held in her hands. Her stomach flipped. Her pulse slowed. "You have a bit of a habit of going through my drawers..." she said, her voice deep, the words pulled from the back of her throat.

Briefly, Tilly's eyes dropped to Kate's semi-naked chest before her gaze darted away.

The school bell rang, once, twice, a third time. With each rhythmic chime, understanding settled, tense and hot.

Silence.

Embarrassment lit a blaze across her skin at the sight of Tilly, scarlet-cheeked and *knowing*.

Carefully, Tilly returned the harness to Kate's drawer. With her bottom lip tight between her teeth, she fiddled about in the drawer, shifting pyjama shorts and T-shirts to cover what she had exposed.

Swallowing over the lump in her throat, Kate stepped forward. "It's okay, Til, just leave it—"

"I'm so sorry," Tilly whispered her eyes refusing to meet Kate's as she pushed the heavy drawer closed with both hands. "I just wanted to put your washing away."

Kate exhaled harshly. Tilly wasn't a snoop, she knew that. It simply wouldn't have crossed Tilly's mind that there was any reason not to open Kate's drawers. "It's fine. Really."

She opened the closet doors and pulled an ironed shirt from the hanger. With her back to Tilly, she shrugged it on quickly. "I, uhh, I thought you were putting the tree up in the convent."

"I was, before, but then it looked like rain and Sister Mary Monica was supervising the girls so I went to get the washing in." Tilly's voice was raspy. "I'm truly sorry, Kate."

Kate's heartbeat pounded as she poked buttons through the holes, watching in the mirror as Tilly grabbed the half-empty washing basket from her bed. Kate cleared her throat. "I have a meeting with Mia's parents," she said. "They're probably already here, so…"

She crossed the room and reached for the gold watch she'd forgotten on her bedside table that morning. Her hands trembled as she fumbled with the bands. She pressed her wrist against her abdomen for leverage.

Tilly lowered the basket to the mattress and stepped around the bed. She reached for Kate's wrist. "Let me…"

Head-spinning, she let Tilly fold the clasp into place. As she carried her gaze over Tilly's features—the slightest protrusion of her chin, her fine nose, porcelain skin—a sudden urge to kiss Tilly overcame her. It was strange, the marriage of anxiety and arousal, the need to run, the equal, all-consuming need to press Tilly back on the bed and discover every inch of her skin in ways Tilly had probably never imagined. With Tilly's fingers curled around her wrist, her thumb pressing the clasp to lock, Kate's fist tensed, contracted like a Venus flytrap.

Tilly looked up.

As though sensing that Kate was on the verge of saying something she didn't want to hear, she suddenly turned. She swiped the washing basket from the bed and held it against her belly like a shield. She wet her lips. "You looked angry," she said, hesitant. "When you came inside…"

Kate released a hollow laugh.

Tilly's eyes widened slightly. "What is it?"

"You remember when we were kids and Mackenzie Henley caught that baby possum? Decided it was our school mascot until Sister Hattie found out about it and made her set it free?"

Tilly nodded. "Vaguely."

"Well, welcome back to two thousand and four. Contrary to the Chinese Zodiac, it appears to be the year of the rabbit."

CHAPTER THIRTEEN

"Kate, do you know that Tilly has mermaid hair?"

Looking up from her steak, Kate locked eyes with Lily across the table. Briefly, her gaze flickered to Tilly, sitting beside the little girl. Her hair was freed tonight, curled slightly with its natural wave. Kate smiled. "I do."

"Lily," Declan said, a playful lilt to his voice as he tapped lightly at his daughter's hand, "Stop touching Tilly's hair and eat your peas."

Lily sighed. "Okay," she said. "It's just shiny, that's all…"

"I know it's shiny," Declan said, winking at Tilly from the head of the table, "but I'd like you to eat your dinner. Look how much your brother has already eaten. See what happens when you don't talk so much?"

Kate glanced beside her. Seated between his father and Kate, Mason looked like he was enjoying the dinner just as much as Kate.

With a sigh, Lily picked up her fork. "Good girl," Declan said, but before he could return his eyes to his own meal, Lily's fork found the placemat again.

"Kate," she started again, shifting in her booster seat, "did you hear that I'm going to be in the Christmas play? At mass?"

"You are?" Kate asked, reaching for the gravy boat. "And what role are you playing?"

"An angel," Lily said. "I even have a...what's it called, Dad?"

"A halo," Declan said.

"Yeah," Lily said, drawing an imaginary circle around the crown of her head, "a halo."

"That's beautiful, Lily," Tilly said, rubbing at the little girl's forearm. "You'll make a lovely angel."

"Your costume is a tad too large, isn't it?" Declan asked Lily.

Lily nodded. "I tripped."

"We'll have to get it mended," he said, "won't we?"

The comment didn't bypass Kate. Subtly, she chanced a glance at Tilly.

"I could fix it," Tilly offered.

"Really?" Declan asked.

"Of course," Tilly said.

"You don't have to do that," he said. "I shouldn't have mentioned it."

"It's no trouble," Tilly said. "The sisters have a sewing machine. After dinner, I'll get Lil to try it on and I'll take it home with me."

"*Or*, we could just give it to the wedding tailor," Declan suggested jokingly. "She's charging enough as it is for Lily's flower girl dress."

Kate's heart lurched at the comment. They had a tailor? Already?

"I'm going to be flower girl," Lily said.

Kate swallowed over a clump of half-cooked potato. "That's exciting."

"My dress is just like Tilly's. We match."

Kate reached for her water glass. "I'm sure you'll both look beautiful."

"Did you have a wedding?" Lily asked.

Kate looked up. Lip worried between her teeth, Tilly's gaze was focused on her dinner plate. "No," Kate said. She set eyes on Tilly. "Have you started thinking about setting a date?"

Slathering his potatoes in butter, Declan smiled. "We're well past *thinking*. We've decided on sometime in March. Date yet to be determined."

Three months. Just three months.

"Will you be coming, Kate?" he asked.

She reached for her glass of water. "To the wedding?" *I'd rather swallow razor blades.* "I'll be in the city by then."

Across the table, Tilly didn't look up.

"Melbourne's hardly a trek," he said. "We're having the ceremony at St. Vincent's, and the reception at Mornington. We've organised a marquee for the cliff top. It's going to be lovely."

Lily grunted as she attempted to slice her steak with a blunt butter knife. Tilly leaned over and cut the gristle away with her steak knife. "Better, baby?" she asked.

Lily looked up at her. "Remember when you fell over at the table? And then you went to hospital?"

Tilly chuckled. "Yes," she said. "I do."

"That was bad," Lily remarked. "It hurt?" she asked.

Tilly nodded. In her peripheral vision, Kate watched as Mason looked up in interest.

"What happened at the hospital?" Lily asked.

"The doctor removed my appendix," Tilly said, leaning back as she tapped at her belly. "But that's okay, I didn't really need it." She grinned at Kate.

"Did the doctor cut you?" Mason asked. "Did you get stitches?"

"Yes," Tilly said. "Just a few stitches."

Lily sat back in her seat, dinner abandoned. "On your belly?" Tilly nodded.

"Did the doctor take them out?" Mason asked.

"No," Tilly said, her eyes meeting Kate's across the table. "Kate did."

As Declan's gaze snapped up from his plate, Kate's face heated.

"Did it hurt?" Mason asked.

Tilly shook her head. "Kate was very, *very* gentle."

Declan's knife and fork chimed against the sides of his plate. "What time will you be heading into the city tomorrow night for your play?" he asked Tilly.

"We're going in earlier," she explained. "Around lunchtime."

"And where will you be staying?" he asked, his eyes flickering briefly to Kate.

Kate reached for the salt. "At the Meriton."

"Why not just take the causeway back to Lords at the end of the night?" he asked. "I understand that you can't get to Lords from Mornington, what with the last ferry leaving at ten, but surely the drive from Melbourne to Portarlington only adds another half hour?"

Kate bristled.

"We had planned on doing just that," Tilly explained, "but a storm is forecast for Wednesday night and the causeway will likely be closed. We don't want to drive two hours to Portarlington and be stuck without accommodation."

"Will you sleep in bunk beds?" Lily asked.

Kate chuckled. "No, sweetheart—"

Abruptly, Declan stood. "I should get the kids into a bath," he said. Easily, he lifted Lily from her booster seat. A couple of peas slipped from the skirt of her dress to the hardwood floor as he shifted her onto his hip. Slowly, Tilly bent to pick them up. "Leave all of this," he said, unconvincingly.

Kate sipped at her water, anticipating the inevitable. "No, no," Tilly insisted. "We'll take care of it." *And there it is…*

Together, they cleared the table. Alone in the kitchen with Tilly, Kate reached for Tilly's plate. She'd left half her potatoes, and while her carrots were gone, half of the meat was still on the bone. Kate's brow furrowed. "You feeling okay tonight?" she asked, pushing Tilly's scraps onto Lily's mountain of unfinished dinner.

"I'm fine," Tilly said.

As Tilly filled the sink, Kate stared at the back of her head. It had been weeks since the surgery and she was slowly getting her appetite back, but tonight, she'd barely touched her meal. "You ate more last night, and the night before that…"

Tilly sighed. "What do you want me to do, Kate? Red meat is heavy and I've never been too fussed on it."

"I know, but—"

"I'm *fine*. You don't have to worry every night that I don't finish my dinner." With the pepper, salt, and sauce containers tucked inside the bend of her elbow, Tilly opened the cabinet above the sink. Then, she tried the one beside it. And the one beside that…

Rinsing sauce from a plate, Kate watched on, satisfaction curling inside her at the realisation that, for as perfectly as Tilly fit into the vicar's home, it wasn't hers—not yet, anyway. Opening the final cabinet beside the fridge and finding it full of plates and bowls, Tilly sighed. She shrugged shyly. "I don't really know where anything goes."

"You'll have to shuffle things around when you move in," she joked to ease Tilly's embarrassment.

Tilly smiled.

"He has a nice home," Kate managed. Gently, she placed his fine china serving dish on the drainboard. "Could do with a dishwasher, though," she said playfully. "*And* a jacaranda."

With a chuckle, Tilly bumped her shoulder. "We can't all afford a terrace in St. Kilda."

"Neither can I." She bent her wrist and pushed her glasses further up her nose. "So was this place ever in your dream?" she asked.

The levity of the question hummed along with the forgotten stove fan. As Tilly stared back at her, the moment pulsed. The invisible string between them pulled.

"No," Tilly said softly. "It wasn't."

Kate watched as Tilly lifted glasses, one by one, into the cupboard. Her deep navy dress, cinched at the waist and flowing to her knees, was far too elegant for washing dishes. Kate's eyes dropped lower, to shapely calves tanned by the very stockings Kate had pulled from the clothesline late that afternoon. A surge of longing arrested her. Christ, Tilly had beautiful legs.

Suddenly, a flash of movement in the doorway caught Kate's eye, and she twisted her neck, her body stiffening as she met Declan's hard stare. She looked away sharply.

"Matilda, would you like to stay the night?" He took the collection of dried plates from the counter beside Tilly and returned them to the cupboard. "The guest room is ready."

"Oh." Tilly's eyes flickered to Kate at the sink, then back to Declan as he hovered behind. "I didn't bring any of my things," she said. "Besides, I couldn't, we're heading away early tomorrow."

"Kate could always stop by in the morning with the students and pick you up."

Bristling, Kate wiped the sink down.

"Really, it's very nice of you to offer Declan..." *But?* "But I still have to pack," Tilly said.

Kate fought against a smirk. So that overnight suitcase full and ready by the cottage door? The extension already unzipped? There was more to go in there?

He sighed in defeat. "Next time then?"

"Next time," Tilly appeased.

Kate chanced a glance across the counter where Tilly stood, smiling that dutiful smile she had always reserved for the sisters.

In the doorway, Lily stopped to say goodnight. "Lily," Declan asked as the little girl showed Tilly and Kate the glow-in-the-dark stars on her pyjama shorts, "would you like to take Tilly upstairs to get your angel costume?"

A charge of anxiety chased up Kate's spine at the prospect of being left alone with Declan after he'd just caught her admiring his fiancée.

Peppering kisses across the top of Lily's head, Tilly passed the tea towel to Declan and led the little girl from the kitchen by the shoulders.

The kitchen fell silent.

"Did you enjoy dinner, Kate?"

Kate soaked the steak knives. "Yes, thank you."

Silence.

"It was important to me that you came to dinner with Tilly tonight," he started, "that I had the chance to get to know you better."

You don't know anything about me.

"Tilly values you very much as a friend," he continued. "You've been very good to her since she arrived at St. Joan's. I think we could even go as far to say that she considers you to be the sister she never had."

Sister. Kate swallowed at the pointed remark. Did this powerful and formidable man think she was a threat? Could he feel his control wavering? "Yeah," Kate said, gathering courage from deep within. "One thing gets me though…"

"What's that?" he muttered, his back to her.

Even if her voice shook, she wasn't going to let it stop her. "If you're aware that we're so close, why didn't you call me?"

At the corner cupboard, he turned to face her. "Excuse me?"

Kate held his stare. "The night she went to hospital…"

"I have a lot on my plate, Kate. You understand that. I was trying to make sure Tilly was taken care of, and the children…"

"You put her in an ambulance and didn't show up at the hospital until hours later when she was in recovery. Fair enough that you have kids and you don't know anyone here yet to call on to babysit in the middle of the night, but Tilly needed somebody with her and you didn't call me. I could have been with her so she wasn't alone."

He sighed condescendingly. "The ferries don't run at night—"

"I would have called a water taxi."

A plate screeched against another as he slid it into the cupboard. "Tilly was fine without you."

Upstairs, Tilly laughed loudly.

Dangerously close to saying too much, Kate reached for the plug. What more could she say? The sink gurgled loudly. That she knew about Vanuatu? That, if he didn't tell Tilly tonight, she would?

She barely had time to consider how best to broach the subject when, suddenly, he was sidling up next to her at the sink. As the hairs stood on the back of her neck, she tried not to tense under the heat of his gaze. "Whatever this emotional affair is that you think you have going with my fiancée," he whispered, "it stops now."

The words set a storm in Kate's heart. Her jaw set hard. How easy it was, she thought, to forget how to breathe.

Lily was loud as she descended the stairs, Tilly's voice soft and agreeable as she followed.

He moved away, out into the hall to the melody of their voices.

Kate placed the sponge by the tap, her heart desperately attempting to find its rhythm as she listened to Lily and Declan disappear down the hall to the lounge room. Moments later, Tilly's heels tapped lightly onto the kitchen tile.

Kate spun. The plastic covering of Lily's costume crinkled in Tilly's arms. Her brow furrowed as she stared at Kate. "Is everything all right?" she asked, hiking the halo up to her elbow.

Kate cleared her throat. "Of course," she lied. "Should we head out soon?"

At the stern of the car ferry, they stood together, looking out into the darkness of Port Phillip Bay as they made the crossing back home. "So," Kate started. "St. Vincent's at Mornington…"

"Yes."

"Not a Catholic Church. Not St. Gerard's? No nuptial mass?"

"If God is our witness," Tilly said, "I don't believe it matters."

Kate believed it had more to do with the fact that Declan was the vicar at St. Vincent's and less to do with Tilly's considerations. For somebody who had wanted to join the sisterhood, Kate knew that marrying in a Catholic church had to be important to Tilly.

"Does he know that you wanted to be a nun?"

Tilly rested her forearms on the railing. "Yes." She fixed her gaze on Kate. "You think that's the allure for him, don't you? That I understand his devotion to God. That I'll understand he is married to both God and myself and I won't dare challenge that."

Kate raised an eyebrow. "Challenge?"

"Resent."

Kate rubbed at her jaw. "No, I don't think that." She paused. "I…"

"Yes?"

"I don't know. I think the allure is that you're a very beautiful, very selfless woman."

Blushing, Tilly rubbed at her arms. She'd left her knit jacket in the car.

"St. Vincent's will be nice," Kate offered, shrugging off her black blazer. "I mean, you don't have to be married in the church for it to be marriage," she said as she helped Tilly into the blazer.

"No," Tilly agreed, smiling her thanks, "But it's important to me to be married in the Lord's house."

The need to know burned hot in Kate's heart like a blue flame. "What did you vote?" she asked pointedly.

Tilly's head whipped around. "Vote?"

"Last year on the marriage equality survey. I want to know what you voted."

Silence eclipsed them. It was a loaded question, one she perhaps didn't have the right to ask.

Tilly's eyes were clear, unveiled as she gazed up at Kate. "I voted 'yes.' Of course I did."

Kate's heart fluttered with relief.

Tilly wrapped her arms around herself. "Church and state are separated, of course. It's just that, I suppose, for me, personally, I would like to be married with God as my witness, in His House." She shook her head, her chin ducking to touch her chest. "You know I can't help it, Kate. It's something I've always held close. It's been ingrained in me since I was little." Tilly stared up at her like she was waiting to be challenged—like she wanted to be challenged.

Kate looked out at the full moon, low tonight. She understood where Tilly was coming from, but it just wasn't something she could embrace. "I think that God is all around us," she said softly. "I think he witnesses everything." She turned back to Tilly. "Don't you think that's a hell of a lot nicer?"

Tilly smiled, acquiescing. "I do. But I also respect the church."

Kate swallowed, hard. "So do I." She shifted to face her, only a breath of space between their bodies. "Churches are beautiful, reverent. But if you look at the bigger picture, I like to think that standing inside four brick walls isn't going to change much. If two people love each other, God's going to bless that—witness that—either way. It shouldn't matter whether you're inside St. Vincent's, St. Gerard's or under a canopy on a beach."

Tilly held her gaze for a moment before she looked out to the lights on Lords, searching. "That's a nice thought," she said. "You've always had nice thoughts. I wish I was more like you."

"Like me?"

"You're brave."

"So are you. There's nothing wrong with being fond of tradition, Til."

"I know." Tilly danced her nails across the chipped black paint of the railing, her gaze focused on the exposed metal. "Sometimes I just feel like the weight of it all is coming down on me. I know where you're coming from Kate, really. Before I went into surgery, I said a prayer, and I felt God's care in a different way. It felt more powerful than being in a church, made the whole concept of tradition seem almost…fruitless." She locked eyes on Kate. "I didn't even say the Hail Mary. I just told God that if it was my time to be with my parents, I was grateful that at least I had found you again." Her voice dropped to a whisper and Kate watched as Tilly's eyes welled. "I just thanked Him for bringing you back to me. And I felt like He heard me."

Kate's mouth grew dry. That Tilly would think of her at a time like that? When she was so scared? In so much pain? Tilly's admission struck her hard. They were so in sync. An emotional affair, the vicar had called it, eyes piercing and jaw set hard. He hadn't been so far off the mark. But it was more than that. It was an unmatched intimacy that they shared, like destiny and fate were each pulling at two ends of a rope, twisting a cord between their hearts without relent.

"I prayed for you every night, Kate."

Their eyes locked. "When you were in hospital?"

"No. When we were children. When you were so stricken over your parents' separation…"

It was a painful thing, resisting the urge to reach out and take Tilly's hand in hers, to feel her fingers wound with her own as they so often used to.

Eyes welling, Tilly turned her face and glanced over the side of the ferry. After a few moments, she turned back to Kate, a weak smile plastered on her face. "I'm so excited to be going to the city tomorrow. I'm excited that we're doing this together, that we get the chance to spend some time together before things change."

Kate licked her lips. "Me too."

"I'm going to miss you when you're gone, when we've both moved on from St. Joan's…"

Would Kate ever move on? She'd been beating herself up for weeks over the fact that seeing Tilly again had unravelled years of hard work she'd put into getting over her. But maybe she'd been lying to herself when she told herself she had moved on from Tilly in the first place.

"I still remember you at seventeen," Tilly whispered. Her fingers reached out and began to toy with the buttons of Kate's vest. "I remember you so clearly. You, at the piano, the two of us, practising…"

As Tilly's knuckles brushed against Kate's abdomen, the touch only slight, Kate's muscles clenched, electrified. She could hardly speak for fear of making confessions Tilly surely wouldn't want to hear. But what was the cost of holding her tongue when in just a few months, she was going to lose Tilly all over again? The thought left her light-headed.

"And I've been thinking," Tilly said softly, "about songs that I might like to have played at the wedding, songs that mean a great deal to me…"

Kate's head swam. "Songs?"

Tilly sucked on her bottom lip. "I was thinking about *Hallelujah*."

Kate's heartbeat grew sluggish, her chest weighted. *No. No, no, no…* She pulled her hand from the railing and clasped Tilly's fingers in hers, stopping their movement. "Don't use that song, Tilly."

Tilly looked up, her green eyes hooded. "Why?" she whispered.

As shadows played across Tilly's face in the moonlight, her long, dark hair fluttering free of its plait, an ache swelled in Kate's throat. Tilly was so beautiful. So, so beautiful. Impulsively, Kate leaned forward, closed the space between them, and pressed her lips to Tilly's.

Gently, Kate nipped at her bottom lip, her heart leaping as their lips met, over and over again. It was chaste, innocent, perhaps the gentlest kiss Kate had ever given. Kinder, even, than those they'd shared as teenagers. The pace was sweet agony, setting an ache deep in Kate's chest as she waited for Tilly to respond. *Please, Tilly, please.* And then it happened. Tilly's lips moved firmly against Kate's. Kate's head swam at the soft, velvety pull of Tilly's mouth against her own. Slowly, Tilly's lips parted. Daring, desperate, Kate's tongue traced her bottom lip.

With a whimper, Tilly pressed a hand to Kate's chest and pulled back. "Kate," she whispered, her voice breaking. "No...we can't."

Releasing her gentle hold on Tilly's hands, she reached up and cradled Tilly's face in her palms. She pressed her forehead against Tilly's, let her eyes slip shut. Tilly's breath came hard against her lips. Heat curled in her gut. Primal, unstoppable attraction.

"I'm sorry," Kate whispered. She rolled her forehead against Tilly's, resisted the urge to kiss her brow, her temple. "You're a pull on my self-control..."

Wide-eyed, Tilly drew back. She shook her head.

"What?" Kate husked, reaching out to link a strand of Tilly's hair behind her ear. "You don't believe me?"

Tilly stepped backward, her hand tight on the railing as the ferry slowed. "I think I should go back to the van," she said, her voice a warning.

Kate's gaze pleaded with her.

Tilly touched her fingers to her lips. "Can I have the keys? Please."

Kate fished in her pocket and handed over the set. In a blink, Tilly was gone.

Kate slid onto the wooden bench and rested her head in her hands. *So I'm not going crazy...* She'd spent months forbidding herself from thinking that Tilly could possibly feel anything for her. She'd spent months trying to convince herself that she'd imagined the sexual tension. But Tilly had kissed her, had held Kate to her and welcomed the intimacy.

The ferry horn blew loudly as they pulled up to the slipway. Heart racing, Kate made her way down into the damp garage, around the cars and trucks that would disembark at East Island.

Through the lightly tinted windows of the van, Kate could see Tilly, elbow propped up in the windowsill, her hand supporting her head. Her eyes were closed. Kate swallowed over the tightness in her throat and pulled open the driver's door.

In the passenger seat, Tilly's eyes snapped open. Kate closed the door. The clip of her seat belt was loud in the silence. They watched as the ramp lowered in preparation for disembarkation. "Are you okay?" Kate asked, her tongue leaden.

Dropping her gaze to her lap, Tilly nodded.

The look on Tilly's face? The shame? It turned Kate's stomach. "We can just forget that happened," she said softly. "You were upset, I was upset…"

Briefly, Tilly's gaze flickered to her.

"We have a lot of history," Kate said, choked. "I think maybe this little…outburst, I think it's been building for a while. It's been a lot," she continued, "being here together again after all these years. You're a different person, I'm a different person. Relearning who we are to each other…I think it's been…emotional."

Tilly's voice was a whisper. "Right…"

"I mean, we had an intense friendship. We were very close." She wet her lips. "And I think you know I've always been attracted to you."

Silence.

"But it was just a kiss, Til. That's all. We can just forget it."

"Okay," Tilly whispered.

"Okay." Kate turned the key in the ignition.

The second Kate drew to a stop outside the cottage, Tilly was out of the van, the angel costume fluttering in its plastic garment bag over her arm. From the van, Kate watched her unlock the cottage door and disappear. She was in such a rush to get inside—away from Kate—that she didn't notice she'd dropped the halo by the door.

Kate locked the van, the lights blinking once, twice, turning the white roses lining the path to red in a fleeting flash. In a stupor, Kate followed Tilly inside and locked the door behind her. A soft glow emanated from Tilly's room but her door was pushed to, shutting Kate out.

Fear gripped Kate. Was this how it would be from now on? For weeks she had lain awake at night, heart aching as she thought about Tilly. Finally, they'd surrendered to their burning need, and now Tilly didn't want to be in the same room as her, let alone look her in the eye.

Possessed by uncontrollable hurt and wrath, Kate crossed the room, wrapped her fingers around Tilly's doorknob and pushed.

By the bedhead, still wearing Kate's blazer, Tilly was focused on tucking the fitted sheet around the corner of her unmade mattress. Her eyes flickered to Kate in the doorway. "Yes?" she said, no more than a whisper.

As Kate watched Tilly round the bed to anchor the other corner of the sheet, she vibrated with trepidation. "He's going to Vanuatu next year and he's asked Sister Ellie to go with him. He wants you to stay here with his kids."

For a long, strained moment, Tilly stared back, eyes calculated. Suddenly, she reached across the bed and picked up a pillow and its case. "Check in at the Meriton isn't until three so I'm thinking we should leave around eleven tomorrow."

Stunned, Kate blinked.

"I'm going to take history with Year Eight first thing in the morning." Tilly tossed the dress pillow toward the bedhead and smoothed the wrinkles from the sheets. "Will you be ready by eleven?"

Kate pulled her clammy hand from the doorknob and slipped it into the back pocket of her jeans. "Of course…"

"Great."

Mind racing, eyes burning, Kate backed out of the room and pulled the door closed.

She locked the bathroom door behind her. Gripping the edge of the basin, she glared at her own reflection. Behind her, the bathroom curtain fluttered. There was a light on in the school, higher in the west wing bathroom.

Kate looked back at her reflection, her short hair swept to the side, barely two inches long on top. Not all that long ago, she herself had been up in that dorm bathroom, doling out free midnight haircuts to the rest of her cohort. After months of having Tilly sit on the basin observing as Kate worked her magic as resident barber, she'd handed Tilly the scissors. Cut mine, she'd said. Goose bumps rose on the back of her neck as she remembered Tilly with the spray bottle, lithe fingers in her hair. *Just a trim.* Tilly's work had been so uneven, so terribly asymmetrical, that it had brought tears of laughter to both of their eyes. She'd only lost two inches on the right side, a few millimetres on the left, but it had been enough to let Tilly know under no-uncertain terms that the first time was most definitely the last. *Never* again, she'd said, tears rolling down her cheeks as they'd giggled and cackled, Tilly sweeping the damp, disparate tendrils of Kate's dark hair into a pile as Kate held the dustpan still to collect the mess.

Kate pressed her fingers to her lips and recalled the sensation of Tilly's lips against her own. The memory of Tilly's horrified stare played in her mind's eye. Never again, she thought. Never again.

CHAPTER FOURTEEN

"Buy me these chips?" Molly asked Emma.

"Why should I?"

"Because it's my birthday."

"Kate literally *just* gave you a whole bunch of screenwriting books. The gift wrapping is still on the backseat of the van."

"So? They weren't from you, they were from Kate. Don't be stingy."

"The books were from all of us, right Kate?"

Distracted by the encounter evolving outside the service-station convenience store, Kate tore her gaze from the window and glanced over the snack shelf at the girls. "It was from Tilly and me," she murmured, returning her attention to Tilly by the van, deep in conversation with a British tourist who had asked for route advice. Kate squinted in the morning sun as she watched Tilly throw her head back in laughter at whatever he had said. What was so funny about the Great Ocean Road? Kate lowered her sunglasses and stared as Hugh Grant leaned a hand against the beam of the petrol bowser, grinning as Tilly talked animatedly.

At least she's talkative with *some* people, Kate mused bitterly as she stepped further up in line to pay. Tilly had been incredibly quiet that morning when she'd returned from the school to pack the car with Kate. The tension was thick, the memory of last night's encounter still raw. Kate had offered to forget it, but that was proving impossible. Since they'd taken the causeway out of Lords that morning, twice she had caught Tilly chancing glances across the front seat when she thought she wasn't looking. Tilly seemed torn between wanting to ignore what had happened and wanting to acknowledge it, and knowing that only made it harder for Kate to resist the hope that bubbled away at the surface of her longing.

Bristling with irritation, Kate pushed her sunglasses to the top of her head. "Where are Grace and Lexi?" Kate asked the other girls.

Molly looked up from a magazine she had pried from the rack. "I think they already went back to the van."

"Good," Kate said. "I'm going to pay for the petrol and go to the restroom. Hurry up and get something if you want it." After paying, Kate cast one last glance outside before she pushed the door open to the restroom, stepping past a woman on her way out.

The whistle of the hand dryer was loud as Kate latched the cubicle door behind her.

A toilet flushed, a cubicle opened. Another flush. Just as she reached for her own flush, Grace's voice echoed across the tiles. "Kate's got it bad for Tilly, hey?"

Her hand froze in midair, hovering above the flush as her entire body rushed with fierce and sudden embarrassment.

Lexi's cubicle door clicked loudly as it opened. "I know, right?"

"I don't know *why*," Grace pondered. "Maybe Kate's just lonely on Lords." A tap turned on, then another. "Like, if I were a lesbian, I wouldn't be into someone like Tilly. I'd be into Kate, though. Maybe. But Tilly? I mean, she's the sweetest thing on the planet, but she's not really hot. Kate must be hella desperate."

"Tilly does seem a little frigid, I guess."

"Frigid?" Grace scoffed. "Tilly's *unfuckable*."

The deafening wheeze of the hand dryer drowned out the pounding of Kate's pulse in her ears. She turned the latch and stepped out.

Grace turned at the hand dryer. Lexi looked up from washing her hands. And never, in all her years of teaching, had Kate seen two girls go sheet white.

She crossed the bathroom to the sinks, the hand dryer continuing its rumble. Finally, it stopped. Silence settled like a plague.

"Oh my God, I'm so sorry," Grace said softly, voice thick and cheeks quickly growing bright. "Kate, I'm so sorry. I didn't know you were in here. I didn't mean it."

Roughly, Kate pressed soap into her palm, her jaw set hard with annoyance. "Exactly which part didn't you mean?"

"All of it," Grace said instantly, blood charging to her neck in a humiliated rush.

Kate looked up into the mirror at their regretful expressions. She dropped her gaze back to wringing her hands. "I can't look at either of you right now. Go and get in the van."

Lowering the iron to the sleeve of her blazer, Kate chanced a glance toward the closed bathroom door of their hotel room. Tilly had been in there for a while—it had been almost forty minutes since Kate had finished showering and declared the bathroom free.

Steam puffed from the iron and Kate yanked her left hand from the edge of the board. *Fuck.* She felt like she was on another planet altogether. She looked down at her watch. The little hand was only on the five and already she was dreading going to sleep that night, only a narrow bedside table between their double beds. As the day had gone on, Tilly had relaxed, but the tension had yet to disperse.

She concentrated on ironing away the largest crease, and when the fold was still visible, upped the heat just enough to be sure the fabric wouldn't mark. Tilly had taught her even this. How many afternoons had they spent in the convent as teenagers, Kate helping Tilly with her ironing chores while the sisters were at evening mass? How many baby-blue habits had Kate spent hours ironing just so she could have her best friend all to herself down by the cove a little earlier?

The bathroom door opened, and Kate's gaze lifted. Her stomach bottomed out.

"Do I look silly?"

Kate shook her head. "No."

Silly was the last word in the English language Kate would use to describe the way Tilly looked in the simple black dress, the neckline scooped below her collarbone, the sleeves tight to where they finished at her elbows. "You look beautiful." Her long tresses were freed, and for the first time ever, Tilly appeared to be wearing *lipstick*. "I just…I've never seen you wear anything above the knee… you know, other than your PJs. For a while there, I wondered if you *had* knees."

Tilly laughed as she gathered her dark hair around her neck to fumble through her suitcase. "Don't get too excited," Tilly said, "I *am* wearing stockings."

Doesn't count.

Kate watched from the corner of her eye as Tilly sat on the edge of her bed and slipped her heels onto her stockinged feet. Silence settled and Kate tried to control her yearning for the tension to dissipate, for them to find that sweet peace that had been theirs up until twenty hours ago.

Suddenly, Tilly's voice broke the silence. "Hey," she said slowly, her attention focused on buckling the thin straps of her shoes, "about what you said last night…"

Kate glanced up, her heartbeat quickening as she watched Tilly fasten the tiny buckle of the shoe around her ankle. *Which part?*

Both shoes buckled, Tilly sat up on the edge of the bed. As she met Kate's stare, her shoulders slipped back, posture perfect. "I know he's going to Vanuatu," she said.

"You do?"

"I've known for weeks. Mason told me that he overheard his father speaking to one of the acolytes." She paused, her gaze flickering to the closed toe of her heels as they dusted along the dark carpet. "I haven't spoken about it with Declan, but I do know."

"Right." She tilted her head. "You're okay with it? Him leaving?"

Tilly hesitated. "I suppose I would have liked to have been informed."

You think?

"But the fact of the matter is that it doesn't bother me." She stood, smoothing her dress over her thighs and adjusting the seam and refusing to meet Kate's eye. "It really doesn't."

The sound of Tilly's laughter was infectious. Kate smiled as she closed the hotel room door behind them and followed Tilly and the girls down the hotel hall to the lifts.

With an arm slung around Tilly's shoulders, Emma's other hand gestured wildly as she spoke in fluent French, Tilly attempting to guess what Emma was saying while Lexi and Molly threw corrections at Emma every two seconds.

"Kate?"

Grace's whisper was soft as she fell into step beside Kate. "I feel dreadful," she said. "What I said was just the worst. I didn't mean it. I love Tilly. We all do. Forgive me?" Grace had timed her apology perfectly—they'd reached the end of the hallway and Molly was holding the elevator door open, hurrying the others inside. But Kate wasn't finished with Grace. A quick "sorry" wasn't going to cut it this time.

The lift was already semi-full with other guests. Kate reached out an arm to stop Grace from following the others inside. "You all go on, Grace and I will get the next one," she said.

Lexi licked her lips, her gaze flickering knowingly between Kate and Grace. "I can hop out too, make some room…"

"No," Kate said. This wasn't about Lexi. "You stay."

"Don't be ridiculous," Tilly said from deep inside the elevator. "There's oodles of room. Just get in."

The other strangers in the lift agreed, but like a gift from Heaven, the doors closed instantaneously and the man holding them open lowered his arm, indifferent. Kate shrugged lightly at Tilly's curious expression as the group disappeared.

Left alone with Kate, Grace's desperate energy vanished. They fell silent, the corridor speaker slipping into a Beatles cover.

Kate ran her tongue along her teeth and exhaled. "Look, I want us to have a good night, okay? I do. I don't want you to be stewing over this all through the play. But I also don't want to hear you speaking about other women the way you did today. You're better than that and we both know it. You call other women words like 'unfuckable,' like 'frigid,' it just makes it okay for boys—men—to do the same thing." She paused, turning to meet Grace's eye. "The things you say in this world have an impact, Grace."

"I know." Grace dropped her watery gaze to her feet. "I've learned my lesson. Forever. I swear to God."

What she had overheard in that roadside bathroom was not a reflection of who Grace was—Kate knew that. She also knew that Grace would remember the faux pas for the rest for her life. "You're forgiven," Kate said softly. "It's done. Forgotten. Okay?"

Grace nodded solemnly.

Kate reached out and pressed the down arrow. "Don't cry, Grace, your mascara will run."

The theatre was bustling when they stepped inside with just ten minutes to spare until showtime. With her hand at Tilly's elbow, the soft ends of Tilly's freed hair teasing Kate's wrist at the cuff of her blazer, she followed closely as Molly led their small group up the marble staircase to the dress circle.

They were stuck behind the crowd at the top of the stairs when fingers clawed down Kate's back. She swivelled against the bannister.

"Hello stranger."

Shock gripped her. "Elodie…"

Looking up at Kate from the step below, Elodie's large brown eyes danced warmly. "Don't I get a hug?"

Kate pulled her close. "Hello," she breathed into Elodie's thick dark hair. She inhaled deeply. The scent of Elodie's hair was still the same. On the step below, Elodie's small frame seemed even tinier. Grinning, Kate pulled back. Elodie beamed, and not for the first time, Kate was incredibly glad that their breakup had been clean, mutual, *kind*. Not long after, Kate had moved to Lords.

Elodie bit her lip. "I was thinking about you yesterday."

"You were?"

Nodding, she shifted the straps of her handbag over her shoulder, pulled her long hair from where it was caught between the leather. "You're going to kill me, but I accidentally broke the nozzle on the coffeemaker."

Kate grinned. "Not *my* coffeemaker."

"I told you that you should have just taken it with you. I'm not equipped to handle fragile objects or small children."

The reference to children set a pang in Kate's chest. Forcing a smile, she looked around. "Are you here by yourself?"

Elodie shook her head. "No, Anna's just checking her laptop bag in at the cloakroom—she came straight from work."

Just like Kate and Beccy, Elodie and Anna had always been close. It was one of the things that had been great about dating Elodie—she'd always understood that a sisterly bond wasn't anything threatening.

Elodie looked to Tilly. "Hi," she said brightly. "I'm Elodie."

Kate stepped back, gesturing for Tilly to move closer. "Sorry," she apologised. "Where are my manners?" Her cheeks heated in embarrassment. "El, this is Tilly."

As Tilly shook Elodie's hand, a look of surprise flashed on her face. She quickly hid it. "You went to school together, right?" She looked between them. "Kate mentioned your name often."

A wave of guilt swept over her at Elodie's polite, feigned ignorance. Elodie knew all about Tilly, about their belltower kisses. For the entire time they'd dated, it had been a private, running joke between them. Every time Kate had teased Elodie for her youthful obsession with straight girls, Elodie had retorted, "Yeah, tease me all you want, Casanova, but at least I never tried it on a nun."

Kate cleared her throat. "Tilly and I teach together at St. Joan's." She gestured to the group of girls in front. "We're on an overnight excursion."

The crowd moved forward. Elodie followed after Kate and Tilly. "You took the position on the island?"

Kate nodded.

Elodie's expression brightened. "Good for you." Smiling widely, she set her gaze on Tilly. She looked her up and down in her little black dress. Her curiosity turned to confusion. "Do you belong to that order?"

Oh God. Oh, Jesus Christ...

Tilly raised an eyebrow.

"On the island?" Elodie clarified. "The sisters?"

Kate wet her lips. "Tilly's not a nun."

Elodie's eyes widened. "Oh my god, I'm so sorry. Kate always said that she had a friend who was a nun." Elodie looked between them. "I've gotten it mixed up." She pressed a hand to her cheek. "I'm so embarrassed. I must have the wrong person."

Kate bit back a smile. Elodie's penchant for pointing out exactly how she was feeling had always been one of the most endearing—and amusing—facets of her warm personality.

Shaking her head, Tilly forced a smile. "Don't worry about it. And you're right—that was me."

Elodie swallowed. "Right."

The last call bell chimed persistently. Lexi turned on the step above. "Tilly, do you have a nail file I can borrow?"

Tilly hunted in her bag. "It's in here somewhere..."

Kate's gaze locked with Elodie's. Understanding passed between them. Smirking, Elodie folded her jacket over her arm. She shifted closer to the bannister, purposely moving out of Tilly's earshot. "We should get a drink," she whispered. Her cheeks coloured as she stared up at Kate. "What are you doing after the show?"

Kate looked down at her. "I'm with the kids. I have to get them back to the hotel."

She looked up. "And after?"

"El…we can't."

"Why?"

"You know why…"

"But you're thinking about it."

The fact that she was considering it was written plainly across her face. It was one thing they'd never been very smart about— knowing when to stop. It was the reason why their breakup had been so long and so painful—because when they'd put an end to it, they still hadn't *put an end to it.*

"Kate, it doesn't have to be a thing. Just…tell me where you're staying."

Kate spared a glance at Tilly, deep in conversation with Lexi. She met Elodie's gaze again. "The Meriton."

"I could come to the hotel bar."

Kate quirked an eyebrow. Elodie had always been so forward, so confident.

She leaned closer. "My number hasn't changed, so if your mind does…"

The six-minute call broke loudly across the crowd. In line to the door, Molly ushered their group over.

Kate slid her hands into her pockets. "I've gotta go. But you look really good, El."

"So do you."

The moment pulsed. There was a lot of history between them. And a lot of it was good. Really good.

"Bye, El."

"Call me later?"

Kate grinned. "I'm on duty."

With a shy grin, Elodie turned and headed to Door Ten.

Quickly, Kate caught up to the group. In the line of patrons outside Door Eight, Lexi was stopped to open her bag for inspection. As she produced her own ticket for the usher, Kate shook her head in apology as the entire confectionary aisle of Woolworths was confiscated from Lexi's bag.

"Eugh," Lexi moaned as they sank into their assigned seats. "That was ten bucks' worth."

At the end of the row, Kate sat forward. "If you hadn't brought it into the theatre, you'd still have it, wouldn't you?"

Lexi leaned over Grace's arm, watching as Grace checked the four girls into the theatre on Facebook. "They let you take stuff in at the cinema," she said mindlessly.

As Tilly grinned at the exchange, Kate rolled her eyes. "This isn't a cinema, Lexi, it's Her Majesty's Theatre."

Between Kate and Tilly, Molly sat forward in her seat and turned to Tilly. "You want to just sit next to Kate so I can sit next to Em?"

Their eyes locked. Tilly smiled a tight line with her lips. "Sure," she said softly.

As Molly swapped seats with Tilly, Kate feigned deep interest in the program, scanning her eyes over the actors' bios and doing her best to avert her gaze from the enchanting way Tilly crossed her legs as she sat. The way she smoothed her hand over her stocking-clad thigh. The way she danced her fingertips against the hem of her little black dress.

Christ… She'd been relieved when they'd walked into the row and Molly had sat between them, grateful to have a buffer. But now, with her elbow balanced on the thin armrest between them, she could feel the heat of Tilly's body, so close, so warm, so *present*. And for the next two hours and fifty minutes—including interval—there would be no escape.

With the girls occupied, Tilly leaned close, her breath hot against the shell of Kate's ear. "Let me help out with dinner," she whispered.

Kate shook her head.

Tilly's gaze was warm on the side of her face. "I know that came out of your pocket…" she pressed. "Let me help. Please."

The lights dimmed and the audience hushed. Kate pressed her finger to her lips and winked at Tilly, who rolled her eyes before she turned her attention to the stage.

The desire to reach over and touch the warmth of Tilly's knee set a desire in Kate's heart that was painfully heavy. Her fingers twitched with the impulse to trace the curve where muscle began below the hem of Tilly's dress. It wasn't difficult to imagine the sensation of the thin denier of Tilly's stockings against her fingertips, the silky roughness at the slightest friction...

In the past, she'd taken for granted how easy it was to reach out and innocently stroke a lover's knee. She'd disregarded how meaningful such a permission happened to be. But even when she'd had that easy intimacy, that sweet softness, such a caress had never garnered the surge of emotion that consumed her at the mere *thought* of touching Tilly in such a way.

Tilly shifted, and as their arms brushed, heat poured through the thin sleeves of Kate's shirt, of Tilly's dress. Longing unfurled in her chest.

It wasn't until interval that Tilly pulled away.

CHAPTER FIFTEEN

With a sigh, Kate collapsed onto her bed. For a hotel, the pillows were decent, much better than her own at the cottage. The night before Tilly had arrived at St. Joan's, Kate had swapped her own therapeutic pillow with the guest room pillow so Tilly wouldn't have to suffer. She'd be lying if she said she didn't miss it.

Kate pulled her eyes from the ceiling and glanced across the room. She watched, enchanted, as Tilly plaited her hair, her skilful fingers working quickly. Damp from the light rain on the walk home, it was darker, wilder than usual.

"The remote's on the bedside table," Tilly murmured, shucking off her light jacket and hunting through the wardrobe for a coat hanger.

"That's okay. I don't really feel like watching TV."

"Tired?" Tilly asked as she disappeared into the bathroom.

Kate rolled onto her side and held herself up on her elbow. "Nah, it's early. Early enough to go out." Early enough to call Elodie and get that drink. It would certainly keep her mind off Tilly for a few hours…

Silence. And then… "What time are you meeting Elodie at the hotel bar?"

Kate swallowed as she listened to a tap turn on, then off. Tilly had heard their conversation on the theatre steps? "I'm…I'm not meeting Elodie at the hotel bar."

"Oh. I was under the impression that you were."

Stunned, Kate remained quiet.

"If you don't have plans," Tilly called out, her voice wavering ever so slightly, "I was thinking we could go and get coffee. That place on the corner was still open when we passed."

Kate blinked in surprise. "Really?" It wasn't a very *Tilly* thing to suggest.

"Sure," Tilly replied, her voice echoing off the bathroom tile. "The girls will be fine. I could go knock and tell them we're heading out for a little while. If you're interested, that is."

Spencer Street was quieter than when they'd returned from the theatre half an hour before. Fluorescent lights from the twenty-four-hour convenience stores and adult bookstores brightened the dampened strip.

Ahead of Kate and Tilly, three girls stumbled in heels, drunkenly arguing whether or not to call an Uber. They couldn't be much older than the seniors Kate had just bid goodnight. What an arduous struggle it had been to pull her students' attention from the Harry Potter film playing on TV. "Girls, are you listening? Did you just hear a word of what I said?" Lexi had waved her arm, her eyes focused on the TV. "Yeah, yeah, you're going out. You have your phone." How did it go so quickly from four girls piled in one bed, scoffing junk food and entranced by *The Chamber of Secrets*, to clubbing and Ubers?

When they arrived at the café at the corner of Spencer and Flinders, like a reflex, Kate brushed a hand against the low of Tilly's back and ushered her inside.

"Go and save us those stools by the window," Tilly said. "I'll order."

Kate rested an elbow on the wide ledge and looked out at the street, trying to shake the feeling that she was like a marionette in a puppet show, so exposed there at the open bay window with her back to the rest of the café.

Tilly danced her nails across Kate's shoulder, smiling as she pulled out the stool beside her.

The historical free city-circle tram rounded the corner, stopping for passengers to disembark at the stop in the centre of the street. At the late hour, only a handful of passengers climbed on and off. Kate smiled as a woman seated at the window of the tram quickly inserted her earphones to drown out the tram's loudspeaker as it spewed facts about the history of Melbourne's South Bank. As the bell rang to announce its departure, the trolley sparked to life. The tram doors closed, leaving Kate and Tilly alone with the soft jazz music of the café. "I can probably recite that entire tour in my sleep," Tilly murmured. "I took that tram every day for four years."

"You did?"

Tilly nodded. "I had a part-time job at the cinema on Little Collins. I'd go from uni to Federation Square and back again." Her lips curved into a small smile. "Gosh, that feels like another lifetime."

Their order arrived. "You know," Tilly said when their waitress disappeared, "I haven't had this much fun in a very long time. I love the city."

She watched as Tilly poured her tea. The soft hairs around Tilly's ears, too short to reach her plait, had curled in the humidity. God, she was adorable. "You liked living here? After you came back from New Guinea?"

"Oh, I loved it. Just loved it. I loved being around people and having the ACU campus to go home to at night. It wasn't like St. Joan's, no, but sometimes that was a good thing. At St. Joan's, I was Tilly the Nun. In the city, I could be myself. I could be different for other reasons—for my humanitarian work, for being a student. And there was something about being in the city, amongst a sea of people, that brought me closer to God." As she stirred sugar into her tea, she sighed. "I've always felt distant from other people because I hold my faith so close." She looked up, the lines in her forehead relaxing. "But you always respected who I was. You never made me feel naïve, or prudish, never treated me as though I was sheltered. And maybe I am all of those things—I'll be the first to admit that. But you always made me feel like my faith wasn't all there was to me."

She looked out at Spencer Street, her voice softening as she seemed to disappear into her own little world. "You still make me feel that way," she murmured.

At the green light at the intersection, a taxi pressed on his horn, unrelenting until the car in front accelerated.

Tilly looked up. Kate held her gaze. The question itched beneath her skin, begging to be asked. Was it the right time? It felt like the right time. "I want to know something," Kate admitted. "And don't feel you have to answer if it's too personal."

"What is it?"

"Why didn't you take your vows?"

Tilly sighed. "When I was a missionary, I met so many beautiful children. Children who had nothing, children without parents. Without love. My heart ached for them, Kate, but it ached for me too. Papua New Guinea changed everything. I came home and started studying teaching at uni and the months passed and I found the song in my heart changing. Joining the sisterhood wasn't the plan I thought God had for me." She paused. "He wants me to be a mother."

Kate sipped at her coffee. "And is that what you want?"

Tilly nodded. "More than anything." She shrugged. "I don't think I would have made a very good sister, anyway." She tore the end off a sachet of sugar and poured it into her cup. "I didn't have the commitment." Her voice dropped to a whisper as she stared down into her tea. "And I'm not as pure as you might think."

Kate's heartbeat fired. She twirled her spoon around the surface of her cappuccino, scraping chocolate from froth. "What, uh, what do you mean?"

Tilly looked up at her through her lashes. "Sometimes I have… thoughts," she whispered.

Kate inched closer on her stool. "Thoughts?"

There was a glint in Tilly's eye that betrayed the shameful lilt to her voice—Tilly was curious. Tilly *wanted* to talk about it. "Mhm."

"What kind of thoughts?"

Tilly looked around the café.

"Nobody can hear us," Kate assured her.

Tilly nodded. Nervously, she played with the empty sachet, twirling it around her finger. "There was this film late one night," she started. "On television. I was about to change the channel, but

I found myself just..." She hesitated. "I couldn't stop watching. It was like I was hypnotised."

As Tilly looked down into her tea, Kate swallowed, hard.

Tilly wet her lips. "When it was over..." she said, her voice low, "...my underwear was ruined. I think I must have had an orgasm." She paused. "Do you...do you think that's what it was?"

The question stole the breath from Kate's lungs. She pressed her fist to her mouth and resisted the urge to bite down. *Must have.* Tilly didn't know. It was suddenly too warm at the window. How could Kate tell her that, no, it didn't sound like she'd had an orgasm—that if she had, she'd know it. How could Kate tell her that without humiliating her?

Tilly's eyes bore into the side of her face, waiting for an answer. "Um, maybe," Kate said, pressure growing in her chest. What if Tilly never knew that kind of pleasure? The thought of Declan's hands on Tilly's body had jealousy leaking into her veins, rich like poison. He was so much older than Tilly, and all the more maddening was the fact that he was slack with disregard for Tilly's happiness. He had already proven himself selfish in so many ways— she could only assume that he would be selfish in that department too. Tilly was only thirty. She had so much life ahead of her. Kate wanted to be the one to make love to her, to worship her body, to pleasure her in ways that would take her to the edge of destruction, to love her hard enough to keep her on that blissful edge for as long as Tilly desired.

"You're human, Tilly," she said, choked. "You don't have to feel ashamed for feeling something that everyone feels. You're not a nun."

"But I thought I was going to be. I can't just stop thinking like one. And yet, at the same time, there's this part of me that feels wicked, a part that I can't turn off no matter how hard I try." She licked her lips. "And Declan...he's a good man."

Jealousy erupted in Kate's lungs. "Do you love him?"

Tilly avoided her gaze. "No. But I could."

"Til...do you really think that's enough?"

Tilly dropped her gaze to her tea. "He's a wonderful father."

"Does he want more children?"

"He says I'd make a good mother."

"To whose children? His? Or yours?"

Uncertainty flickered across Tilly's expression. Quickly, she veiled it. "Ours."

They looked up, watching from the open window. "It's started sprinkling again," Tilly murmured. "I hadn't even noticed."

Kate didn't want to press the issue—really, she didn't—but she couldn't just let it go. "Have you talked to him about having more children?"

A light blush inked Tilly's cheeks. "I don't feel comfortable talking about things like that with him. He's not very open to it. It's personal. Intimate."

Tilly lifted the small teapot, the same colour as the stone on Tilly's finger. As she raised the spout to the lip of the cup, Kate watched the weak tea swirl inside. If Declan was so closed-off about such a thing *now*, she could only imagine what he would be like once they were married. Once they were lovers. The thought of them in bed together made it almost impossible to swallow her coffee. Would Tilly ever know what it was to be loved passionately? "Has he ever touched you?" Kate whispered. "Have you ever touched him?"

Tilly looked up, her gaze bright with surprise. She chewed at her bottom lip.

"He doesn't try to touch you?" Kate pressed.

"He's *respectful*," Tilly said, shaking her head with a contrived little grin that made Kate deeply uncomfortable. As Tilly sipped at her tea and stared out at the street, her smile quickly disappeared. She looked to Kate, her lips parting. She stopped herself.

"What?" Kate asked. "What were you going to say?"

"It's just that sometimes I wonder if he's even attracted to me."

"That's not true." Kate saw the way he looked at Tilly. He wanted her. He may have been using her, but he desired her too. How could he not?

"It is true," she said indifferently, as though she'd resolved herself to the fact a long time ago. "I think he may still be in love with his wife." She paused, her eyes trailing over Kate's face. "I mean, you must think it's strange that he isn't interested in touching me, right?"

Kate bit her tongue. She couldn't lie to Tilly, not when Tilly could read her like an open book. "Do you want him to touch you?" she deflected.

Tilly licked her lips. "I don't know."

Kate's fingers left her cup. She reached out and danced them along the inside of Tilly's wrist, felt the ridges of her veins beneath her fingertips. Confessions burned on the tip of her tongue. *I'd do anything to make you happy. All I want to do is kiss you all the time. I can give you everything you want.* She could feel Tilly's eyes on her thumb as it gently careened back and forth across her pulse, so slow it was barely a movement. "Has he ever kissed you?"

"He's kissed me a few times on the cheek to say goodnight," Tilly confessed. "I've only ever…I've only ever been kissed by you."

Desire hit her like a freight train. Her thumb froze over Tilly's pulse. Everything but Tilly ceased to exist—the whirl of the coffee machine, the slush of tyres on the wet road.

"And how did it feel?" she whispered over the noise of the bustling café. "When I kissed you?"

For a long moment, Tilly was silent. Kate's thumb ceased its caress. Had she gone too far?

"Gentle," Tilly suddenly murmured.

Kate looked up.

Tilly's eyes focused on her lips. "Soft. And warm." Her hand turned in Kate's. She pinched the cuff of Kate's blazer between her thumb and forefinger and Kate's heart lurched. She shifted slightly on the stool to ease the growing pressure between her legs. Slowly, Tilly's dainty fingers crept underneath the fabric to feel the bare skin of Kate's wrist. Her fingers settled over Kate's pulse. It wasn't enough. Kate turned her hand and linked her fingers with Tilly's.

Tilly's eyes were hooded, lips slightly parted. The attraction was all-consuming, a magnetic pull Kate wasn't strong enough to resist. A noise caught at the back of Kate's throat. How easy it would be to close the space between them, to press her lips against Tilly's and finish what they'd started on the ferry. Not a soul in the café would care. Here they were, just two women on a midnight date, shyly, desperately wanting.

"Kate…" Tilly whispered. "What are we doing?"

What were they doing? They were testing the limits, playing with fire. Finally, the floodgates had been opened and if the moment felt dangerous for Kate, she could only imagine what it felt like for Tilly. Tilly, who had only ever been kissed by Kate. Tilly, who blushed at the most innocent of suggestions. Tilly, who was *engaged*. In a trance, Kate stared down at the sapphire on Tilly's finger. It wasn't supposed to be like this. In a perfect world, it was supposed to be *Kate's* ring on Tilly's finger.

The thought shocked her out of her stupor. An ache fluttering in her heart, she dropped her gaze and withdrew her touch. "Come on," she said over the lump in her throat. "Let's head back."

As they made their way down the empty street, the impulse to reach out and take Tilly's hand was painfully acute. Desperation surged within her. If Tilly was any other woman, Kate would surrender to the temptation, lead her into an alley and claim her. But who was she kidding? She'd never feel compelled do something so animalistic with any other woman. She'd never had these kinds of impulses with anybody *but* Tilly. Kate swallowed. Christ, if Tilly could read the carnal, fervid fantasies playing through her mind, she'd run a mile and get a restraining order.

The hotel lobby was empty. Kate forced a smile for the concierge behind the desk. Silent, they waited on the elevator. When Kate stabbed at the up arrow a third time, Tilly let out a little sigh. "Kate. It can't go any faster…"

Kate clenched her jaw, hands tingling with impulsivity. She slipped them into her pockets. As they stepped into the empty elevator, Kate jabbed at the button to the twenty-third floor. Fucking hell. What was the point of having a door-close button if the doors didn't close the second she punched it?

Leaning against the wall, Kate stared at her feet. Finally, the doors came together. Immediately, the air thickened with tension. In the middle of the elevator, Tilly didn't dare look her way. The hairs rose on the back of Kate's neck. So she wasn't imagining it. She raised her gaze and watched as the digits ticked over and the elevator climbed higher.

"I think about you, Kate." A beat. "I think about us."

Her breath caught. She watched in the reflection of the mirrored walls as Tilly glared straight ahead at the line in the elevator doors.

"I was jealous of that woman when she touched your arm at the theatre. When she looked at you the way she did."

Kate's eyes slammed shut. How was she supposed to respond to that? When she wanted so badly, just *speaking* was dangerous. What if some kind of salacious confession escaped her without her permission? Something she'd regret in the light of day? "Just don't say anything else, Til."

"I'm sorry," Tilly whispered. "I can't help it."

"Just don't say any more, okay?"

As twenty-two checked over to twenty-three, the elevator pinged. The doors opened on their floor and Kate shot out.

Tilly fell a few steps behind her, her heels clicking across the tile until they reached the carpeted corridor. Kate slid her key card into the handle. The little red light flashed once, twice. She huffed, tried it again. Red. A third time. *You have got to be kidding me…*

Kate could feel Tilly's gaze hot on her face. In a second, Tilly was slinking closer and tapping Kate's hand away, inserting her own card. As the green light flashed, Tilly pushed down on the handle and held the door open for her.

Kate immediately went to the bedside table between their beds and reached for the remote. A rerun of *Dr. Quinn* drowned out the silence. There. Good. Blowing air from her cheeks, she took her pyjamas from her bag and headed for the bathroom.

Standing beneath the jet of a hot shower, Kate tried to regulate her breathing. Maybe it wasn't a shower that she needed. Maybe she needed to go down to the hotel gym. Or the bar. What I need, she thought, is my own fucking room.

She rested her forehead against the steamed glass. Ever since their kiss on the ferry, she hadn't been able to think of anything else. The little whimper Tilly had breathed into Kate's mouth, the way she tasted. The memory of Tilly's lips against hers had driven her crazy all day.

The spray of the shower rained down her back, soothed the tense muscles in her neck. Of all nights, why had their kiss happened then? The tension hadn't been given time to breathe and now look what had happened. Regardless of how receptive Tilly had been to Kate's kiss the night before, how daring she had been just then in the elevator, Kate couldn't rid herself of the memory of Tilly's horrified expression when she'd pulled away from the kiss. When reality set in, deep down, Tilly didn't want this. She was confused. And as much as it excited Kate to know she could have such an effect on Tilly, she had no intention of playing games. Not with Tilly. Not ever.

She throbbed between her legs. God, she was so riled up from their moment in the café, so tight with—

She opened her eyes and her skin sparked *hot*. Across the bathroom, their eyes locked. Her pulse slowed as Tilly's gaze dropped to stare blatantly at Kate's nakedness.

Wiping the water from her eyes, she stared back. The lace hem of Tilly's cream slip stopped mid-thigh. Kate pulled her gaze higher. The neckline of the slip dipped low, and beneath the harsh light of the bathroom, the crucifix glinted upon Tilly's flushed, heaving chest. Through the thinness of the satin, it was obvious Tilly wasn't wearing a bra.

Kate's body flared with excitement at the sight of Tilly gazing across the bathroom unabashedly. In all her years of being intimate with women, Kate had grown from self-conscious to indifferent, but this...this was new. This was electrifying. She could only imagine what had possessed Tilly to make it this far.

Tilly released her grip on the door. Barefoot, she stepped forward.

Heat burned between Kate's legs at the sight of Tilly's eyes on her body, dark with desire.

Closer. Closer again.

Tilly reached out, her fingers brushing the silver push pad of the shower door. She stared past it, her gaze focused on Kate's breasts.

The weight of what they were about to do settled thick like steam. Finally, they were about to release this lecherous thing that had chosen the two of them.

As Tilly's hand settled against silver, Kate's heart hammered. Only a thin panel of steamed glass was keeping Tilly's body from her own. Her body ached with the need to have Tilly's body against her, to trace Tilly's warm, wet skin with her bare hands.

She couldn't stop herself. She had to meet Tilly halfway. She had to. With a trembling hand, she reached for the handle.

Their gazes locked. Something behind Tilly's eyes turned, twisted from dark to light, and like she'd been in a trance from the moment she'd stepped into the bathroom, Tilly *snapped*. Her hand dropped and she swivelled, almost tripping over her own feet as she charged out of the bathroom, the door slamming behind her.

Fuck. Kate reached for the taps and spun them off, grabbed for the nearest towel. Quickly, she dried and dressed.

She ran a hand through her hair and stared at her reflection. As she took in her flushed cheeks, a rush of satisfaction gripped her. Had she ever experienced anything as erotic? Her head spun. God, they hadn't even touched. She drew her hands over her face. *Fuck...*

Hesitantly, she opened the bathroom door.

In the middle of the room, Tilly stood before the muted television in her slip, her arms crossed, biting her nails. Her eyes were wide, expression panic-stricken.

Kate wet her lips. "Til, it's okay..."

Her expression crumbled. "It's not okay. It's so far from okay. I'm getting married."

Kate's gaze dropped to the ground.

Tilly shifted. "I don't know why I did that. I'm sorry. I'm so sorry. I just...I thought that maybe we could move past this if we just got it out of our systems...just once."

The breath caught in Kate's throat. Her eyes snapped up. She would never have considered a thought like that could cross Tilly's mind let alone impassion her so much that it could drive her to act on it. She'd underestimated Tilly's courage, and the realization made her head spin.

Kate shook her head. "But I don't want to get you out of my system." The words were pulled from her throat. "And it wouldn't work. I am telling you now that if it happened once, it wouldn't work." *Not with us. Not with me.*

Meaning turned behind Kate's gaze. Tilly's eyes widened. "I don't know what I want."

That wasn't true—they both knew *exactly* what Tilly wanted. Therein lay the problem.

Tilly's gaze was hot enough to light Kate on fire. "Kate, you're the only one I've ever..."

The broken sentence left Kate aching to know what Tilly had intended to say. Out of their control, the bond between them fizzed and crackled, like a short circuit in high-tension wires. It didn't help that Tilly was gazing at her like all she wanted was for Kate to close the space between them and silence the insatiable need that had been clawing at them for months.

Across the room, Tilly pressed a hand to each of her cheeks. "I feel like I'm losing myself to something I don't understand."

Kate stiffened. Was Tilly really attracted to her? Or did she just like the safety and familiarity that Kate offered? Did her body inflame at the sight of Kate's nakedness? It had interested her— that had been plain as day—but had the sight of Kate's skin made Tilly pulse with arousal the way green eyes focused on her breasts had made Kate throb? Or did she just like that Kate felt like home?

Kate swallowed, hard. "In the elevator, you said that you think about us." She paused. "Do you like the thought of my hands on your body? Touching you? Is that something you think about?"

Tilly's cheeks reddened. She drew a shaky breath.

"When we were in the bathroom...did you come in there because you wanted me to touch you?"

"Kate, please..."

"Or were you doing it because you think it's what I want? Because you always give people what they want. Because you're scared of losing me if we *don't* do this?"

Tilly stared back at her, eyes pleading. The moment stretched. "I'm scared that I'll lose you if we do and I'm scared that I'll lose you if we don't."

Kate sighed heavily. She brought her hands to her hips and ran her tongue across her teeth. Her eyes burned with tears. As she crossed the room to her bag and pulled out jeans, the pain was almost crippling.

Tilly stared in confusion. Kate swallowed. "I'm going out."

"What?" Tilly clutched at the base of her neck. "Where? Are you going to see that woman from the theatre?"

It took every effort to peel her eyes away from Tilly's nipples, so apparent through the thinness of her slip. Kate groaned internally as she took her blazer from the hanger. "No. Of course I'm not going to see her."

Tilly stared like she didn't believe her. "Then where are you going?"

"I don't know where I'm going. I'll take a walk."

The walls were caving in. When she closed her eyes, the images that played beneath her eyelids were brazen. She couldn't be in that room with Tilly, sleeping so close, lying awake and listening to Tilly breathe. And what if Tilly wanted to talk about it like she always did? Kate couldn't. Tilly could look at her with that wide, yearning stare all she wanted, but their reality was heartbreakingly simple: Kate didn't stand a chance of ever being anything more than Tilly's friend. It would destroy them.

Her name fell from Tilly's lips in a raspy plea. "Please, stay. It's the middle of the night."

Kate slid the room card into her back pocket. As she passed Tilly, she slipped a hand around the back of her neck and pressed her lips to her temple.

Tilly released a shaky breath, but her hands remained at her sides.

Kate pulled back. "I have my phone if you need me."

CHAPTER SIXTEEN

Their eyes locked across the hotel breakfast room. As Kate watched Tilly's features soften with relief, an incessant brand of guilt grasped her. Tilly looked away sharply.

At the small breakfast buffet, the clatter of cutlery and dishes only contributed to the unrelenting headache Kate had had since she'd watched the sun rise over the Southbank River from a park bench at five a.m. She glanced across the breakfast room. Perched on high stools at a bar table, her students had their faces in their phones. She glanced at her watch. Check out was in forty minutes.

As she crossed the buffet to the coffee and tea dispenser, heat crawled up the back of her neck the closer she came to Tilly. With only the selection of travel-sized cereal boxes between them, Tilly stood at the conveyor toaster, patiently waiting. Kate's gaze tracked over her body as she fiddled with the takeaway cups. Her tight black jeans hadn't made an appearance for weeks, and paired with the heeled brown boots, Tilly's legs seemed to go on forever. Her thin grey jumper was warm, soft. Kate had folded it with the clean washing at least half a dozen times and she knew what the cashmere felt like against her fingertips.

Tilly's slice popped from the conveyor belt and Kate pulled her gaze away. She selected her coffee preferences on the machine and listened as it churned slowly. Tilly clicked her tongue in frustration. Kate glanced across the counter. The slice two shades too light for Tilly's liking, Tilly reached for the tongs and slid it through a second time.

Out of the corner of her eye, Kate could feel Tilly's gaze on her as Tilly leaned back against the counter and folded her arms across her chest. "Your hair is wet," Tilly observed. "And the back of your blazer."

"It just started to sprinkle."

"Sister Mary Monica called—the causeway is closed after the storm. We can't drive through Portarlington. We'll have to drive to Mornington and take the car ferry."

"*Fantastic.*"

Tilly's toast popped into the tray. "Would you like some?" she offered, reaching across the condiment arrangement for a butter square.

Kate tore at two sachets of sugar. "No thank you. Not much of a breakfast person."

Tilly's brows furrowed as she pinched open the foil. "You eat it every day at home."

Kate sighed as she watched the coffeemaker drip into her cup. "That's because I do it to keep you happy."

She regretted it the moment she said it. Heels tapping across the tile, Tilly tossed the butter packet into the bin between them and reached for the jam. Kate glanced over. Tilly's jaw was set hard, her lips twisted as, with more effort than necessary, she spread jam onto her toast. Kate returned her gaze to the dripping coffee. *Jesus Christ, I do not have the energy for this…* "Do you want me to make you a tea?" she asked, trying.

"I already have one." Tilly's tone was short. "I packed your things."

"Thanks."

"I left a spare set of clothes on the bed in case you wanted to change."

"Great. I will."

"But, by all means, don't do it just to keep me happy."

Fuck. She watched as Tilly sliced the bread in half. "Til—"

"The girls think you've been upstairs all morning in the room. Don't tell them otherwise."

Mind foggy, she pressed the lid onto her cup and headed for the lobby. As she passed her students at their breakfast table, she deduced from snippets of conversation that they were picking pictures from the night before to post on Instagram.

"Kate?" Molly asked. "Aren't you eating with us?"

Shaking her head, she gestured to the elevator. "I have to send a few emails," she lied. She looked from one girl to the other. "Are you packed upstairs?"

Grace and Molly nodded.

"*All* of you are?" Kate clarified. "Lexi?"

Lexi pulled her gaze from her phone. "Yeah. Almost."

"*Almost* isn't good enough when we leave in half an hour. Pull your socks up with breakfast and go upstairs and get your act together."

As she crossed the lobby to the elevator, she hoped she could follow her own instructions.

Vibrating with exhaustion and an overload of caffeine, Kate squinted against the glare of the water and cursed herself for leaving her sunglasses behind in the van. Even with the midday rainstorm pelting the windows of the car ferry, the glare of the sun burned brightly between charcoal clouds, awaiting its turn.

The ferry jolted against the waves as it slowly reversed from Mornington Pier. Kate flinched in shock as Tilly's hand shot out to grip the back of the chair beside her for balance. Attempting to regain her footing, Tilly glared down at her outstretched hand that held a takeaway cup. Black tea had leapt from the mouth of the cup and onto her thumb.

Tilly's gaze flickered from her hand to Kate's stare. "May I sit with you?" she asked, so softly that Kate could barely hear her over the noise of the engine and the storm.

Kate nodded. "Yeah," she said, her voice husky from so little sleep. "'Course."

Sinking into the seat beside her, Tilly crossed her legs. Kate tried not to stare as Tilly lifted her wrist to her mouth and kissed the droplets of tea from her hand. "It's gloomy today," Tilly murmured.

"Mmm."

"And rough."

"Won't notice it once he picks up speed."

God, can we open a window in here? The ferry was stuffy with humidity and Kate felt sticky, sickly.

"Where did you go last night, Kate?"

Kate picked at the corrugated cardboard sleeve of the cappuccino from the Mornington Pier café. "Nowhere. I just walked around."

"All night?"

"If you're asking if I saw Elodie, I didn't. I just walked around." There had been a visit to a bar around two thirty, but Tilly didn't need to know about that.

"You must be exhausted."

Kate shrugged. She looked across the aisle. Lexi, Molly, and Grace talked quietly amongst themselves while Emma rested, eyes closed, hand pillowed between the vibrating window and her temple.

Tilly's hand that wasn't holding her coffee slipped between her crossed legs. "I'm so sorry, Kate. For last night..."

Kate took a sip of her coffee. "We're okay," she murmured.

"I'm not," she said, whisper soft. "I'm scared, Kate."

Kate looked at her, searching.

"I'm scared that I'm being used, that everybody can see it but me." Her green eyes bore into Kate's. "I'm scared to think of going to bed with him." She paused. "And I'm terrified that, deep down, I wasn't scared of that with you last night. Not in the slightest."

A potent mixture of satisfaction and relief stole the air from Kate's lungs.

Tilly's lips parted and for a moment, she struggled—not to find words, Kate thought, but to voice them. "I don't know who I am anymore." She searched Kate's gaze for an anchor. "I don't know what to do."

"I can't tell you what to do, Tilly," she said raggedly. *I can't tell you who you are.*

Tilly leaned across the armrest, so close Kate could feel her breath on her neck. "But you know me better than anybody."

Kate looked out at the water. Tilly's disappointment was palpable. It seemed Tilly was expecting some kind of pleasing, titillating response. If Tilly was looking to be seduced, she'd come to the wrong woman. There was nothing Kate wanted more than to have Tilly in her arms, but the threat of consequence rattled those fantasies close to death. Making love with Tilly…it could destroy them.

When we were in the bathroom…did you come in there because you wanted me to touch you? Or were you doing it because you think it's what I want? Because you're scared of losing me if we don't do this?

I'm scared that I'll lose you if we do and I'm scared that I'll lose you if we don't.

Hope had dissolved into fear in an instant. The mere thought of Tilly regretting her? *Resenting* her? The last thing on earth Kate wanted was to pressure Tilly when her judgment seemed as clouded as the midday sky.

"Kate, look at me."

"I'm tired, Til. Can we please just let it go?"

"Maybe you wouldn't be so tired if you'd been an adult and stayed and talked it through with me last night."

Kate turned. "You didn't want to *talk* after the ferry kiss."

Tilly's eyes gaze locked on hers. "You're the one who suggested we forget it."

"Because you pulled away. Because you *ran* away." *Because you're always running away.*

Kate's stomach somersaulted. Memory barrelled at her at full-speed—Tilly's horrified expression on the ferry, Tilly's hand on hers in the café, Tilly in the elevator, Tilly running from the bathroom. Tilly's uncertainty was a roller coaster. And here they were, halted at the steepest point of the track, suspended upside down, ready to surge full circle and claim that blood-rushing thrill, that mind-numbing charge. *Stuck.*

Kate shivered. "I think we need to put some space between us."

"Space?" Tilly's eyes brightened with unshed tears.

"What happened last night can't happen again." *Because it's breaking my heart.* "You have no idea what it is that you want and you're engaged to somebody else," she said bluntly. She looked out the window. Ahead, the hills of Lords were shadow-speckled. They were minutes from pulling up to the slipway. Lords Pier stretched out like a helping hand to welcome them home. "Until you figure out what you're feeling," Kate said woodenly, "I think maybe you should move into the convent for a while."

The suggestion fell heavily on the breath of air between them, and for a moment, Kate didn't dare pull her gaze from outside. It wasn't a good idea for Tilly to move out—Kate knew that. If Tilly moved from the cottage, there would be questions from the sisters, and worse, it would drive a wedge between them, only serve to sever the chord of friendship that had already frayed to expose a live wire.

Tilly's stare was hard, undeterred. "You've had that up your sleeve for a while, have you?"

Kate shook her head. "No."

The horn sounded, sudden and sharp. Across the ferry, the girls cackled as Emma pulled her head from the window in shock.

Tilly uncrossed her legs and shifted to the edge of the seat. Squaring her shoulders, she leaned closer. Clarity burned hotly in green. "Well I'm not going to do that," Tilly said. "I'm not moving anywhere."

Kate's gaze chased the sway of Tilly's hips as she crossed the aisle to the girls. *God, grant me the serenity to accept the things I cannot change, courage to change the things I can, and the wisdom to know the difference.*

"You're going for a walk?"

In the open doorway of the cottage, Kate stilled.

Tilly closed the fridge. "I'll come with you. Just let me get changed."

A ball of lead sank in her stomach, tugging on her resolve as she watched Tilly hurry at wiping the last plate. Going *without* Tilly was the whole point of going. Truly, a run was the last thing she felt like after her sleepless night wandering Melbourne. But getting out of the cottage for an hour or so was a break from Tilly. Earlier in the night, when Tilly had stepped into her office and insisted she stop marking and come back to the cottage for dinner, Kate had given in, sat through perhaps the most uncomfortable dinner of her life for politeness' sake. What were they supposed to do now? Sit and plait each other's hair in front of the TV? It was only nine. Even though she was exhausted, she couldn't go to bed—she had checks in an hour. She adjusted her glasses. "I, um, I think maybe I should just go by myself."

Tilly's face fell. "Oh. I get it. I won't bother you again." She turned back to the sink, but after a moment, she spun. "*You* kissed *me*, Kate. *You* started this." Her stare was heavy. "Why *did* you kiss me?"

Why? *Because I wanted to. Because I've always wanted to. Because I love you.*

Kate's silence was met with a shrug, a scoff. "Guess I'm just not worth the trouble, huh?" Tilly drew the dishrag through her hands and dropped her gaze to the floor. "The confused straight girl still isn't really worth it?"

Kate swallowed as Tilly's bottom lip disappeared between her teeth. "I know gay people," Tilly said. "Lesbians. I've heard the way they talk about girls like me—they don't sleep with straight girls, don't want anything to do with us."

Eyes boring into Tilly's, Kate did her level best not to betray the sadness that gripped her at the suggestion. She had keep this torch burning for Tilly for *years*. If Tilly truly believed that Kate would throw it all away on an attitude so ridiculous, she obviously had no idea just how invested Kate was. And that…that was devastating.

"You think I want to put space between us because I'm…what? Because I'm arrogant?" The moment pulsed. "Is that what you really think?"

Tilly refused to meet her eye. She gripped the back of a kitchen chair. "I don't know what to think any more, Kate."

It was borderline offensive—for somebody to know her so well and think so little of her. Kate's grip tightened on the edge of the door. "Well when you figure it out, you know where to find me." Carefully, she closed the door behind her.

Wet, sandy gravel spat at her ankles as she started down the road, heartache swimming through her veins like poison. In the quiet of her heart, she knew she was being selfish—she wasn't avoiding Tilly simply because she didn't want to pressure her, or because she respected her engagement. There was more to it. In the hotel room, on the ferry, Tilly had made no suggestion that she had any intention of leaving Declan. To let it go any further and then lose Tilly? Kate wasn't so sure she'd ever get over it. What they shared wasn't something to be experimented with. What they had was becoming all or nothing, and without Tilly giving her any kind of hope for a future, *nothing* was quickly proving to be the safer option.

She rounded the steep track. As much as she despised Declan, as poorly as he treated Tilly, it did nothing to suppress the fact that what she was doing with Tilly was deceitful and illicit. Tilly had made a commitment to another person, and this…it felt like an affair.

Frustration bloomed in her chest, spread its wings between her ribs. Tilly thought she didn't care enough to fight for her? Screw that, Kate thought as she navigated the sharp turn down to the pier. Tilly needed to learn to fight for herself.

Kate yawned loudly as she slid onto a long wooden bench in the middle of the dining hall and dropped Molly's script onto the table. She sipped at her steaming mug of coffee. If there was one advantage to waking at the crack of dawn to help Molly edit her play, it was that she hadn't had to face Tilly.

"It's so weird to be in here without anybody else," Molly said as she climbed onto the bench opposite Kate, a slice of toast pinched between her fingertips. She licked strawberry jam from her fingertips. "Thanks again for helping me with this."

Kate turned the pages of Molly's script—the final draft before she left for Scotland at the end of the month. "Don't sweat it."

"I know, but you've edited it for me five hundred times and you got up so early to do this."

"It's fine, Mol."

"It's just that I'm kind of in a rush at this point. I have to print twelve copies to hand out when we start the program and I need to get them bound and everything on Monday afternoon. Thank God it's a long weekend and I have the staff development day to write. I really only have this weekend to finish."

Thinking, Kate tapped the pencil against the pages. "I'm a bit swamped this afternoon with phone calls so I won't be able to get it back to you before you get the ferry back. Is it okay if I scan the pages and send it to you tomorrow morning?"

"Yeah, of course, that'd be great," Molly said. "Or, I mean, are you going to Tilly's engagement party Sunday night?"

Kate's eyes snapped up.

"I'm staying at my cousin's in Mornington this weekend instead of going all the way home, and my cousin's going to the party," Molly explained. "You could just give it to her, save you the hassle of scanning thirty-eight pages…"

Kate pushed her glasses to the top of her head and rubbed at the bridge of her nose. "Your...your cousin was invited to that?"

"Yeah. And her husband."

Kate's stomach hardened. Molly's older cousin, who simply worked in the vicarage, had scored an invite? Tilly had said it was just a small dinner with Declan's family. "No," she said. "I'm not going."

"Oh."

Mind racing, Kate lowered her glasses. She turned the page.

"He's a lot older than her," Molly said.

"Mol...I can't discuss them with you."

"Right. Sorry. I didn't mean it in a bad way. It's just that Tilly's so young and sweet and I mean, I've only met him twice, but he seems kind of...domineering. With my cousin, anyway. She's always having a bitch about how he likes things *his way* in the office, how he gets cranky when she organises things the way she used to when the old vicar was there."

Kate fixed her with a look.

"Sorry," Molly said, sheepish. "I'll stop talking."

Kate cleared her throat. "That's all right." She scribbled a correction above a typo.

"I'm sorry," Molly said again. "My head is kind of all over the place right now with this script. I've been so nervous I can barely eat and I think my blood sugar is low."

It left Molly's lips disguised as a joke, but it reached Kate's ears as a cry for help. She looked up, brows knitted. "Are you okay, Mol?"

Molly's lips pursed and Kate watched as a veil of deflection clouded her gaze. "Yeah, I'm fine."

Kate held her gaze for a moment before she looked back to the work before her. "You'd come to me if you weren't?" Kate asked, her eyes scanning Molly's words. "Right?"

Molly picked up her pen and scribbled a correction between the double-spaced lines of the new edits. "Right," she murmured.

Tortured by the knowledge that Tilly's engagement party was that coming weekend, Friday passed slowly for Kate. The conversation with Molly about the party played on her mind until the evening, when it got the better of her.

"Making tea at this hour," she murmured, joining Tilly at the kitchen counter. "I'm surprised you're still up."

Tilly looked at her strangely. "It's only quarter past ten."

Kate reached for a glass and filled it at the tap. She looked out the kitchen window at the illuminated statue on the hill. "I just mean, you know, you're probably exhausted. You probably have a lot to organise before your engagement party on Sunday."

Tilly was quiet.

"The sisters haven't asked me to drive them over to Declan's—that's where Molly tells me your party is—so I figured they weren't invited either. I guess that's probably for the best—it would be pretty awkward for Sister Ellie after the position he put her in. Probably not her idea of a *party*—"

"It's not a party. It's a small dinner."

"Can't be *that* small—Molly's cousin is going."

Tilly dunked her tea bag slowly. "I didn't think you'd be interested, considering the way you feel about him."

There was more to it than Tilly's awareness that she couldn't stand Declan. To not invite Kate was one thing, but Sister Ruth? With Sister Hattie's death, Sister Ruth was the closest person to family Tilly had left. Would there be anybody there with whom she had shared more than a handful of polite hellos?

Tilly reached for the sugar. "And about Sister Ellie…I spoke to Declan this morning about his mission trip to Vanuatu," she said. "He's not even certain that he's going. The whole thing was blown out of proportion." There was a bitter edge to her tone. "So it's all fine. Everything's fine."

"Right." *Like hell it is.*

Kate slipped into the bathroom. She was vigorously washing her face when there was a knock at the cottage door. Moments later, Tilly called her name.

Towelling her neck dry, she stepped out to find Molly hovering just inside the front door.

"I need to talk to you."

Kate started. "Mol, what on earth are you doing back here?"

"I needed to speak to you so I took the ferry from Mornington." As Molly's eyes grew wide, worry struck Kate. "I think I'm about to have a panic attack."

Instantly, Kate reached out and curled a hand around Molly's elbow. "Come over here and sit."

Together, the two of them sat on the edge of the lounge. For a long moment, Molly was silent as she pulled at the sleeves of her jumper. "I can't go to Edinburgh," she said.

The room stilled. This is what Kate had been anticipating for months. "Yes," she said. "You *can*."

Molly shook her head. "I can't." Her eyes welled. Instantly, she pressed the cuffs of her jumper to her eyes. "I've been texting with the girl from Sydney who won and I sent her my play and she sent me hers and…mine is *so fucking shit*."

Sinking back into the lounge, Kate sighed. "It's not, Mol. It's brilliant." She stole a look at Tilly. Across the room, her grip was tight on the back of the recliner. *A little help here?*

"Molly," Tilly started, taking a seat on the recliner, "We've both read your play. It's incredible." She clasped her hands, emphasised each word with a gentle shake. "*And you were selected.*"

Molly pulled her hands from her face. Her eyes were red-rimmed, the sleeves of her jumper darkened with tears. "But hers is so much better," she ground out. Her glassy gaze fixed on the small nativity scene Tilly had set up beside the television. "I don't think I can do this."

Before Kate could speak, Tilly stepped in. "You don't have to do anything you don't want to, Molly."

Kate's eyes snapped up. "Don't tell her that!"

"Kate, she's almost an adult. She can make her own decisions."

"Til, she wants this. You don't know her." God, it was *exasperating*. Where the hell did Tilly get off saying something like that? Letting an anxious, impressionable teenager think it was okay to keep that mindset? She turned back to Molly. "I'm not going to let you give up on this just because it's hard, not when you've come so far. You're going."

Tears slipped over Molly's cheeks as she dropped her head. "I'm going to be the shittiest writer there. I am. I mean, what if they only chose me because I'm the token Aboriginal?" she whispered.

Kate sat forward, elbows on her knees as she ducked her head to catch Molly's eye. "I assure you, that is *not* true. And about the writing thing? Look, I hate to be the bearer of bad news, but hear me when I say this: there's always going to be somebody in a room who is better than you in some way. It's how we grow—how we improve and become better learners, better *people*. You might get there and, okay, sure there'll be more criticism for some more than others, but you'll be in the smartest of company, and that's going to *make* you better. You're not there to blow your own trumpet. Like every other kid in the room, you're there to be better. To learn. And let me tell you, you're going to teach some other kid something, Mol, because you're just so clever." She paused. "But that's not the hard part, is it?"

Molly pulled her hands away from her face and locked eyes with Kate.

"It's the getting there," Kate guessed.

Visibly swallowing, Molly nodded. Her voice was a whisper. "I keep think about saying goodbye to Mum at the airport and I think I'm going to have a heart attack."

In her peripheral vision, Kate watched as Tilly tucked her legs beneath herself. Kate gripped Molly's shoulder gently. "So you ugly-cry in the Qantas terminal? So what? You and half the country."

That pulled a small smile to Molly's lips.

"It's two weeks," Kate continued. "You go there, you learn, and you come home a better writer knowing that you've done this for yourself, that you've given yourself this once-in-a-lifetime chance. All you have to do is get on that plane, Mol. Once you've got your bum in the seat, you'll be fine. I *promise*."

Conflict flickered across Molly's face as Kate's words took effect. Finally, she pulled her gaze from the floor and met Kate's stare. "Can you come to the airport too?"

CHAPTER SEVENTEEN

She'd almost forgotten.

It wasn't until the car ferry was docking at Mornington and they were waiting to disembark that a radio advertisement for a concert presale jogged her memory. Sitting forward in the driver's seat, Kate turned down the radio.

As silence settled, the tension they'd entertained for the past few days sharpened. Tilly pulled her attention from watching the current of rainwater drip from the steep metal staircase that led to the passenger cabin above. She fixed her gaze on Kate. "Is something the matter?" she asked hesitantly.

Well, if we're being completely honest with each other, tonight you're celebrating your engagement to somebody else—so everything's turned to shit. Kate shook her head. "Everything's good. I just…I remembered that I have something for you."

Tilly's lips slipped into a thin line. She pushed a strand of hair behind her ear. "Oh," she said nervously. "You do?"

Kate rolled down her window. The humidity swept into the van with a deafening roll of thunder. "Jesus," she murmured lowly as the sky's roar groaned on and on. The first early morning storm had brought rain so torrential that it had made it impossible for Tilly and the sisters to make it to the mainland for Sunday morning mass. Finally, at ten thirty, the flooded dip in the island road had cleared, making it possible for Kate to navigate the van down to the slipway. Now the storm was finding its voice all over again.

She leaned across the car to open the glove box. The sky growled loudly as her wrist brushed Tilly's knee. "Sorry."

"That's okay."

She felt into the corner of the glove box. Turning her head, she met Tilly's curious stare. "Close your eyes and hold out your hands."

As Tilly's eyes slipped closed, she took a moment to study her face, the way her features tensed for a second as Kate clicked the glove box closed.

Careful to keep the face of the pendant turned up, she lowered the sterling silver chain into Tilly's cupped hands. "Okay," she said. "You can open them."

Silent, Tilly stared down at the pendant of St. Lucy—the gift she'd passed on to Kate at their graduation. It had once been Tilly's favourite keepsake, given to Tilly at her confirmation when she'd chosen St. Lucy as her patron saint. "I can't accept this," Kate had said at the time. *But you have to, Kate—it's all I have to give you.*

Tilly's brow furrowed. "I can't accept this," she whispered.

"Sure, you can. It's yours."

Tilly's teeth sank into her bottom lip.

A flash of lightning lit the dark, morning sky. Kate wet her lips. "I was at Mum's the other weekend and I remembered I still had it in my old trinket box." Her voice dropped to a whisper. "And I know today's her feast day, so…"

Tilly looked up, eyes wide and glossy. "I think I'm going to cry," she whispered.

Oh, God.

Kate drew a deep breath. "I didn't want to upset you."

"I know." She paused. "I'm sorry. It's just that I've hated this week, feeling this distance between us…I mean yesterday you spent all day in your office avoiding me, and I thought you couldn't stand to look at me…and now you go and do something sweet like this…"

Heat rose to Kate's cheeks, partially fogging her glasses. Tilly tipped her head back and blinked away tears, swiping hastily beneath her eyes. Quickly, Kate opened the glove box for a Kleenex.

"Thank you," Tilly whispered as she took the tissue from Kate and dabbed at the corner of her eyes. She leaned forward and slipped the pendant back into the glove box. "You'll keep it there for me?" she said. "Lily has an obsession with jewellery at the moment and I couldn't stand it if the chain snapped…"

Throat growing tight, Kate nodded. "Yeah, sure. I'll just leave it there." The last thing she wanted to talk about was Tilly's future stepdaughter. "So…ten o'clock ferry tonight? Don't worry about asking him to drop you down to the dock. I'll swing by and pick you up on my way back from Mum's."

Tilly hesitated.

Kate arched a brow. "What is it?"

Tilly licked her lips. "Declan's invited me to stay in his guest room. I'm…I'm not coming back on the ten o'clock."

Jealousy sank in her stomach like a hot ball of lead. "Oh."

"Sorry. I thought you would have assumed when you saw my bag…"

Kate glanced down at the larger handbag beside Tilly's feet. A devilish pressure grew in her chest. "Right. Yeah. No. I didn't realise."

Their eyes locked.

What could she possibly say? *Are you sure you want to do this?* was too loaded, too weighted with memories of stolen glances in hotel rooms, of almost-declarations in kitchens. Her stomach rolled. "Til?"

"Yes?"

"Please don't use *Hallelujah* as a wedding song."

Tilly stiffened slightly. "I—"

"That's for us. It's our song, okay?"

Tilly nodded. "Okay," she whispered.

Averting her eyes, Kate inhaled deeply. "Well…I'll be coming home on the last ferry. You have your phone." *If you need me.*

Wide-eyed, Tilly nodded.

The car ramp screeched its way down to meet the slipway. Last on the ferry, they were first to reverse off. From the driver's seat, Kate could see Declan's car was already waiting there for Tilly.

Kate cleared her throat. "You ready?" she asked.

Tilly nodded.

At Colin's instruction, Kate started the engine.

A crowd was quickly gathering, grinning in amusement as Kate called her niece's name for a third time to no avail. Reclined peacefully on the racing car bed of the display bedroom, Karlie's eyes were closed, one arm bent above her head as she feigned sleep.

"Karlie, *please*."

Karlie's eyes fluttered lightly, barely. Kate knew the five-year-old well enough to recognise the ever-so-slight hollowing of her cheeks for a suppressed grin.

"This is the last time I'm going to ask, Karlie."

An elderly woman chuckled.

Great, Kate thought, her cheeks heating with embarrassment. *Just what I need—a performance in the heart of Ikea.* She looked past the gathered group. Where the hell had her sister wandered off to?

"Better this than a full-blown tantrum," the elderly woman murmured to Kate.

Kate turned to look at her. The frizzy mass of her auburn hair was held back by two alligator clips pinned above each ear. There was something about her that smelled so familiar, too light to be perfume, stronger than fabric softener... Realisation dawned. Sister Hattie's powder. She swallowed. "To be honest," she told the stranger as they both watched Karlie, "I've never seen her have a tantrum. She's a pretty good kid."

The woman laughed. "Then I take it she's not yours?"

Smiling, Kate shook her head. "She's my niece."

"I was going to say, you don't look alike."

"She's going to be a big sister next month," Kate found herself saying. "We're not too sure how that's going to go."

"Have faith," the woman said playfully, "I think she'll enjoy having an audience of her own."

"You're not far off." In her "sleep," Karlie tossed and turned, earning herself a laugh from her spectators. Kate rolled her eyes. "Excuse me."

She crossed the room and scooped Karlie up.

Karlie groaned. "*All right.*"

"Do I need to carry you like a baby or can you walk yourself, Juliet?"

"Who's Juliet?" Karlie asked as Kate planted her on her feet. She took Karlie's tiny hand in her own and dragged her down the arrowed aisle.

They took a left, then a right, and found the nursery rooms. Leaning against a cot, Beccy looked up from an instruction manual. "What took you so long?" she huffed.

"Sleeping Beauty decided to take a nap." Brows furrowing, Kate plucked the pamphlet from Beccy's hands. She looked between the model on paper and the display item. "You're not actually considering this one, are you?"

"No," Beccy said sarcastically. "I just thought I'd catch up on some light reading while I had a moment to myself to think."

"No," Kate said decidedly. "You're not getting this one. It's not strong enough. Get that hard timber one over there."

"The one in the corner?"

Kate nodded.

"No. I like this one. Besides," she added, like an afterthought, "this one is half the price."

"Yeah, because it'll last half the time. Bec, this one is crap. The side doesn't even lower."

"I didn't even use the drop-down side on the old one for Karl. You don't know everything, Kate, and you certainly don't know anything about babies."

"Did I say I knew everything? Honestly, I can't believe you just got rid of Karlie's cot."

"I didn't *get rid* of it, I gave it to my best friend."

"So get her to give it back."

"Her bub is only thirteen months—she's still using it."

"You know you can just say her kid is a year old, right?"

Karlie sighed and crouched low in a squat, elbows rested on her knees, head cradled in her palms. "Can you stop fighting so we can go and get meatballs upstairs?"

Kate pulled her niece to her feet, spun her beneath her hand like a ballerina. "Yes, yes, yes we can," she said, and Karlie threw her head back with a chuckle as she tried to find her balance on the spot. She turned to Beccy. "Let's go, Bec. You can tell me all the reasons why I'm wrong on our way down to the warehouse to pick up the one in the corner, okay?"

Beccy smoothed a hand over her protruding belly. "Honestly, I don't know how Tilly lives with you. You're insufferable."

Ten minutes later, they were down in the warehouse, finally settling on the more expensive cot.

Kate loaded the three flatpacks into the trolley and, much to her niece's delight, lifted Karlie up to sit atop the secured tower.

"I really can't afford this," Beccy argued.

"You don't have to—it's on me."

Eyes widening, Beccy shook her head. "No, it's not."

"Bec, can you just leave your pride behind here in Section B, Aisle Six? Please?"

Beccy fixed her with a glare. "Fine," she huffed as Kate pushed the trolley—and Karlie—toward the checkout. "But I'll pay you back over the next few months. And I'll pass it on when you have kids."

After dropping Tilly off with her ready-made family that morning, Beccy's innocent comment hit like a jab at Kate's already-bruised heart. She laughed it off. "You better pass it on, considering I'm the one who's going to build it."

"Please, I think I can assemble a flat pack," Beccy said. "I don't need your help."

As it turned out, Beccy *did* need her help. And that was how Kate found herself spending the afternoon in her childhood bedroom, sliding A into B and G into H and having a few tantrums of her own. After dinner, she returned to the nursery with Karlie to finish the job. "When my baby sister gets here at Christmas," Karlie had said, "I want to tell her I built it for her all by myself."

"Want a cuppa?"

Kate looked up from teaching Karlie how to work the Allen key to find her mother, Susan, in the doorway. "I'd love one."

"I'd love one, too," Karlie said, shifting in Kate's lap where she'd been plonked for the better half of twenty minutes. Kate grinned at Susan as she readjusted her niece in her lap. Karlie was tiny for her age, but Kate was halfway to pins and needles.

Susan bent low to pick up the empty juice cup Karlie had left behind at lunch. "Why don't you stay the night? No point rushing back to Lords," she said. "Unless Tilly's waiting, *of course*."

"What's that supposed to mean?"

"What's *what* supposed to mean?"

"That comment, about Tilly. That '*of course*'…"

Susan quirked an eyebrow. "I didn't mean anything. I'm just suggesting that, if you don't have anybody waiting on you, you might as well stay the night. These days, you don't stay over half as much as you used to and we miss having you."

Kate licked her lips. Her mother was right. There wasn't any point in going back to Lords. Staying at her mother's was a much better option than spending the night alone in the cottage consumed by thoughts of Tilly. With the next day being a staff development day for the following year, as a temporary teacher who wouldn't be returning next year, Kate—like Tilly—had the day off. She didn't have to be at Mornington until six on Monday evening. Who knew, maybe Tilly wouldn't even be home before then.

She hadn't told anyone about the engagement party—not even Beccy. What would it imply to her family to know she wasn't invited? Her mother would certainly want to know what that was about, and Kate didn't have the confidence to go over it with anybody. What would her family think of her if they knew that her relationship with Tilly was a whole lot less innocent than it seemed? *Hey Mum, I'm having an emotional affair with the woman who used to be my best friend. You know, the girl who was fixated on becoming a nun? Tilly, yes, that's right. Tilly who's engaged to a widowed Anglican vicar in Mornington.*

"Okay," she said simply. "I'll stay."

"Good. I'll change the pullout."

Kate looked across the carpet to where a forgotten pile of screws lay beside her phone and wallet.

She picked up the instruction manual. "Karls, can you go over there and grab me a screw that looks like this?"

Karlie squinted at the page. "Okay."

She bit back a groan as Karlie climbed out of her lap, seizing the opportunity to stretch her legs. *Hallelujah, praise be to Jesus...*

"Aunty Kate?"

"Yeah, baby?"

"Your phone is flashing."

Tilly and Declan stood beneath the porch light, deep in conversation, but as Kate drew to a stop, they glanced toward the van.

The narrow street was so packed with visitors that Kate was left with no option but to double park. Buzzing with the awareness that she was being watched from the porch, Kate got out, walked around the van and leaned back against the passenger door. Her sneakers sank into the damp grass of the nature strip. She wanted to feel pity for Tilly, really, she did, but Tilly's text kept racing through her mind, filling her with a sense of ungodly relief. *Kate, I need you to come and get me, please.*

Silhouettes moved inside the front room window and Kate could hear the laughter, the chatter of the guests who had gathered to celebrate. A cold shiver passed across Kate's skin, pricked the hairs on her bare arms as she watched Declan reach out and rest his hand on Tilly's upper arm. He slid Tilly's large handbag off her shoulder and a few words were exchanged as Tilly insisted on carrying it, much to his protest.

With Declan falling a few hesitant steps behind her, Tilly—sans bag—started down the cobblestone path.

Kate pushed off the van, palms sweaty. As Tilly stepped through Declan's front gate, their eyes met. Nervously, Tilly pushed a strand of hair behind her ear. "I'm fine," she said as she drew closer, Declan out of earshot. "Don't say anything about this to him, please," she breathed in a rush.

Kate opened the passenger door for her. "I won't," she whispered.

Tilly didn't even give her a chance to close the door, just reached for the interior handle and pulled it shut with a bang.

In surprise, Kate blinked twice.

"Kate."

She pivoted. Standing before her with Tilly's bag outstretched in his grip, Declan's eyes held a strange focus.

Kate wiped her palms on the back pocket of her jeans and accepted the bag. But he held on, waiting to let go until she dared meet the richness of his glare. A silent acknowledgment charged between them, muffled like voices down a telephone line—whether or not Tilly thought she *wanted* to be married, she wasn't ready, and he knew it. And yet here he was, letting Tilly go ahead with something that clearly brought her distress.

"Drive safely," he said.

Kate nodded.

As Kate pulled the van away from the gutter, Tilly wound down her window.

Biting her tongue, she continued down the vicarage's street and onto the main road.

"You'll need to change lanes here," Tilly said. "Just up ahead…"

"I know."

"Just here," Tilly noted.

"Yep. Been here before."

"Right."

Silence settled. Kate adjusted her glasses. "Can I ask what happened?" she said softly.

"Nothing happened." Tilly paused. "I just…"

The need to know crawled beneath her skin, desperate. "You what?"

Tilly sighed. "I had a panic attack in his bathroom before dinner."

As Kate paused at a stop sign, her head whipped around. "You did? Are you okay?"

"I'm fine." Tilly crossed her legs. "It was hours ago, don't worry."

"Well I *am* worried."

"Well *don't be*." Tilly brought a hand to her face and covered her eyes. She wasn't crying, no, but from the shake of her head, Kate could tell that she was frustrated. With herself? Declan? … Kate? Tilly groaned softly and heat pooled low in Kate's belly at the sound.

Eventually, Tilly sighed. "You think I'm ridiculous."

The indicator ticked. "I'm not thinking anything, Tilly."

"Of course you are. You're always thinking. You think louder than anybody I've ever known."

She sighed. "I don't want to argue with you."

Tilly rested an arm against the window ledge and watched the houses as they drove by. "I'm not arguing. I'd just like to know what you're thinking, Kate. That's all…"

No, she thought, you really don't. She reached forward and turned the radio up, and for the next ten minutes, neither said a word.

"It's three minutes to ten," Tilly said quietly as Kate made a left onto Mornington Peninsula Road. "We're going to miss the boat."

No analogy was better fitting, Kate thought. They'd always be the pair who missed the boat.

CHAPTER EIGHTEEN

"I couldn't do it," Tilly called down the pier. "I couldn't stay in his house."

Kate's long, exasperated groan was swallowed by the sound of the waves crashing against the shore, against the pilings of the pier. Running a hand through her hair, she stared out into the dark void of Port Phillip Bay. The lights had gone out over on Lords, the dim lights of East Island hidden behind it. And that goddamn ferry, already so far away. A few minutes earlier and they would have made it. What was she supposed to do now? Take Tilly back to her mother's house?

Tilly's heels clomped loudly down the pier, taunting. Closer. Closer still. Kate's body hummed dangerously. Swiftly, Kate pivoted, setting her hot gaze on Tilly. At Kate's stare, Tilly halted midstep.

Kate swallowed harshly. "I don't want to patronise you but I don't think you understand just how close we are to making a very, very bad decision." The words escaped her in a rush. "If you want to keep your promise to him, then you need to just go back to the van and give me a minute here to just cool—"

"I haven't made a promise yet."

Kate's eyes slipped closed for a second. *Yet.* What part of that statement did Tilly think Kate would find helpful?

When Kate's eyes opened, Tilly stepped forward. Kate raised a hand. "Don't."

"It wouldn't be a mistake."

"I never said it would be a mistake."

"A *bad decision.* You said it would be a bad decision."

"It would be."

"Why?"

"Because you're straight, Til."

"But what if I'm not?" Tilly asked shakily. "I want you the way you want me."

"Tilly. Don't."

"I see the way you look at me," she said, moving closer. "You think I don't see it but I do. You've been looking at me that way for months. Since the day I got here. In the convent kitchen, when I was telling the sisters about Declan…you were just staring at me like…like…"

Kate's breath hitched. "Like what?"

At the sight of Tilly's unfaltering gaze, heat crawled beneath her skin. "Like you loved me."

Cheeks burning, Kate swiped her hands over her face in frustration. The handle she had on her resolve was wavering, and with every ardent comment from Tilly, like the tide, her will to resist slipped further away. They were teetering on the edge and it wouldn't take much to lay their truth bare. Any further and they couldn't go back.

Tilly reached out, smoothed her fingers across Kate's cheek. Instantly, the hairs stood on the back of her neck. "It's always been so easy for me—to remain abstinent, to not give in. But I've never been tested—not really." Kate's eyes slammed closed. A thumb traced Kate's bottom lip, tentative, then firmer. "But now I can't go a day without thinking about what your body feels like. The way you'd love me."

Kate opened her eyes to find Tilly's hooded, her focus dropped to watch the pad of her thumb pull at the fullness of Kate's lip. Suddenly, she looked up. Their eyes caught. "I look at him and I feel nothing. I look at you and I feel like my skin is on fire."

Christ. "You're scared. March is getting closer and you're scared."

Withdrawing her touch from Kate's mouth, Tilly shook her head. "I've felt like this since that night on the ferry. No, before that. Sitting under the jacaranda in that backyard in St. Kilda." She paused, drew a deep breath. "Kate, I think I've felt like this since we were sixteen." She dug her palm between her breasts, rubbed it there as though she could roll away the ache. "I am so certain in my heart and it terrifies me."

Gently, Kate drew Tilly to her by the waist. The press of Tilly's hips against her own was maddening. As their breath mingled, desperation erupted inside her. She bunched the thin cotton of Tilly's dress in her hands. "You're marrying somebody else," she whispered.

Long, slim fingers smoothed the collar of Kate's shirt, tracked low until they twitched against the top of her breasts. "I have never felt more married to somebody in my heart than I do to you."

The breath caught in Kate's throat. "The thought of you with him…it makes me feel like I'm dying—"

"Kiss me?"

Kate captured her lips.

Tilly's hands were manic—on her neck, locked in her collarbone, flattened on her breastbone. As Tilly licked into her mouth, Kate burned with the raw desire to pleasure her. No longer did she care about holding back, about scaring Tilly with the extent of her lust. Their time was *now.*

Kate drew Tilly hard against her body until there wasn't a breath of space between them. Her heartbeat fired against Tilly's chest as Tilly's fingers raked into her hair roughly, her other hand clutching at the back of her plaid shirt.

When her mouth found the pulse in Tilly's neck, Tilly pulled back. Her eyes were hooded, swollen lips parted as she fought for breath. "I want you to take me somewhere," she whispered. "*Now.*"

Mornington Peninsula Cabins and Trailer Park wasn't exactly the Hilton. It was, however, their only option within a ten-kilometre radius. More hostel than vacation park, Kate had stayed in the cabins a few times when she'd pushed her luck and missed the last boat. Twenty-five dollars a night wasn't too much to ask for a single bunk bed in a shared cabin for four. Sometimes, if she was lucky, nobody would show after ten and she'd end up with an entire cabin to herself. Tonight, if she was able, she'd ensure that was the case.

Kate stepped into the reception cabin, Tilly close at her heels. The woman behind the counter stubbed her cigarette into an ashtray beside the keyboard. "Missed the ten o'clock, did ya? There's nobody in Six or Two at the moment, but a few backpackers called through earlier so I can't guarantee they won't show up to bunk with ya—"

"We'll rent an entire cabin, please," Kate said. "Whichever one is without bunks if it's possible."

She looked down at Kate's credit card on the counter, and then up.

"You want a whole cabin?" she clarified. "With a double bed?"

"Yes, please."

Her gaze flickered between Tilly and Kate, and slowly, the corners of her lips twitched. "Oh." With a wrinkled hand, she slid the credit card across the counter and swiped it off the edge like a poker player. "PayPass okay?"

Kate nodded.

She pressed Kate's card against the machine. As they waited for the beep of approval, the woman set her gaze on Tilly. "Aren't you the one engaged to the vicar at St. Vincent's?" Her eyes narrowed as she looked down at Tilly's hand.

Tilly stiffened beside her. "Yes," she said softly.

She looked between them. "Right…" She slid a keychain across the counter to Kate. "Cabin Twelve. Aircon's broken, but the windows are open. Fridge conked out around five this arvo, but there's a vending machine between cabins nine and ten."

"That's fine," Kate said.

The track to Cabin Twelve was dark, the short garden lanterns doing little more than outlining the winding path. Kate took Tilly's hand in hers again. They'd only let go in reception, and a small part of Kate worried that it had broken the spell, that the tension had softened. Was Tilly having second thoughts? Just as Kate was about to ask if they were moving too fast, Tilly linked their fingers and squeezed, pressed her body tight against Kate's side. They took a right at Cabin Eight and started up the hill.

Past Cabin Nine, the path grew sandier. Tilly tugged on her hand. "I need to take off my heels," she said, her voice raspy the way it always was after a full day of teaching. She reached low, but Kate stopped her, bending to unstrap each shoe. Wordlessly instructing Tilly to lift her leg, she smoothed a hand up under the hem of Tilly's long skirt and innocently palmed her calf muscle. At the brush of Kate's hand against her bare skin, Tilly made a noise, barely audible over the crashing of the waves down below at the cliffs, and a deep heat curled low in Kate's belly. *Fuck.* She pressed her forehead to Tilly's thigh and swallowed. She pulled herself to her feet. "Come on," she ground out.

Inside Cabin Twelve, Kate lowered Tilly's shoes to the mat. When Tilly stepped over the threshold, Kate locked the door quietly.

She crossed the room and turned on the bedside lamp, watched as Tilly looked around the outdated cabin. Worryingly, the comforter looked to be from the nineties, and worse, its godawful floral print matched the faded art piece hanging above the bed. On the bedside table, an old clock radio blared red digits. Outside, somewhere down below, waves chased into the bay from the Bass Strait and crashed wildly and loudly against the cliff face. Kate fiddled with rolling down the blinds, closing them. "I hope this is okay," she murmured.

"It's fine."

In the soft glow, their eyes met. With the windows open, the blinds fluttered.

Tilly licked her lips. "It smells like the sea," she whispered.

Kate's heart pounded. "Yeah." Stopping at the end of the bed, a few feet between them, she reached behind herself and wrapped her fingers around the wrought iron rungs of the end frame. "We don't have to do anything, Til," she said slowly. "I know you're... waiting until marriage. We can wait together," she said breathily, her gaze dropping to her bare feet. "I'll wait for you."

As the levity of Kate's proclamation settled upon the quietness of the cabin, Tilly's eyes locked on hers. Tilly slid the ring off her finger and set it on the low table by the door. "I don't want to wait," she whispered.

Tilly set her eyes on her. Kate watched, enraptured, as Tilly touched a hand to the top button of her dress. Slowly, she flicked the buttons open until she reached the tie at her waist. As her hands fell to her sides, the top of the dress gaped, revealing a long strip of creamy skin between her breasts.

Kate's pulse slowed as she set eyes on the hint of white lace between Tilly's breasts. She gripped the base of the bed. "You need to tell me exactly what you want," she husked. As much as she was desperate to have Tilly writhing beneath her *now*, control belonged to Tilly and only Tilly. If Tilly regretted this in the light of day, Kate wouldn't be able to live with herself.

Tilly's chest rose and fell with sharp breaths. Her eyes pleaded.

Feeling like her feet were made of lead, Kate pushed forward. With her index finger she brushed her knuckle lightly against Tilly's sternum. She stopped the caress of her finger at Tilly's diaphragm, her nail scratching ever-so lightly against hot, smooth skin she wanted to map with her mouth. Tilly shuddered, her muscles drawing back at the sensitive touch.

A ripple passed through the room. "What do you want?" Kate whispered.

"I want you to undress me."

"And?"

"And I want you to touch me."

Kate reached out and took Tilly's face in her hands. "I'm going to take care of you, okay?" She pressed her forehead against Tilly's. "I'm going to make you feel so good, I swear to you—"

Tilly captured her lips in a bruising kiss. In her arms, Tilly was like a woman possessed. Her lips grew eager, her kiss bold, and a bolt of need gripped Kate. She pulled Tilly against her, palmed her behind with a desperate grip. God, she was about to come out of her skin. Nothing would ever be as beautiful as this. Nothing would ever compare to the two of them together, their history clawing at the walls, their bodies finally, *finally* fusing. When Kate moaned into her mouth, Tilly took her hand from kneading her hip and brought it to the tie at the small of her back.

"Yeah?" Kate gasped.

"*Yes.*"

She tugged.

As Tilly pushed the sleeves down, the dress fell over Tilly's slim hips to the floor. Kate dropped her gaze between them.

No slip. Underwear. White lace. Legs that went on forever. Pale skin, flat belly. A purple scar, no longer than an inch, that dipped from the crease of her belly button. Kate's throat tightened.

"This is the body that God gave me," Tilly said.

Kate's eyes snapped up. "And you were given a beautiful body," she avowed. The chain of Tilly's crucifix was rough against her tongue as she sucked at the dip of Tilly's collarbone. "God, Tilly, you're so *beautiful*."

"Really?" High-pitched, breathy.

"Are you kidding me?" Her hands warmed over Tilly's ribcage, the plane of her belly, the jut of her hip. "I've been dying to see you like this since we were sixteen."

Tilly gasped as Kate toyed with the lace band of her underwear.

All the years of pining and here they were, her heartbeat firing against Tilly's fingers as they worked frantically to unbutton Kate's shirt. Fourth button was enough, Kate decided, reaching down to yank it over her head as Tilly's hands shot to the button of Kate's jeans. "Help me," she rasped, hooded eyes locked on the swell of Kate's breasts.

Pushing Tilly's hands away, she pulled at the zipper and shoved denim to her ankles. Tilly's eyes grew wide. Unabashedly, Kate flicked the clasp of her own bra and let it fall. Taking Tilly's hands in hers, she slid them up her sides until Tilly's touch found purchase.

Her eyes snapped shut.

"You're so soft," Tilly whispered, her touch growing deliberate.

Kate cradled Tilly's face in her hands and tilted her head into the kiss. Her fingers threaded through the fine silk of Tilly's long hair, body pulsing with promise as Tilly's tongue slipped against hers. Groaning, she stepped out of her jeans.

Kate linked Tilly's arms around her neck and walked her backward, her fingertips slipping under the band of Tilly's bra. As Tilly whispered her name, the blinds rustled loudly in a gust of wind. Kate yanked the covers back and gently, pushing at Tilly's shoulders, urged her to lie down.

Straddling Tilly, Kate painted kisses over her chest to the line of her bra. Tilly's fingertips whispered up and down her spine as Kate kissed through thin lace, and lower, over the two matching scars on either side of her abdomen.

Seemingly too far gone to entertain modesty, Tilly closed her eyes and drifted her hands up Kate's sides to feel the fullness of her body. "I know how two women make love," she whispered.

Kate groaned, her chest growing tight at Tilly's show of determination. "Yeah?" Her tongue traced the curve of Tilly's ribcage. "You do?"

Hand raking into Kate's hair, Tilly gasped. "Yes."

Kate's mouth drifted lower. There were so many things to show her. So many beautiful, intimate things for them to share. *Slowly. Slowly.* She pulled back slightly, and suddenly, at the sight of the dark patch on Tilly's underwear, her heart skipped a beat. At the pull of want, her eyes slipped closed.

Pulse racing, she crawled up and buried her face in Tilly's neck. Her hands slid over Tilly's belly. "I'm crazy about you." Higher, to the band of her bra. "Can I take this off?"

Tilly arched from the bed to find the clasp at her back, and at once, Kate's hands were tugging the straps from her shoulders, flinging the garment to the floor. Holding herself above Tilly, she lowered her chest. Tilly dropped her gaze, her chin trembling as she watched their softness mould together.

Kate swallowed. "Are you okay?" The sensation was mind-blowing for her—she couldn't imagine how intense it must be for Tilly.

Tilly held her gaze. Taking Kate's hand from her waist, she skimmed it low until she pressed Kate's fingers over her core. Her hips twitched up into Kate's caress. Kate groaned. Softly, her fingers parted Tilly through lace. Tilly's eyes slipped shut. Kate bit her lip, teased lower, pressed. Suddenly, Tilly's eyes snapped open. Her lips parted.

Awareness chased down Kate's spine like ice water. At once, her hand froze. "Too much?" she whispered, hoping her gaze was as soft as she intended.

Tilly's hips rolled against her stilled touch, searching for pressure. "No. I want...so much, but that's..."

Kate slid her hand higher, across her abdomen. She smiled, understanding. "We won't do that. Okay?"

"I'm sorry."

"*Don't.* Don't be sorry." She pressed a tender kiss to the corner of Tilly's mouth. "I don't have to be inside you for this to be everything. It already is, okay? It's already everything." She expelled a breath against Tilly's jawline. "We can stop. We don't have to do anything more. I don't want your mind to be anywhere but here with me."

Hands clutching at the small of Kate's back, Tilly shook her head. "I am. I'm here. Touch me, please." She pushed Kate's hand lower. "I don't want to stop. Please." As Kate circled her through lace, Tilly wrapped her hands around the posts of the bedframe. Her hips shot up from the mattress. "Kate. Kate…"

A groan caught at the back of her throat. "How does that feel?" Kate rasped.

Tilly's eyelashes fluttered. "Don't stop."

Kate kissed Tilly's shoulder, the dampness of Tilly's underwear at her fingertips making her dizzy with desperation. She lowered her mouth to Tilly's ear and kissed the point of her jaw. "I want to kiss you where my fingers are."

Tilly whimpered.

Kate had to be sure. "Is that something you want?"

Tilly nodded. "Yes. *Please.*"

"Are you sure?"

"Yes. *Kate.*"

Fuck.

Edging Tilly's knees apart, Kate sank between them. She littered kisses on the insides of soft thighs. Higher. Kate exhaled sharply and Tilly squirmed, breath hitching. *Yes.* Gently, she lowered her lips to the apex of Tilly's legs, where lace was dark, saturated. With a gasp, Tilly arched from the bed.

At the sound of Kate's name leaving Tilly's lips, Kate held back a moan. Hooking her fingers around the band of Tilly's underwear, she drew it down her legs.

Her eyes held Tilly's as she pressed kisses to the inside of her knee. A flicker of apprehension glossed over Tilly's expression, her legs drawing together self-consciously. *No way.* Kate smiled softly, and pinned Tilly's legs apart. With exquisite gentleness, she linked her arms around Tilly's thighs and flattened her hands on the subtle swell of Tilly's hips.

At the first touch of Kate's tongue, Tilly groaned, raked a trembling hand into her hair. The surprised exhalations that reached Kate's ears sounded almost scandalised. Pride burned hot in Kate's chest. Was Tilly even aware that her hand in Kate's hair, gripping, *pulling*, was holding her there, keeping her against her?

Something locked into place in Kate's heart. Even when she'd been with other women, even Elodie, this was all she'd ever wanted. Even when she'd tried to forget Tilly, tried to put her out of her mind, it had still been *Tilly Tilly Tilly*. She'd only ever been attracted to women with sweet smiles and kind eyes, dignified, feminine women who smiled timidly and touched carefully. Long ago, she'd guessed she'd never love anybody the way she'd loved Tilly, and now she was certain.

Tilly's sighs twisted into moans. Kate could feel herself throbbing, clenching. Beyond the point of inhibition, she dragged her body against the bed, heart pounding as Tilly writhed against her. It was all building, fast and raw. The past few months had been the most agonising foreplay of Kate's life—the moonlit walks around the island, the breakfasts. Tilly teaching and Tilly in elevators and Tilly in the doorway of a hotel bathroom. Tilly wide-eyed at Kate's bureau, leather straps between her fingers.

Kate held back to draw out the moment. Slowly, she told herself. *Slowly.* Tilly had never been touched let alone experienced an orgasm—she was beyond sensitive. Kate didn't want to overwhelm her, really she didn't, but as Tilly's fingers skated across Kate's scalp, she decided there was no point in taking this slowly—they were already too far gone. They'd fallen fast and hard, given in to this thing with palms raised and eyes wide open and there was nothing that could be done to stop the onslaught of need. An overwhelming rush of excitement gripped her at the thought. She closed her lips around Tilly.

Crying out, Tilly shot up onto her elbows. Suddenly, her hand tightened in Kate's hair and with a gasp, she tugged, hard. Kate raised her gaze. Looking like she was ready to splinter in two, Tilly's lips were parted, her eyes wide as she stared down. Kate moaned against her and Tilly's eyes slammed shut, legs twitching as Kate raised the tempo.

"Kate…" She whimpered. "Kate…stop that."

Instantly, Kate pulled back. She wiped her face against the heat of Tilly's thigh. "What's wrong?"

"I think I need to go to the bathroom."

Kate bit back a moan. "You don't." She breathed hard against Tilly's core, trying to catch her breath. "I promise." They'd been so close. So close.

Kate ducked her head and continued. Gasping Kate's name, Tilly almost shot from the bed. Her eyes were alive with panic, black with arousal.

She pulled back. "It's okay, I promise. I'm going to make you come, okay?"

Tilly's eyes were hazy. Sympathy pulled in Kate's chest, and suddenly, her eyes burned with tears. She rested her forehead against the heat of Tilly's belly, pressed a gentle kiss to where dark curls began. "It's okay. It's just me. Just us. Let me show you."

Closing her eyes to shield her tears, she pressed a hand between Tilly's breasts, encouraged her to lie back. Blindly, she fixed Tilly's thighs back over her shoulders.

With renewed desperation, Kate returned to what she now knew Tilly liked, what had had Tilly crying out for a reprieve just moments before, and with her lips pursed, hungry and adamant, she carried Tilly to the edge.

Tilly came with a strangled cry, a hand gripped at the back of Kate's neck, the other clenched in the pillow.

Wiping her face against Tilly's thigh, Kate nipped at soft, creamy skin. She throbbed between her legs so forcibly it was almost painful. Reaching down and slipping off her underwear came like a reflex. She didn't expect a thing, not a single thing, but the need to feel Tilly against her came as natural as breathing.

Tilly's shaking hands held her face firmly, her eyes boring into Kate's. Kate grinned, her lips latching to Tilly's jaw as Tilly gasped for breath. "I thought I was going to pass out," she said. "I think I almost did."

Lightness curled inside her at the sound of Tilly's laugh. Mindlessly, her lips found Tilly's. When Tilly gasped sharply, stunned, Kate froze. *Fuck.* Slowly, Tilly's lips parted, her tongue flitting along Kate's bottom lip, and surprise took root in Kate's heart.

She pressed herself into Tilly. Tilly's hands slipped to her sides, sighing prettily, a sweet mixture of relief and comfort. Burning, Kate grasped the back of Tilly's knee and locked Tilly's leg around her hip, pulled it tighter. Tilly's core pulsed against her skin. She exhaled shakily. "*Oh.*"

It was all so fucking inevitable, Kate thought, so good and right. Her heart drummed ferociously, panicked by the speed at which they were travelling. Kate tried to slow, but Tilly was looking up at her, eyes blazing, hands clutching at Kate's sides, murmuring words of encouragement that only urged her on and on and on.

Together, they quickly found a rhythm, Tilly's eyes slipping closed as awareness took hold. One of Tilly's hands raked up her back, hard enough to draw lines, and curled into Kate's hair. The sensation drove her higher. She ached to feel Tilly inside her, but it was enough, *more than enough*, to have Tilly beneath her, warm and eager and falling to pieces.

Kate gripped Tilly's waist, her touch rougher than she'd ever dared. As Tilly arched into her hold, Kate's hand slipped to the small of Tilly's back. She pulled Tilly's lithe form against her. Her hips rolled, firm. "I love you." Emotion welled inside her, sudden and strong. "I loved you in that belltower and I still love you now."

Tilly gasped for breath. Kate released her back onto the bed and shifted into a sweeter position. Tilly was silent as she stared up at Kate from the pillow, her mouth falling open. "I…"

She couldn't hear it. Not when Tilly had made no promises, when there was so much uncertainty. She grasped Tilly's chin between her fingers. "Just kiss me."

Their lips met, slowly, without finesse, and when Kate opened her eyes, she found Tilly's pupils blown. She looked turned on beyond belief. Her belly undulated against Kate's, her pointed nipples dragging against Kate's chest. Kate pulled gently at one of her nipples. "Don't we feel good together?"

Tilly moaned.

Kate dipped her head and licked the sweat from Tilly's clavicle. Just the sound of her wanton little whimpers was going to make Kate come fast and hard. Knowing that Tilly wanted this just as much as Kate was lovely and beautiful and soul-cleansing, but it was also painfully erotic, driving Kate to the brink with each roll of her hips.

Tilly looked close to coming again. Hair was stuck to her neck, spilling over her breasts. Her face was flushed, skin salty against Kate's tongue. "Can you feel it?" Kate gasped.

Tilly's nails marked crescents against Kate's ribcage. "Yes."

Kate was almost there too, ridiculously, embarrassingly close. When their eyes met, green on blue, it almost felt like too much. She buried her face in Tilly's neck.

Trying to hold herself back from the edge, Kate slipped a hand between them. In seconds, Tilly was shuddering beneath her, the muscles in her thigh tensing for Kate, and quickly Kate was flying into an orgasm, pulsing against Tilly's leg and crying out.

Boneless and breathless, she smoothed a trembling hand over the sweaty strands at Tilly's temple. Beneath her, Tilly twitched. *Yes.* Kate reached between them, her hand spreading lightly, but slender fingers shot down to grasp her own. "Not again," Tilly husked. "It's too much."

Fighting for breath, Kate rolled off her.

Tilly clutched the sheet against her flushed chest. Rolling onto her side, she fixed her smiling eyes on Kate.

Silence settled. "What?" Kate asked hoarsely.

"You make love like you do everything else—with unbelievable arrogance."

Over the sheet, Kate ran her hand across Tilly's belly. Warmth seeped into her touch. "I can't help it if I know what I want." Her hand skirted higher. "What *you* want."

Tilly's eyelids fluttered shut as she drew a shaky breath.

Kate curled her index finger beneath Tilly's chin and tilted her head up. Slowly, Tilly's eyes opened. "You liked it?" Kate whispered. *The way I was? The way we were together?*

It wasn't so much a question as it was a declaration. Tilly had revelled in Kate's dominance in a way that surpassed simple compatibility. Their dynamic, as it turned out, was explosive. In her arms, Tilly had given herself over to Kate's certainty, her practised touches and desperate hands. Tilly's eyes were clear, focused. "Yes," she said, voice steady.

As their gazes held, the significance of what they'd done sank in. Kate leaned in and pressed her lips to the corner of Tilly's mouth. Beneath the sheet, her hands swept across Tilly's waist, pulling her closer.

When Kate's tongue skated across her neck, Tilly gasped. And then, sudden and strange: "How many women have you done this with?"

Kate's kisses slowed as she attempted to make sense of the question. It didn't matter, she could say, but it would be untrue. She'd never been one for casual sex. Each and every woman she'd been intimate with had changed her in some sense, loved her in their own way. It didn't compare to what she had with Tilly, but those experiences had still mattered, had still made her who she was. "Don't ask me that," she said against the curve of Tilly's neck.

"Why?" Tilly asked as Kate pulled back and dropped her head against her pillow.

"Because I don't want to think about it right now." She gazed up at the ceiling, trying to regulate her breathing.

"I've never felt that before." Tilly reached out and slipped a hand between their pillows. "That...release."

Kate licked her lips. After their discussion in the city café, she had gathered as much. "No?" she asked carefully, her voice as neutral as she could manage.

Tilly shook her head against the pillow. "How many times do you think it can happen?" She paused. "An orgasm," she clarified.

That familiar heat curled low in her belly. "As many times as your body wants," she murmured.

Tilly's green eyes bore into hers. "And what if my body still wants?" she said, raspy.

Kate pulled back the sheet.

CHAPTER NINETEEN

As Kate fixed the last button on her shirt, she leaned back on the mattress and traced her gaze over Tilly's sleeping form. Her palm sank deeply into the pillow they'd tossed to the end of the bed sometime in the early hours of the morning. Tilly had fisted it so tightly that it had half-slipped from the case, and near the edge of complete exhaustion, neither of them had had the energy to fix it.

"Til?" she whispered.

Deep in sleep, Tilly didn't move.

Tracking her gaze over Tilly's relaxed features, she adjusted her glasses. She whispered her name a second time.

God, it was like trying to wake the dead. Tilly hadn't stirred at the sound of the shower running, hadn't even shifted in her sleep when Kate had tripped over her own sneakers in a quest to locate her bra. Gently, she reached out and touched her hand to Tilly's bare shoulder.

Tilly's eyelashes fluttered. Slowly, her lips parted.

"Tilly."

As Tilly's eyes opened, their gazes locked.

"I'm sorry," Kate said softly, "but we have to check out in half an hour and I wasn't sure if you'd like a shower before we go…"

Shyly, Tilly sat up, the sheet modestly pressed to her chest. She looked to the end of the bed where Kate had laid out her dress from the night before. Hidden beneath it was the underwear Kate had peeled from her body. "You should have woken me earlier," she said groggily.

Kate yanked the towel from where she'd hooked it on the bottom bedpost and rubbed at her wet hair. "You were really out of it."

A smirk broke across Tilly's face, half-bashful, half-knowing. She pulled her messy hair around one shoulder. Timid, she looked past Kate to the bathroom, then down at her nudity. A blush tinged her pillow-creased cheeks pink.

Kate held the towel out to Tilly. "Here. You know, in case exhibitionism isn't your thing."

With a shy smile, Tilly took it from her. "I can't thank you enough for the gift of this saturated towel," she joked.

Kate grinned. "You are *most* welcome."

Tilly's eyes sparkled.

Kate wet her lips. "Would you like me to get your bag from the car? If you have a change of clothes, your toiletries…" she rambled.

"That would be great. Thank you."

She brushed her lips against the corner of Tilly's mouth. "Be right back."

When she returned, Tilly was in a towel, her long hair wet down her back. Kate sat on the edge of the bed, watching as Tilly hunted through her bag one-handedly, the towel pressed tightly to her chest with the other. "Can't find my damn toothbrush…" Tilly said, scowling. "I'm sorry, Kate, I'm trying to hurry…"

"That's okay, we have time…"

Holding the softness of Tilly's cardigan in her hands, a surge of need gripped her, powerful and demanding. Declarations burned on her tongue, begging to be voiced.

"Oh, here it is!" She rushed back to the bathroom, a change of clothes and toiletries in hand.

The hum of the hairdryer was loud in the small cabin. At the far side of the room, Kate stood by the window and looked out, beyond the trees, to the ocean below. It was a dull, cool morning, and streaked with whitecaps, the sea looked turbulent. Desperate for fresh air, she pushed the window all the way open. The wind howled, and unbeknownst to Kate, grabbed the screen door on the other side of the room. *Bang!*

The hairdryer shut off.

"Kate?" Tilly called out. "Is everything okay?"

Quickly, she closed the window. "It was just the door in the wind."

In a blink, Tilly was back and dressed in a long, short-sleeved cream dress tied loosely at the waist. Swiftly, she folded last night's dress into the bag and charged across the room for her heels by the door.

"It's all right, Til, you can slow down."

Tilly swiped the engagement ring off the end of the dresser and slipped it into her bag.

Looking away sharply, Kate busied herself pulling up the covers, untwisting the sheets.

"What's wrong?" Tilly asked.

Kate looked up. "Nothing's wrong."

Tilly wrapped an elastic around the tail of her plait. "You look tense."

Tense? Kate dropped the pillow to the mattress. "I'm not tense." She exhaled sharply. "I'm just…feeling a lot right now."

Eyes widening slightly, Tilly nodded. For a long moment, she held Kate's gaze.

She smiled for Tilly. Tilly smiled back.

"I'm going to return the key," Kate said. "We have about three minutes and they're pretty strict here with check out."

Tilly nodded. "I just have to get my stuff together and put my sandals on. I can pull the door behind me and meet you at the van?"

When Kate came out of the office, Tilly was leaning against the van, waiting. "Are you hungry?" Kate asked as they clipped their seat belts.

Tilly sighed. "Starving, actually."

"Perfect. Let's grab something before the ferry," she suggested. "Something will be open down by the pier."

Nothing was open down by the pier. All three cafés were closed, and the kiosk at Mornington Pier café was only serving coffee. Outside Doug's Seafood, a woman wearing an apron was shifting a chalkboard easel out to the footpath. Putting the car into park, Kate turned in the driver's seat. "How long has it been since you've had fish and chips for breakfast?"

Down by the water's edge, a father baited his young daughter's fishing hook. As Kate slid the carton of fish and chips from the paper bag and arranged their tartare sauce, she watched Tilly, watching them.

"Sometimes I wonder what my life would have been like if I'd been raised by my parents," Tilly said.

The child cast her line out into the dying flow of a wave.

"Pretty different, I guess." Kate pinched the wedge of lemon over her portion of fish and ignored the seagulls that flocked to see what they had to share. "Growing up in a convent made for an unusual upbringing."

Tilly nodded. She picked out a chip and dusted the extra salt against the corner of the box. "I doubt God would have played such a strong role in my life."

Kate examined her. "You're probably right," she said honestly.

"Yeah," Tilly said, squinting at the glare off the water. "Probably."

Clearly, Tilly was upset. It must be a horrible, sinking feeling, Kate thought, to feel as though everything you valued was borne of circumstance. Kate chose her words carefully. "I think that if your parents survived and you hadn't been raised by Sister Hattie, you still would have felt God's spirit. Maybe just in a different way."

Tilly searched her gaze. "In a different way?"

Kate leaned back, palms on the grass. "I mean, you live your life thinking that God is inside all of us, right? All around us?"

Nodding, Tilly unbuckled her sandals and slipped them off.

"So maybe you wouldn't feel Him the way you do now—in churches and in prayer—but your parents were good, genuine people with kind spirits."

Tilly's brow furrowed in confusion.

"So you already had God's love in them, right? You didn't need to step foot on Lords to find it." She paused. "Maybe when you lost them, God just happened to take the more obvious avenue to keep you close."

Tilly searched her eyes. "Do you really believe that?"

"I don't really know what I believe." Gently, she nudged Tilly's shoulder with her own. "But I *do* believe in making you feel good about yourself."

Tilly ducked her chin to her shoulder. "You do make me feel good about myself," she said softly.

Kate nodded, a strange wave of emotion washing over her as Tilly's eyes burned across her skin. God, it was too early in the morning to be feeling this much. "I'm not just telling you what you want to hear," she said. She sat forward and squirted lemon over her grilled sole. "I'm just saying 'maybe.' That's all."

As they ate, Kate told Tilly about her small group of friends in the city. She hadn't seen them in months, she said. She missed them, wished she'd invited them to Lords—wished they'd offered to visit.

"Are your friends mostly women?" Tilly asked.

"Mostly." Sated, Kate slid her fork into the bag and reclined on her side on the grass. She looked up at Tilly. "What about yours?"

"It's a mixed bunch. Most of my friends have married, a few have children..." Delicately, she bit at a chip. "Things change when they marry. You don't think they will, but they do. I do miss their company," she said, "the company of female friends..." She set down her own fork and brought her knees to her chest, mindfully fixing her skirt.

"When I first arrived in Papua New Guinea, for a good few months, I was the only female missionary. The local women I worked with were so kind to me, so warm, but with the language barrier, it was difficult. There were men who spoke English, Australian men, too, but...I suppose that it was the first time that I realised how much I needed women in my life, how they made me feel safe and understood. I mean, I was raised by women—by *so many* women." Her features softened, as though she was reliving something sweet. She pulled her cardigan around her body. "I know you don't like Sister Mary Monica, but she was just as much of a mother to me as my aunt. She cared for me when I had chicken pox, and bronchitis, and she taught me how to shoot a netball, how to ride my bike..."

Kate sipped at her water. "It's not that I don't like her, Til. She just doesn't like me."

Arching a brow, Tilly tilted her head.

Kate grinned. "Okay so maybe it goes both ways. But the fact that she had to make a point of making sure our dorm room door was open every night didn't do her any favours…"

"I forgot about that," Tilly murmured. Silent, she tossed the remaining chips to the hovering seagulls. "You know, I've had a hard time reconciling the fact that I feel what I feel for you and being Catholic. I've prayed about it. A lot."

Kate studied Tilly's features, the way she refused to look at Kate. "I don't know what to tell you, Til," she said honestly. "I can't really relate to that." Religion had never been something that Kate had held dear. By the time she was old enough to think for herself and consider what it was that she truly believed—*if* she believed—judgment was already set in stone: even if Kate was interested in God, he wasn't too fussed on her. If she wanted religion to play a part in her life, she'd have to go out into the real world and find a church that distinguished tolerance from acceptance, one that welcomed her for exactly who she was.

Deep down, Kate wasn't sure religion was something that she had any interest in seeking. A lifetime ago, her sexual awakening had beat her spiritual awakening to the finish line. At the time, one thing had been made clear: when it came to spirituality, for girls like Kate, there were extra hurdles to jump, and at the end of the race, she was already well and truly out of breath.

Was that history the root of Kate's indifference? Perhaps. Perhaps not. She resented religion for being the one thing that had kept Tilly from her. She'd always viewed faith as the other woman with whom she could never compete. Faith had always been prettier and kinder and offered Tilly a purpose Kate never thought she could. But now, things were different. Life had changed, and so had they. It didn't have to be one or the other.

"There are churches," Kate started, "Christian churches that will open their arms. You just have to seek them out."

Tilly sighed. "I think we both know that's like finding a needle in a haystack."

"Yeah, but they're out there. It's not one or the other, Til. There are options."

Tilly forced a smile. "You sound like my therapist."

"You were in therapy?"

"You look surprised."

"I am."

"Why does it surprise you that I was in therapy?"

"I'm not sure," she said honestly. She considered it for a moment. "Maybe because I thought you'd go to a priest for counselling." She paused. "Or maybe because you were so confused in Melbourne—you know, in our hotel room—like you didn't have the...the..." *God, what's the word for it?*

"The *what*?"

"I don't know, I guess the *tools* to figure out how to handle what you were feeling."

Tilly scoffed. "Well, I wasn't talking to Doctor Fennel about *this* three months ago."

"No, I know, that wasn't what I was trying to say..." *What am I trying to say?*

"You know, I haven't spoken about this with anybody," Tilly said.

"I know."

"All these months, I've kept it close to my chest," she said, voice strained. "The good and the bad. All of it. I haven't told *anyone*."

Kate hated to see the hurt so plainly written on Tilly's face. She wet her lips, tasted salt from their breakfast. "Maybe you should tell someone."

Tilly's eyes widened slightly.

"Therapy," Kate clarified. "I mean, the city is only an hour or so away. It could help if that's something you're used to doing."

"Yeah," Tilly said. "Maybe you're right." She fixed her gaze on Kate. Her lips parted as though she were about to say something, but she stopped herself, looked back out at the water.

Curiosity burned. "What?" Kate asked.

Gaze averted, Tilly smirked. "I was going to tell you something but then I imagined the smug look you'd get when you'd hear it and it turned me off the idea."

Kate arched an eyebrow. "You can't say something like that and then *not* tell me."

Tilly let out a shuddery little breath. "Fine." She paused. "Doctor Fennel advised me against coming here."

"He didn't think Lords was good for you?"

"He advised me against coming here with *Declan*," Tilly clarified. "Against the move, against the engagement…" Tilly traced the tendons on the top of her bare foot. "He thought I was trying to fill somebody else's shoes. And that I was being taken advantage of."

Kate plucked at the grass. So it wasn't just her who was so against Declan. It wasn't just deep-seated jealousy that made her skin crawl at the thought of Tilly sharing her life with him. There was a *reason*. For a therapist to voice such an opinion, there had to be other things that Kate didn't know about, insights Tilly had shared about things that had happened before they'd moved from the city to Mornington. In her heart, curiosity burned bright in a pit of sympathy. What on earth had warranted such a response from a therapist? And why had Tilly ignored the advice? Kate's conscience purred. *Does it matter anymore?* Tilly was safe with her. Finally, they'd found each other—really, truly found each other. And the wanting? Kate bit the inside of her cheek. Their night together hadn't done anything to quell her desire. She wanted it again. All of it. Over and over and over again.

Tilly sighed. "Well go ahead. Say whatever it is that you feel compelled to say."

"All I want to do is kiss you."

Tilly's gaze softened.

Face growing hot, Kate looked away. It was silly, to feel so bashful when last night they'd been skin against skin. Still, she couldn't help it.

Tilly's hand skittered across the grass, inches from her own. "You're so experienced," she whispered.

Kate stripped a blade of grass. "Not really."

"Yes. You are."

Tilly slipped down to lie beside her. Between them, the paper bag crinkled. The tips of Tilly's fingers grazed her own. Kate wove their fingers together. "You were so beautiful last night," she said.

Tilly breathed her name, sheepish.

"You've never done that to yourself?" Kate whispered. "You haven't tried?"

Tilly flushed. "You know I haven't."

Kate swallowed. "Do you know how it makes me feel to know that you shared that with me? Something so special?"

Tilly's eyes slipped closed, and Kate watched as Tilly's teeth sank into her bottom lip. Kate's jaw set hard with emotion. After all that Tilly had confessed on the pier the night before, Kate's heart was full with hope that this was it for them—Tilly wanted a future together. But Tilly hadn't made any revelations about what she now planned to do. She hadn't asked Kate to take her back to Declan's to end it. Instead, here they were, waiting on the passenger ferry to carry their secret back to Lords.

Tilly couldn't marry him—she'd said it herself. She hadn't returned his ring to her hand. Tilly knew it was over, Kate knew it was over, and judging by the way Declan had glared at Kate the night before, he knew it was over, too. But *over* wasn't *ended*. Tilly needed time, and for Kate to expect anything *more* right now was juvenile. The last thing Kate wanted was for her passion to come off as demanding. Pressuring Tilly would make her no better than *him*. That wasn't fair.

"We don't have to rush this," Kate said. "I know there are other things to deal with...to take care of. I just want us to keep talking about what it is that we want, about how we're feeling. I don't want us to slip into how we were after Melbourne."

Tilly's eyes opened. She released a breath. "Thank you."

This—right now—was enough. Being alone with Tilly in the real world, away from St. Joan's, was enough. In fact, it was something she'd once fantasised about. The simplicity, the normalcy, had always seemed so out of reach. "You know, when we were kids," she said, "I used to think about what it would be like to date you. Where I'd want to take you..."

Tilly's thumb slipped over her knuckles. "And where did you want to take me?"

Maybrook Maze wasn't the largest or most impressive of the two mazes on the peninsula, but what it lacked in comparison to Carol Gardens—fancy tearooms and the costly display of handcrafted miniature steam trains—Maybrook made up for in serenity. Three walls into the maze, they'd only passed two other couples, the privacy a blessing Kate hadn't anticipated when she'd paid their entry at the gates.

For the third time since they'd ventured inside the hedge maze, they arrived at a bottleneck. "This way?" Tilly pointed to the shadier of the two routes.

Kate shrugged. "Where you lead, I will follow."

Tilly quirked an eyebrow. "That sounds dangerous."

Kate grinned. "It probably is."

They turned down the right passageway and Kate was glad for the reprieve from the sun. The day had turned surprisingly hot and Tilly had shed her soft cardigan in the van. She watched, amused, as Tilly sipped incessantly at the straw of her cup of lemonade. A nervous quirk? Tilly's pink lips puckered tight around the straw. Want bubbled in Kate. They hadn't kissed since the cabin that morning and Kate was itching to feel Tilly's lips against her own. Since she'd confessed the desire at breakfast, she could feel that Tilly was anticipating it too. Maybe, if Tilly would stop sipping away like the straw was surgically attached to her lips, Kate could make a move and indulge them both.

Deep in the maze, they could still hear the soft, sweet melody of the busker they'd passed outside the boundary. "I used to busk when I was in uni," Kate said offhandedly.

"You did?" Tilly asked. "Where?"

"A few places. Swanston Street in front of the state library. Southbank, sometimes. Mostly the tunnels at Flinders Street Station, though."

Tilly frowned. "I used to sit on the grass in front of the state library and study in the sun. I never saw you."

"It was mostly nights, rush hour. And I'm talking early days— eighteen, nineteen. You would have been overseas. I was kind of desperate for cash and Rebecca Mason got me into it. We played guitar together sometimes when she came into the city from Ballarat. We did Joni Mitchell to death down in the tunnels. Ten years later and I still can't hear *Both Sides Now* without feeling claustrophobic."

They turned a corner. "When we were young, I was jealous of the way you looked at Rebecca Mason," Tilly said casually. She sipped at her drink.

Kate had looked at Rebecca Mason a certain way? Maybe. Rebecca had been a year older, and there had been fleeting moments, she supposed. It *had* been nice to revel in Rebecca's attention at boarding school where it was every girl for herself. Okay, so she'd had a little crush as a kid. But when she'd reunited with Rebecca to busk, it hadn't been like that. Not at all. Not even a little bit.

"I'd get so jealous when she'd invite you up to her room to tutor you and you'd jump at it," Tilly continued. "You were a better guitar player than her anyway—you didn't need tutoring. Her pretence was pathetic."

At the note of irritation in Tilly's voice, Kate bit back a grin. *Interesting.* Reaching a junction, Kate turned right, but Tilly reached out and tugged her left, the gravel grinding beneath her sneakers. Kate laughed. "Nothing ever happened with Rebecca."

"But she wanted it to."

"Maybe."

"I bumped into Lisa White a few years ago and she said that Rebecca's a lesbian now."

"I'm pretty sure she was a lesbian then too."

Tilly halted, her hand tightening in Kate's. As Tilly fixed her with a look, Kate grinned.

"You know what I mean."

A young family rounded the corner. They shared smiles as they passed, pram wheels crunching the gravel. When they rounded the corner, out of sight, Kate pulled Tilly down a shallow dead end. Carefully, she backed her against a brick pillar.

Their eyes locked. "Don't be jealous," Kate breathed. "I wasn't following *Rebecca* up to the roof to 'study.'"

Tilly's green eyes shined with anticipation and Kate's heart lurched to her throat at the raw vulnerability she found there. The moment swelled. Against hickory brick, Tilly's hair shined reddish-brown. *So beautiful.* Low in Kate's belly, the pool of want seared hotter than ever before and suddenly, it was as though everything they'd shared in the past three months caught up to them in a turbulent rush. This...it was more powerful, more demanding than any moment they'd shared. She ached with an incessant need to be somehow closer to Tilly, to live inside her skin. Gone was the angst of yesterday. The void had been filled with an insatiable hunger that bloomed a pretty little blush on Tilly's neck. Tilly felt it too.

Heart pounding, she linked her arms around Tilly's waist, and Tilly stiffened slightly in surprise. "Kate..." she said breathily.

Between them, the icy lemonade cup pressed against Kate's chest, soaking a tiny patch through her plaid shirt. Kate dropped her forehead to the crook of Tilly's neck. "We should go back up there…" she husked against her skin. "To the belltower. For old time's sake."

Tilly's body was hot through the thin cotton of her dress. "Why?" She scoffed playfully. Her fingers dug into Kate's side. "You want to see if, after all these years, I'll finally let you under my skirt?"

The words were so bold that Kate was glad her face was buried in Tilly's neck. The last thing she wanted was for her surprise to discourage Tilly from *trying*, *testing*, discovering this new, sensual part of herself that was suddenly blossoming.

Smirking, she pulled back. "No." She took the lemonade from Tilly's hands and held it away from them. Tilly huffed and Kate grinned wider. She tightened her arm around Tilly's waist and drew her hips flush against her own. "Because I want to kiss you up there knowing what I know now."

Tilly wet her lips. "And what is it that you know now?" she asked coyly.

"That I can make you happy."

"Mmm?" Tilly asked playfully.

Kate tilted her head to brush her lips against Tilly's. "Really, really, *really* happy."

The whisper of Tilly's breath against her lips was maddening, the nervousness cloaked in flirtation drawing breath from Kate's lungs. "Oh?"

Kate's eyes slipped closed. "And that in your heart, you feel married to me."

Tilly's lips met hers with a different kind of electricity. Soft, *familiar*, sweet like lemonade. Need burned inside her as Tilly's hands bunched the front of her shirt roughly. Maybe they should have gone straight back to Lords, to the cottage. All she wanted was Tilly molten and messy over her sheets. Tilly pressed a hand against her chest and drew back.

"What's wrong?" she breathed.

Breathless, Tilly blinked up at her. "My lips are tingling."

Kate smirked. "Good." She lowered her mouth to Tilly's.

Again, Tilly pushed her away. "I'm having a reaction."

Kate blinked. "Huh?"

"To the sunflowers." Tilly winced as she unclenched her hand from Kate's shirt and scratched at the back of her neck.

Kate's eyes widened as her gaze set on the rash on the side of Tilly's forearm. With a gasp, she grasped Tilly's wrist. "Jesus Christ, your arm's the colour of a lobster. Why didn't you tell me?"

"You were so sweet about coming here—"

"Oh my god, Tilly, you should have said something earlier!"

"I didn't realise there would be an *entire sunflower labyrinth* on the other side of the boundary wall! You said it was just a *hedge maze*."

A pink, patchy rash was blooming on Tilly's neck, creeping down to her collarbone. "Jesus Christ. How do I not know that you're allergic to sunflowers?"

Tilly grinned. "I'm fine," she said coolly as she reached out to take the lemonade from Kate's grasp. "But I'm *completely* parched."

"What are we having for dinner?" Lexi asked, the wheels of her cabin bag rolling loudly across the gravel of Mornington slipway as she made her way toward Kate later that night.

"Rabbit stew," she said dryly. "And *good evening* to you too."

Lexi rolled her eyes. "*Hi.* What are we *actually* having?"

"Consider it a surprise and consider yourself glad that you abandoned that vegan phase before it began."

"So *meat*?"

"So-*I-don't-know*."

Cassie brushed past them, heading for the ramp of the car ferry for boarding. "Hi, Kate."

"See?" Kate called out to Lexi as she watched the two of them board. "It isn't so hard."

Kate glanced across the slipway. A few yards away, Tilly and Grace were seated on the bench, chatting away. When Kate approached, they both looked up. "Grace, may I talk to Tilly for a sec?"

Grace reached across the seat for her backpack. "Sure."

As Grace wandered off toward the car ferry, Kate sat down. The heat of Tilly's arm was warm against her own. "How's the rash?"

Tilly smiled. "You make it sound like I contracted a venereal disease."

Kate raised an eyebrow.

Her eyes widened. "Okay, I just heard how that sounded."

Kate grinned. She looked up to the second level of the car ferry. A group of her Year Eight boarders were outside, leaning back against the railing—out of earshot, but close enough to see if Kate took Tilly's hand in her own. "By the way," she said softly, resisting the urge to reach out, "that's not anything you have to worry about."

"Okay." Tilly looked to her feet. "Thank you." She paused. "I'm going to put my ring back on," she said solemnly. "In case the sisters see and ask. Or one of the girls." She looked up. Their gazes locked. "But I wanted to tell you that's why. I want you to know that's the *only* reason."

Throat tightening, she nodded. What could she possibly say when Tilly was reading her face with a bottomless intensity, as though what Kate felt and thought was all that mattered? It fuelled her with relief.

As Tilly slid the band back onto her finger, the hairs rose on the back of Kate's neck. For as right as this was, how they were going about it possessed an undeniable element of deceit. They'd been living in their blissful bubble all day—it was the reason they hadn't returned to Lords earlier—but once reality set in, it wasn't going to take much for guilt and shame to squirm their way into the equation. "Til?"

She looked up.

"Until you tell him, I think maybe we should—"

"Stop?"

"No…but I think we should sleep in our own beds."

"Because I'm being unfaithful?"

If only my moral compass was that strong. "No. Because I don't want to pressure you, Til. I think we need to take it slowly. I don't want this to become too much, for you to suddenly start feeling… like it's wrong or something. I don't want you to regret this."

"Oh," Tilly said softly. "Okay."

The moment hung, suspended.

"Thank you for today," Tilly said.

"You're welcome." She took Tilly's arm. The rash had calmed from its angry pink. Lightly, Kate trailed her short nails over Tilly's arm.

Tilly's eyes closed. A long breath slipped from her lips. "That feels nice."

"I should have taken you to the lighthouse," she said jokingly. "I bet *it's* sunflower-free."

Tilly's eyes opened. "Cape Schanck lighthouse?"

She nodded. "It was on the list."

Tilly stared at her the same way she had the night before in the cabin as she'd placed her ring on the dresser. Kate's stomach flipped. She glanced up to the ferry. The girls had gone inside. "I'm sorry today was spoiled," she said.

"It *wasn't*."

Kate tilted her head in disagreement, but Tilly's response was interrupted by the headlights of Emma's mother's car pulling into the bay.

Quickly, she retracted her touch. "Later?" she whispered.

Tilly nodded.

Together, they stood.

CHAPTER TWENTY

The summer storm was at the height of its late-night rage when Kate's bedroom door creaked loudly. Her eyes shot open, body stiffening as she glared at the fluttering venetians. At the hiss of floorboards, she sat up and locked eyes on Tilly's outline. She threw the covers back, heart hammering as she reached for Tilly's hand.

The breeze raised the hairs on the nape of her neck as Tilly crawled into her bed and hesitantly straddled her lap. A noise escaped her involuntarily and Tilly sighed in response. She smoothed her hands over the heat of Tilly's skin, felt her heartbeat beneath her ribs. "What are we doing?" she asked, voice rough.

"I don't know," Tilly said breathily. "I was lying awake thinking about us, about last night, and…"

This was a bad idea. They needed to slow down, to stop and think and…

Tilly ghosted her lips over the curve of Kate's ear. "I know what we said earlier, at Mornington, but I can't help it."

Kate shivered at the heat of Tilly's breath against her jaw.

"My body wants your body."

Reaching low, she peeled Tilly's nightgown over her head and cast it to the floor. She dropped her teeth to Tilly's neck and earned a gasp, her heart racing with a surge of arousal. This was different to their first time. Perhaps it was that they were at St. Joan's, safe inside the cottage, or that touching each other wasn't so completely new, but each press of Kate's tongue to Tilly's naked chest consecrated the bond that quivered between them.

"Til, we should stop," she said. Gasped. "Do you want to stop?" *I don't want to stop.* "Maybe we should stop."

Tilly's hands swept under Kate's shirt, across her stomach and higher, to fondle her softness. In her embrace, Tilly pressed her body closer, whispered her name. Slowly and deliberately, Kate's hands roamed Tilly's back, felt the fineness of her bones. Her touch swept low, encouraged Tilly to her knees so that she could slip Tilly's underpants down her legs.

Tilly returned to her lap, eyes dark with determination. Kate's heartbeat quickened. "What is it?" she whispered.

With a tight, unwavering grasp, Tilly took Kate's hand and coaxed it low between their bodies.

Oh, god. Her skin burned. "Tilly...wait."

"Shh..."

"Tilly..."

"Come on. *Please.*"

No anticipation, no hesitance. Just perfect, maddening heat.

Tilly gasped suddenly, astonished. Her eyelashes fluttered, lips parted. In the semi-darkness, their eyes locked. "It doesn't hurt," Tilly said, her voice heavy with surprise. Testing, her body gripped at Kate's fingers.

Fuck. Kate swallowed, hard. As Tilly's fingers relaxed their grip around her wrist, a ripple of excitement crafted over Kate's skin. She shifted her wrist infinitesimally and the thighs at her hips twitched.

They hadn't done this the night before. They'd come close, sometime around two a.m. when Tilly had taken her hand just like this and pressed her fingers tightly against her, but Kate had pulled away, resisted. Tilly's hesitance earlier in the night had made her cautious.

"Are you sure?" she asked.

Lips slightly parted, Tilly's back bowed. "Oh," she breathed, her eyes drifting closed in pleasure as Kate's thumb settled against her. Kate pushed the sheets back roughly. Jaw set hard with barely restrained desire, she curled her touch, and Tilly sighed peacefully.

When Tilly began to respond, fervent and quivering, Kate dropped her head to the juncture of Tilly's neck. It was all building to a crescendo too quickly. She felt dizzy with fulfillment. All she wanted was to take Tilly apart, again and again until Tilly couldn't stand it. Tilly whimpered into the kiss, hips giving half-hearted movements as she came closer and closer. Kate's arm tightened around her waist. "The window's open," she rasped. "You have to stay quiet."

At the demand, Tilly keened, moving hard, faster on Kate's hand.

Kate was surprised. She'd unlocked something. "You have to be quiet," she said. "*So quiet.*"

Tilly came hard, crying out into Kate's kiss and collapsing in her arms.

Kate drew her closer against her body, pressed her lips to the corner of her lips, the curve of her jaw. "That was beautiful," she professed. "You were beautiful."

Relentless, impassioned, Tilly undressed Kate in a daze. The night before, in the cabin, the soft light had fuelled their lovemaking with gentleness and wonderment. Now, in the dark, each touch was marked sharp with intent. Tilly pushed her back to lie down and crawled over her.

Kate *burned.* Touching Tilly had left her almost quaking with need. Roughly, Tilly's fingers raked through her hair, and as Tilly's lips found her breast, a noise pulled from the back of Kate's throat. Her mind escaped her. "I want your mouth on me," she whispered brokenly.

Tilly's frenzy slowed to a standstill, her lips barely moving against Kate's skin.

Oh God. Kate's heart pounded, her eyes squeezing closed as the enormity of the confession pulsed between them, untamed. That was too much. Too, too much. *What have you done?* She shivered as Tilly lowered her forehead to rest on her sternum, breath hot across her flushed skin.

"I'm sorry," Tilly murmured as she pulled back to sit astride Kate's hips, "I just need a minute. I can barely feel my legs."

A bright flash of lightning lit the sky and Kate caught Tilly's glassy, apprehensive gaze. It took another moment for her eyes to adjust to the darkness again. Reaching out, she kneaded Tilly's hips.

"You okay?" Kate asked softly. Tension swung like a pendulum in the breath of space between them.

Tilly exhaled slowly. "I'm fine," she said. "I'm just trying to figure where to start. Because I want to. I do." She paused. "It's all new," she said, and there was something unsettling stitched to her voice, a patch of shame as though she felt the need to explain her inexperience. "I don't know if I can do that yet," Tilly said, voice wavering as she lowered her trembling body. "I don't know if I'm ready."

Reverently, Kate slipped her hands up to hold Tilly's waist. Her touch was light, leisurely. "I know. I shouldn't have said it. It just slipped out."

The rain grew louder.

"I want to touch you," Tilly said.

Kate wet her lips. "You don't have to. I can take care of…"

Tilly's touch swept across the taut muscles of her abdomen. Kate stiffened in anticipation. Tilly's hand stilled, *so close*. "What do you like?" she whispered. Without waiting for an answer, she pressed her lips to Kate's.

Kate's need was almost deafening in its dominance, but the timidity of Tilly's kiss set a lump in her throat. It was suddenly too dark. Kate needed to be able to look at Tilly, to know that her mind was here and only here, that she knew this was nothing but pure and good. She needed to be able to look in Tilly's eyes and know she felt safe. She pushed Tilly back to rest on the pillows and pressed a gentle kiss to the dip of her collarbone. "Let's shower."

Incredulous, Tilly's voice grew in pitch. "Together?"

Kate lowered her chest to Tilly's, the contact lighting fires beneath her skin. Kate licked at the curve of her neck. "It'll be nice."

She could almost feel Tilly holding her breath at the suggestion. "I'm not sure…" she said shyly.

The mere thought of seeing Tilly's body beneath the soft, kind glow of the bathroom light was enough to elicit a poorly concealed groan. "You don't want to?" she whispered.

"I…" Tilly gasped sharply as Kate's teeth linked around her earlobe lightly.

"You wanted to in the city," Kate rasped. "In the hotel." She skimmed a hand beneath Tilly's thigh and lifted it against her hip. "Didn't you?"

Kate played her body like an instrument. Tilly's legs parted at her touch. She hummed a noise of agreement to Kate's question.

"Please?" Kate implored as her mouth dipped to Tilly's chest. "I want to see you, be with you..."

"You *are* with me," Tilly breathed.

"But I want more."

Tilly was quiet for a long moment. "Okay," she finally whispered.

Beneath the hot spray of the small shower, it started slowly, languidly. Kate was careful, *aware*. She took her time, every touch calculated to soothe, not to push. She tried to ignore the slipperiness of Tilly's skin against her own, to focus instead on smoothing the conditioner through the ends of Tilly's long hair. But as Tilly leaned back into her, the tempo slipped.

Tilly stepped out of the spray, leaned against the tiles, and as Kate blinked water from her eyes, she found Tilly's stare decidedly less demure. Her timidity that had urged Kate to invite Tilly into the shower, into the light, swirled away down the drain.

And it changed.

Their kisses grew ruthless. Their fingers wove together, frustrated, and before Kate could comprehend how to ease the ache that breathed between them, always wanting more and not quite certain how to take it, she was kneeling on the floor, staring up at Tilly. Tilly's eyes were dark, her lip caught between her teeth. Kate's cheeks burned at the desire that had flushed across Tilly's skin.

She likes this the most, Kate thought, the tiles biting into her knees as she wiped water from her eyes and brought Tilly's leg over her shoulder.

Tilly was quieter than usual as Kate carved her release. In desperate craving, Tilly's nails scratched her scalp. It was slower, less intense than earlier. When Kate stood, Tilly breathed hard against her lips, searched Kate's stare with hooded eyes. Kate pinned Tilly against the wall, relishing in the feeling of their heartbeats slipping into sync. "What does it taste like?" Tilly whispered, her eyes trained on Kate's mouth.

Kate's heart soared. She slid her hand between the shower wall and the curve of Tilly's lower back. "It tastes like I want to do that for the rest of my life."

Tilly's eyes widened slightly.

It was the second time she'd made a comment like that, and the enormity of the declaration echoed off the ancient floral tiles, swept about them in the steam. Dropping her head to Tilly's neck in embarrassment, Kate's hands slipped low and she brought Tilly hard against her, palmed her behind, hands kneading roughly. Tilly groaned.

Kate's declaration had brought a certain melancholy that both eased the ache between her thighs and set her heart to a dangerous rhythm. This was all new to Tilly, but it was new for her too. She'd shared intense, intimate experiences with other women, nights much wilder than a midnight rendezvous in the shower, and yet, just the feeling of Tilly's wet, flushed body against her own brought her body alive like never before. She needed and wanted and yearned for more and more, for something unknown and intangible. What was it that she was searching for? That she needed so badly? An answer, her mind drawled.

You want an answer.

"You're so beautiful," Kate gasped. It was impossible to stop the roll of her hips against Tilly's when Tilly was keeping her so close. She wrapped her lips around the pulse in Tilly's neck and sucked.

Tilly's nails left her sides, her hand slipping between their bodies. Suddenly, Tilly's mouth was at her ear. "Don't distract me this time," she said firmly.

Knees threatening to buckle, Kate planted her hands on the tiles above Tilly's shoulders. Warm water slipped over her lower back, down her legs. Even though she was the one looming over Tilly, pinning Tilly to the wall, vulnerability hit her like a charge of homesickness. "Are you going to ask me what I like again?" she murmured against Tilly's chin, the waver of her voice betraying her confidence.

Tilly's fingers danced low. Her green eyes blazed with intent. "I don't think I need to."

CHAPTER TWENTY-ONE

When Kate was eight years old—before St. Joan of Arc, before Tilly—her best friend at Mary MacKillop Primary School was Meredith Elson. During the summer between fourth and fifth grade, Meredith went west to stay with her grandparents in the country for the entire holiday break. Before school returned at the end of January, Kate's mother sat her down and explained that there was a reason Meredith wasn't returning her phone calls. There had been an accident in the country—Meredith had gone swimming with her cousins in her grandparents' dam, got her foot stuck in a yabby trap and drowned. She'd been dead for thirty seconds before her uncle had been able to resuscitate her.

The morning when Kate returned to school, Meredith had told Kate that they were lying when they told you what it was like to die. "Your whole life doesn't flash before your eyes," she said. "You get to relive one moment. *Just one.*"

"What did you relive?" Kate had asked, sceptical. Blunt as ever, Meredith claimed she'd "relived" the moment her foot got stuck in the yabby net. "I don't know if that counts," Kate had said.

"Oh," Meredith had said, "it counts."

With Emma beside her and the others trailing far behind, Kate looked out at the cityscape of Melbourne. The bright lights were cast against a canvas of stars, the moon glowing full and clear. For the first time since the beginning of the year, they'd hiked a different track, deep through the bush that led them to the point on Lords where they could best see the city. Last time, when she'd found herself at this point with Emma and Molly, the three of them had tried to convince themselves that, if they concentrated hard enough, over the crashing waves at the base of the cliff they could hear the screams from St. Kilda's Luna Park. Not tonight. Tonight, all Kate could hear was the muffled sound of Tilly's laughter as she caught up with Molly, Lexi, and Grace. For the first time in a long time, Kate's heart felt full. I'll die happy, she thought, if *this* is the one moment I get to relive.

"I can't believe this is over next year," Emma said. "No more Sunday night ferries and breakfasts in the dining hall."

"You still have nine months of breakfasts in the dining hall," Kate reasoned as the others joined them at the cliff's edge. "*And* tomorrow before the ferry. It's not over yet."

"I'm glad it's almost over," Grace said as she fell to lie down on the grass. "I don't know how I'll get through another May of saying The Angelus every day."

Kate rolled her eyes. "I think you'll survive."

Lexi sighed as she collapsed beside Grace. "This is so depressing. Everyone is going to leave me at the end of next year."

Emma scoffed. "As if you're not going to love being the eldest."

Tilly moved closer, and with the brush of her fingers against the back of her hand, Kate felt the affection right down to her core. In the dark, the gesture was infinitesimal, nothing compared to the touches they'd shared behind closed doors since Monday. A wave of calmness settled inside her. She was always so intensely aware of Tilly, and after spending the past three nights sleeping together, it was quickly growing apparent that perhaps the feeling was more requited than she'd first assumed.

Living in this bubble would come to an end on Saturday night when Kate left St. Joan's for good—but they had yet to discuss where the coming week would take them. There was hope in the fact that Tilly hadn't gone to the mainland for Tuesday night dinner at Declan's, but still, on Wednesday afternoon, Kate had returned to the cottage to find Tilly at the sewing machine, the kitchen table covered in glitter from the hem of Lily's angel costume. Quickly, Tilly had packed up the costume. Of course she was still going to the Christmas play. Regardless of what was happening between Declan and Tilly, Tilly would never let the little girl down. It would be ridiculous for Kate to expect anything less.

Between overthinking everything that was happening between her and Tilly and coming to terms with the fact that her time at St. Joan's had reached an end, Kate felt emotionally exhausted. And she wasn't the only one. "Can we just sleep tonight?" Tilly asked when they returned to the cottage alone.

They hadn't done this for *years*. Kate loved it—the cool night air breezing through the opened windows, the warmth of Tilly's body spooned against hers. With her pointer finger, she drew patterns on Tilly's back through her satin summer pyjamas, pressed kisses to the ridge of Tilly's spine where the collar gaped, lips skimming the tiny hairs at the nape of Tilly's neck. It didn't have to turn into anything more. Just the scent of her hair made Kate warm all over. A memory gripped her and her finger stilled in the feminine dip of Tilly's back. Tilly shifted into her, eager for Kate's touch to return to tracing patterns.

"You know," Kate said softly, "each time I'd go back to Mum's for the school holidays, I'd pinch her Chanel Number Five and spritz it on my pillow just so it felt like I was home with you, back in our room…"

Tilly hummed a laugh and Kate smiled. After graduation, she'd even bought a bottle for herself. Although she never wore it, within six months, it had been empty in her bedside drawer. As Tilly turned onto her belly and slipped her arms beneath the pillow with a contented sigh, Kate decided to keep that part to herself.

She listened as Tilly's breath evened out. Clasping her hands beneath her head, Kate stared up at the ceiling. It was a balmy night and the ceiling fan spinning sporadically above—furious, then slowing, and back to erratic—wasn't helping any. Just as she focused on a blade, the motor kicked in and it disappeared into the blur. Great. Another thing she'd have to take a look at before she left on Saturday night.

She had no option but to go. Cynthia was returning from her Europe trip on Sunday—Christmas Eve—and with the pipes still out of order in the teacher's suite in the boarding house, Cynthia would need a room in the cottage. The auction for the St. Kilda terrace had been delayed for another month, in the meantime, so Kate would be staying at her mother's.

Tilly, however, wasn't going anywhere. Regardless of the fact that the teaching term was over, Tilly had made an offhanded comment about wanting to remain on Lords to be there for Sister Tessie's medical assessment. Kate knew she was using it as an excuse—she'd always planned to stay until the wedding. But now, if there wasn't a wedding, there was no real need for Tilly to be there. Tilly had options. And leaving with Kate was one of them.

The fan ceased its rotation. The heat was suffocating. Careful not to disturb Tilly, she sat up in bed and stripped off her singlet.

With a sigh, Tilly rolled over.

She winced. "Sorry..."

"I wasn't asleep," Tilly murmured. Gingerly, she reached out, and like it was second nature, rested her palm over Kate's heartbeat. At the contact, Kate's body sighed in relief.

"Do you think I'm a lesbian?" Tilly whispered.

Their gazes locked. Worried that Tilly would read her surprise for something else, she looked to the ceiling again. "It's hard to take that question seriously when your hand is an inch from my nipple..."

"Try harder," Tilly said evenly.

She could feel Tilly studying her face intently in the dark. "I can't tell you who you are, Til." She sighed. "I don't know who you've been attracted to in the past...if you *have* been attracted to anybody in the past..."

Over the rattle of the venetians in the night breeze, she could hear Tilly thinking. "There was a boy—a man—when I was a missionary. An Islander. He was a medic." Her hand shifted on Kate's chest. At the inadvertent tease of Tilly's nails across the swell of her breast, Kate's eyes fluttered closed. "I liked him very much. Nothing ever happened but...I thought about him for a long time after I came home," she confessed. Her hot breath blessed the skin of Kate's bent arm. "And then in university there was a professor."

"Oh?"

"Australian Literature," she murmured. "She was beautiful."

As she covered Tilly's fingers lightly, solace fluttered warm in her belly.

"But it's never been like this," Tilly whispered. With a tired sigh, she shifted back onto her belly. "Good night."

Wide awake, Kate blinked at the ceiling, watching on as the blades spun quickly, unrelenting.

As a teacher at St. Joan's, this was the last thing Kate would ever have to do.

At Lexi's request, she'd granted an extension and left her exam until, quite literally, the last moment. In just fifty minutes, the passenger ferry would return, ready to collect the last of the girls at Lords Pier, and now, as Kate stepped into the music room and found Lexi waiting at the piano, pale as a spectre, the depth of her melancholy truly hit her.

Lexi looked up. Kate smiled encouragingly and closed the door behind her, spying Grace and Emma watching curiously from the end of the corridor. No doubt they'd have their ears pressed to the music room door in a matter of seconds. The room fell silent but for the faint voices of Sisters Ruth and Tessie down in the quad garden. "Would you like me to close the window?" Kate asked. "Will they distract you?"

Lexi shook her head. "I need the fresh air otherwise I might pass out."

Kate frowned. It was only her Year Ten exam. And this was *Lexi*. Nothing bothered Lexi. Kate didn't know if she should be glad Lexi was taking it so seriously, or worried she was taking it *too* seriously.

She slung her blazer over the back of a chair and sat down, squinting against the onslaught of the midday sun. Her report book fluttered in the warm breeze. "All packed?" she asked.

Lexi nodded. "I just have to do this and then I can go home," she said, seemingly more for her own benefit than for Kate's. She wiped her hands on her uniform skirt and stared at the keys.

Kate sat forward in her seat. Christ, why am *I* so nervous? she thought. "Okay, Carole King, show me what you've got."

Lexi's performance left her speechless. Pride welled inside her as she listened to every practised note. Lexi gave her *everything*. Kate bit the insides of her cheeks and willed herself not to cry. She'd loved this year, these students—she'd probably never be as close to a cohort ever again. St. Joan's fostered a magic found nowhere else and now, the year was reaching its grand finale.

When she was finished, Lexi's hands remained on the keys as she stared at her opened songbook, as though just then realising she could have used it.

Kate sat forward and pressed her pen to the report line where a graded letter belonged. "Well," she said, marking the page, "I think I just felt the earth move under my—"

A choked sob broke across the room and Kate's eyes snapped up. Lexi swivelled on the piano seat and with her back to Kate, burst into tears.

Just *watching* the much-anticipated performance had been nerve-wracking for Kate—she could only imagine how overwhelming it had been for Lexi. She moved across the room. Gently, she placed her open report book on the baby grand. "Why are you crying, Lex?"

Sobs slowing, Lexi drew her hands over her face. "Because I've been practising for months and I needed to do well and I wanted to impress you and now it's over."

"So you're relieved?"

"No." The tears stopped. With red-rimmed eyes, she looked at Kate. "Maybe." She swatted at her cheeks. "I'm just worried that I'll never get another chance."

Oh, honey. Kate slid her book across the lid of the piano.

Curious, Lexi's eyes darted to the book, then to Kate, and back to the book. Puffing air from her cheeks, she reached out and pulled it toward her.

"Still want that second chance?" Kate asked.

Lexi grinned.

Kate swallowed over the tightness in her throat. She nodded toward the door. "Go on," she said, "it's time to get out of here."

With her toiletries bag already filled to the brim, in the dull light of the bathroom, Kate slowly packed half a dozen half-empty shampoo and conditioner bottles from the bathroom cabinet into a calico shopping bag. There was no other way to distract herself from the low feeling that came from farewelling the girls at the pier. She'd finished writing Lexi's report to mail on Monday, packed two suitcases worth of clothes, the four boxes of her books were ready to go, and Tilly had insisted that she didn't need help dicing vegetables for their dinner.

The bathroom door and window were both open to clear the steam after Tilly's evening shower and over Tilly's monotonous chop-chop and an episode of *Masterchef* on TV, Kate could hear the closing notes of *Silent Night* drifting from the chapel across the road. Earlier in the evening, the choir from St. Gerard's had come to rehearse for Christmas Eve mass with the sisters of St. Joan's. Now, after a light, midsummer's night supper in the quad, they were back at it again.

"Maybe you should walk on over and see if they need a pianist fit for the Sydney Conservatorium of Music." Surprised, Kate turned to see Tilly standing in the doorway in her nightgown, arms folded across her chest.

Forcing a smile, Kate turned back to the cupboard. "I didn't get in—I was only waitlisted, you know that. I wasn't good enough," she said softly.

As though Tilly could sense her sorrow, she slinked up behind Kate and linked her bare arms around her waist. Gingerly, through the thin cotton of Kate's T-shirt, she pressed warm lips against her shoulder. "You were plenty good enough."

She scoffed. "Maybe for Sunday mass at St. Gerard's."

A sigh. Tilly's hot breath and the whisper of her name. "You tried, Kate. You went to Sydney and auditioned." She paused, her forehead rolling across the ridge of Kate's spine. "We were all so proud of you," she said. "*So* proud. I never wanted to pressure you into going, but I was so glad you did that for yourself. That you gave it a shot…"

Kate lowered the calico bag to the tiles and spun in Tilly's arms. Their gazes locked. "I was serious," Kate said.

"You were serious?" Tilly repeated, confused.

"In the cabin. When I said I would wait for you if you weren't ready. I was so serious."

Tilly licked her lips. "I know."

Kate's chest tightened. *Do you?* "I meant I'd marry you if that's what you needed—"

They didn't make it to the bedroom. Instead, they ended up on the lounge, surrendering to an urgency they hadn't met until now.

It was desperate, nothing like the tender, excruciatingly slow sex they'd been having. It was hot, her hand beneath the hem of Tilly's nightgown, nestled between soft thighs, working her to the brink of insanity, Tilly's fingers clutching at her back, hips canting up into Kate's as she pressed her into the cushions. It was also risky— the front door was unlocked and while the sisters were across the street with their choir guests, it wasn't uncommon for Sister Ruth to enter the cottage without knocking. Tilly had to be thinking it too.

Lips curved over Tilly's throat, Kate's tongue flattened to feel the vibrato of Tilly's moan as her fingers sought the undoing of Tilly's pleasure. And then, suddenly, Tilly's hand was slipping below the waistband of Kate's shorts, into her underwear, and together they were working each other to a high, Tilly's head tipped back in frustration as the ache for each other escalated and escalated, beating loudly like a drum.

This was worship. Tilly arched restlessly, eyes fluttering open and locking on Kate's, pleading.

Before Kate could give Tilly what she so desperately craved, her own orgasm caught her off guard, hard and fast. She gripped the back of the lounge, trying to gather herself as Tilly writhed beneath her, so close. Swallowing harshly, she focused on Tilly. Her mind, however, was elsewhere.

It hadn't been Tilly's gasps, or the pull of Tilly at her fingers that had taken her to the edge. No. She'd been thinking about Tilly at Mornington that afternoon, dipping her feet in Port Phillip Bay and calling out that the water was freezing. At the memory, Kate's body had snapped.

CHAPTER TWENTY-TWO

For being Kate's last day *on* Lords, most of Saturday was spent *off* Lords.

The night before, her mum had dropped her car off at Mornington Pier so that she could drive it across on the ferry the next day and pack her belongings to leave that night. It had worked out well. Tilly had arranged to meet a young graduate student in Hastings on Saturday morning to purchase a secondhand car advertised on Gumtree, so with her own car at Mornington, Kate was able to drive Tilly over to the suburbs on the other side of the peninsula.

They'd caught the island shuttle down to Lords Pier, taken the nine a.m. passenger ferry to Mornington, driven over to Hastings in Kate's car, and satisfied with an inspection, Tilly had made her purchase of the 2011 Hyundai i30.

"Let's celebrate," Kate had said when she'd closed the driver's door for Tilly. She'd leaned through the open window of the new car and, without thinking, pressed a kiss to Tilly's cheek. "We can have lunch by the water. I know a great little place about five minutes away if you want to follow me?"

"I'd rather just get back," Tilly had said flatly.

At first, she'd thought Tilly's reluctance had been due to embarrassment. The student and her father had still been hovering by the garage, watching, when Kate had kissed her.

But it wasn't about that—it was what Sister Tessie had said to Tilly that morning before they'd left.

Now, Kate stood in the doorway of Tilly's bedroom, watching as Tilly zipped up the emerald dress she was wearing to the Christmas play at St. Vincent's. In the reflection of the dresser mirror, their gazes met. "You look beautiful," Kate said, watching as Tilly closed the back of her studded earrings.

Tilly smiled. "Thank you." As she hunted in her bureau, she caught sight of the front of her dress. Clicking her tongue, she swatted at her sternum. "I pulled Lily's costume out of the plastic and now I have glitter all over me," she said, waving absentmindedly across the room to where the angel costume hung from her dresser, the hem sparkling in the afternoon sun. "I had to reglue some of the glitter, too, so hopefully it will dry. I mean, it's only five thirty now and the play isn't until seven thirty," she rambled, "so hopefully it'll be fine."

Rolling off the doorjamb, Kate took the balled thigh highs from Tilly's hands. "Sit. Let me."

As Tilly sat on the edge of the bed, Kate sank to her knees before her. Outside the open window, cicadas screamed into the hot, late afternoon. Carefully, Kate rolled the stocking so it wouldn't ladder. "Last week at the beach I said that I wanted us to keep talking about our future, what we want…" She lifted Tilly's arched foot and slipped it into the cocoon of nylon. "We haven't really talked about what happens after I leave tonight."

"I know," Tilly whispered.

"We haven't even spoken about when we'll see each other next. I know that you probably have a lot on your mind tonight, what with seeing Declan and telling him that we're…" She stopped herself short. Pointing out the obvious would only make Tilly anxious. She exhaled sharply, suddenly anxious herself. "I guess what I'm trying to say is, let's fix this. Let's figure it out now."

Now wasn't a good time. In any moment, Sister Ruth would be knocking on the door to drive over to Mornington for dinner with Tilly and Declan's family before the play. *Now*, however, was all they had.

Tilly sighed. "I'm sorry. I thought you would have brought it up by now and when you didn't I…" She twisted her ankle to help Kate slip the material over her heel. "I didn't know where to start."

So they'd both been too cowardly to upset the bliss they'd created in chaos. Kate's throat constricted. "That's okay." She forced a smile and set Tilly's covered foot against her thigh, like a footrest. "I've felt the same way. I didn't want to pressure you. I mean, I thought maybe you'd want to go over to the mainland at some point to talk to him, and then you never went so…I wasn't sure."

A soft, strange sound tore from the back of Tilly's throat. "I feel like a terrible person," Tilly mumbled. "I keep thinking of those poor little children." Kate brought the top of the stocking to Tilly's knee, and she lifted her thigh for Kate to slip her hands higher. "Once on our way from the city, when Lily was sick in the car, her father couldn't seem to help. She kept looking up at me like she needed me." Her voice dropped to a whisper. "Like I was the only one left on Earth who could love her the way she needed."

I need you, Kate wanted to say. She smoothed the elastic garter high around Tilly's thigh. Just as she was about to pull away, Tilly covered her hand, stopping her. Their eyes locked. Tilly seemed to search her gaze for understanding.

I *do* understand, Kate wanted to say. But it was hard to throw Tilly a buoy when she was in desperate need of a lifeline too. Kate dropped her gaze and began gathering the second stocking into a doughnut. Again, she cupped her hand around the back of Tilly's bare heel and encouraged her foot into the stocking. "It's not your job to sacrifice your own happiness for somebody else's, Til."

They were quiet as Kate worked the nylon up her leg. When the elastic garter was secured to the top of Tilly's thigh, she pulled her hands away from hot, soft skin and got to her feet. Jealousy walked her across the room. With her back to the dresser, she faced Tilly. "This is about Sister Tessie's dream last night."

Tilly's eyes widened. "No, it's not."

She shifted against the dresser, the sequins at the hem of Lily's dress scratching at her bare calves. "It is." She folded her arms across her chest. "You were fine this morning when we woke up together, and then I noticed you were quiet on the ferry, when we were picking up the car…"

It wasn't until they'd come back from the mainland that Sister Tessie had also indulged Kate in the story of her dream: Sister Tessie had found Sister Hattie in the garden. Sister Tessie had asked her if she'd seen Tilly. She hadn't, so Sister Tessie had taken it upon herself to tell Sister Hattie all about Tilly's engagement. Sister Hattie had been over the moon for her niece.

"It's not some prophecy," Kate said softly, "or divine intervention. He was going to love you and leave you—for God knows how long. He just wants you to look after his children. Sister Hattie wouldn't have wanted that for you, Til. That's not a marriage. That's not an equal partnership. That's you being his *nanny*."

Tilly's eyes squeezed closed. She brought a hand to pinch the bridge of her nose. "I don't know what you want me to say, Kate."

Fear twisted her stomach into knots. "I need to know that you're going to tell him tonight."

Tilly stared down at her lap.

Kate cleared her throat. "You're going to tell him tonight, right?"

The room fell silent. Tilly reached across the floor to where her heels sat at the base of her nightstand. She crossed her legs and slipped the right shoe onto her stockinged foot. "I don't know," she said softly.

Kate's jaw set hard. "What the hell do you mean you don't know?"

"I don't know if it's the right time. Christmas is in two days. I'm supposed to be having lunch with his family—"

"Is this why you never brought it up? Because you had no intention of breaking it off tonight?"

Tilly fixed her with a tired look. "There are children involved, Kate. Children whose Christmas would be ruined if I do this tonight. Please don't be like this."

"Be like what?" she asked, choked.

"Be *selfish*."

The words speared indignation between Kate's ribs and robbed her of breath. Would she always come second for Tilly—behind God, behind clergymen, behind *people to be fixed*? Hurt seized her, lit her skin hot with irritation. Once upon a time, Kate had been the troubled, enraged, depressed girl who had been Tilly's number one priority. Back then, she'd held Tilly's attention, her love. Now, Kate was healed. So why did she feel as fragile as a dream?

As she watched Tilly buckle the strap of her shoe, she reached behind herself and clutched the lip of the dresser with both hands. Anger chased through her, white-hot. "So after the week we've had, after every night you've been in my bed…you're just going to sit there in the front row and nod along to his homily at midnight mass? Play the vicar's good wife? Have Christmas lunch with him and the kids on Monday? I don't think you can do that knowing what you know, knowing what we did—"

Panicked, Tilly looked to the gap in the bedroom door. "Can you please lower your voice? Sister Ruth will be here any moment!"

Kate scoffed.

"It just feels so soon, Kate, like it's all coming out of nowhere…"

"*Out of nowhere?* Honey, he knows it's over. He knew it the moment he handed your bag over on Sunday night. And if he's happy to pretend that it's not, to continue playing happy families even though he knows that marrying him is not what *you* want, then he's even more pathetic than I thought—"

"He's not pathetic."

She fixed Tilly with a glare. "He doesn't respect you. You have to be able to see that."

"Don't look at me like that!"

"Like what?"

"Like you don't think I have the courage to end it with him! I'm going to end it. You *know* I am. You *know* I'm yours."

"So end it tonight. I know you—if you don't, the deceit will tear you apart. Us aside, you need to end it with him."

Tilly's eyes turned electric green. She stood. "*Us aside?* Don't pretend this isn't about you too. Don't play the martyr. You said you weren't going to pressure me and that's exactly what you're doing!"

"I said I wasn't going to pressure you into something you weren't one hundred per cent sure you wanted! But I think that changed over the past few nights, don't you?" The sarcasm tasted bitter on her lips. "You want this, Tilly. *You* came into *my* bed."

Tilly's eyes bugged as Kate pressed off the dresser and moved closer. Kate swallowed thickly. "You…" She shook her head, eyes burning at the memory of the intimacy of Tilly's encouraging touch. Her response. Anguish coiled in her chest and she dropped her gaze. She couldn't look at Tilly knowing that she intended to spend the rest of the weekend pretending to belong to somebody else. She turned. "I'll go see Sister Ruth and then I'll see you on the ferry."

As she turned out of the bedroom and into the living space, Kate halted. Her stomach dropped.

Standing by the front door, Sister Ruth was wide-eyed, her lips fused in a tight, straight line.

Oh fuck. A rush of vertigo hit her, casting a hot flush over her skin. "H-how long have you been here?" she husked.

Sister Ruth wouldn't meet her eye. "Long enough."

The moment Sister Ruth was out of the front seat of Tilly's car and disappearing up the staircase to the cabin of the ferry, Kate unclicked her seat belt and climbed from her own car.

Slipping between the cars parked in the steamy, dank undercarriage of the ferry, she pulled open Tilly's passenger door. Tilly jumped in her seat, her gaze darting madly after Sister Ruth.

Yanking the door shut behind her, Kate sank into the seat. "It's all right, she's already upstairs. Are you okay?"

Tilly's features were pinched with mortification. "How much do you think she heard?"

Kate fixed her with a look. *All of it.*

"Oh no." Tilly looked like she was going to be sick. She covered her eyes with a hand. "She didn't say a word from the cottage to the pier." For a split second, she paused. "I need to tell him. Now that she knows what we've done, I couldn't live with myself going along with it when she knows, when she's judging me. I have to tell him tonight, it's the right thing to do." She pulled her hand from her eyes and looked at Kate. "What do you think she heard?"

Kate blinked, trying to keep up as Tilly jumped from one problem to the next. What did she think Sister Ruth had heard? Seriously? Tilly had seen her expression too, had halted right behind her in the bedroom doorway. *Christ, Tilly, do I need to spell it out for you?* "I think she heard me say that we slept together."

Tilly exhaled shakily. With her elbow on the windowsill, she held her head in her hands. "What have I done?" she whispered, pained. "What on Earth have I done?"

Heat broke out on Kate's skin. "You haven't done anything wrong."

Tilly laughed bitterly. "I cheated on my fiancé and slept with my best friend."

Kate sank back into the seat. Not knowing what to say, she watched as Colin began the slow process of raising the ramp from Lords Dock. She sighed. "It's more complicated than—"

"I've always told myself that St. Joan's was my home," Tilly said, lost in a reverie as she stared at the electronic pad of the radio, "but there was always something beneath the surface, you know, as though I always knew it was just a lie I told myself so that it wouldn't hurt so much to think that I didn't belong anywhere."

Kate blinked, a lump growing in her throat as she listened.

"But these last few months, I've felt like maybe it wasn't a lie. I was just starting to feel like maybe I'd really, truly found home here. But now all of your things are gone and it's just the cottage and I'm here all alone. And now Sister Ruth knows," she rasped. "She knows what I've done and every time I look at her all I'm going to be able to see is that she thinks I'm an entirely different person." A tear slipped to Tilly's jaw. "I feel like I'm being pulled in every direction and I don't know where home is."

Kate's eyes burned, but before she could say anything, a knock on the back window startled them both. They twisted in their seats. "It's just Colin," Kate murmured. She opened the passenger door and poked her head out. "Yeah, give us a minute, will you?"

He shook his head. "You know the rules, Kate. You can't be in your vehicle while we're moving."

"So turn a blind eye and give me a fucking minute." She slammed the door closed.

Shaking his head, Colin crossed in front of the car and headed up the staircase.

"We should just go up," Tilly said, sounding like she was headed to her own funeral.

Kate's hand covered hers over the seat belt clip. "You could come with me."

Tilly's expression blanked. "What?"

She wet her lips. "There's no real reason for you to stay on Lords." *Especially after what just happened.* "There's room at Mum's. You could pack up tonight after the mass and drive over tomorrow and spend Christmas Eve with us." She paused. "And after."

Tilly blinked. "You're asking me to move to your mother's with you?"

"Bec's moved back into the main house with Mum now that she's so far along, so I'll have Nan's old granny flat to myself. It's not a whole cottage but..."

"Kate..."

"I just want you to know that you have other options in the meantime."

Tilly's brow furrowed. "In the meantime?"

"Before next term starts. You know, while you're figuring out where you want to rent in the city again to be close to St. Matthew's."

The way Tilly's eyes tracked over her face—curious, reticent—made the hair stand on the back of her neck. Had she said the wrong thing? *Oh God.* The ramp lifted higher, splitting the sunset and making it harder to read Tilly's expression. Higher, higher. Finally secured, the ramp locked loudly. Darkness set in.

If it wasn't for the sunlight streaming through the narrow divide between the ramp and the undercarriage, Kate wouldn't have been able to see the torment in Tilly's eyes. "You know, nothing'll change." Her hand relaxed around Tilly's. "We can take it so slowly. I mean, you could have the granny flat and I could sleep on the pullout in my niece's room, in the main house. I just...I want you to know that you have options, Til. You don't have to stay holed up at St. Joan's being made to feel ashamed."

"But I like it there. I feel safe—"

"You feel safe with me too," Kate interjected, her hand jumping from Tilly's to caress the muscle above Tilly's knee. "I know you do."

For a long moment, Tilly was quiet. "I never said anything about renting in the city to be near St. Matthew's," she whispered.

Kate sat forward. "Yeah, I just assumed that was what you'd do considering it's what you did last time you were at St. Matthew's." There was another option?

Tilly's lips wavered. "I have to tell you something."

Kate's heart slowed. "What?"

"I haven't accepted St. Matthew's. I...I've been offered a position at St. Joan's for next year." Her voice tore at the edges. "Full-time."

The hot air in the car grew thick. As Tilly wiped at her cheeks, Kate pulled her hand from Tilly's knee. "Oh."

The sudden onslaught of light was blinding. Kate shielded her eyes to find Colin standing in front of Tilly's bonnet, torch in hand and pointed on them. Growling, Kate reached over Tilly and smacked her hand in the centre of the steering wheel. At the quick blast of the horn, Colin jumped through his skin.

Kate held up two fingers, shook them at him as Tilly chuckled through tears. *Two minutes, Colin. Please.* In a huff, he lowered the torch and headed off again.

Not even the sweet sound of Tilly's laugh could quell the fear swelling in her heart. "Til...you *cannot* take St. Joan's for next year. Please."

Nervously, Tilly pinched her crucifix between her thumb and forefinger. "If something happens and the St. Kilda house falls through, or if that interview you have lined up for Lawson Grammar doesn't work out, maybe you could come back next year too?" Her gaze was downcast, like she already knew Kate's answer. "I'm sure they'd love to have you stay on. I know Cynthia's moving into the cottage, but she could move back into the boarding house once we get the pipes fixed in her old suite."

Is she hallucinating? "Til," she said slowly, "...Sister Ruth *knows*. There's no way I can stay on. It would be so uncomfortable. For *both* of us."

"We could just tell her it was a misunderstanding. We could go up there now and tell her."

At the consideration of what Tilly was asking, pressure grew in Kate's chest. "I can't do that, Tilly."

"Why not?"

"Because it's not an option," Kate said sternly. "I am not about to start lying. I just want live with you like a normal couple, with our own lives and our own freedoms."

"But we've been really happy here."

"And we could be *so much happier*. Please don't take the job at St. Joan's. Please. You already have St. Matthew's for next year." She took Tilly's hand in hers and squeezed it gently. "*Please.*"

Biting her lip, Tilly stared at the console. Kate could see that, deep down, Tilly knew what was best for herself—that staying on wasn't the right thing to do. Suddenly, Tilly looked up, eyes glassy green. "I don't want to hurt you, but I can't go to your mother's. After tonight…I mean, imagine what it would look like to Sister Ruth."

"Like we're together?"

"No," Tilly said firmly. "Like I'm a coward."

Kate nodded. She was right. "I…I wasn't expecting you to say yes. I just want you to know that you're welcome to stay with us if you want to."

Tilly was quiet.

In the dark underbelly of the ferry, the rocking motion crafted a dizzying spell. "What are you going to do about Sister Ruth?" Kate whispered.

"I don't know," Tilly said, despondent. "But I guess I'm going to have to figure it out within the next few minutes."

"I don't want to just leave you alone to deal with this. Do you want me to come upstairs with you?"

Tilly's eyes widened. She shook her head. "I think maybe it's best that you don't."

"Right." She drew a deep breath. "Well, I'll call you tonight—"

"I'll call you, okay?"

Kate blinked. "Oh. Okay." She twisted her hands together, nauseating worry settling in her stomach. She reached for the door handle. "So I'm going to head up…"

Silence.

In the darkness, she leaned over the console. Gently, she pressed her lips to Tilly's cheek. "Bye, Til." Slowly, she pulled back.

Suddenly, Tilly gasped. "Oh Christ!" she cried.

Kate's eyes bugged. "What, baby?"

"I forgot Lily's costume!"

CHAPTER TWENTY-THREE

"Aunty Kate, watch me climb all the way to the top!"

From her seat at the outdoor table, Kate peered through the fence of the children's play area. Beneath the fluorescent glow of the lights, the sunburn was evident on Karlie's little arms. They'd spent most of the day in the shade, but her niece was much fairer than the rest of their family. Tilly would have burned too, Kate thought, and quickly squashed that thought as she applauded her niece's climbing skills. *Unless you'd like to have a cry in a McDonald's restroom, we're not going down that road again...* She returned her attention to the newspaper.

Across the table, Beccy whacked at her arm. "Bloody mozzies. Thank God Mum decided to just go home, she'd never stop whinging." A cool breeze lifted the napkins in the centre of the table. Kate weighted them with her takeaway cappuccino. Beccy sighed loudly as she sat back. "God, I am so glad Christmas is over. I thought it was never going to end."

Kate smiled. She had to agree. For the first time in days, sitting alone with her sister in the dimly lit quietness of a McDonald's at eight p.m., Kate felt like she could breathe again. Regardless of the merry Perry Como song playing on the overhead speakers, Christmas was finally over.

After a big meal of leftovers at the Boxing Day beach barbecue with their mother's side of the family, Kate and Beccy had decided to give in to Karlie's backseat pleas and stopped for a snack on the drive home. Half an hour in the play area would knock Karlie out, Beccy had said as Kate unbuckled the youngster from her booster seat. And as much as Kate adored her niece, knowing she'd be spending twenty-four seven with Karlie until she moved out at the end of January, she hoped for the same.

She flipped through the *Escape* section of the paper. "There's a cruise going cheap for March," she murmured, the idea of getting away suddenly growing in appeal. "Ten nights to Vanuatu—nine hundred and seventy-nine dollars per person for a twin cabin. That's a good deal, less than one hundred a day…Oh, it stops at Mystery Island, I haven't been there."

Beccy sat back in her seat and ran a hand across her belly. "Who the hell are you going to share a twin cabin with?"

"You could come with me…"

Beccy fixed her with a look that so reminded Kate of their mother. "Yeah," she said sarcastically, "I'd just love to pump breast milk in a bikini on Mystery Island." She cleaned up the contents of Karlie's half-eaten Happy Meal, slipping the three-nugget packet into the larger box. "You could go with Tilly," she said. "I'm sure there's a chapel on board to keep her in God's good books."

At the mention of Tilly, Kate stiffened. After almost a week of agonising over their last interaction, it was equal parts lovely and devastating to hear her name. She wanted to talk about Tilly, let her name roll from her tongue, but at the same time, she *couldn't*, especially not with Beccy, who was always commenting about how Kate was so "annoyingly tough." "Kate left her tear ducts in utero," Beccy would tell people, "and seven years later, I got hers as well as my own." Somewhere along the line, Beccy's claims had hardened Kate, made resisting the sting of tears absolutely essential.

Mustering nonchalance, Kate rolled her eyes. "She's not as religious as you think she is."

"*Please*, she's basically the Virgin Mary."

Kate's throat tightened. She reached for her coffee.

"You haven't mentioned her much this week." Beccy pinched a ring of dark red lipstick from her straw. "Or, at all."

Kate took a long sip, trying to gauge what her sister was implying. "Well, I haven't *spoken* to her in three days," Kate said shortly.

"I used to be jealous of Tilly," Beccy said, absentminded. "It was always *Tilly this* and *Tilly that*. I thought you liked her more than you liked me and I could just never figure out why. Before Mum sent me to St. Joan's, Tilly was always this elusive character to me."

Eyes on the paper, Kate scoffed. "Don't worry, she's elusive to me too," she mumbled.

At the comment, Beccy's gaze burned into her for a moment. Feigning easiness, Beccy reached for the miniature toy doll from the Happy Meal. Fiddling with it, she plaited the blue synthetic hair. "Tilly's whole religious thing starting to take a toll?"

Kate's eyes snapped up to meet her sister's. "No. I've never complained about the fact that Tilly's religious."

"You used to. When we were kids, I mean."

"No, I didn't."

Beccy lowered the doll to the takeaway tray. "You did. All the time. It pissed you off that she always had to be at Sunday mass and couldn't stay over because of it. You bitched about it nonstop."

"Whatever. I didn't." She hadn't. She'd remember that... wouldn't she? "It doesn't bother me that she's religious."

"So what *is* bothering you?"

Kate looked up and met her sister's gaze. So Beccy *was* fishing.

"Aunty Kate! Mum!"

They turned at the muffled call, at the incessant knocking. With her face pressed against the convexed fiberglass window at the end of the highest tunnel, Karlie waved for attention. Kate's heart pounded as she waved back, trying to anticipate what Beccy would say when Karlie crawled back through the tunnel.

When Karlie was off again, Beccy turned in her seat. "What is it?"

Kate looked across the patio to the garden bed. "I don't know if I want to tell you."

"Tell me."

Kate hesitated.

"*Tell me.*"

"We've been…"

"You been what?"

Kate rested her chin on her palm. For a long moment, she stared at her sister. "We slept together."

Beccy's eyes widened. "Tilly? You slept with Tilly? Are you serious? She looks about as straight as an arrow." She sat forward. "Was this in Melbourne?"

Kate shook her head. "No. After that. We missed the last ferry one night and we had to stay at the cabins and…" Kate stopped herself. "It just happened."

"She's *engaged*."

"You think I don't know that?"

"And she's like…she's *Tilly*. She was going to be a *nun*."

"Yes. I'm well aware."

"Shit, Kate." Beccy paused. "What was she like?"

Kate's eyes narrowed. "What the hell do you mean?"

Smirking, Beccy leaned back in her chair. "I'm sorry, I just didn't think her legs opened up."

Irritation coursed through her. "Don't be crass." She swallowed, her mouth growing dry. "Don't make it crass," she said, voice hoarse. "It wasn't like that."

"But she let you…do that?"

Kate scowled. "*Let me?* What do you mean *she let me*? I didn't talk her into anything."

"I didn't say that. I'm just surprised that she was into…*that*."

At her sister's inquisitive stare, Kate scoffed. "I'm not giving you details."

"But it…like, you had actual sex? Not just making out, right? You've been having an affair?"

Kate bit at her bottom lip. "Yeah," she said. "We…yeah. But I don't know if I'd call it an affair. That isn't what we've been doing."

"Well, yeah…" Beccy disagreed. "You kind of are."

"I'm not sleeping with her anymore."

"But you *were*…"

Kate rubbed at her temples, her throat burning with the threat of tears.

"Oh, Kate."

"I don't need you to *Oh Kate* me, okay? I know it was fucked up. It only went on for a week—that's all." She drew a shaky breath. "I just couldn't *not*." As she reached for her coffee, she felt her cheeks heat. "I'm a mess."

"You're a mess? I'm twenty-three and pregnant with my second kid, single and living with my parents who are practically paying to raise my kids." She paused. "So what the hell happened with her?"

Kate explained their argument in the cottage, Sister Ruth standing stunned in their kitchen, how, when Tilly had realised she'd forgotten Lily's costume behind, Kate had told Tilly to go on to dinner with Sister Ruth and Declan's family. Kate had been the one who had caught the six o'clock passenger ferry back to Lords, raced up to the cottage for the child's dress, hopped on the return ferry, and delivered the costume to St. Vincent's with five minutes to spare until showtime. "That was three nights ago," she said. "And we haven't spoken since I met her in the carpark and gave her that fucking angel costume. She hasn't called...or answered any of *my* calls."

"Are you in love with her?" Beccy asked gently.

Kate nodded.

"Do you think she feels the same way?"

"She hasn't said it, but...yeah."

Beccy thought that over for a moment. "It was her first time?"

Kate nodded, her heart swelling at the memory.

"Think back to how huge that is," Beccy encouraged. "Maybe she needed more from you, some kind of promise, something that made her feel like she could trust you, something solid to hold on to if everything turns to dust..."

"Oh, I gave her something," she rasped, struck with the memory of what she'd proposed. "Maybe that's the problem. Maybe she went away and overthought it. I mean, I didn't give it a whole lot of thought after I said it because we had so much going on at once, but maybe it was too much."

"Too much?" Beccy shook her head in confusion. "What did you say?"

Kate paused.

"Tell me," Beccy implored.

"I said..."

"You *said*?"

"I said that I wanted to marry her."

* * *

As she took the sharp exit to Tullamarine, Kate couldn't remember the last time she'd been so wired with adrenaline and anxiety. And *guilt*.

She'd been selfish. *So* selfish. If only the last-minute call for the job interview hadn't come four hours before she had to meet Molly and her family at Melbourne Airport. If only the principal from her potential new school hadn't been half an hour late to the café and then droned on and on, going an hour over time. If only Kate had said, *No, I'm sorry, but I can't do today, it's New Year's Eve and I have a prior commitment.* Nothing could erase the memory of Molly's disappointment and panic when Kate had called halfway through her interview when the principal had left to go to the bathroom. *Mol, I'm so sorry but I'm not sure if I'm going to make it to the airport in time.*

As she jogged across the street to the Virgin Australia domestic terminal, not even waiting for the lights to change, she knew the odds of Molly still being on this side of the check-in gate were low, but by God, she was going to try.

The automatic doors parted, and as their eyes locked across the terminal lounge, the room began to spin. Each step was a mission, heavy and weighted with disappointment, and as the doors closed the warm night out, Kate came to a stop.

She pulled her gaze from Tilly's and looked toward the check-in desk. Molly was long gone.

Seeing Tilly was like salt in a wound. In a bright white collared, sleeveless shirt tucked into the high waistband of her pleated skirt, Tilly's flushed skin was obvious. Attraction twisted in her belly as Tilly nervously tightened her high ponytail, shifting the sunglasses perched there.

Tilly cast her gaze up and down Kate's body, her boots, her linen suit. "She's okay," Tilly said when her eyes finally met Kate's. "I think it helped her nerves that her first flight is just to Sydney—"

"How long did I miss her by?"

Tilly wet her lips. "Twenty minutes. Her family just left."

Kate rubbed at her face. "Fuck."

"When I got here, and you weren't here—"

Roughly, Kate pulled her hands from her face, set them on her hips. "Why *are* you here?"

"I wanted to be here, surprise her… And I'm glad that I was."

Kate chewed at her lip. She understood why Tilly had come, but if Molly had already left, why the hell was Tilly still there? Was she waiting for Kate?

Tilly's car keys jingled as she switched her wallet from her right hand to her left. "I remembered that you told Molly you'd wait in the terminal in case she came back out. I mean, she didn't ask me to stay, and she seemed to be keeping it together remarkably well…" she rambled. "But I remembered that you promised her you'd stay in the terminal for half an hour after you said goodbye, and then I had a feeling that you would turn up just to try to see her, because you always *try* when these things happen, you always just try, even if there's very little chance—"

A beeping cart zipped through the terminal, around the check-in counters. They broke further apart to make way. As the cart disappeared around the corner, their gazes brushed. Nervous, Tilly shifted from foot to foot. Her eyes flickered from Kate to the chain of linked seats by the wall. "Sit with me?"

Kate nodded.

The check-in area was unusually empty. Across the lounge, over by the corridor to the gates, a young woman and her boyfriend— Kate assumed—were wrapped up in one another, a boarding pass loose in the woman's grip as her arms dangled around his neck.

Kate sank into a chair in the corner. Tilly followed, placing her wallet and keys on the narrow strip of metal separating their seats. Kate's gaze dropped. Her skin flushed—Tilly's ring finger was bare.

Her eyes snapped up. "How are you?"

Tilly shrugged lightly. "Things haven't been the best at St. Joan's."

Kate twisted slightly in her chair. "No?"

Tilly shook her head. "And not because of what happened. I mean, with Sister Ruth and…us." She hesitated. "Sister Mary Monica came and woke me on Boxing Day night. Sister Tessie had woken and left the convent. They'd found her in the garden." Tilly paused. "It was a hot night and she'd taken off all her nightclothes, didn't have a clue where she was. She wouldn't let the sisters dress her and help her back to bed. I was the only one she'd let close. It was…it was horrible." She sighed tiredly and Kate sensed there was more to the story that Tilly wasn't sharing. "I'm just so glad the girls weren't there to see it."

Kate sat back in the seat and rubbed her thigh. "They were good girls. They would have known how to behave—that it wasn't funny."

"I know," Tilly agreed. "But Sister Tessie would have been horrified." She held Kate's gaze. "It's not safe for her on the island anymore with the beaches and…" she trailed off, her throat bobbing as she swallowed, "…the cliffs. The sisters have decided it's best to move her to a nursing home on the mainland."

Kate nodded tersely. "That's probably a good idea."

"I think so too."

She lost herself in Tilly's soft gaze. "Yeah…" She cared about Sister Tessie, of course she did, but it was hard to focus when Tilly was sitting beside her, so nervous, so unsure.

"I saw your missed calls," Tilly said. "And your messages. I wanted to call you on Christmas Day" She dropped her gaze, broke eye contact. "I just…I didn't want to interrupt your family. I wasn't sure if you did lunch or dinner…"

"You wouldn't have interrupted."

Tilly glared at the carpet.

Look at me, Tilly. Please, look at me.

"I ended it with him," she whispered. Kate's heartbeat pounded between her ears as Tilly's eyes met hers. "I didn't tell him about us but…it's over. It's been over since the night you left."

"Then why haven't you answered any of my calls?"

Tilly caught her bottom lip between her teeth. "I don't know."

Headlights from a car stopped in the No Standing bay shone through the window of the terminal and lit Tilly's hair scarlet.

"I do know that I miss you," Tilly said breathily. "I'm complicated Kate. We're complicated together. I know I'm too religious for you and that I have ideas that need to evolve and that's not going to change overnight. You challenge me to think about things that have been drilled into me all my life. And I want to be challenged. I *want* that." Her eyes widened slightly. "I'm hard to love. Maybe even hard to like. I probably need to go back to therapy so I can be…happy." She reached out and covered the hand that rested on Kate's thigh. "But I'm willing to work on myself. For us."

Kate leaned across the chair. Her nose barely brushed Tilly's before Tilly turned her head, stiffened.

The moment stilled.

Tilly's eyes flickered across the terminal. "I'm sorry," she rasped. "I didn't mean to…"

Devastation gripped Kate. She pulled back, sank further into the seat. "I know."

Tilly's stare caught hers, implored her to try again.

Kate shook her head. She turned her hand over in Tilly's and let their fingers link. "If I kiss you now," she rasped, "right here where anyone could see…you'll resent me for it."

"No. Please. I don't know why I reacted like that. *I'm sorry.*"

She squeezed Tilly's hand. "You don't have to be sorry—I don't want you to be sorry. It's just…you're not ready for this, Til. And it's not your fault. But we can't start this if you're ashamed."

"I'm not ashamed," she said, too quickly. "And I'm only staying on Lords until the end of January. I'm going back to the city. I've already started looking for a rental—"

"Right. That's great. It is. I just, I think…I think that, before things get messy, we should take some time apart. Do this right. You can figure out what it is you're feeling, what it is you want—"

"You think I'm repressed." Tilly's eyes glistened.

"No," she said instantly. Hesitated. "Yes." She swallowed. "I can't be the only reason, Til. We need time apart, for you to be sure. My sister is a few weeks off her due date and I'll be tied up at home…"

Tilly's eyes searched Kate's.

Her mouth grew dry. "What?" she asked.

"Are you seeing somebody?"

Kate fixed her with a stare. "No, of course I'm—"

"Good."

At Tilly's immediate response, a rush of satisfaction spiked in Kate's blood. To know that Tilly was jealous? To see possessiveness etched so plainly on her face? It was intoxicating.

Tilly crossed her legs. "How much time do you think it will take?"

"I don't know, Til. Maybe a few months…"

"Months?" Tilly's hand twitched in Kate's, but she didn't argue, and for that, Kate was glad.

"Yeah," Kate said hoarsely. "It's not that long, not really…I'll start a new job, hopefully, and you'll be off Lords, finishing your book…back at St. Matthew's…"

Tilly's gaze bore into her own, destitute. "What if you meet somebody in the meantime?" She leaned forward. "A woman who's ready for somebody like you."

The idea was almost comical. "Trust me, I'm not going to meet anybody."

"You don't know that."

Her chest ached as she watched Tilly bite at the perfect swell of her bottom lip. "But I *do*."

Tilly's stare was intense. "You left linen in the cottage—the afghan quilt and a few pillowcases." The attempt was needy, *suggestive*. "Come by to pick it up sometime next week. We can have dinner—think about if we really need so much time."

Instantly, she shook her head. If she was alone with Tilly in the cottage again, surrounded by the memories of everything they'd shared together in that perfect little space, she'd lose her damn mind—and the willpower to resist temptation. Couldn't Tilly understand that she was doing this for Tilly? For *them?* "I think it's best that you be by yourself for a bit."

Tilly's grip tightened. "I may be confused about a lot of things but I *know* that I love you. Isn't that enough?"

Kate's heart twitched painfully. "It is. But we've already made so many bad decisions. We need to start treating this the way it deserves and this is the right thing to do, the *smart* thing to do." With all the strength she could summon, she released Tilly's hand. "I'll call you in February. Okay?"

"Okay," Tilly said, her voice wavering. "February," she whispered.

"Yeah. February."

The hint of a sad smile tugged at Tilly's lips. In a heartbeat, her eyes glossed over. "You need to leave now before I start crying."

Kate nodded. She leaned over and pressed her lips to Tilly's temple. "Bye, Til."

Outside the terminal, she raised her gaze to the sky, watched as an A380 made its ascent in the distance. Molly would probably be waiting at her boarding gate. Kate hoped she'd been okay getting through security. It was the part Molly dreaded most, knowing that once she was through screening, there was no turning back. Knowing Molly's phone would be switched off to prevent being triggered into anxiety by a good luck message, Kate could only hope that an apologetic email would suffice.

Kate jabbed the pedestrian button with the heel of her palm, watching on as a large group of travellers gathered on the other side of the terminal road. *God, I could do with a holiday right about now…*

She weaved between the crowd and headed for the lifts inside the parking complex. Did she feel lighter after seeing Tilly? Yes. Did she feel confused? Cautious? Definitely. In the days since she'd ended it with Declan, Tilly hadn't reached out, hadn't answered her calls. That meant something. And then there was the way Tilly had pulled away from her kiss. What choice had Kate been left with but to tell Tilly that they needed time apart? She had very little control over what happened from here on. It was up to Tilly now.

As she made her way across the rooftop of the car park, the ding of the other elevator was faint.

"Kate, wait."

She spun.

Tilly slipped between the cars, heading toward her.

Excitement gripped her. "Did you follow me up here or…"

Tilly's hand smoothed beneath Kate's suit jacket, and clutching her waist, pressed her against the driver's door.

"What are you—"

She cradled Kate's face in her hand and with a staggered breath, kissed her.

As Tilly's lips parted against her own, eager, no holds barred, it took a moment for her mind to catch up to her body. Her fingers dug into the swell of Tilly's hips, drew her firmly against her body. Tilly's wallet hit the concrete with a thump as her hand spread across Kate's lower back. The press of keys against the base of her spine was sharp, distracting. She wove her fingers into Tilly's hair and Tilly hummed, her fingers finding Kate's jaw. But however confident Tilly's kiss seemed, there was no mistaking the way Tilly trembled in her arms.

Kate broke the kiss. Clarity settled as she focused on her swollen mouth, her darkened gaze.

"Til—"

"Don't say anything. Please."

As though trying to burn it into memory, Tilly focused on her own thumb, watched as she swept it over Kate's chin.

Tilly smiled softly, sadly. "Happy New Year," she breathed, and with one last look, she was gone across the rooftop.

CHAPTER TWENTY-FOUR

I missed it. The thought was hard to swallow. But as Kate rested her palms against the ledge of the nursery window and stared at her two-and-a-half-kilo newborn niece swaddled in a pale pink blanket, she couldn't bring herself to care. There'll be other houses, she thought, other auctions. *This* was what mattered. And maybe, she thought, some things just weren't meant to be.

Kate sighed tiredly as she looked at the clock on the far wall of the hospital nursery. Seven o'clock. It had been twelve hours since her sister had been admitted, fifteen since she'd gone into labour. After a day split between hospital rooms, labour suites and entertaining Karlie in hospital cafés, the day was catching up with her. She couldn't imagine how her sister was feeling.

With Beccy resting in her room down the hall and her Mum having already taken Karlie home, Kate had taken the opportunity to see her sleeping infant niece one last time, to say goodnight. Inside the nursery, Beccy's nurse looked up from the desk and waved, said something to the other nurse and gestured warmly for Kate to come inside. Kate shook her head. She was on her way out, she mimed.

She wandered down the hall and took the elevator down to the main floor. In the back pocket of her jeans, her phone vibrated. For a split second, she hoped it was Tilly. A sudden impulse to tell Tilly about her perfect newborn niece gripped her. It had been six days since their last contact—a brief chain of text messages—and it hadn't been enough to satisfy the longing that had consumed Kate since they'd said goodbye at the airport almost a month ago.

The text was from her mother, with an attachment of two pictures. They wouldn't load. Kate wandered from the elevator lobby to where she'd found a stronger signal earlier that day when she'd phoned Beccy's best friend. As the picture of her two nieces loaded—Karlie holding her baby sister for the first time—Kate's heart clenched. A bundle of joy swaddled in soft cotton, baby Madison was a sister for Karlie to love forever.

As tears sprang to her eyes, Kate swallowed against the well of emotion. A want bubbled inside her that she couldn't name, an incessant, all-consuming need for *something*.

Thank you, she typed to her mother. *And Happy Birthday, again, Mum. January 23rd is definitely a day for the books, huh?*

Starting back down the hall, Kate stopped at the door of the hospital chapel. A feeling akin to homesickness beckoned, offered a respite before she went home to her mother and Karlie. *I suppose I could just pop my head in, for a second…*

As she pulled open the door, the breath caught in her throat. The baby-blue habit was almost camouflaged against the curtain on the far wall, but the moment she read the perfect posture of the woman kneeling at the pine prie-dieu at the front, her back to the door, Kate knew with utmost certainty who she'd found.

Sister Mary Monica turned. Their eyes locked and Kate forced a smile. Had she ever found herself alone with Sister Mary Monica for more than a few minutes? She hesitated in the doorway. *She's already seen you. You can't run from a nun, Kate.*

Perhaps it was that she was running on exhaustion, or that the empty, windowless chapel was far more spacious than the narrow seating of most churches, but as she slid into the second pew, she didn't feel the dread she expected to overcome her at the thought of being alone with Sister Mary Monica. After genuflecting in the centre of the short aisle, Sister Mary Monica joined her.

"How are you?" Kate whispered.

"I'm well, Kate. And you?"

"My sister just had her baby—her second. A little girl."

Sister Mary Monica's lips twitched into a smile. "Congratulations, Aunt Kate."

"Thank you."

"What did they name her?"

"My sister named her Madison."

Sister Mary Monica didn't miss the emphasis Kate placed on the fact that her sister was a single mother. Her eyes held Kate's. "Beautiful," she said. "That's beautiful. Madison…York?" she clarified by way of asking if the child had been given her mother's surname.

Kate nodded. "Madison York."

"I'll have to go up to the nursery later," Sister Mary Monica said. "Take a peek at Miss Madison."

Kate's heart swelled with pride.

Sister Mary Monica turned her attention to the altar. "Rebecca was always a good girl. Your parents raised two good girls."

It took everything in Kate to keep her expression neutral. It was perhaps the nicest thing Sister Mary Monica had ever said about her. Kate wet her lips. "What are you doing here?" She glanced down at her watch. "It's after seven…"

Sister Mary Monica sighed. "There's a parishioner from St. Gerard's upstairs in palliative care. Today is…" She took pause. "Well, today has been a particularly difficult day." Kate watched as her lips tightened into a thin line. "Father gave Last Rites a few hours ago. I'll stay with the family for a while."

"That's really nice of you," Kate said. "To stay."

Sister Mary Monica nodded woodenly.

A wave of sadness gripped Kate—not for the dying patient upstairs, but for Sister Mary Monica. She'd always wondered how deeply the sisters confided in one another, the degree to which they shared their hardships. From what Kate had seen in the past year, while their support system was strong, they tended to carry their burdens alone. As much as it seemed a fulfilling life, it also seemed unbelievably lonely. What would it be like for Sister Mary Monica to lay her head on her pillow tonight knowing the sadness and unspeakable sorrow that the day had bought? At the end of a long day of offering a shoulder to cry on, who offered one to Sister Mary Monica?

It had been a month since Kate had ventured inside any kind of religious space. The chapel was warmer than the rest of the air-conditioned hospital, and while that familiar citrus hospital scent clung to the walls and dark maroon carpet, there was something about the soft glow of the flameless candles above the prie-dieu that felt cosy.

She focused on the rosary beads in Sister Mary Monica's grip. At the end of the chain of black beads, separated by a few Our Fathers and a Hail Mary was a medallion. Saint Joan. "I heard about what happened with Sister Tessie," Kate whispered. "I'm so sorry that you had to move her."

"Yes, well…" Sister Mary Monica's sentence went unfinished, her wrinkled cheek hollowing as the line of her jaw drew tight with emotion.

"It's funny the way things work out sometimes," Kate offered.

"Yes. It is. In fact, I said the very same thing to Matilda just this morning."

At the mere mention of Tilly, Kate felt the immediate need to steer the conversation to safer territory. "I don't know if you heard but I got a job at Lawson Grammar. Permanent full-time. Head of the Music Department."

"Tilly did mention that you had an interview. Lawson Grammar. My, you'll have your hands full."

"It's not a boarding school—it'll be a breeze."

"I don't doubt it. You certainly managed very well this year as housemother."

"Thank you. I had help. You all helped."

"And Matilda."

Tersely, Kate nodded.

Sister Mary Monica cleared her throat. "I'm sure Tilly would like it if you visited before she heads off tomorrow afternoon."

Kate stiffened. Tilly was leaving Lords tomorrow?

A tired chuckle forced its way between Kate's lips and she cursed herself as one of Sister Mary Monica's thick eyebrows arched in question. A wave of nervous energy tingled over her skin. *Don't play coy, Sister.* Sister Mary Monica wasn't stupid. Even if she was completely oblivious to the fact that something romantic had happened between them, she had to be aware there was a reason why Tilly's broken engagement had coincided with Kate's departure. Kate balled her fists and dragged them up and down her thighs. "I don't think…that's probably not the best idea right now. Tilly's probably too busy…"

After a few seconds of silence, Sister Mary Monica made a sound of disagreement. "I don't think Tilly has ever been too busy for you, has she?"

Kate's hands ceased their movement. Was it her imagination, or was Sister Mary Monica implying that she knew about the two of them? She couldn't possibly know. Sister Ruth would never tell her, and there was no chance Tilly had.

The moment grew long and heavy. Then, in a show of affection so strange, so unfamiliar, Sister Mary Monica reached out and patted Kate's knee once, twice. "I have to get back upstairs." Slowly, she stood. She looked down at Kate and drew a deep breath as she set her shoulders in perfect alignment. "I hope we haven't seen the last of you on Lords, Katherine York. You've been a blessing to us all."

And with that, she was gone.

No sooner than Kate set foot inside the passenger cabin of the interior, Captain Bob Sheppard sounded the ferry horn. She tripped over the threshold in shock. "Old jackass," Kate mumbled beneath her breath, lunging out to steady herself on the back of the nearest chair. So she'd held up the ten o'clock to East Island for a few minutes? *Big whoop, Bob…*

Attempting to catch her breath after running the length of Mornington Pier to make it, Kate glanced around. Had anyone seen her trip through the door? For the ten p.m. trip, the cabin was fairly empty. There were a few East Island residents on board, but most were outside enjoying the warm night, or puffing away on the lower level.

Across the cabin, Kate locked eyes with a woman seated by the open door opposite. She was older than Kate's mother, but younger than the sisters of St. Joan's. On the seat beside her was a large checked bag, filled to the brim. Kate couldn't help but notice the sole half-unstuck from the bottom of her heel. Beside her tattered shoes, a square sheet of creased cardboard had fallen to the floor. Kate couldn't see what was written on it—it was face down—but she could only imagine that it read the kind of message that would prompt Tilly to invite this woman into her home and offer her a meal.

Headed for the other side of the ferry, Kate crossed the cabin and stopped by the door. The woman looked up, curious. Kate dipped her hand into her pocket, feeling for the notes she'd shoved low when she'd bought lunch for Karlie and herself at the hospital cafeteria. She pulled out a twenty. "I think you dropped this outside," she whispered.

Their gazes held. After a moment's deliberation, the woman reached out and plucked the red note from Kate's hand. "Thank you."

Kate just hoped the woman had somewhere to stay when the ferry reached East Island.

She ventured outside. The moonlight was strong. From her spot on the deck, she could see her car parked at the end of the beach by the café loading zone. She'd been so late for boarding that the car ramp had already been drawn—she'd had no option but to leave her car behind at Mornington.

Resting back against the exterior wall of the cabin, she inhaled deeply. *Is this too soon?* She stared up at the Southern Cross. *Give me a sign…*

When Kate had asked for time, she hadn't just asked for Tilly— she'd also needed time to come to terms with the complicated mess of it all. On New Year's Eve, the prospect of them being together had seemed nothing short of a risk. Perhaps it was still too soon. Perhaps Tilly still wasn't ready. But there was something about Sister Mary Monica's words that had encouraged Kate's burning impulse to run to Tilly and never look back.

Things were changing, shifting again just as they had twelve years ago when she'd been handed a diploma and lost her best friend. This kind of love only came around once in a lifetime—of that she was sure. And Tilly? She had turned up in Kate's life *twice*. That had to mean something.

The light at the end of Lords Pier, merely a faint glimmer in the distance, sent a rush of panic through Kate. How would Tilly react when Kate turned up on the doorstep? Over the past month,

Tilly had been persistent with the text messages. At least twice a week, Tilly's name popped up on her screen, the messages short and sweet, but the flirtation had been limited, leaving Kate with no real indication of where they stood. What if, during their month apart, Tilly had realised that she didn't want this? After all, that was why Kate had given her space—to consider it. What if Tilly needed more time?

A droplet of rain fell from the gutter and splashed onto her hairline. Quickly, she pushed off the wall, swiping it away as she wandered down the starboard deck until she reached the stern.

Suddenly, every worry swept away like the pull of the tide.

Her heart lurched to her throat at the sight of Tilly standing in the corner, grip loose on the railing and hair dancing in the breeze as she stared out into the dark void of the bay.

Kate bit down on her lip, and watched, enchanted, as Tilly's freed hair danced on the warm wind. If only her seventeen-year-old self could know, she thought, that one day she'd meet Tilly Wattle at the stern of the cross-bay ferry and they'd find their forever.

With hope threatening to burst from her chest, Kate's feet carried her down across the deck, around the "wet floor" safety sign, closer, closer… As she stepped off the anti-slip flooring, her shoe screeched loudly against the sealed floor. Tilly swivelled on the spot.

Tilly's eyes widened briefly. Relief crossed her expression, and as though she knew their struggle was over, her gaze beckoned Kate forward. The familiar, flowery scent of Tilly's perfume was alluring. Kate sidled up next to her at the railing, only a breath of space between them. As Kate rested her forearms on the warm metal, feverishness surged through her.

The moment drew long. "So," Kate started, "I guess I'm not the only one irking Bob Sheppard tonight asking him to stop at Lords."

"Asking Bob to detour doesn't make him cranky."

Kate quirked an eyebrow. "Maybe not when *you* ask."

"What's that supposed to mean?"

"You could ask Bob Sheppard to navigate you to the tip of Italy in his tinny and he'd stock up on six months' worth of fuel to get you there."

Tilly smacked her lips together. "That's not true."

"It is—you've got him under your charm."

"Don't be silly. He's old enough to be my grandfather."

"So was your fiancé."

Tilly's cheeks hollowed as she bit back a grin. "Not quite."

Kate tilted her head and surrendered to the tug at the corner of her lips. "Not far off…"

They fell into an easy silence. The day's news burned on the tip of Kate's tongue, aching to be told. A colony of flying foxes soared overhead and together they raised their gazes to the starlit sky until the bats disappeared into the darkness of the bay. "My sister had her baby today," she said.

Tilly gasped. "On your mum's birthday! That's lovely! Beccy's okay? And the baby?"

Kate nodded. "Beccy's fine. And Madison is very cute." A rush of emotion welled inside her as Tilly repeated her newborn niece's name, so softly it was barely a whisper. "She's perfect," Kate rasped. "You should see her little nose."

As Tilly turned and settled against the railing, the bare skin of their arms brushed and sent a charge through Kate. She licked her lips. "I think I might even get one of my own."

Tilly grinned. "And how exactly do you plan on going about that?"

The urge to kiss Tilly was acute. "Not sure yet. Think you could give me a few ideas?"

Tilly's breath was hot against the shell of her ear, and Kate could hear the smile in her voice. "Did you miss that lesson where they taught you how babies were made?"

Kate chuckled softly. As Tilly turned, the heat of her arm pressed against Kate's. Smoothly, Kate took Tilly's hand in hers.

Together they listened to the rush of the waves, relished in the warm breeze as the ferry crossed the bay. Softly, Kate traced her thumb over the spot where Declan's sapphire once trapped sunlight tauntingly.

"That feels nice," Tilly whispered.

Kate swallowed over the emotion that welled high in her throat. "How are things with Sister Ruth?"

Tilly sighed. "It's getting better. We ignored it for a while but I just couldn't live like that. We had a chat and I told her that I couldn't accept the position, that I wanted St. Matthew's. That I wanted to be with you."

Kate's eyes snapped up. "You did?"

Tilly nodded. "And I told Sister Mary Monica about us as well."

Sister Mary Monica's parting words replayed in her mind. *Oh.*

"I don't want to keep this from people. I'm trying, Kate."

She couldn't help it—her eyes dropped to Tilly's mouth. "I know you are."

Tilly's stare bore into her own. "Were you on your way to see me?"

"No, I'm on my way to East Island actually—Bob asked me to dinner and I couldn't resist."

Tilly's sweet laugh tugged loose a knot in her chest. Shifting, Tilly pulled her hand from Kate's and playfully pushed on her shoulder, but Kate was too quick, seizing the opportunity to slip her arm around Tilly's waist and pull the heat of her body against her own.

She lowered her forehead to Tilly's. "I missed you." The truth spilled from her lips, effortless, unguarded. "Every day."

Tilly hummed a sound and hunger hit Kate like a blow to the stomach. "I missed you too," Tilly said, her breath hot against Kate's lips. "Kiss me. *Please.*"

She did—long and slow. Satisfaction curled hot in her belly as Tilly's hand smoothed over Kate's shoulder and up her neck. When Tilly moaned into the kiss, Kate cradled her face in her hands.

"I bought it," Tilly whispered against her lips.

Kate grinned. It had been a good kiss. "Good. I *meant* it."

"No." Tilly pulled back, trying to regain her breathing. "St. Kilda. At the auction. I bought your house."

Her heart was like a drum in her chest. "You bought my house?"

"Yes." Tilly's eyes searched hers, desperate. "I went to the auction because I thought you'd be there and I wanted to see you, to talk to you. *Support* you. And when you didn't show, I just…I knew how much you wanted the house and that you wouldn't miss it for anything and I knew there had to be a reason why you weren't there. I asked the agent if she'd heard from you and she said your sister had gone into labour and that you hadn't organised for anybody to bid for you. That you'd just thrown in the towel." She paused. "So I bid. I just did it. It went for one point four and I signed a cheque for the deposit. Not that I expect to live there—with you. It's yours, not mine, so we'll have to figure out some sort of—"

She pulled Tilly against her, kissed her deeply. Happiness pulsed through her, a fulfillment so rich she felt dizzy with relief. She had trusted her instincts and the universe had rewarded her—rewarded *them*. Her arm snaked around Tilly's waist as she pressed her slender frame against the railing. Certainty bloomed inside as Tilly's heart settled against her own.

Tilly slipped a hand between their bodies and pushed at Kate's sternum. She pulled back gently, watched as Tilly's long eyelashes fluttered. "You can't stay with me tonight," Tilly said. "I have company."

Kate grinned. She linked her arms around Tilly's middle. "I know. I'll just stay on board and do the loop back to Mornington. I wasn't really planning on hopping into your bed with Cynthia in the next room. It might give her a coronary."

Tilly's lips twisted. "No…I don't mean Cynthia. The pipes were fixed and she's already moved back into the boarding house." She nodded toward the passenger cabin. "There's a woman inside. I met her in the city…"

It wasn't difficult to put two and two together. "Bloody hell, Til…"

"I couldn't help it, Kate. I was tossing away my leftovers from lunch and she asked me for the rest of my sandwich and my heart just broke for her." She paused. "I bought her lunch and we got to talking and it turns out that she knows the sisters—Sister Ruth invited her to stay years ago—and I thought that since I'm moving out tomorrow she could stay in the cottage for a few days and…" Her eyes scanned each of Kate's, first the left, then the right, as though one could harbour greater sympathy over the other. "Please don't be mad."

"Oh, I'm mad."

Tilly smoothed her palms over Kate's biceps. She arched an eyebrow. "You are?"

Kate nodded, a smile tugging at the corner of her lips. "Absolutely *livid*."

She dipped her head and captured Tilly's lips in a slow, promising kiss. Nobody, she thought, could solve a problem like Matilda.

Bella Books, Inc.

Women. Books. Even Better Together.

P.O. Box 10543
Tallahassee, FL 32302

Phone: 800-729-4992
www.bellabooks.com